D0453947

WHISKEY COVE

DENISE FRISINO

BOOK PUBLISHERS NETWORK

Book Publishers Network
P.O. Box 2256
Bothell • WA • 98041
PH • 425-483-3040
www.bookpublishersnetwork.com

10 9 8 7 6 5 4 3 2

Printed in the United States of America

LCCN   2011938709
ISBN   978-1-937454-07-4

Cover Design: Laura Zugzda
Topography: Michele Savelle
Interior Design: Stephanie Martindale

To my father, Joe, who made writing look easy and who gave me the support and courage when my attempt at the written word appeared impossible.

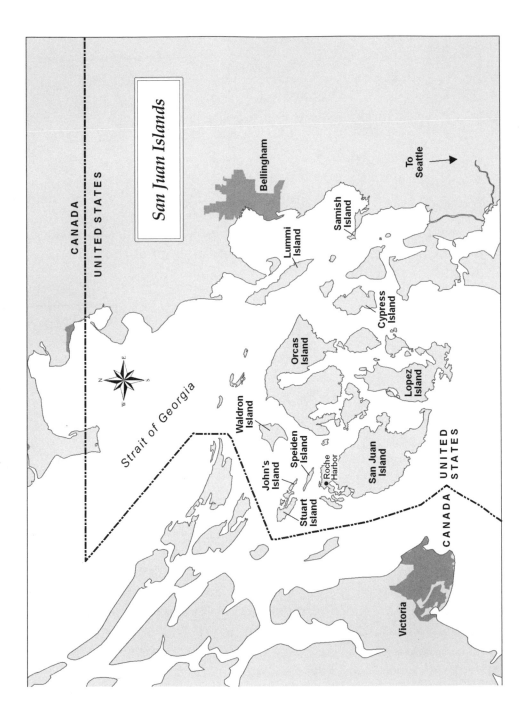

San Juan Islands

Acknowledgments

In the early 1970s, as my summer job for college, I was lucky enough to work at Roche Harbor in the San Juan Islands, which flank the border between Washington State and Canada. It was there a friend, Nick Nash, whose family had fished those waters for generations, told me his grandmother had been a rum runner during Prohibition. And thus, the seed for this story was planted. I ran an ad in the local magazine, *Senior World*, dragged along my father, journalist and editor for the *Seattle Post-Intelligencer*, and began my interviews of those who remembered the world of bootleggers. With the help of several historians, including Ann and Jim Faber, Murray Morgan, and Paul Dorpat, my story took shape.

Thank you to my parents, especially my father whose last words to me were concerning this book, "It better be a damn fast boat, Dece."

And thank you to professor Randolph York Hennes for helping me discover that best "damn fast boat" to use.

Thanks are also in order to Barbara White, the Clarks, Tartes, Phillys, Jack, and my friends and family for their support.

John Dayton, ever the constant guide, allowed me the gift of a lifetime while working with him and introduced me to Katharine Hepburn, who introduced us to her favorite whisky.

Hats off to my publisher, editor, and graphic designer, who patiently pulled it all together for me.

Thank you to Elizabeth Jean, who has spent her life making others' dreams come true.

And thank you to my husband for continuing to love me through the mayhem.

———⟫•⟪———

This story is fiction, based on the facts I uncovered, written from the heart with no intent of injury to those who read it. I apologize now for mixing up the islands and shaking up history.

CHAPTER 1

The task at hand confounded me. I matched the numbers on my torn, yellow piece of paper with those that hung from the fence post halfway down the driveway, leading to a long, reddish house. This was no easy task as the middle numeral was missing, leaving in its wake the sun-faded image of its former self against the old wood. My eyes narrowed in confirmation, 304, then traveled over the yard.

What a tangled, desolate mess. The vines of time had grown untouched and were choking the life from what, at one time, must have been a pleasant setting. Roses, thick and thorny, mixed with sun-dried weeds, flanked the fence leading down the driveway. Across the brown lawn, another bed of questionable foliage marched unevenly along a small shed, turning an unruly trail down the border. A square, drooping patch of browned blossoms marred the only portion of semi-green grass.

The state of this yard was the reason for my journey to this seaside cliff home. The garden and I were to tango. I would orchestrate this disaster into a tidy and unequivocal landscape of order. I adore order.

Encouraged by the task surrounding me, I picked my way to the door, intent on delving into my job. No time for idle small talk. I was here for one reason only. The sooner this job was accomplished, the closer I was to graduation and my teaching certificate. Order. Get the job done and finish my final class.

I had never intended to go back to work before my studies were complete, but then I had never intended on falling in love. At least not then. Being a young woman of precision and schedules, I felt the sting of not reaching my goals. I had let love sidetrack me, and now I would not be among the graduating class of 1972. The affair had been costly. But now, I had dusted off my life, left behind a good job and a broken heart, and had my new target in sight. With what I had saved and this new job, I could finish my studies at Western Washington University fall semester and be on my way to success. I smiled at myself for streamlining my past. Life was so simple with nothing in it.

The back door of the home rattled a little with the force of my knock, as an old, faded white chip of paint drifted to my feet. I braced myself and tried to remember if, with this small scrap of paper, I was handed an image of the owner as well. No. Mrs. Goldsmith, from the student center at Western, had only said there was an elderly widow who needed to have her yard cleaned.

This point on Samish Island, just south of Bellingham, Washington, where the garden and house hung over the sea, was unknown to me. I couldn't see Samish Bay from the back door, but I had glimpsed it as I turned down the drive. It had taken me exactly twenty-eight minutes from Nash Dorm on campus to this spot, cruising a beautiful, winding path over Chuckanut Drive, drifting past blue waters with emerald green islands. At Bow Edison, I turned to cross the flats before climbing the cliff road to Samish.

The job intrigued me. I had taken it more for the change of scenery than for its future promises and my abilities with greenery. Having reasoned long into the night that outdoor, active work would be a welcome alternative for this summer, I had hurried to accept the offer. It was to last only two weeks, which fit neatly into my schedule.

Exactly 7:49. The hands on my wristwatch never lied. Was she awake? The morning sun was struggling to be seen, hidden behind a dense mist that was rising just off the water's edge. Once burned off, it promised to be a blistering day for late June. Taking note of my newly purchased garden gloves and bandana, I rocked back onto my heels in assured confidence. This was indeed the proper occupation for a grappling, young student.

"Older widow," I mused as I rapped on the door again. Maybe she had difficulty walking. My breath stopped in my throat. Older widow. The elderly love to embroider their past, thread by thread, in the hopes of leaving behind a neat and tidy tapestry, a wall-hanging of their life to be viewed and admired from a distance. I had no time for long-winded stories. I began to sweat with unease.

I was no stranger to the misty memories of the old. My parents' small house in Cle Elum with its flat, dry plains of Central Washington toyed with my memory. So did old man Saunders who lived down the block. As children, we ran if we saw him coming, not wanting to get caught up in his rattling, often the same slow tale.

Please don't let her be a talker, I silently prayed. My schedule could not bear any more interruptions. Keep on target.

I turned toward the yard to inspect further my new project. There were not two weeks' worth of work here. Possibly, I could squeeze in another job. Maybe I should just leave now and find other employment. A deep sigh emitted from my lungs, and my shoulders followed in a defeated sag.

"Hello."

I jumped at the high-pitched, sing-songy voice and turned to face its owner. The light voice did not match the keen blue eyes that looked down at me. A shock of dyed red hair topped the image.

"Hello. Mrs. McKenzie?" I fumbled the yellow paper into my pocket, unnerved by the sturdy blue gaze. "I'm here from Western. Uh, University. For your garden."

"Yes, I know, dear. How do you do? Jean, isn't it?"

She extended her hand, thin and freckled, which I took with some caution.

She smiled as we shook, her thin, copper bracelets chiming with the rhythm. Then with lightning speed, she flipped my hand over into both of hers and jerked it up close to her face. The puffs around her eyes wrinkled into a squint as she examined my hand.

"You haven't worked with your hands for a long time," her voice was as calculating as her stare.

I opened my mouth to protest, but her eyes told me it was pointless. She was right. Not about the working. I had worked but not with my hands. And my soft, pink hand, which still rested in her surprisingly strong fingers, told her as much. My heart stopped, as did my prospects for the job.

"I can do it." I gently extracted my virgin limb.

Somehow, those squinting eyes scrutinized me even harder.

"I've done some yard work before," my voice was almost breaking with fear. I quickly added, "And I loved it."

A smile smoothed out the deep creases across her forehead. "Good. Don't waste your time on a job you don't like to do. Now, come in and let's chat."

Chat! My frame froze. *Don't go,* a voice from within warned.

She smiled, "Come in, Jean. The work ahead of you will take some strong coffee."

She turned to go, and I followed. To this day, I don't know why, but follow I did. Possibly, it was the use of my name, or her voice had lost its sing-song lilt to a booming strength. It could have been her height or the strawberry tinted hair. Whatever the reason, I was unaware of how this spider's web worked.

Reluctantly, I followed her through the arch of the door into the afterthought of a laundry room, glancing about for signs of tools that might be helpful in my chores. Instead, I saw the kitchen with turquoise countertops and heavy, copper pans hanging from the wall. Two empty, rose-patterned plates were set in anticipation of a meal at the small, round, dinette table in matching turquoise with metal sides and matching chairs. Just beyond, another arch led to the dining room and a bank of large windows. I relaxed with the thought she had company or possibly someone lived with her. Good. I would soon be about my business.

"Tea or coffee?" She raised one brow in invitation while waving me toward a chair with a well-practiced gesture. Her long index finger had a slight bend just below the tip, as if once broken, which pointed me toward my seat.

"A small cup of coffee."

As I followed the finger to my chair, I attempted to guess her age. Her eyes were a clear, bright blue. Her skin, wrinkled with the deep lines of age, still held its youthful smoothness across her high cheeks. The fingers that wrapped around a pink flowered cup she extended toward me had a charming grace and spoke of their hidden strength.

A yellow parakeet fluffed his feathers, scampered across a wooden peg, and pressed one eye against the side of his cage. He watched me closely from his perch.

"That's Pretty Boy." The old eyes fixed on the bird as she continued in a hushed tone, "He's all I have left now. If I wrote a book, no one would believe all I've lived through."

My empty cup clinked against the saucer and snapped the spell triggered by memory and the sight of the bird.

"Sorry, where were we? Oh, yes. You were telling me about yourself. So you're going to be a teacher?"

I quickly tried to surmise where she had obtained that information. She must have done some research on me, and I wasn't altogether sure the feeling was a comfortable one.

"What will you teach?" The break wasn't long enough to slide in an answer before she started off again. "You aren't very old. Are you about eighteen?"

"Twenty-two," my answer came quickly, my inflated ego punctured by this slight.

"Well, yes, that's much better. Have you ever not been in school?"

No answer emerged to that question.

"I mean, what is it exactly you plan to teach? Have you lived enough to take on such a great responsibility? Why, you've been in school and haven't had time to live, to see things, to know the dif—"

"Music. I want to teach music." I did? I was getting an early education degree. But this woman was making me nervous, and music sounded more dramatic.

Pretty Boy twittered loudly, then fell silent. Even he knew I wasn't telling the truth.

Her head bent toward me, and she whispered, "Don't you wonder where we've met before?"

The look of amazement screwed up my face. I would have remembered that hair if not those piercing eyes. Panic was setting in.

"Maybe in another lifetime?" She waved away my confusion and sat back in her chair.

I regretted taking the first step inside, and that must have shown on my face too.

"Oh, I know you're in a hurry to get to your work, but why did such a pretty girl like you pick teaching as a course of interest? Surely, it is an honorable course to follow. But life is the lesson, and people, people are where the truth lies. How they choose what they do and then what they do with what they choose." She laughed, a surprising low sound, "Christ, sometimes I sound so trite."

"I really had better get started."

"Sit, sit, sit," it was the lilting voice again. "It's so nice to see such youth."

Frustration wormed its way into my organization of daily events. How to escape into the garden so that I could be done with what I came for? The prospect of graduation was dissolving before my job had even started. I couldn't breathe.

"Really," I punctuated my statement by standing.

Relenting, she also stood. "All right. Rush, rush, rush. Let me show you around so that if you need to ask me any questions you'll know where to find me."

She shrugged her shoulders and led me out of the kitchen into a large, open room. Behind me, the walls were covered in polished, split-cedar panels that shone copper with age. The floor was dark wood and so were the large beams that hung overhead. To my right, the cliff side of the house, floor-to-ceiling windows captured my attention.

"Do you like the sea?" Her words rushed against my ears as the waves hit against the beach below.

Mesmerized by the sight, I nodded.

She was watching me, but I could only stare at the blue water that eased across the bay to where a small island grew in the middle, tall and green.

Her words drifted toward me, "Then I've made the right choice."

I turned toward her to ask what choice, but she was gone. Glancing back at the wall of windows stretching the length of the room, I wanted to stay but, instead, started off in the direction of the mumbling that invited me further down the hall.

My mind lingered on the sight of the pounding salt water that churned below at the foot of the massive glass windows. The garden with its killer vines was drifting from my consciousness, like an old piece of cork on water, the vines surfacing in my mind maybe every other wave.

"I am a woman of rhythm, not entirely in the musical sense, my soon-to-be music teacher," her voice found my ears in the tightly shuttered room. "Therefore, it is to this room that I come daily to make my dance." She was searching in the darkness, her long thick fingers groping the top of a small table. "Damn, now where have I put them?"

"Can I help you with something?" It must have been the darkness or the sense of the snug quarters or her comment about music and dancing that pulled me back to the reality of time.

"Ah, here you are, you little devils." The burning match startled me as she pushed it closer to my face. "No, thank you, dear. I've found them."

The kerosene lamp proved my suspicions about the size of this room—little and inky dark with shutters drawn tight. It had a chair, small table, and a cluttered desk. Papers protruded from stacks that resembled the yard, in need of some attention. The walls were solid with books, and stacks of newspapers and magazines lay scattered about. Pictures and memorabilia struggled for space.

"Jake was rewiring this room before he left me so suddenly. Maybe someday I'll get it finished. But I like it this way. It's wonderful. More secretive. We all have secrets. Some more so than others." Her voice was low as she held the lamp close to my face again, hiding hers from me. "Maybe someday I'll tell you some of mine."

There was nothing ominous in her voice. It was a voice of the old longing to relive snatches of her prime. Still, I wanted nothing to do with the ramblings of time. I only wanted to be in the garden and about my own business.

"Yes, maybe. Sure. Well," I started to back out of the room, mumbling in my confusion, "I'd better get started."

I was in the hall, now, heading for the large room. "Do you have any tools? A rake or shovel or something?"

She blew out the light. "Follow me," she commanded and, with two quick strides, passed me. We were back in the large windowed living room. She turned toward a black, wrought iron, spiral staircase at the far corner in front of the slate-blue stone fireplace. Just before the stairs, she ducked into an alcove that held a wooden door and looked through the round portal window.

"You should be able to find everything you need out there in the shed." She pushed the door open and strode into the sunlight across the worn path. Not bothering to take a breath, she continued, "Jake liked everything in order. He ran a tight ship."

"Oh, your husband was a sea captain?" I hurried to keep up with her.

"That's light terminology for what my husband was."

Unable to decipher all that lay behind that statement, I quickly decided not to pursue the subject since the garden was now in sight.

Mrs. McKenzie extracted a long chain of keys, which now hung from her neck and dangled inside the plaid, cotton shirt. Her bracelets jangled as she chose the precise key and flung the door open, her voice echoing off the wall in the darkness, "Here. But I warn you. These tools are sharp. Jake always believed in keeping all blades razor sharp. You never know when trouble comes to call."

She left me alone then, for which I was grateful. Twenty-six minutes had passed, and I was anxious to put in a full day's work. My fresh garden gloves felt rough against my milky white hands as I pulled them on and examined my options. She was right; everything was in impeccable order and condition.

The shed was thin and long, barely wide enough for the cars of today. A workbench skirted one side with various wood-handled shovels and picks adorning the walls like an art museum of the gardener. I selected a pointed shovel and claw-shaped rake. They felt good to the grip, well balanced. Marveling at my own genius, and with complete ignorance, I marched forward into my new occupation.

Bending in the burning sun that was now directly overhead, I firmly grabbed at the deep roots of a dead corn stalk that refused to give. The choice of where to begin had been difficult, but the jagged edges of the square garden presented the most likely solution. Progress had been slow as the small patch of newly exposed earth attested. A long-legged spider crawled across the uneven earth toward my hoe. I poked at his hairy legs with a stick. In my haste to accept employment, I had forgotten my distaste for things that crawl close to the ground. Again, I stabbed at him, but his determination was as strong as his gait.

"Persistent buggers, aren't they?"

McKenzie's approach had gone unnoticed. I did not know how long she had been watching. The large-brimmed hat she wore concealed her expression as she stepped into my light, casting her shadow across my face, cooling it.

"You've been out here all morning. Time for a break. A man's only as good as his strength."

The brilliant sun blinded me again as she stepped away. The wood handle made a thud against the dirt as I turned my aching limbs toward the house. Time had slipped by with thoughts of the odd woman and the project ahead of me. I could not afford to encourage her loquacity. Yet for now, my tired and parched body welcomed the coolness of her home.

"Hope you like oysters. I bread them and then chill them overnight. Oh, and always pick the small ones. The large ones are no good unless you're making a stew. Next time, I'll let you shuck them, teach you a trick. Bathroom is first door on your left."

The plate she put before me was enticing. Aromas and arrangements met my starving senses as she sat across from me.

"How did you like the work?"

"I like your cooking better."

Her laughter brought a squawking from the cage above us as Pretty Boy ran back and forth across his perch, echoing the old woman's mirth.

"That's good because there's always plenty of cooking going on around here. I used to cook up North for the boys in a logging camp before I got involved in my own business and teamed up with Jake."

I knew it was a lead into a narrative, and I tried to stop the words from sliding from my lips, but the coolness of the kitchen was thawing my muscles and obviously my ability to think correctly, "What kind of business was that?"

I lowered my eyes onto the breaded oysters and lifted a bite to my mouth.

She waited, watching, then posed her question, "Pearls of the sea. Like 'em?"

There was no reason to fib. "They are delicious."

My mind settled into the silence that followed, well aware that the red-haired widow watched my slightest gesture. Thankful she had not started in on a long-winded journey through time, I kept my trap shut except to fill it with the delicacies she had expertly prepared.

Pushing the empty plate away, I smiled across at her, readying myself to make a quick beeline for the garden.

She bent toward me, hovering over her cup of coffee, eyes narrowing, calculating her next question, "Do you smoke?"

"No, thank you. I never have liked—"

"Good," she sighed. The aged limbs relaxed back into her chair. Suddenly, she sprang in my direction again. "I used to love it. Fashion. Hell, everybody used to. But Diesel Rose cured me of that. God Bless her."

The image of Diesel Rose emerged before me, big, strong with a tattoo on her right arm and maybe one somewhere else. I bit my lips to keep them shut as I nodded across at her. No questions, no encouragement.

McKenzie turned from me toward the windows of sea. "Christ, every damn man on the dock used to chase her when she'd snatch their butts they'd leave lying around." Her body heaved with a quick laugh. "What a sight! They'd run after her yelling and cursing to beat the band. Then she'd casually drop the burning cigarette into the water and play dumb. She was anything but dumb. But they never should have done that to her. Saved our lives once, my little Diesel Rose."

Little? I quickly rearranged my vision and drew a blank. For I couldn't conjure up a "little" Diesel Rose.

"Well," I started picking up my plate not wanting to engage in further conversation, "I'll just wash these up and head back out."

"Leave them," her voice a hollow sound. She did not turn back toward me but kept her gaze on the waves, gently lapping below on the incoming tide. "I'll get them later. I'm tired now."

Her words pulled an invisible shroud of age around her. She sat motionless. I turned to go, then stopped at the door, and looked back on the silent image. She suddenly appeared so frail, not the bubbling woman who had cagily inspected my hand to ascertain my value as a laborer. Something akin to pity tugged at my heart. She had probably lived a quiet life here in this blissful setting. Yet, no matter how docile a life, an end comes to everything. I tore my mind from the scene and stepped out into the sunlight.

Like any project put off, nothing had changed in my absence except my limbs felt weaker—and the dark, moist dirt I had exposed had turned a light shade of gray in the heat. A beetle waddled across the craggy mounds of soil. I hate bugs. But, I reasoned, the job being short, I would force myself to tolerate them.

The hoe pressed against a sensitive patch on my hands, where work was quickly taking its toll. Mrs. McKenzie had been right. I had tried other odd jobs but had decided on what I like to do first, or thought I liked. My arms throbbed with every new blow to the tough ground. Maybe I had been wrong in my choice of work. Maybe I should quit today, find something less exhausting. This was clearly going to be a lot more difficult than I had, at first, imagined.

The sweat dripped into my eyes, burning them closed when I heard a high-pitched ping. The hoe had struck something. Slowly, I lowered onto my knees to dig with my hands, a posture I had assumed several times that day when the rocks proved too big for my simple tool. I pulled on the hard dirt form, but it did not budge. I started to excavate down its side and was surprised by its depth. Whatever it was, it was round, long, and thin, like a cylinder. I tugged again. Suddenly loosened, I found myself on my back clutching the object with a large, hairy, black spider crawling up my arm. I screamed, brushing the black bug with my glove while the dirt-encrusted object rolled across the cleared patch to rest under a withered mum plant.

The back door opened, and Mrs. McKenzie was standing over me, hat in hand, critically eyeing the situation.

"You all right?"

"Sure." My voice struggled to be strong as I tried to brush away my embarrassment with the dust covering me. I lied, "I slipped."

Her expression didn't change as she looked around. "Well you've done quite a bit for now. More than I expected. Why don't you just call it a day and get a fresh start tomorrow. Sun will be cooler and ground a bit softer."

Wiping the sweat from my forehead, I left a streak of mud that caked on my face. Shifting, I prepared myself to tell her there would be no tomorrow. I was sorry, but this was really not the job for me.

"Look at you," she slapped her hip, bracelets jangling, and cackled with glee. "Damn if you don't remind me of me. Jake McKenzie would have taken a shine to you. Yep, I've made a good choice." She coaxed me toward the door. "Now run on in and clean up before you head out. Don't fret. This yard isn't going anywhere."

A mirror is a bad liar. I looked like hell. Dirt clung to the sweat that pressed damp brown curls against my forehead and down my neck. My face was a shade darker with its new coat of dust. I could barely lift my arms. The cool water made my blisters tingle and burn.

A feeling of complete helplessness and failure overtook me as I watched a single tear clear a path down my cheek. I could not return. I must tell Mrs. McKenzie immediately.

Gathering my strength, I emerged from my wash. It was only one day's work. It would mean nothing to her. She would understand, see my weakness, and dismiss me.

The big-brimmed hat could not hide the twinkle in those incredibly blue eyes. She rocked forward onto her toes. "You've done a fine job. Just fine. Now run on home and get some rest. We have a big day ahead of us tomorrow." Her hand waved through the air, bringing her words with it, "You've given me a gift. You've breathed new life into these old bones of mine, and I'm very grateful."

I looked at her smile and the practiced speech disappeared into jumbled words, "Yes, but I—"

"No, Jean. You've taken this job, and you're doing fine. We'll go slower tomorrow."

Her happiness tore into my guilt. I had taken the job and now was going to let her down. I could work one more day I reasoned.

"All right," my shoulders sagged as I gave in. "See you tomorrow." I started down the path toward the road. As I worked my legs past the partially exposed patch, I noticed the tools were gone and so was the dirt-encrusted cylinder-shaped object.

"You do good work," her words followed me. "We would have welcomed you on board. Now there's a job I think you would have loved. I did. And you would have had a hell of a lot more fun than teaching. A lot more dangerous too. But exciting."

I turned back to look at her, the big brim shadowed her expression. But nothing could have prepared me for what came next.

"You see, my dear Jean," her voice was low and calculating, "rum running was the highlight of my life."

She turned and was gone before my mind digested the full meaning of her words.

CHAPTER 2

The hot bath oozed the pain from my limbs but did not stop my ranting to the translucent bubbles surrounding me. Rum running? Who was she kidding? I angrily splashed at the water, and the scalding liquid stung against my sunburned face. The pain was a relief from the torment of my mind. It was obvious the old bat McKenzie was toying with me.

The light, lime-green, cotton dress stuck to my still-moist back as I dashed through the lobby of Nash Dormitory. Cheap rent for the summer in the dorm was well within my budget if I kept this job. I was in the passageway of full-length windows that arched over the parking lot below when I stopped to catch my breath. My watch reported it was already 6:20, leaving me a mere forty minutes to find out what I could.

The warm air brushed through my damp curls as I crossed the street and took the path along the Ida Baker Bird Sanctuary that ran to the front steps of Wilson Library. The ornate, black iron doors were wide open in the evening sun.

Inside the thick stone walls, the coolness made me shiver. Not breaking my pace, I headed for the east wing, the older section, past the antique wooden file cabinets that held the Dewey decimal cards, to the research section.

Lissa's small form was easily overlooked in the high ceilings of the campus library. She sat, as usual, behind a tall counter, bent over a stack of books, her straight blond hair folded around her face. A shaft of soft purple light from the old stained-glass window fell across her delicate hands as she sorted through a stack of cards on her desk.

"Well, Jean," she smiled invitingly up at me, her soft voice teasing, "how does your garden grow?"

"Very funny." My mood carried across to my friend, blocking any attempt at cordiality.

"Going to quit?" she parried. "I can see it in your eyes. The same look you had when you quit Brian last year."

"Brian wasn't right for me. Besides, he wanted me to settle down on a quiet farm and be a nice wife. I wasn't ready."

Lissa ignored me.

"But this work is horrible."

She didn't blink so I tried again. Starting slowly I began, "Just look at me. My body is sore from head to toe." Seeing no response I pointed to my face, thinking visual aids accompanying my speech would solidify her compassion and enlist her support of my leaving the job, "I'm sunburnt." In desperation, I thrust my hands under her nose, my voice rising an octave. "My hands have blisters on them." I hated to stop, but I'd run out of available limbs and complaints.

Lissa quietly slipped a card into the jacket of another book. "I rather thought the color agreed with you." She rested the cards on the desk, eyeing me, selecting her words carefully, "You know, you just can't up and quit every time something doesn't go your exacting way."

"Besides," I hurried forward, remembering my biggest objection, "she's cuckoo. First, it was the past life bit, 'Where have we met before?' and then, it was some babble about rum running. I'm not going back." I sat on the edge of her desk, arms crossed, defying my friend to counter.

"A rum runner? That's interesting." Lissa's inflection perked up as she soundlessly pushed back her heavy oak chair and disappeared down a long row of books, her straight hair swaying with each step. Her voice trailed behind her, "Maybe she was."

Drawn in by the web McKenzie had wrapped around my thoughts earlier, I followed my friend's steps to find her hunched over a shelf in the history section. "Ah, here we are. Prohibition. Check these out and see what you can come up with. If nothing else, you can work this information into a research paper or lesson plan of some sort."

My arms dropped with the books piled in them. They strained against tired muscles. Why had I come to this dark, musty womb that harbors centuries of knowledge? My anger grew into frustration. Lissa sought books only for the answer to any problem. That fact I had been made painfully aware of one year ago when I struggled to my feet again after my unsuccessful flirtation with love. She had even gone so far as to get me a job with her, but that library proved no place for me. The breath of silence sought by some only echoed within my troubled mind and I spent hours hunched over, longing for an active outdoors challenge. Life isn't fair.

The irony of my situation cracked the anger from my face, and a smile slid forth.

"Good," Lissa encouraged and clapped her petite hands together. "Now, get out there, Jean, and stay with this job. See it as a game. Have fun."

Confusion carried me and my load of books from the library over the red bricks to the fountain. The urge to toss the entire stack into the large, spraying structure was great. My subconscious must have been hard at work and sent the top book sliding. I watched in horror as it tumbled toward the chlorine-scented liquid. A hand, strong and sure, reached from seemingly nowhere and caught the thick volume before it splashed into ruin.

"Wow, what a catch." I followed the hand to the face, and my breath stopped short.

"Actually, I'm the pitcher," his smile was broad, and he seemed to be enjoying his own comment. But his countenance changed when he placed the book back on the stack in my arms and caught a glimpse of some of the titles before observing, "Those are some books you have there."

I gaped helplessly, unable to respond to the figure towering over me as his intense green eyes took me in.

"Hey," a voice from behind him pulled his attention away from me. "We're late." He smiled and shrugged at me as he turned and jogged in the direction of his friend.

I let myself study the two departing figures, which was an easy task as they were a striking pair. Similar in height, the curly haired blonde patted his friend on the back, laughing at him, teasing. I stood admiring the long, reddish hair topping the bronzed muscles of the man who had just saved the book. How could a body like that know about books? I watched as he rounded the far side of an old pale green Chevy pickup and pulled open the driver's door. Suddenly, I realized he had paused and was returning my gaze with a look of confusion. Caught in the act, I forced my body into motion and continued past the fountain. With relief, I heard the truck sputter to life and pull away from the curb.

Restless, my feet kept moving back across Highland Drive. I reminded myself of two facts: One, I had no time for men; two, I had no interest in the likes of my book catcher, preferring brains over brawn.

I sought the lookout area next to the Viking Union Building with its sweeping view of Bellingham Bay. But it was the almost exact view from my dorm, and it bored me. I found no comfort in watching the various sized ships that lazed along this stretch of waterway.

Lissa, my neighbor in dorm life, my confidante, had failed to go along with my decision to quit. I felt lonely. I had made a huge error, and this slight could cost me my graduation. I would have to stay on the job.

—————⇒▸◦◂⇐—————

The stack of books sat untouched on my desk, drawing me toward them. I had attempted every avenue of avoidance: a walk, magazines, and even TV. Nothing budged them from their stubborn perch. It was three a.m. when I snapped on the light and picked through the pile to begin to read.

By five thirty, I closed *The Dry Years* in mixed interest and annoyance. Clearly, as Norman Clark had pointed out, Prohibition, the

"Great Dry," was a hot spot in recent history. "The Noble Experiment," as President Herbert Hoover coined it, was an experiment that failed miserably, as I was about to do.

My bed offered no solace as I twitched this way and that. Finally, giving in to the brilliance of the early sun, I planted my feet squarely on the cool floor. Why would an old lady such as Mrs. McKenzie make up a story about her involvement in rum running? If it was true, that old bird must have been one lively dame.

⇒•⇐

Mrs. McKenzie flung the door open before I could knock. "There you are. Isn't it a beautiful morning? Won't be as hot today. We'll be able to get more done." She strode past me and opened up the shed.

Not questioning her eagerness for work, I followed in her tracks across the dew on the grass.

"Here," she handed me the hoe with an encouraging tone, "let's see if we can't get the rest of that garden dug out today."

Gloves over my bandaged paws, I proceeded to whack at the earth before me. She was right—the sun was not as hot, and the ground moved readily under my tool. Her long legs bent as she eased toward the ground, grabbing the clumps of upturned overgrowth I left in my wake. Nimbly, she shook the dirt from the old roots, tossing the dead foliage aside. Within minutes, we were a team, surging across a brown field, destroying old life to make way for new.

A cool breeze from the bay chilled the sweat beaded on my brow. I could not keep silent any longer. "Mrs. McKenzie, were you really involved with rum running?"

"Alex," her voice was commanding. She didn't look up as she scattered the loosened soil. "Call me Alex. That's what they called me. Short for Alexandria, you know. Mary Alexandria Barry McKenzie to be exact. Born March 17, 1906, in Bellingham, Washington, to Irish-German parents. I've seen a hell of a lot in my time. Too much."

Her looks, my calculations, and her actual age were three different categories altogether. Realization stopped my progress.

"You mean you were my age when you were involved with smuggling booze?"

Her head tilted back, and she looked me right in the eye, her voice strong, "You bet." Seeing my reaction, she chuckled. "Don't worry, it didn't get real dangerous until I was about twenty-six or so. And hell, back then, that was middle age."

"Yes, of course," I stammered. Turning back to my digging, I tried to envision myself in such a predicament as she must have been in to do that kind of work. Why else would anyone in her right mind do something so crazy and dangerous?

"I did it for the adventure," she continued, unaware that she was picking up where my mind was letting off. "I never really fit into any of those highfalutin social circles. I was much better on my own or on the sea. My father was a sea captain, and I was the son he never had. So, I could out-drink and out-maneuver most of the captains on the waters around here. All except Jake and Stoney Black, that is."

She fell silent, hunched on all fours. Her body trembled, her face hidden from me. "Christ, it's hard to watch so many die before you."

Alex sat back onto her knees, moisture clung to her eyes as memories cling to the spirit. "Come on, it's time for a coffee break. Give me a hand here, Jean."

Her arm extended toward me, and I grasped it as gently as possible while steadying her to her feet.

"Old bones, don't rattle," she encouraged her limbs as she limped across the yard, stiff from her zealous effort.

The refrigerator closed behind her. Alex worked the foil from a platter before she placed several sandwiches before me.

"Coffee will be just a minute. Hello, Pretty Boy. Miss Mama?"

Alex was moving quickly again, having shaken the cramps from her limbs. "Jean, just try to think about it."

I was taken aback and puzzled by her seriousness. My mind raced. Think about what?

"One· day you could drink, and then, poof, they took it all away from us. Not a drop, unless you brewed it in secret or bought illegally. That's when all the tomfoolery started. You see, the state of Washington always wore pristine skirts. It was December 31, 1915, when the state went dry. Before that, no woman or Indian could enter a place of drink. In fact, the establishments had to have all these windows so people could see into the bars, just to be sure. I think they made that law so old lady Henley could find her husband. The Henleys were very well-to-do, pillars of the town and church, but he loved his drink.

"In the early 1900s, Bellingham had fifty-one churches and fifty-one saloons. And those saloons were rank, stinky places. People wanted to get rid of them so badly that they invited Billy Sunday out to preach his no-liquor talk. Everybody got together, and they threw up this tabernacle. The thing was an entire block long, cone-shaped with cheap, tar-paper roof, rough lumber seats, and six inches of sawdust on the floor. But damn, when old Billy Sunday—he was an ex-professional baseball player, you know—well, when he stepped down from his podium after his Evangelist speech, he'd converted even the saloon owners. So, Bellingham voted to go dry early on. And if you wanted a drink, you'd have to get yourself down to Sedro Wooley. They were still wet. Or you found other ways, other places. Damn, I used to love some of those honky-tonks.

"Then, in January of 1919, the Eighteenth Amendment got its vote. The entire nation went dry. I heard that back East they had a parade with coffins marked with booze bottles and all, and everyone was wearing black. Quite the funeral procession. Out here, our front page read, 'Better to buy shoes than booze.' Hell, it was my shoes that got us into all this trouble."

I smiled faintly at the shoe comment, and I waited politely for her to sit before grabbing at the delicious, thick sandwiches before me. Absently she waved me on, and I bit into the soft bread.

"It started one summer's night, on a lark. More of a mistake than anything. It was late August of '26, warm as they come. And still, the stillness before a storm. I wandered down onto the dock with Diesel Rose for a little exercise and to feel the coolness of the water.

On account of the new moon, it was real dark that night, except for the stars. There were just a few shooting stars left playing across the sky." Alex slid into her chair, her finger slightly arched up as she pointed at me. "Always know your moon, Jean. Many a cargo was lost, people were even killed, because that old moon had come out of nowhere and shone like the noon-day sun on night-time doings." Her finger bobbed with the chanting of her speech. With a snake-like move, she recoiled her finger, signaling the end of the warning, to continue her tale.

"Where was I?"

I hurried to swallow the sumptuous bite of sandwich before answering, "You were on the dock."

"Oh, yes. Well, I thought it was just the two of us down there, but I was wrong. Diesel had run on ahead, her short, little legs beating a rhythm on the old planks. Pretty soon, she came running past me with a cigarette butt in her mouth, leaving a little wisp of smoke as she scurried by.

"'I'm going to kill that damn dog.' It was Stoney Black, and he was hot as a pistol as he came toward me."

"Dog?" I choked out.

"Of course, Diesel Rose was a terrier mutt of sorts, the best in the world. Body by committee, a bit too long here, too short there, but a damn fine creature."

My nod seemed to encourage her forward.

"So I stepped out of the dark, right in front of Stoney, scared the bejesus out of him. 'You'll have to catch her first,' I spoke right up to that big galoot. Could have knocked him over with one finger. He ran his burly hand over his black beard and just stared at me as if we'd never met. That's when I knew something was up, and I planned to find out what.

"'Whatcha doin' here, Alexandria?'

"'It's a free country. Maybe I came to spy on you.' He didn't like that and just kept shifting his feet.

"'Ah, why don't you just run on home like a good girl?'

"That got my goat. I started to go past him down the dock, and he moved in front of me. So, I tried again, and again he blocked my path with his powerful bulk. So I said good-bye, whistled for Diesel Rose, and left. Only I didn't leave, you know. I just went up there and waited a few minutes with Diesel, then took off my shoes, and snuck back down onto the dock. That crazy mutt, she knew I was up to something because she crept just as quiet as can be right next to me.

"I don't have any idea what possessed me to do such a thing. My mother used to always tell me that I would get into serious trouble if I didn't learn to keep my nose where it belonged. Well, so there we were, and suddenly I saw this boat I'd never seen before still rocking slightly, so I knew Stoney had gotten into it. Oh, she was a beaut, sleek and fast as all get-out. Sea sleds they called them. Originally built by Boeing so he could show off for his girlfriend, it was that fast, could do up to 45 mph on the open water. But no one wanted to buy them—too fast, not practical—until the Prohibition came along. Then they were all bought in one day for cash.

"Diesel whimpered and moved further down the dock, and luckily, I took her cue and slid behind a piling just as two large figures emerged from the boat and disappeared up the dock. With my ear to the dock, I could hear the retreating feet. We waited a half-minute then climbed aboard. I put my shoes under the captain's chair and was snooping a good look at the craft when footsteps signaled the arrival of those two dark figures. Diesel's tail was wagging furiously, so I grabbed her, and we ducked below into a small berth forward. The hatch door opened, and a coat landed on us, smelling of cigars and oil fumes. And then, we felt the boat begin to drift and a big thud as the line hit the floorboards, and then someone landed on the bow above us. When I checked out the portal, there were no running lights reflecting on the water; it was dark as death.

"Weren't you frightened?" I hadn't meant to interrupt. It had just slipped out.

"Frightened? You bet. Not about being on a strange boat but about what Stoney would do to me when he found me. And I had no idea who the second person was and what this boat was about. When the engine kicked into gear, I fell so fast I knocked my head. But there were still no running lights, and that meant trouble.

"Whoever was skippering knew the waters. Only once did I hear what sounded like 'dead head' warning of floating logs or some object to avoid. Smooth as silk, we glided along for quite some time. I was lulled to sleep in the dark comfort of the hull. It seems we had headed south around Lummi Island to Orcas and were off Grindstone Inlet when I heard the engine start up again, and it woke me up. At first, I thought I was aboard my dad's vessel but then remembered my father had died some months back. Waiting, I listened intently for any clue. There was the soft shuffle of feet from above. I felt the weight change as someone moved aft to check the engine. Then the weight shifted again as the person moved forward and halted. The engine cut so suddenly I slipped forward and knocked against the hatch door with a curse and a thud. The running lights came on.

"The hatch flew open, one of my shoes came out of nowhere and hit me in the arm, and a strong beam of light was shining in my eyes. Diesel started to growl so I was trying to put her behind me.

"'What in blue blazes is that?'" Alex imitated a deep voice. "Now, I've been called many things before, but 'that' was never one of them. It got my Irish up.

"'Get over here,' a voice commanded, and my knees went weak. Suddenly I was damn scared because it wasn't Stoney talking.

"'Now,' it barked, and I hurried to comply. I left Diesel below, scampering over the mid seat to the aft deck, the beam of light constantly in my eyes.

"The two voices exchanged hushed remarks, the anger evident in both sides. Then, not far off, a light appeared and shone on the water. At first, I couldn't tell if it was another craft or someone on shore. The flashlight on my face snapped off, but I still couldn't see, and fear wasn't allowing me to breathe. The lights across the water were coming straight for us.

"Stoney went below and reappeared with a blanket. The other figure was bent over the floorboards between the captain's chairs.

Stoney tossed me the blanket and started to strip. I was mustering up a lecture when he disappeared over the side into the dark, chilly water.

"The second guy scooped up Stoney's pants and shirt, tossed them at my feet, and hid a gun under them. Before I knew what was happening, he was undoing the top two buttons on my blouse and shoving me down on the cool floorboards, drawing the blanket over us.

"'You got yourself into this, Red,' he whispered as he put his arms around me and pressed his lips against mine. He started kissing me like there was no tomorrow.

"I started fighting back because I realized it was Jake McKenzie. Jonathan Edward McKenzie. He'd called me 'Red' since I was in knickers. I hated him for it then. I could tell I was losing the fight, and maybe not minding so much, when the second boat bumped against our starboard side. I was so dizzy from the intoxicating kiss and frightened by the gun, I didn't realize another man had boarded us until I heard him speak.

"'Isn't it a little late for you to be up, laddie?' His Scottish brogue was thick with mockery as he leaned into us. Sergeant Drummond's badge caught the light as he shone his torch around the boat. 'And where did you find this fine specimen? Sure she's a fast one.'

"I began to wiggle with my reply but the sergeant didn't allow me to speak.

"'I was speaking of the boat, mum,'" her imitation of the strong accent getting bigger.

"Jake loosened his grip on me to fold his arms behind his head. He looked so relaxed, but I could feel his heart beating swiftly. 'Never too late for an evening on the water.' Jake kissed me on the forehead, and I snuggled closer, suddenly liking this dangerous game.

"Officer Thompson's figure, short and stocky, appeared behind Drummond.

"'Mind if I look around, mum?'

"Suddenly in command, I yawned in Drummond's face, which brought a low chuckle from my bed partner. 'Be my guest.'

"The light remained on us when suddenly there was a warning growl from Diesel Rose, and Thompson backed out of the cabin.

"'Like my new guard dog?' Jake whistled, and Diesel came and sat on our feet as Jake slid his hand down toward the gun.

"Drummond couldn't help but laugh. He crossed the boat and sat on the side rail right where Stoney had slipped overboard.

"'What have you been up to, Jake?' the sergeant was attempting friendliness.

"'Fishin' and look what I caught.' Oh, Jake could be cocky.

"But Drummond wasn't having any of it. He started for the blanket, but Jake and Diesel stood their ground. Thompson appeared empty handed and frustrated. The tension built. It was suddenly hot down there out of the wind. I could feel the sweat dripping down my body.

"Drummond and Thompson started for the starboard side and slid over into their craft when he turned back. 'Just remember, then, Jake McKenzie, I enjoy my job. I like knowin' where you are and what you're doin'. Always keep that in mind. Night, mum.'

"The boat rocked as they pushed off and were on their way, the fury of their idle search erupting in a cavalcade of waves that beat against our boat.

"I began to relax when Jake jumped up, tugging the blanket with him as I slid across the deck.

"'Is-is-is it cl-clear … yet?' a voice from the darkness barely whispered.

"Jake leaned over the engine and helped Stoney, a shivering mass, aboard. The blanket went around Stoney's shoulders, and Jake began patting him on the back. 'We got him good that time.'

"'You b-b-bet.' Stoney sputtered, smiling, his teeth chattering and the cold water dripping from his beard and hair.

"I stood beside them, watching. Stoney sat on the side rail, trying to warm himself, drying his foot. Suddenly, they both remembered I was there and turned toward me.

"'Now weren't you our …,' Jake did his best imitation of Drummond's accent as he drew out the words, 'lucky lass, Red. And not a bad kisser either.'

"That got me up and going. I was as mad as a hornet in a woman's Sunday hat. I swung my best haymaker, but Jake ducked, and I hit

Stoney square in the jaw. I caught him so off guard I knocked him right back into the water. Jake was laughing so hard he couldn't even help Stoney back on board. When Stoney did finally crawl back on deck, I thought I was going to be the next one in, but he started into laughing too. Pretty soon, Diesel Rose got into the act, and that was our beginning, as the four of us howled in the moonless night. What a sight we were."

Alex sat back in her chair, and silence filled the room. She closed her eyes adding, "There is so much to tell. But that's enough for now."

The bird decided to fill the void that followed with his chatter while I sat digesting my food and the story.

"We'd better get back to it, Jean. I want to get the garden patch cleared before you leave today." She was up and shuffling the dishes to the sink before I could respond.

The sun was still hiding behind the clouds when we returned to our work. I tried to concentrate on what she had just told me when suddenly I realized she hadn't told me why the boat had gone out that night.

I wanted to ask, but her concentration was so intent on the rubble of the overturned earth I didn't dare disturber her. She was picking through it meticulously and appeared to be looking for something. I remembered the object I had unearthed yesterday. Was that why she had transformed so suddenly? Was there more to uncover?

I pocketed my questions for later and went back to churning up the earth.

CHAPTER 3

It seemed as though days had passed in the silence of the afternoon. The aches and pain had long since dissolved into a comfortable rhythm as the shovel and I became one.

Mrs. McKenzie wandered from house to garden, encouraging my progress as a pit crew does a racecar driver.

"You're doing a fine job. Looking good. Keep going. Almost there," she would sputter, always with a constant eye on the ground I was exposing.

It was almost five. Exhaustion had passed into delirium. I looked at the garden area I had finished some time ago. *Enough*, my mind was screeching at my body. Yet, all Alex had said was what appeared to be an exasperated, "Holy crap," then swiftly turned me toward the long stretch of brown foliage inching up the driveway.

"Dig, Jean, dig," became her mantra.

It was a command backed by a hidden urgency. I could feel the traces of that need as I began to ply the new patch of ground. She stood behind me, imitating my moves, as if her dancing in my shadows would speed my shovel in its search. I wasn't quite sure when the knowledge had passed between us of the hunt, but like a well-trained animal, I had picked up the scent. What was it, though, I was looking for? The mystery hastened my motion. Images of treasure chests dripping with jewels, a few cases of rum with a stash box stuffed with money, a dead body, or parts of one. Whatever it was, I was lost to it. My shovel and mind committed with feverish stokes. I worked the soil, hitting it again, harder and harder.

The shovel struck something solid, vibrated in my hands, and loosened my grip as it twirled to the earth with a decisive thud. I was on the ground, my face inches from the dirt, the smell filling my nostrils, as my gloves worked frantically to unveil the object. It was large and hard. A boulder.

I felt the sigh of disgust from behind me. Now Alex scurried back to the neatly edged garden. She fell to her knees and, with her bare hands, began to root through the dirt. Like a dog digging for his beloved bone, the old hands scooped at the soil littering the soft grass.

Her mumblings came in broken drifts, "It must … Jake, you son … put the damn thing?"

The garbled words stopped. She pointed her long arching finger at the garden. It hovered as if it had its own mind.

"You," the rumblings came from deep within, "you can't do this to me, you son of a sea bitch." Tears sprang from her blue eyes to run down the smooth, aged cheeks. They glistened in taunting pearls, then rested at her chin, too tired to complete the journey. "Why, Jake?"

I watched in agony, glad for the distance between us. She rocked gently, catching the drops with the back of her hand. A thought came to life within me like a budding flower in sunshine. Was I witnessing the disjointed meanderings of an old mind? A mind lost to the realities surrounding it? Yes, that had to be it. There was really nothing lost except the mind of the red-haired widow, whose tear-streaked face was now hidden from me. The hunched figure was silent and motionless like the many rocks I had plucked from the garden, solid, etched with time.

Stretching to a stand, I began to dust myself off as if my brisk slaps would awaken my trust in this venture. How had I gotten so caught up in a search I knew nothing about? I put it down to exhaustion. This job was dangerous, I realized. It was taking far too much out of me. A surge of red found my cheeks as I looked around to be certain no one had witnessed this event. This would convince Lissa I should quit.

First things first, I attempted to bring order back to this sad scene. Get Mrs. McKenzie calmed down, then leave quietly. Get home. Get Away. Most important, get another job.

"It's here somewhere, Jean," the tired voice interrupted my thoughts. "I know it is. I can feel it."

"What is it you are looking for?"

"Something that Jake gave me a long time ago. I need it. I need it to go on. I lost the damn thing. But now I need it," her voice dwindled to a whisper of hope.

"Of course," I humored the slumped shoulders. "But, ah, well, it's late. Maybe we should get some rest and get an early start tomorrow."

"Yes. Yes, you're right. You will be a good teacher someday, Jean." Her arm lifted through the air as if hailing a taxi in a heated city.

I went to her, and like a human teeter-totter, we swayed to our feet.

"I hate getting old. It's a pain in the bum to have to be helped like this." She kicked forward, a wooden puppet marching, easing the stiffness free.

The coolness of the house and the chatter of Pretty Boy were welcomed by both of us. We sat across from each other, sipping cold water, silence the only thing spoken between us.

How to tell her? A lifetime could be spent in a search, and from the grave would come the echo, "I know it's here somewhere, Jean." I shoved the atrocity of that thought aside.

"What was Jake doing on the water that night?" The question formed by my lips surprised all who heard it. I jumped. Alex knitted her brow, while the bird raced back and forth on its perch. Pretty Boy paused long enough to press a startled eye between the bars to look down at me as if I were an intruder not to be trusted.

Slumping back against my chair, I sputtered, "I-I was just curious." The need for truth had spoken for me. I had to know before I quit. Holding my arms, I waited for an answer.

Her tongue moved over her teeth, her upper lip bulging, carrying the thought from one side of her mouth to the other before she could spit out the answer.

"That's good, Jean. Good. But remember, miss," she leaned forward extending her long finger, that bent nemesis, in my direction, "curiosity killed the cat."

"Satisfaction," I squirmed, eyeing the arched appendage, daring to form the words, "brought him back."

The bent finger, with its strong sense of power, disappeared as she slapped her side, emitting a small puff of dust.

"My God, Jean, you have guts. I like that." She lowered her voice to continue, "There was trouble in Seattle. Big Trouble. The Barbecue Pit had been raided, and Doc had been arrested. Doc was one of Jake's customers. I'll never forget the first time he took me to see the famous old speakeasy. And you wouldn't believe the high-class clientele. Why, most nights the curb on East Union in Seattle outside the Barbecue Pit was lined with society's elite rides. Some places were more discrete. One mansion on Capitol Hill had a driveway that went under the house with a huge area for parking. They had this disk that you drove your car onto, and it would spin so they could load that underground parking up, and no one knew how many cars there really were down there.

"There were codes used to get in and everything. Doc's door had a small peek hole that would open if need be. And Jake had his very own code, prayer to the wind god, he called it.

> Now I sail me to the dock,
> Pray that I won't hit a rock.
> If you get me safely in,
> I'll give up beer
> But not my gin.

"Doc had dancing, gambling, and the best gin fizzes in town. But he got raided because the Feds were trying to find the gang of hijackers that'd murdered some Canadian suppliers. The Eggers gang shot Gillis and his son. Someone spotted Gillis's trawler drifting off

Waldron, up toward the border. When they got on board, they found bullet holes up top and below, sloppy work. Seems the gang had not only killed them but cut them up and tied a 150-pound anchor to their dirty work. Feds caught two of the bastards for it. But they didn't get the real leader behind that."

Her head shook, trying to loosen more words, but her smile faded. "Anyway, Jake got word of the shooting from O'Leary up on Whiskey Ridge—they renamed it Carnation after Prohibition—and so Jake called a meeting. A convention we called them. Of course, it was nothing like the big convention of 1930, held right in downtown Seattle, mind you. That one had to do with the intrusion of the mob from back East. It was a dilly. I was awake for that one.

"You see, Jake had several men working for him and wanted to be sure that after the killing everyone was still with him."

Alex pushed herself up and started towards the window.

I followed her, and we both stood watching the exposed sand on the outgoing tide sparkle in the light, glistening with moisture. "Did many leave him?"

"Jean, those were rough times. Both sides thought they were doing the right thing. But, it was risky. Thrilling. We wore armbands the day of the Gillis funeral. Those hijackers were a bad lot. Took the load, of course. But they put fear in everyone. They had no morals, no sense. But the worst was yet to come.

"The same night, it seems, some righteous Feds busted up the Rosewood Bar in Seattle. Broke my heart. It was such a beautiful place, all hardwood from around the Cape. Big expensive mirrors. The damn fool Fed Hinkley hollered he'd teach 'em a lesson. Marched right in the place with his men, and they all had axes and went to it. Destroyed everything. Useless. Stupid. I get so damn mad when I think of it. Those saloons were only providing a service. Hell, there were very few judges and lawyers that didn't have their own private stash, built-in secret closets to store the booze. I know. I was at their homes.

"Homes on the waters were famous for their hidden passageways for the boats to go right under their homes, like at Smugglers Cove. It was thrilling to outwit the Feds. But the Feds had their tricks too.

That first night I hooked up with Jake and Stoney, the Feds had some-how heard about their meeting and were working the waters. The conference was almost over when old Chief Roaring Thunder pulled up alongside and warned Jake some of his fishermen had spotted Sheriff Drummond's boat. And he knew Jake would want to get his men out of there fast. Jake thanked his old friend. They respected each other so much. In fact, Jake tried to keep his booze away from the chief's men. Some fool Canadian tried to get the Indians to run while they paddled from island to island but soon stopped because the Indians drank all of the liquor before it was delivered." Her chuckle held wistful memories.

"Jake took that warning, and he and Stoney, and me, of course just waking up, and headed right toward the area where Drummond had been spotted. He was trying to draw the sheriff away from his men. Jake was like that."

The water below us churned foamy white wisps that rushed over the sand, consuming it, only to retreat, build up its strength, and surge forward again, reclaiming its own path with dizzying freedom. The unending ballet of the sea.

Mrs. McKenzie drooped onto the couch that faced the windows. "I'll see you tomorrow morning, Jean. We'll dig. I know it's there." She looked tired, remorseful.

I couldn't help but be drawn to her. Like a mystery game board, a chancy roll of the dice could unfold pieces to the past.

Something inside clicked, and pity was replaced with anger. It became clear why this temptress had hired me. It wasn't to clean her garden. I was not here to straighten her yard. I was here to dig for something she'd never lost. I was convinced of that now. I was being tricked, used. This idiocy needed to end.

Our eyes were locked. She was watching my changing expressions as if they were pages in a novel, reading my hidden innuendos. I, like the retreating wave mustering strength, needed to reclaim my own path and be free of her control.

The back door opened and closed. Neither of us moved. The bird chirped a greeting as the spry steps brought the intruder to the window beside us.

I turned to find an old man, about my height, with tan skin and gentle, brown eyes. His face wrinkled as he smiled at me, bowing slightly. He smoothed the ornate robe, his knuckles gnarled, as they passed over the rich material. There was a large intricate gold ring on his pinkie, just below the fingernail. The nail extended in an arch at least one inch beyond the tip of his finger.

"Chin, you've come. How grand." Alex struggled to her feet.

The two old friends smiled at each other and much passed between them in their slight gestures of courtesy and love.

"Mr. Chin, his real name is LiFan Ho Chin, I'd like you to meet Jean Bowen."

"How do you do?" I smiled at his happy apple face.

"I chose wisely, don't you think?"

McKenzie was talking about me, and I shifted my feet in annoyance and embarrassment.

"Yes, Alexandria. You have the eye of many great men."

"Will you stay and have some tea with us, Jean?"

"No, thank you, I must get going. But there's something I—"

"That's all right," she cut me off. "I'll see you tomorrow then."

She led the way to the kitchen. I scooted past her and continued toward the back door.

"Good-bye. Nice to have met you, Mr. Chin."

"And you," again the nod.

My hand rested on the doorknob, my head was pounding. *Tell her you won't be coming back.* My resolve swelled within me. *Now,* that irritable voice insisted, but I hesitated a moment before turning back toward them.

They had slipped back inside the safety of the turquoise and wood kitchen.

"Oh, Chin, it was an exhausting day," Alex's tone reflected her state of being as she lowered her tired bones into the steel framed kitchen chair, her back to me.

The old man passed into view with a teapot in his hands, his words barely audible, "Did you find what you were looking for, Alexandria?"

"No." It was a sad, pitiful sound.

Ever so quietly, I backed out of the door, softly closing it behind me. A new wave of emotion propelled me past the carnage of my day's work. Chin's words resounded loudly in my muddled mind, *"Did you find what you were looking for?"*

I would have to come back, be her tool in a search I knew nothing about. At least not yet.

CHAPTER 4

I woke with a start, thankful to be wrestling with my sheets and not the tall man with the thick accent who was trying to push me off the bright silver boat that streaked across the water without anyone at the helm.

Lying back, I snuggled deep into my pillow. The pain was not worth the product. I had no time to chase ghosts. She must understand. Forcing my toes to the cold linoleum floor, the rest of my limbs slumped after. I stood bent and cramped, a prehistoric figure in a youthful body.

My feet dragging, I opened my eyes wide to find my calendar. There it was in my exacting penmanship in bold black and white: June 20–24, Mrs. McKenzie – Garden. And in my thoroughness, I had calculated the amount of pay and neatly added this amount to the week's end: Sunday, June 26, $225.00. My eyes scanned further, and the next Sunday also boasted pay of $225.00. The following weeks remained blank until early August: Mrs. Rebstock ? cleaning.

My shoulders slumped even lower. I crawled back into bed, pulling the covers tight around me for protection from the world, a big, ugly monster, too frightening to face. If I quit this job, I would fall in the category below starving student to one called non-student for lack of funds.

Why hadn't I taken a summer desk job? Why did I have to pretend to be so damned independent and clever? The sheets gave no solace to my query.

The loud ringing in my ear rattled my bones. I flipped the cover back and swatted at the annoying keeper of time. Whoever invented alarm clocks should be placed in a hell of never-ending ring … ring … ring.

Yet, submissively, I obeyed. Beaten before I'd begun, I trudged to the bathroom to prepare my hands for another day's toil.

<hr/>

"Time for a break, Jean."

I hadn't heard that voice all morning. When I had arrived, the shed door stood open, inviting me to proceed at once with my duties and, as I had hoped, without interruptions.

I was tired. The shadow dancer of the prior day had left me little energy. I had begun slowly, exposing and examining, inch by inch, up the long driveway. Every now and again, the newly tanned skin of my lower arms caught and ripped open on the old, large thorns of the evenly spaced rose bushes that dotted the way.

Pushing myself up, I spread my legs and arched my back so I faced the bright, cloudless sky. The brim of my new hat was edged in dirt and stained with sweat. So much for neatness. She was watching me now, I knew, as she had from different vantage points all morning. I didn't need to check, I could feel her. Throughout the morning, different windows had darkened with her shadow as she moved from perch to perch like Pretty Boy in his cage, thrusting an ever-watchful eye closer for inspection.

The chirping of the busybody parakeet and the smile of the old woman greeted me as I entered. To the unobservant eye, the scene would play as a kindly, elderly woman fixing a treat for her helper. Yet, from my vantage point, my shield of armor was up to ward off the craft of this beguiling witch. Macbeth himself would have feared this redhead far more than the Ides of March.

I sat. The aroma was of strong, dark coffee.

"A piece of cake?" She had never meant the remark to be a question but a command. The spongy, brown slice was before me.

Eye of newt and toe of frog, wool of bat and tongue of dog, Macbeth's witches chimed in to warn me. As my mind spun, the lips stayed sealed.

"How do you bake a cake, Jean?

I wasn't sure where this was leading, except that my shield was slipping as I glanced down at the tender morsel.

"A cake?"

"What do you put in it? The cake?"

The question seemed far too simple for a trap. I answered dutifully, "You mean like eggs and flour and milk?"

"Exactly." She drew out the word as if she'd won the game.

"And butter," I hastened to add.

She laughed then leaned across the table toward me, her arched index finger out and ready, pointing at the cake. "And just how damn easy do you think it was to get butter, let alone eggs or milk, during the depression?"

I was beginning to follow the concept.

"That cake doesn't have any milk, eggs, or butter in it. Now go on, try it."

Where a few seconds before my mouth had watered at the tempting, moist wedge, my throat was now dry. I eyed the cake and prepared myself as I took my first bite.

The fork left my lips, and what remained was a rich coffee flavor with a spongy texture. "It's wonderful." My reaction was genuine.

"That is what is known as the Great Depression Cake. It was real popular after the stock market crash of '29. Sugar, strong coffee, raisins, there's shortening in it and flour, but it's the baking power and soda that make it rise. I also put in some walnuts, cinnamon, a pinch of cloves and nutmeg. Recipe's there in that brown book."

I looked at the book that was wedged between two jars holding dried herbs of some kind on the counter. It was thick and had a few ripped-out recipes protruding high above the other pages. Her kitchen bible bulged with many secrets.

"I remember one Christmas I made twenty-five of those dang cakes. Only I put a ten dollar gold piece in them, see, like the Greeks do with wedding cake."

Alex shifted in her chair, smiling, settling in to further her tale. "Jake and Stoney and I thought that was a pretty good one. Our neighbors who were real hard up weren't expecting to find an expensive cake sitting on their porches. Mrs. Aspelund's dog got to hers. She tied him up and waited for poor old Juno to pass that coin as if she was waiting on Santa himself."

She leaned back into her chair to continue. "I swore I'd never make another one of those damn cakes again," her finger poked in the direction of the remaining cake. "And I swore I wouldn't dwell on what happened back then, I mean the bad things. And look at me." She pushed herself up from the table. "The past walks with me like a shadow, closer sometimes."

She began pacing. Pretty Boy, feeling the tension, followed suit by keeping pace back and forth on his wooden perch. Two old birds in unison.

I fingered the bandage covering my blisters, eyes on the cake, waiting for what I knew was the build-up to more of her incredible tales. But, I reasoned, these glimpses might help me discover just what it was she was looking for.

"Times weren't easy. People did what they had to do. You can spend five seconds doing something you wonder about for the rest of your life. It was New Year's Eve. I was wearing this deep blue satin dress. It was rather daring, cut to the waist in the back and low in the front too. But hell, it was Jake's party. He liked to entertain his city clientele to keep everything running smoothly, if you get my drift.

"Anyway, I had these new shoes too. Cost almost as much as the dress. They were gold, with open toe and straps that went around the ankle with the sweetest bows in the middle. Oh, and high. We wore real heels back then. We were in the down below, that's what I called it. What a night. It started out just grand. Jake had his men positioned with lanterns so we could make our way out of those catacombs in case the Feds showed up."

She stopped and turned toward me speaking with some urgency, "Have you ever been down there?"

"Where?" my voice was soft so as not to disturb her line of concentration.

"The Underground in Seattle. The fire of June 1889 destroyed Seattle, so they built on top, leaving the old buildings below. Someone got smart and turned part of it into a speakeasy. Lots of ways to run, places to hide. Oh, it was not as fancy as the speakeasy built under downtown Tacoma. That one was made of pink marble, mind you. These were wild times. Women got a taste of liquor and took to it like water. Anyway, after an exceptional year, Jake threw a New Year's Eve party to remember. Jake was courting Judge Warren, you see. Wanted to make sure our backsides were covered. Hell, free booze and dancin' brought out the best lawyers and judges every time.

"But that night, toward the end, someone else showed up uninvited."

The next words she spat out, "Antonio Vitrona." She sat as she said his name, the weight of his memory pulling her down. "Oh, he was a handsome devil, all right. Not rugged good-looking like Jake and Stoney, but all slicked back Italian style. He had a slight scar across his cheek. Impeccably dressed and mean as a shark. He loved blood.

"Nobody knew how he'd found us. But the room shifted, and tension replaced the laughter when he came in with his goons. We'd met before, and it hadn't been pretty, barely escaped. His Italian Mafia, Camorra, was trying to take over the Northwest with his back-East pockets and guns. They were trying to squeeze the life out of us. The guys were all riled, but Jake told them to let him stay and only nodded in his direction. Should have killed him right there and then.

"We settled back into the party, and I was dancing with Stu, one of Jake's men, when Antonio cut in and took my hand. Stoney was on his feet, and I saw Jake slowly start toward us. The room had hushed, but Antonio just kept on dancing me around the floor, the scent of his cologne makes me sick to this day." Her fingers ran through her red hair, leaving a strained path.

"Jake took my hand from Antonio's, and it was shaking. 'I believe you have something of mine,' his voice was a smooth threat.

"'Not for long.' Antonio's accent was thick, Italian and Brooklyn mixed, his words calculating. He kissed my hand before letting go, and what he said next set our world upside down, 'For now, firebird.'

"Jake's arm was around me at that, and he guided me to the table, which quickly filled with his men. I took off my shoes, not only because I was nervous, but because my feet were killing me. A dance floor is no place to break in a new pair of heels. My nerves were just settling down around my Scotch and soda when I saw one of the guys signal Stoney and Jake. Stoney headed my way, and Jake headed toward Judge Warren's table all smiles as if nothing in the world was wrong. Within minutes, we were all sliding through the back exits to follow the lanterns. The Feds were coming to wish us a happy New Year.

"Well, I was trying to get my shoes on. I had one on, but Stoney was rushing me so, and the other slipped out of my hand. I tried to go back for it, but once Stoney got movin', nothing could stop that bull. Especially my little gold shoe with all those straps. And I was not happy about losing my new shoe.

"We were twisitn' and winding through those damp, dark paths. There was a blue lantern swinging up ahead. That meant come fast, the car was waiting. Suddenly there was a loud crash from behind.

"'Alex,' Stoney barked, 'Jake will kill me himself if anything happens to you. Now get to the car and stay put.'

"Then he turned back and was gone. I limped in the direction of the blue light. I wasn't afraid, but my foot was wet and cold. And I'd run my silk stockings on the rough path. I wanted my shoe.

"I heard someone behind me and just kept on going, thinking it was Stoney or Jake. I was just about at the blue light when a hand went over my mouth and a body pressed up against me, dragging me into the shadow. I felt something pointed press against my back.

"'You are a beautiful woman,' the accent slurred. 'I want you and should take you right now. But I can be patient. I will have you, firebird.'

"He held me, breathing heavy down my neck, his hand moving freely down my skin." Alex shuddered and her words seemed to shake with her. "That cologne."

"I tried to get away. I bit him, but he just laughed and licked the hand where I'd drawn blood.

"I was so scared I could barely speak, 'Get out before Jake kills you.'

"'Jake will never kill me. Why? For returning a lady's shoe? You are always leaving me an easy trail to find you.'

"He dangled my shoe by its strap, and I snatched it from him. Then he grabbed me and began to kiss me. I was hitting him with my shoe when there was a noise behind us. Antonio put his hand over my mouth and pressed his lips to my ear. 'I will be back for you.' His words were chilling. I was breathless as he left me and slithered deep into the dark.

"'Alex,' Stoney bellowed, steaming toward me, 'I told you to keep going. Come on.'

"He had my arm, and we were off, up a ladder to the street, and into the car before I could say Canadian whisky. The judge and his wife were in the back seat. Stoney and I slid in the front seat next to Jake, and we sped off in silence that lasted until the judge was delivered safely to his mansion on Capitol Hill.

"'That's my girl,' Jake patted my leg, attempting to break my dark mood. 'The Feds show up, and Alex remembers to grab her dancin' shoes.'

"In his own way, Jake was commenting on my dancing with Antonio, and I knew it bothered him. That he'd brood about it. But, it was Stoney who stared at me now as he noticed both shoes were securely strapped to my feet. I never wore those damn shoes again."

CHAPTER 5

The impact of her story followed me up the driveway to my rake, hoe, and shovel. Choosing the shovel, I snatched it up and, with a mighty blow, struck the dry swath of earth with its tiny crack that ran from the base of the old roses outward. I felt as if my life was as depleted and boring as this patch of brown earth, and I hated the new sensation.

We were the same age when she was flirting with the law in the bootleg world running whiskey. For me, it was books, a broken heart, and now these dried-up, overrun flower-beds. On the horizon, if I graduated, lay the hope of settling into the quiet of teaching, which appeared lackluster in comparison.

A spider legged its way across my shadow. I did not pull back but moved closer, observing my enemy from a short distance. If I were brave, I told myself, I'd touch that fuzzy thing. The thought alone made me recoil. The spider, suddenly exposed to the light, jumped and was off hiding behind a small clump of dirt.

"Get," I yelled at the intruder, in no mood to play hide-and-seek with a creepy crawler. And with explicit instructions not to kill worms or spiders because of their advantage to the garden, I vented my frustration by striking the earth, close to the creature. He moved inches to the nearest rock. I parried. He dodged a few more steps.

Obsessed with ridding this disgusting intruder from my life, as if this small, hairy, creature contained all that thwarted my efforts to live a more exciting life, I began chasing the blackish spider with my shovel.

"Get, get, get," I spat in its direction. Each blow came a little closer, hitting the earth with more force.

"Well, I declare, I believe you have sunstroke, child," her voice, the now annoying sing-songy one, held a hint of laughter.

I looked at the large bonnet that shaded her expression. A tin bucket swung in her hand. Suddenly, I wanted to chase Mrs. McKenzie with my shovel too. She had lived so much. It was unfair. I wanted some excitement in my life.

"Jean, I fear my story has upset you."

"No," slipped out like a child whose toy was being taken. She was considering my ability for this job. My grip tightened around the shovel as I rushed on to make my excuse. "No, it was just one of those damn spiders, just got to me. That's all."

She shifted, briskly lowering the empty bucket to the ground. "Let's call it a day for now. Would you run by Paulson's Drugs for me and pick up my prescription? It's all ready for you."

Her back to me now, I watched her ease behind the wooden door and disappear.

Prescription? The word drained my rage at her enticing exploits and filled me with an unsettling fear. Was she sick? Collecting my tools, my analytical mind gathered facts on her agility, presence of mind, and coloration. No, she didn't appear sick. Probably just another attempt to play on my sympathy. I remembered a line my older brother used about an ancient, cardboard-faced aunt I was fond of. He constantly reassured me the frail old being would be late to her own funeral. I started to laugh. Not only would Alex McKenzie be late, but she'd be directing the entire proceedings.

⟫•⟪

The prescription rested on my desk under my lamp, a beacon of mistrust. I had not opened the small white bag with the emblem, which sealed the contents, boasting of the livelihood of drugs, but crawled onto my bed exhausted.

Closing my eyes, I attempted to envision the scene of that New Year's Eve party, wondering at my own reaction to such an ordeal. The excitement, the risk, being on the wrong side of the law, yet respected by some. Not to mention those they helped in those terrible times. I tried to envision a world without alcohol. No ads on TV blaring which booze is the best to consume on various occasions, pushing hot buttered rums for winter and iced margaritas for the warmth of summer. My mind drifted back to Jake. No face floated before me. She had said he was handsome, but that was all. There must be pictures somewhere. Her private room, that small dark space left unlit, unfinished like so many lives, must have pictures of him. Why weren't there any up around the house?

Don't let your mind get away with you, that hated, well-versed voice of reason cautioned. I rolled over, too tired to argue even with myself, and let sleep overtake me.

———»-•-«———

"Jean?"

"What?" I bolted up shaking off the dream of spiders pinning me to the ground with their sticky strands of webbing.

"Sorry," Lissa half whispered as she entered my room. "I saw your light on and thought you were awake.

"What time is it?" My eyes were adjusting to my half-dark room.

"Ten thirty. You still gainfully employed?" she eased onto the side of my bed, drawing closer for the ribbing.

I draped my hand over my thigh, palm upward, the half, soft light from my desk lamp, exaggerating my wounds.

"My God, Jean. What are you doing?"

"Working."

"Well, maybe you should quit. That looks awful."

I couldn't tell if she was baiting me, so I was slow to answer, "Yeah."

"When?" her voice sounded urgent.

"Friday, I guess." I cupped my hand back toward the warmth of my chest and let my lids fall. It was an invitation for Lissa to exit. I was too tired to talk.

I heard her step toward my desk lamp. The movement stopped and was followed by the crinkle of paper. "Are you sick?" my friend's tone was now soft and caring.

"Naw. It's for old bird McKenzie. I'm delivery girl now."

The paper rattled back into place while darkness engulfed me with a snap, and Lissa silently left my room.

———•◦•———

The white bag remained unopened on the turquoise speckled linoleum of the kitchen counter. Pretty Boy hadn't missed a trill when I'd placed it there. Neither had Alex rushed to snap it up. What was in the bag wasn't important, I told myself.

Stepping into the hazy morning, I felt replenished by my long sleep. The new bandages across my hands did not smart as much as they had yesterday. I could finish the row of roses and then move on to the other side of the yard by the shed. Then what? No. Then I would quit. There was no needle in this haystack.

I walked past the rusted, tin bucket that sat in the shade by the back door and stopped short. It was full. Small shells, cream colored with hints of gray blue, stacked up midway. My mouth watered as I watched the small, tan necks extend into the clear water and spit, cleansing themselves of the mud and sand they lived in. I hoped these clams were to be our lunch and reminded myself of the one small benefit of this job. My stomach reacted to the momentary thought of returning to morbid dorm food. There was indeed a lure attached to the age-old pleasure of good cooking. The sumptuous meals by those strong and elegant hands would surely be missed.

The shed was cool. The sweet, summer smell of dampness lingered in the air. I paused, looking around. It felt different, larger this morning, as if in the night an extension had been added. Collecting my equipment, I put it down to an overactive imagination due to the surroundings and sallied forth.

Alex had soaked the ground at the base of the roses, and the earth gave way to my shovel with ease. This implied I was still to be digging, still looking. *Stay clear of this trap*, my mind continued to warn.

My hands required I move a bit slower this morning. The breeze was gentle, and I let it soothe me as I worked. Pleased, I looked down the neat line of bushes and onto the cleared path of garden. The opposite fence, with its jagged disarray of brown and bent flora, was now an eyesore compared to the polished accomplishment of my four days of work.

My stomach told me it was time to pause, but there was no beckoning from the sealed doorway. I started slowly across the yard, whistling, clattering my equipment, attempting to draw her attention. The bucket was gone, a sign that bode well with my desires. I chuckled. If she wasn't going to get to me with her wild tales, she certainly could own my soul through my stomach.

It seemed an eternity before my productivity of the early afternoon was broken by the sputtering of a battered, tan car. The engine coughed and died away.

"Japanese junk," was followed by some mumblings as Mr. Chin scurried down the driveway, carrying a small, red silk box, somewhat concealed by the voluminous sleeve of his brown Chinese coat.

"Good morning, Miss Jean. So sorry I am late. Chinatown is very busy."

The peeling grayish-white door slammed opened. A frazzled looking Mrs. McKenzie stood there, hands on her hips, eyes wild. The old Asian was ushered inside by the joint squawking of the redhead and bird.

She hadn't even glanced in my direction. Hunger controlled the shovel. It struck without conviction. I couldn't go on. I had to eat now. I started for the door to tell my employer I was going out for lunch, I'd return as quickly as possible. However, on this tucked-away stretch of island, I wasn't quite sure where "out" was, but that was indeed where I was headed.

Mr. Chin answered my hesitant knock and led me into the living room. Alex sat on her long couch facing the windows. Her hands were busy covering an object with a magazine. They moved over to the small red box Chin had brought with him, snapping it shut. A golden dragon, mouth open, shimmered in exquisite embroidery on the top. Holding it fast, she stood, taking the box with her.

"How about some clams?" As she moved, her leg bumped the corner of the magazine, which slid slightly, barely exposing the tip of a syringe.

CHAPTER 6

I would have left right then and there but felt limp with hunger. I had slept through dinner, had had a piece of toast with peanut butter for breakfast, and was about to faint for clams. I sat numbly watching and waiting. What could be in Mr. Chin's dragon-covered box, and why a syringe?

Too fatigued to move, I gave in to the whim that an adventure lay in those answers.

"Don't overdo clams. Just clean them good. Keep them in cool, clean saltwater overnight, throw in some cornmeal so they don't starve. Some people put in a beer and what have you when they steam them. I like mine with a little garlic, celery, onion, and fresh herbs. Try fresh oregano. It'll knock your socks off. Makes the broth rich and flavorful. Most fools throw out the broth."

She was moving with her usual clip now. The edginess of the woman at the back door had mellowed. Within minutes, a large bowl of steaming clams, the shells opened and inviting, was placed in the middle of the table. Bread, dunking butter, and some greens accompanied the meal. Mr. Chin added a pot of tea.

"When you dig, get the small ones. Not too small. As long as they're larger than thumb size, you're fine." She scooped a ladleful into Mr. Chin's bowl as she lectured. They made a tinkling sound as shells hit china.

The savory clam slid down my welcoming throat. They were sweet and beyond compare. My fork found another of the small delicacies. Taking a chunk of warm sourdough, I dunked it into the succulent nectar of the sea gods. I busied myself with mass consumption, filling the hollow that longed for this meal.

"I don't like the city. Too big now." Chin broke into my mindless concentration, riveted on my plate. He put down the chopsticks that I hadn't even noticed in my haste. "Too many relatives after my money."

His appearance, tough and impeccable, was not one of wealth. Drab would be the word I would pin on his brown coat. Then I remembered the elaborate robe he had worn at our first meeting. There was obviously much this man was hiding. His smooth, ageless face beamed at his own thoughts, the twinkle in his eye captivating, challenging.

"Chin, you crafty old dog. They would have sung over your grave years ago."

His old eyes squinted in my direction as he spoke, "All of these children and grandchildren after my money. This would not be, except for Jake."

They both nodded as reverence for that which is only spirit now passed between them.

"Jean," her hand slid in my direction, the tone was teacher to student. I waited for my exam. "In those books you said you thumbed through, was there anything in them about the Chinese crossing from Vancouver, Canada, to Washington in the early days?"

"Not that I remember. There was something about drug running, I think." I hit the word drug hard and scrutinized them both.

"Yes, opium, nasty stuff. But what was worse was the human running." She picked up her bowl, filling the space with her elbows, so she could sip the clam nectar. Her eyes, now tender, fell on Chin.

I followed her gaze. His jaw was now set, his eyelids half-closed over expressionless, dark beads.

"Jake's dad was a fisherman. Gill netter," her attention returned to me. "There was a huge Chinese population in Vancouver back in the late 1800s, desperate to come to America to work. They were wanted for cheap labor on the railroads. One old scalawag, Kelly, who lived up sound, was constantly dodging revenue cutters as he worked the "hole in the fence," as they called it, smuggling opium and booze. Maybe someday, we'll go by Kelly's Point on Guemes. They say he never ran Orientals, but it's hard to say for sure."

Her finger snaked out at me. "The going price was fifty dollars to pick up one illegal and take him to American soil. Lots of Chinese paid, but not all of them made it."

The silent, old gentleman stirred, nodding her forward with the tale.

"The mean skippers, bad ones, would get the Chinese on board, chain them, then once they'd crossed into U.S. water or if pursued, they'd dump them over. Chains and all."

My eyes moved from face to face, as if observing a painful ping-pong game. I snapped my mouth shut, for my jaw had loosened and was hanging. Where does this fit in? I wanted to scream, but my eyes were the only part moveable, and they focused from one face to the other. Waiting.

"Babies float." Her old lips moved into a sickeningly sweet smile. "It's some kind of built-in protection device. When Jake's dad drifted out of the fog, following a scream and loud splash, he only saw what he thought was a deadhead floating just off starboard. It looked like an old piece of driftwood. But then it moved just as it went under. He fished it out with one of his nets. It was our Mr. Chin."

The horror of the deathly cold water with an infant, alone and afloat, made me shudder and softly ask, "What happened to your parents?"

"They say they washed up in Deadman Bay. Mr. Chin was placed with a family in Chinatown for a few months and then sent, by my father-in-law, back to China."

"Yes, I studied hard and saved money so when I was eighteen, I could return to Mr. McKenzie to pay back for my life. At first, Mr. McKenzie did not want me. But I would not leave. So, I started to follow young Mr. McKenzie, Jake. Finally, I swore my life to protect Jake, and his father accepted my offer." He nodded, looking at me, continuing, "But now I am a very old man, and still I do not die." The lines at the corner of his eyes deepened as his cheeks pulled up in a devilish smile.

"And we wouldn't be sitting here talking if it wasn't for Chin pulling my royal Irish behind out of the sling every now and then."

Chin demurred, glancing at his chopsticks as he toyed with them. The light caught the gold ring he wore on his pinkie, just below the long fingernail curving in an arch. Rising from the gold was the spine of a dragon, nostrils flaring in warning. With practiced grace, his hand sailed toward the steeping pot, his voice a soothing pitch, "Tea?"

The redhead exploded in laughter. Pretty Boy joined in her shrill sounds.

Missing the joke and tempted by another large slab of fresh sourdough, I reached for the bread. The left hand of Alex snapped around my wrist, and she twisted in my direction, holding my arm. Her bent finger, used much like a pointing stick, snaked between my eyes. "You be damn careful when an old silver fox like this one offers you a cup of tea."

Drugs. They were going to hold me down and fill me with drugs. I was captive. My arm lightly jerked against her now-iron grip.

"This man is a wizard." Her brows arched with the dance of her pointer.

I sat frozen.

"Herbs," she whispered. "He can heal you. Or," she glanced at him, pausing slightly, "he can make you violently ill."

I followed the finger as it recoiled to rest gently with the other hand, which had now released me. Then my gaze went to the face opposite me. His smile held a puppy-like innocence.

He filled my cup, holding back his long sleeve so he did not disturb the items on the table. I didn't budge but cautiously eyed the brown liquid.

"Not to worry, Miss Jean. Only once, and only in an emergency, did I make those miserable intruders sick."

Alexandria grabbed her cup, hurrying to stop him, "Not now, Chin." She smiled, big, broad, overdone. "To our health."

I reached for my cup of tea.

Alex sipped from her cup, closing her eyes, savoring the aroma.

Mr. Chin, having drunk deep, precisely returned the porcelain to its spot.

They watched me and waited for some movement.

"Good heavens, girl. Don't be silly. If you don't trust us, then we have nothing that sticks. Trust is like glue. It holds you together and makes you strong. And if you lose trust and break apart, well, you can spend the rest of your life trying to rebuild, re-glue that trust. If you can."

I had to drink it, of course. The taste of green slid down easily.

"Jasmine. Mr. Chin owns several stores, which sell a variety of imports. But his specialty is herbs."

"And tea. You will come and visit someday," it was a command and invitation rolled into one.

The light pink note with the flowery script attached to my door could only have come from one person. I plopped onto my bed and eased the seal open.

Dear Blisters,
Pizza night. Come celebrate quitting your job tomorrow.
                              Love, Lis

The note slid from between my tired fingers. I would welcome Lissa's company, but the other two, Barbara and Kitty, with their noses permanently adjusted to high society, rarely included me in any other events except Thursday night pizza and beer. They were the boring ones. But I knew I would join them. For, if nothing else, they presented a great distraction.

Life was getting difficult. Quitting. I felt the tug of war inside me begin at the mere thought. Mrs. McKenzie and her ancient friend had ventured into the garden on one pretext or another a few times while I toiled through the afternoon.

My imagination was expanding into so many new areas in this myriad of events, old and new, that I found the silence of my work a comfort. Time to piece this puzzle together. Questions tumbled forward, but these bits of information I had so far seemed to have nothing in common. What was jagged here was smooth there. What was she searching for? Why wouldn't she tell me what it is? Should I leave tomorrow?

My mind demanded order. I sat at my desk and began to scribble my thoughts in the only way I knew how to proceed.

1. I was hired under the pretense of cleaning up a garden, but possibly to dig up a lost, unidentified item. (That makes it easy.)

2. Feeling satisfied, seeing the order I am creating in the garden

3. Syringe?

4. Mr. Chin, watch out for him?

5. Guilt re: quitting

6. Am beginning to enjoy the excitement of the adventure and Alex's stories.

7. What to believe?

I dropped my pen in frustration. This wasn't a puzzle. It was a joke, and I was the fool.

Pushing away from the desk, I headed for the shower. I'd stuff myself with pizza, drink some beer, and plan yet another exit speech for tomorrow.

I left the bright sun outside as I entered Magnano's Pizza, our hangout. The smell of stale beer and cigarettes was occasionally overpowered by wafts of baking deep-dish pizza and garlic. "I Heard It through the Grapevine" was being accompanied by some who had obviously already partaken of beer and unfortunately knew the words to the song but not the tune. I drifted toward our usual table in the dimness of the tavern.

Lissa's soft pink shift matched that of her writing paper. "Here she comes," her voice hurried me along with the beckoning of her wave. The other two regulars on our girls' night, Barbara and Kitty, smiled and shifted to accommodate my tired frame.

"Show them your hands, Jean." Lissa's eyes were bright with mischief. "Go on," she urged at my reluctance.

"Are you going to tell my fortune?" I placed both palms face up, where peeling blisters were giving way to calluses.

"Yes." Barbara, an image of pale yellow, matching her overtreated hair, leaned closer, her sharp tongue always ready for a dig. "It says right here, get a new job."

I smiled bleakly at their laughter. Barbara could barely spell the word "job," let alone entertain the thought of having one. Her only goal was to marry rich. Her perfect white teeth, courtesy of her dentist father, flashed in my direction. It was rumored she would not leave home if her panties and bra did not match.

"What tales have you brought for us today?" Lissa, more animated than usual, filled my waiting, empty glass and pushed it towards me.

Kitty's button nose shot forward with interest. Too vain to wear the glasses she needed, she struggled for attention in the shadow of Barbara in her pursuit of perfection and husband, rich, of course. I bit my lip at the two fraternity girls, who, deep down, were good but were caught in the uncertainty of their own expectations. Their goals were so different from mine, Barbara with the fake smile and hair, Kitty with a blue-and-white striped dress which hugged her a bit too tight for her curves, and contemplated where to start.

I began slowly replaying the snatches of conversation, steering clear of the syringe, Mr. Chin, and the search for the hidden object. Mrs. McKenzie was enough for them. They listened intently, questioning here, thrilled there.

"When are you quitting …?" Lissa started in her innocence.

"Oh, she can't now," Barbie interjected as she polished her nails on her napkin in the event a speck of sauce had inadvertently landed there while eating with her hands.

"I would," Lissa countered, attempting to protect me.

"Not me," Kitty's voice was half muffled as she busied herself retrieving the piece of onion that had slid down her cleavage.

I sat back and let them chase each other in their quarreling over my future. Things had changed. I don't know when or how, but they had. It was odd being the center of their attention and not having the usual conversation over which hunk on campus to pursue. I felt in control and yet at a loss. The dizziness of the prim, pastel females surrounding me at the table twisted my feelings into tighter knots.

"Well, are you?"

I became aware all heads were turned my way. I shrugged, "I don't know."

"But it's going to be such fun," Barbie insisted, eyes bright with the excitement.

"They say there's going to be a lot of guys there," Kitty added, not wanting to be out-done.

"Where?" My confusion was evident. I hadn't been following the conversation.

Lissa piped up, "You know, the big party tomorrow night at Tom's house. You promised to go with me."

"Oh, yeah." And remembering my social etiquette, I asked the expected question, "What are you going to wear?"

That set them squealing again amongst themselves as they planned for the event. I attempted to follow along but became disheartened. Nothing seemed to lighten the load of my troubled mind. The company of the girls had offered no solution. The pizza and brew had given no inspiration. Using the excuse of an early morning of work, I left them and drove home more perplexed. I turned up the volume on the radio singing with Otis Redding to try to soothe my soul, "I'm sittin' on the dock of the bay ... watching the tide roll away."

Crooning with Otis helped a little, but the sea and its tides, like the push and pull of Mrs. McKenzie, continued to be a mystery to me.

CHAPTER 7

The shed was locked. I turned toward the peeling back door and observed my trail of footprints in the soft dew of morning. My eyes fell on the small patch of tangled mess before me. There was no wind, just stillness. No leaves budged. They sat waiting for me to pull their dead brownness from the earth. I would dig deep, excavating the roots, the hidden life, leaving no trace.

I breathed deep the cool moisture with the taste of the sea. The scent was beginning to possess me. Now my lungs longed for its briny freshness.

Proud of my accomplishments of the week, I surveyed my work. Not bad for my novice attempt. Add a few new plantings and let mother nature grow the green of new life. My meditative state was broken by the sound of the peeling door opening.

"Come in, Jean." A smile accompanied the request.

My gait was slow, calm. Like the windless morning, my turbulent mind of the last few days was still. Peace sparkled like the dewdrops on the grass. Life was good.

Alex was cloaked with a matching aura as she hummed her way between table and stove. Even Pretty Boy's lilt was light and airy.

"It's a beautiful morning." Her words held a hint of mischief. "The sea gods are with us today." McKenzie slipped into her chair facing the big window, proclaiming to the glass and waters below, "Just perfect for what we're going to do."

I let the statement glide by. We sat in silence, mesmerized by the nothingness of the morning.

"Isn't it something?"

I turned toward the windows, for the first time noticing how thick the fog was, hanging just outside the large glass. The entire window was filled with a soft light of moisture. The sky was all one opalescent color, the sea lost in its shroud.

Gathering my cup, I headed to the large panels of glass, where the light refracted through the moisture, at times creating shards of colors. I felt surrounded and alone. It was as if I could walk into the soupy mass and disappear a few feet away. The fog gently clung to the cliff, holding me spellbound with its emptiness.

"My God, what you couldn't do on a day like today," memories and longing guided her voice to me. "We were on our way to meet up with Duke and Axle Hanson, boat builders. Jake wanted to add a couple more 'fast freighters,' as Axle called them. Oh, we had the Boeing sea sleds, but one got wrecked, and it was my fault. She was such a great craft. Sleek and fast. You put her in a mist like this, and she would purr, slowly, soundlessly along. Then in the open, no one could catch you. Sledding in the mist like this," her arm waved toward the gray wall outside, "was what made it all so thrilling. You become one, you think like one, act like one. You have to. The slightest wrong move could be your last. And that's what I miss the most, the thrill of the oneness with my Jake." A deep sigh covered her in silence.

I held my breath in the hope she would continue.

"Oh, we weren't a big 'rum fleet' like the King of Seattle, Olmstead. But, he ended up in jail too."

My breath made a squeaking noise as I sucked in even more.

She rose and repositioned herself on the big couch, the excitement of her tale gathering momentum with each step, "Heck, the boat builders had it the easiest. We'd pay cash up front, and there could be no complaints after delivery, if you catch my drift. And all the best builders were into it. Blanchard, Coolidge, Hillard.

"The Feds thought they'd gotten smart one time. Just as Axle was finishing up a boat, they stationed a man down at the dock. Poor fool owner couldn't get near his new boat to take it home. Ruined Axle's business for a while."

Alex chuckled, then sipped her coffee before continuing, "Those boats were real fast back then. They had 400 HP Liberty aircraft engines in them. They'd roar like a storm when under the gun, up to 40 knots. They also had quiet diesel engines, too, for sneaking around. Long bow, fast, and smooth as silk. We'd paint them black and gray, called them 'runners' or 'blacks.'

"At first, the poor Coast Guard had a fleet of tow tugs as its rum chasers. They couldn't chase their grandmothers. Poked along at 12 knots. Slow, but some mighty crafty captains. But then they caught on and had sleek new chasers made. Heck, some dry docks were building chasers and runners side by side."

She shifted with discomfort as her memory spilled forward. "But with the hijackers, Feds, and then Antonio's gang trying to muscle in, it got bloody for a while."

In her silence, the mist took on a deep red hue. Blood possessed the sky. My heart beat faster at the vision.

"Ah," she started up again, and the grayness returned, "those were dangerous times. And you could never tell what was going to come at you out of mist like this. Yet sometimes you needed this for cover. Well," her arm drifted through the air carrying her words, as though her action controlled the heavens, "this and a damn good captain.

"We were cutting across the channel, not always wise in pea soup, but for us, the best action. Not good to be seen with the builders. It was just Jake and me and Diesel Rose. I was below when Jake stomped his foot. I came running up and could barely see him standing next to me. It was so thick you could cut it and serve it.

"His voice was low. He expected danger. 'I heard something. Get up on the bow. Careful.'

"It wasn't cold, just damp. Diesel followed me forward, and we sat up there, watching the rainbows play across the mist. They were everywhere, magical. I was just about to tell him his hearing was in need of repair when I heard it too—a rhythmic creak, moving to the slap of the gentle waves.

"The sound was from the starboard and close now. Jake cut the engine back even further. We were barely moving. Luckily the swirls of fog thinned, and then I saw it, and my arm went up, pointing. A dinghy. One oar was in the water, lapping with the wave, producing the rhythmic bump of wood on wood, the other oar missing. A bloody hand protruded listlessly, the body hidden by the gunwale of the boat.

"We didn't recognize the skiff. But it smelled of nothing but trouble. I began soundlessly aft on the starboard side. Jake was heading toward me, motioning me below. He pulled his pistol from the belt. He liked having his gun ready, especially in the fog."

A sad smile formed on her lips, a sadness that filled the room. I could feel Jake's presence, just outside in the heavy mist. I shifted, the movement spurring the redhead forward.

"Well," she put down her cup, "Jake was ready as the boat came up alongside. I was pretending to go below, but my head was poking out, and a good thing too because just then Diesel Rose let out a low growl and began to whimper. I turned in her direction to hush her when I saw it coming at us out of the grayness and let out a yell.

"Jake leapt to the wheel and gunned the engine. I grabbed Diesel and held on tight. Seconds later, we heard the sound of the small craft being crushed by one of the mosquito fleet steamers. The big hull just smothered the small boat and its scene of death.

"We were lucky. That white bow was so big and close. I suppose we didn't hear it because we were concentrating on that rowboat and the bloody body. My sweet Diesel Rose, that little ragamuffin, was our best guard." In her sigh, the pain was apparent.

"We heard rumors. Turned out the body in the skiff was just a kid. Must have got caught up in some filthy business. Antonio and his gang were trying to enlist the hijackers to work for them. Ugly. They never found the body, and we never told what we saw. Oh, I was sick about it, and Jake was mad as hell. Fightin' mad. That's when it all really got started. That was the spring of 1930."

To be there now, my mind sought the mist, ready for battle with my cargo of whiskey, tasting the danger. Visions of sleek crafts drifted toward me through the haze, large ones, small ones. I longed to step through the gray into Alex's world.

"It'll lift soon, and then we'll go."

Go? I snapped back to the present and turned toward her.

She answered my gaze, reassuring me, "It'll be nice and calm out there. Just right."

CHAPTER 8

In the gentleness of the morning, a gull cried somewhere in the haze. With some effort, Alex pushed herself from the couch.

"These old bones need some sunshine pick-me-up." As she passed my slumped body, she eyed my dusty tennis shoes, nodding. "Good. Time to rattle on. It'll be clearing soon."

I stayed a moment longer, anchored by the weight of the grayness. Where we were going I could not guess, but like a child following the Pied Piper, I would go. Of that, I was certain.

The commotion in the kitchen subsided. Pretty Boy watched from his perch as footsteps made their way toward me. My eyes caught sight of the basket and thermos, worked their way past the sweatshirt, the smile, to the big straw hat.

"What'd I tell you?" she nodded toward the window, her voice carrying her thrill at being correct.

The fog was lifting. The heaviness gave way to a thin white with streaks of blue. Below, the beach was barely visible in spots, the rocks and sand steaming with the promise of heat. The homes on either side of the U-shaped inlet were poking through the mist. Reality was taking shape.

"You be good, Pretty Boy," she sang out.

Following her along the row of large windows, we passed the dining table, just off the kitchen, to the sliding glass doors on the southeast corner of her home. The dewdrops were melting, and the slightly long grass left damp streak marks on my dusty tennis shoes.

I had never been past the windows on this side of the house. I had only seen the top of a short hedge, the few large rocks that dominated the smaller ones along the shore, and the water below. But now on the crest of the cliff, a whole new arena opened up before me. The horseshoe bay glistened with the moisture, which was evaporating in the sun's lazy light. The tide was gentling toward the beach in an attempt to reclaim the stringy pieces of kelp, seaweed, and bits of driftwood it had left behind, like a ribbon snaking along the beach as far as the eye could see. Here and there, boats sat motionless, clinging to their buoys, fearful of unforeseen powers of the now smooth, ice-blue waters. It was still. No wind met our faces as we watched from our perch.

Mrs. McKenzie handed me the basket. "Be careful, Jean. These boards will be slippery as hell." The big brim disappeared in an opening in the hedge. My eyes watched the straw hat as it flounced down the old wooden stairs, a hand secured to the railing. I followed suit, the steepness of the journey not unnoticed by my pounding heart. Where the path zigzagged, we came upon a small landing that had been hidden by the hedge from above. There sat an old boathouse with rail-car tracks to carry a boat leading to the water. The door and window of the small building were fastened tight.

She did not stop or glance back but continued in her practiced pace. Not daring to hesitate, I tagged along down the remaining steps, captivated by the rusty metal tracks, a train to the sea.

The hat did not slow at the base of the steps, but with determined stride, she picked her way over glistening rocks across a flat of wave-sculptured sand, straight for the water's edge. Alex arched her back, breathing deeply of the spicy air.

I scurried up next to her, waylaid momentarily by the side-winding of a small, eager crab.

"Ah. The sea is life. Or death," she let the words hang between us before continuing. "A ruthless wrestler on a journey to the unknown."

Bending, she scooped some of the chilly liquid and splashed it on her cheeks. The salty drops clung to the layer of soft, red wisps surrounding her damp face, spilled down her blouse and slid between her toes, claiming her as one with the sea.

I followed her gaze to a piece of driftwood bobbing in the shallow tide. The peacefulness of the vision gave way to the horror of a baby struggling against this merciless element. Mr. Chin was born a survivor.

Mrs. McKenzie stood and started back towards the sandy beach, her imprints in the thick sand flats filling with water, disappearing. How quickly one's life gets consumed by the incoming tide.

"Shall we? It won't be that far of a carry."

What I had missed from the bank above was now apparent from where I surveyed the shore. The blue hull of a small rowboat protruded like a colorful sand dune, restless, waiting, above the curve of the seaweed of last night's tide. I suddenly recognized it as the boat that had hung from the rafters in the shed. That explained why the shed had felt so large, so open, yesterday.

How and when the wooden hulled craft was moved, I could not guess. But the image of her curved finger casting a spell that floated the boat down the cliff was one I could not easily dampen.

Alex reached the upturned mound of boat. "This side," she nodded her instructions. "We'll flip *Old Blue*, then carry her down."

We hoisted the boat side up, lowering it gently onto its back. I gathered the oars hiding under the belly of *Old Blue*, loaded them, and then picked up my side to begin our haul to the water's edge.

"It's pretty heavy." The sound of crunching barnacles on a small piece of driftwood I stepped on made me concentrate on my path instead of the awkward pull on my arms.

"A boat is not an it. All ships are she's." From under the brim of her hat, her eyes regarded me with distaste. "Schools," she snorted. "There's a school for you. Out there."

I tried to change my expression to one of complete agreement, as if hauling a boat across a beach was what we did at school between classes.

We must have looked the odd pair. Alex, the old sea sage, brim flapping in the wind, presented a calm appearance. Whereas I, the eternal student, struggled to keep the agony of the strain on tender palms off my face, which dripped in sweat, exuded discomfort.

But that was not enough. She began in a low voice. Her words setting the dance to her calculated stride across the soft sea earth.

We always call a ship a she, and not without a reason,
for she displays a well-shaped knee regardless of the season.
She scorns the man whose heart is faint and doesn't show him pity.
And like a girl she needs the paint to keep her looking pretty.

That's why a ship must have a mate: she needs a good provider;
a good strong arm to keep her straight, to comfort her and guide 'er.
For such, she'll brave the roughest gales and angry seas that
    crowd her,
and in a brand new suit of sail no dame looks any prouder.

For love she'll brave the ocean vast, be she gig or cruiser,
but if you fail to tie her fast, you're almost bound to lose her.
She's happiest beneath the stars, a time for speculation,
and has a hatred for all bars, just like a Carrie Nation.

The ship is like a dame at that: she's feminine and swanky.
You'll find the one that's broad and fat is never mean or cranky.
Yes, ships are lady-like indeed, for take them all together,
the ones that show a lot of speed can't stand the rougher weather.

On ships and dames we pin our hopes; we fondle them and
    dandle them,
and every man must know the ropes or else he cannot handle
    them.
Be firm with her, and she'll behave when skies are dark above you,
and let her take a water-wave, and praise her and she'll love you!

Alex's breath was coming shorter, and with a quick nod, she motioned the lowering of the boat at the white, foamy edge of the bay. She stood, hands on hips, catching her breath, staring out to sea. With the back of her sleeve, she dreamily wiped the moisture from her brow, then scooped up the cool water, and splashed it over her face.

Tossing her wet shoes inside the boat, she chuckled, "Good heavens, I haven't said that in years. Pretty good for an old coot like me. I used to repeat that to Jake every time he'd get mad at the old *Moon Beam*. That was my favorite boat we owned, a thirty-six-foot Blanchard. God, I loved her. All teak cabin. Oh, not as pretty or big as *Gitana*, but modest. Our dream boat. Had her built. Ran with her a little, but she was more of a family boat, not a working one like the sleds and blacks.

"Well, anyway, there we were on the old girl one late moonless night in August with a rather large load. We'd just picked up from the mother ship, the *Mowhata*. She was a four-master that would sit just off the four-mile limit between Canada and the U.S. A floating warehouse of booze. One of our pick-up stops. Usually, we'd run to Canada. But this time we just met the boat.

"We were up by Stuart, just trying to make it to Samish Bay, when one of our damn two-thousand-dollar engines began to sputter. See, right after the war, those aircraft engines could be bought out of California boating magazines for around seven hundred. But, supply and demand caught up with them. Pretty soon, the price jumped and kept right on jumping. I heard they reached around four thousand. We didn't need any more by then. We had enough trouble."

She looked straight at me for the first time, her eyes blending in with the blue of the water, the strength of her voice reflecting her pride, "Integrity. That's what Jake had. Jonathan Edward McKenzie never opened a bottle unless he was going to drink it. Some of those buzzards doctored up their booze for more profit. But they got it in the end. Not as bad as my best friend, poor Ginny Dillard. She went blind from bad booze. Jake named one of our sleds after her, *The Dancin' Gin*."

The hat hung over the soft mutterings, her hand grabbed the bowline, and she headed for the stretch of sand that had not yet been consumed by the incoming tide.

I splashed toward her, not wanting to miss a word.

"Glory be, that gal could dance. Died a few years later. Killed herself."

She sunk into the sand, line in hand. "We were lucky that night. Since we were just breaking those engines in, we decided to hang close to shore. My job was to tie a rope to each of the gunny sacks." Her fingers toyed with the line she held. "See, twelve bottles were sown inside a sack. Now this rope had a sack of rock salt and a buoy attached to it too. Sack with booze, rock salt, buoy. In an emergency, we'd throw the whole thing overboard. The rock salt would sink the buoy. Hours later, as the rock salt dissipated, the buoy would rise, eventually popping up on the surface, and if lucky, we'd swing back later and haul in our bottles of Canadian whisky.

"So, Jake was cursing mad at the engine. Just shut it down and sat on the stack of bagged-up booze, swearing and kicking.

"'Treat her like a lady,' I tried to make him laugh.

"'She's no lady. She's a bitch of a sea hag.'

"I knew he was hot, but that made me even hotter so I started in the poem. He didn't much take to that.

"'Put a lid on it, Red.' He was hollering. I just went right on with that poem. And when I hit the part about Carrie Nation, I thought he was going to send me overboard. We were topside now, screaming and yelling like people in love do, and we weren't paying attention to what the old gal was doing. While we were yelling to beat the band, letting everyone know for miles around where we were and what was up with our powerful voices, the boat took charge. A current found her beam, and we were slipping right into shore.

"Those damn currents. They pull you along in life, fast, slow, this way, that way. But it's the undercurrents that can be dangerous, the ones down below that you can't see. Jake always said we were like undercurrents, the way we lived our lives under the surface of society."

She paused for a moment, startled by the cool water that had now reached her toes, tickling them.

"By the time I'd finished that prose and Jake had run out of roar, we were dangerously close to shore and a set of rocks.

"'Ah, for Christ's sake, Red, now look what you've done.'

"Men like to blame a woman as much as possible, but I was only trying to defend the boat. So Jake starts back toward the engine when Diesel Rose starts to growl.

"'Treat her nice,' I was being sassy.

"'I'll treat this damned boat any damn way I please.'

"We weren't paying attention to Diesel so she barked. That's when I saw the real trouble. The Coast Guard had just gotten some new boats to give us more to think about. These revenuers were black hulled and fast. The 'Black Pups,' they were called, and they kept a regular schedule. Now the only thing that was stupid about those boats was their bright copper smokestacks, made them visible from far off.

"In fact, one night a bunch of the boys got drunk, went home, and got their wives' copper polish. Then they snuck on board the Pups tied over at Bellingham and began shining up those smoke stacks. Wanted them real bright so we could see them better. Got caught too, the fools." She rocked back, laughing, her words choppy as she continued, "Had to give money to the wives to bail them out."

"So," her finger waved in the air, returning both of us to the story at hand, "there was that smokestack coming right at us.

"'Jake,' I'd lowered my voice.

"'I don't want to hear another word out of you.' His back was to the Pup as it eased closer.

"'Jake, there's the—'

"'Tarnation, woman.'

"'All right then,'" I pouted back at him, folded my arms and sat, waiting. My heart was racing, and I couldn't talk. I thought we were done for. All I could think of was who was going to care for Diesel Rose and the stew meat in the fridge would go bad.

"Suddenly, Diesel ran back and forth between Jake and me. As we weren't paying her any attention, she bit Jake in the rear and he spun around steaming. But he cooled real quick when he saw that smoke stack.

"I was delirious with fear and felt someone grab me. It was Jake.

"'Damn you, woman,' he hollered at me as he quietly began lowering our load.

"'Well, you never listen to me,' I screamed back, helping him as fast as possible.

"'The hell, I don't,' echoed across the waters as we worked the last two bottles.

"'That's what I think of you and your manly manness.' Plop. I tossed the load into the darkness. But I wasn't watching, and the last bag caught on a cleat.

"Jake leaned over to loosen it. The rum chaser was just about on us but had seemed to slow in its approach. 'Well, little missy, Miss Alexandria, that's where you can go,' the rope finally got free, 'straight down.'

"I watched the phosphorescence outline the sack, salt, and buoy as it sank. My Irish was so up, and I think I was still scared and all. Besides, I'll take a challenge anytime, so off came my clothes. "We'll see about that," I shouted back. I dove into that black, cold water and was still yelling, cursing him as I swam the short distance to shore.

"Jake just stood there with his big mouth hanging, and the Coast Guard revenuers came aboard. They'd heard us fighting and got an eyeful when I went in, I suppose. They must have figured Jake had enough on his hands because they just took a quick look below, didn't find anything."

"'Domestic problems?' the skipper had asked Jake, who was still squinting at my progress as he nodded.

"As they shoved off, the skipper hollered back at us. 'No fool would be dumb enough to carry a load and holler that loud. But, I do like that poem. Live by it.' His crew was still laughing at us as they headed back out to deeper waters."

Alex pulled her feet from the thickening sand as she pushed herself up, love and pride shining in her eyes.

I suddenly realized my feet were covered with the cold water, and it sparked my questions, "Weren't you freezing? I mean when you got to shore?"

"I did cool down a bit, you might say," she replied with a wink. "But it was a warm night. And pretty soon, I heard the splash of the anchor, followed by another as Jake put the little dinghy in. There they came, Diesel Rose in the bow, Jake with his cap back off his forehead, all that thick sandy hair. My God, he was handsome. And he was whistling, "Oh, when the saints, come marchin' in," she led the tune.

"When the saints come marchin' in." I joined her.

Her hand went to her forehead in a salute, signaling more of the story. "'Permission to come ashore.' He gave me that smile from a few feet out.

"Heck, I was standing there, shivering a tad, naked, my hair dripping, 'It's a free country.' I had to let him know I wasn't that easy."

Her voice went low, imitating Jake, 'Thank you, ma'am. Don't mind if I do.'

"That rascal pulled the boat up and came ambling on over to me. 'Looks like you might need these.' And he handed me a book of matches. 'Nice outfit.'

"'Didn't you bring in anything else?'

"'Like what?' He tired to sound innocent.

"'Like my trousers or a shirt?'

"'I have an old blanket,' he gave me that devilish grin, 'but the blanket's mine.'

"I got moving as fast as I could to build a fire. I knew his game. It was fun, the way you make up after a fight. 'Fire's mine.'

"He rolled out the blanket a ways away. 'You can have it.'

"Diesel gave him a look and came and sat by me. Well, that didn't last long. He told me he never would have let me go straight down like the whisky, not with the way the phosphorescence illuminated my body in the water. We watched meteor showers until dawn.

"The next tide, the rock salt melted, and up popped the cork markers, dotting the water. So we rowed back out to the buoys and pulled in our wet cargo, just like pulling in crab pots. Then off we went.

"By the time we got back, Stoney was there with the boys ready to load fast and drive like hell. Only those young boys were looking at me funny." She started for the rowboat that was now drifting free and floating. "We hired young, strong kids, fifteen or so, to run the cases from the boat to trucks. Stoney would clock them and pay each boy a dollar a case they carried. Only the fastest would be asked back. Anyway, they were eyeing me suspiciously. Seems Stoney'd heard the story from a friend with the Coast Guard that we were having domestic problems and I'd taken a naked dip right in front of all of them, and God, for a long time after that, all of Jake's cronies wanted me to teach their wives to swim. Oh, there is nothing like swimming naked at night in these waters after a long hot day. The water's like silk."

She splashed at the salt liquid with her foot. "Come on. These old bones can't take the cold like they used to."

CHAPTER 9

Mrs. McKenzie rolled up her tan slacks as the water was now threatening to darken them with its wetness. I followed suit. We stepped knee-deep into the sea. The weight of the craft dissipated into the water, becoming fragile, buoyant, and tipsy.

"I'll head us out, then you can take over."

"Me?" my voice raised in horror. "But I've never—"

"I figured. That's why I brought lunch. We have all day. Now, climb into the stern," she employed her visual aid, the crooked finger, to tell me exactly where I was expected.

The back of the boat sank a little with my weight as I settled into the rocking motion any slight movement created. I'd almost swamped it but for her swift reaction and counterbalance. Alex walked the bow out a little further before she lifted one long leg over the side and then the other, motioning me to shift to the opposite side to steady the craft. Using the oar like a pole, she pushed us, and we gently eased away from shore as *Old Blue* drifted into deeper water.

"I love to row," her exuberance evident as she put the oars into the oarlocks. Alex's voice drifted across the water. "Jake bought me my very own rowboat as a wedding present." With a few deep strokes, she set her pace. "Damn. I'm just so mad at him for leaving me." We slid across the smooth surface, her wet and dripping legs straddling mine. Her toenails were painted a fiery red, matching, I calculated, her temperament.

"Oh, God. I loved that time of our lives. You see, one day Jake just up and asked me to be his wife. Said we were the same and that we belonged together."

I watched the glittering drops that fell from the oars as they continued with their own beat. Creak, silence. Creak, silence.

"I was tickled pink, you know. He gave me this brooch, a half-moon with pearls and diamonds like the sea and stars. Said he wanted it to help anchor me down. He was quite the man. His smile was magic." She fell forward on her oars chuckling, the exercise and memories having softened her anger. "If I don't sound like a lovesick school girl."

She steadied the oars in the water, halting our progress. "Time to switch. Always boat your oars when you are changing position or pulling in pots," she began as she hoisted them aboard. She took them out of the oarlocks, and the water puddled around them where she had placed them on either side of the boat. "It's a mite slow, long ride home without them.

"Now," she crouched low, pulling her legs toward her, "I'm going to the right, starboard; you come over here on portside. Stay low, don't stand. Makes it top-heavy."

Blue rocked as we traded seats. I adjusted and readjusted my bottom, attempting to be exactly center as she instructed. My heart was racing. It seemed like hours before I could even get the oars into their holders and in the water.

"Find your stroke, Jean. Pull evenly. Jake was captain of his rowing crew before he had to quit the University of Washington. He loved rowing in those Pocock racing shells."

I tried. One board went in deep while the other skimmed the surface, splashing Alex.

"That's all right, dear," she laughed and sank back further into the stern. "You'll get it. I'm counting on you."

We circled, sputtered, giggled, and limped around the bay.

"More on the left. Full reach of the arms. Straighten those legs a bit. Put your back into it. Feel that on your belly? You're getting it," accompanied my virgin attempts.

Alex's body wavered as we jerked along. I was getting it all right. But more important, I was thrilled by the power and the beauty, the freedom of rowing.

Soon, Mrs. McKenzie was relaxing into my stride. "It was 1927, March." Her head was toward the shore. "Springtime. There had been a thick fog like this morning. A little harder on the left," she interrupted her own story. "Jake, Stoney, and I were headed up to celebrate a wedding of the daughter of one of our suppliers in Canada. We had decided to split up to travel so we flipped to see who was going by car and who by boat. Jake and I got tails for the car.

"Booze was legal up there, remember. Canada exploded, making whisky for Americans to get drunk on. And that was "whisky" with no damn *E* in the word, just plain old whisky. The Irish and Brits added the *E*, and so later on, the Americans picked it up. But I like my Scotch whisky. No *E* for me." Her head nodded in affirmation of her statement and then picked back up her train of thought. "Famous brands were started up back then, like Canadian Club. They were making it and selling it as fast as they could. If runners didn't want to go to a mother ship, and there were several of them out there, *Moonlight Maid, Lilyhorn, Malahat, Principio*, you could go to any liquor store. Heck, they even built special docks and sold right on the piers.

"Some Americans loved Canada for that. Ever heard this ditty?" She began to sing, her scratchy, high voice echoing across the flat, still water of the bay. I now understood how easily it must have been for those revenuers to hear Alex and Jake fight that night. The song, set to the nursery rhyme, stopped my progress.

> Four and twenty Yankees, feeling very dry,
> Went across the border to get a drink of rye.
> When the rye was open, the Yanks began to sing,
> "God bless America, but God save the King!"

She finished, an arm raised high above in the pose of a reverent evangelist. "Come on, music teacher. Give it a try."

She began again, and I followed, a beat behind. We sang, or at least made a racket, as we jollied along, faces to the heavens, the sea below. Life was good. Life was simple. I did not realize how captive I was.

"Some of us Yanks sang that song at the wedding. We had a grand time," she said as she settled back into her tale, "dancing to that great band and, of course, enjoying the best booze money could buy. The McKnights, our hosts, had this mansion, the Casa Mia, all stone with rolling green lawns, so well kept that your heels got caught in it when you tried to walk across the sprawling landscape. The place had a long circular driveway with a fountain. It was on a cliff so McKnight could watch his ships. He also owned the house next door. There were two tunnels that ran underground, one to the second house and the other to the sea in case they ever needed to escape by boat.

"But who would want to leave that wonderland? A room for everything, billiards, swimming pool, shuffle board built into the floor tiles. You name it, this place had it, and if it didn't, they'd go and get it for you. Real generous. When Jake had his trouble, they sent money.

"After dancing until the wee hours, we went back to the boat to drop Stoney off. Jake and I weren't really an item then, but I had hopes. Stoney knew I was soft on Jake, but he kinda liked me too, you know." She dipped her fingers in the water. "Stoney just smiled with that black beard and told us to be good. Famous last words.

"So, it was Stoney's turn to slip through the 'hole in the fence' with the cases that had already been loaded. He was going to stay on the boat and head out the next day. He didn't mind, especially as he was tied up to his old friend, Lars. Those two partied all night. The gods had other plans for us."

She brought her hand to her lap and wiped the fingers dry, shifting with the story. "Lars Nelson lived down south in Des Moines and loved his vodka, being Swedish. He'd built himself a storage place for his stash—an outhouse. At least it looked like one. And that's what a little Boy Scout thought it was until he tried to use it. Oh my,

Lars took a lot of, shall we say, crap for that one. Damn Boy Scout told about what he found, and that was the end of the Swede's stash below the outhouse."

We both laughed at that image.

"Well, we left those two on their boats, knowing the worst that could happen was if one fell in the other was there to help him back aboard. Jake took only a few bottles. He didn't trust the land. So many people were running by land. They even built special cars. The Hump-mobile was the most popular. Had a custom-built, big tank to haul the booze built right in under the seats, a hidden customized cash box, and they were fast. Thunder road. But not Jake, he'd be kind of like a fish out of water. Besides, the border patrol got slick and had these big mirrors they would make the cars drive on to check underneath the autos to be sure you weren't carrying anything."

She scooped up some water with her hands, idling it through her fingers.

"There were extra inspectors at the border at Blaine. They'd got-ten wind of the wedding. The Feds and local authorities were heatin' up, so we decided to slip across Mount Baker Highway. No need to attract attention. Jake had the booze between us on the floorboards so he could toss it out quickly if need be.

"There was a little moon, and I was in the mood for a drive. It was spectacular—tall evergreens on either side of the road, like a winding green ribbon. The thick trunks looked even bigger in the shadows. I slipped off my white shoes that matched my white-and-blue polka-dot chiffon dress, tossed them in the back, drew my fur coat closer, and let the calmness and strength of the passing trees lull me to sleep.

"I woke up with a start as Jake turned sharply into a side road by the Nooksack River. He flipped off the lights. Watching.

"You get to know danger. It rides with you always, especially in our line of work, a constant companion. And I sensed fear crawl from Jake to me. I didn't say a word, but my heart started beating fast. I was bone scared in the darkness.

"We were being followed. We couldn't outrun them, weren't familiar with the terrain. And instead of them picking the place, Jake had gone to the one thing he trusted the most. Water.

"'Get down by the river and get ready to float.' His voice was low and steady. There were no lights behind us now, a bad sign. I did as I was told, slid the door open, and the minute my bare foot hit the ground, I knew I was in for it." Her laugh was heavy. "Damn shoes. Always getting me in trouble.

"When I reached the Nooksack, it was running hard with melting snow, hard and loud. I realized I couldn't hear if Jake needed me. And I also realized how very much I loved him. So, I crawled back up the bank, just under a lip of overhanging rock and root.

"Bright lights from the other car now illuminated the scene. There were three men around Jake. I'd never seen any of them. But I came to hate them all. They all wore heavy coats and hats and underneath, faces long and drawn by the angle of the light. I couldn't tell if they were Feds or locals or what. I could tell who was talking by the puffs of steam as they spoke. One of the guys held up our bottle of booze and Jake's gun. Trouble.

"Then I saw the light catch on steel. It was a knife, and it was sliding down the inside of one man's coat.

"Jake shifted, and I knew he'd seen it too. Two of the men turned and headed right for me. I took off my big fur coat to cover my legs and dress and tried not to breath or move.

"They stopped at the edge of the bank, from here to the end of the boat." Her hand waved through the air, demonstrating the distance.

"I learned, then, something that always stayed with me. If I was going to be killed, I wanted to see the man who was going to do it. So, I shifted slightly and watched them closely. The one who hadn't said anything yet was obviously the boss. He reached into his long coat, and the other did likewise. The boss lifted a cigar, and his monkey lit it. The small flame gave me just a glimpse of his face. I would never forget. Handsome. Evil.

"My heart beat as fast as the river pounding below. 'What da we do?' the monkey asked as he lit his own cigarette, his accent telling me he wasn't from here. He looked mean; small, squinting eyes, fat face, tight lips, and short stubby fingers.

"The smoke of the cigar preceded the boss's answer, 'Kill 'em. And leave my mark so they know this is my territory now.'

"'Si, Antonio.' The heavy figure hesitated, then licked his chops as if he was about to bite into a juicy steak, and headed back to the car. Antonio hummed above me, lipping his smoke, adjusting his expensive coat.

"I waited, fear dripping down my body in the cold of the evening. I couldn't move. I couldn't see or hear what was going on at the car. And that disgusting man just stood there, indifferent, his back to the dirty task he had ordered.

"Suddenly there was the sound of footsteps running toward the bank.

"'Boss, I told ya I seen two heads.' My white shoes were dangling from his short, fat fingers.

"'Bravo,' a sickening smile moved the cigar. 'Finish him, and let's have some fun, eh.' He flicked the cigar onto the dirt and stomped it with the heel of his polished shoe. He was impeccable and deadly.

"They were leading Jake into the woods. All three of them. I slipped back to the car. They'd taken the keys, but they hadn't searched all of the car after they'd found the booze and taken Jake's gun. The door was open so I sank behind it like a shield and reached under the seat; the other gun was still there. Skirting the lights, I got behind a big tree, thankful for the broad girth of its trunk. Boy was I dumb. The river was on the other side of me now, and those guys in between. I'd never do that again. Always have an escape route.

"The fear I tasted in my mouth was of bile. Sickening. It was my first time. I mean I'd shot before, Jake had made sure of that, but I'd never pointed at a human. Whole different cup of tea. My hands shook so I put the gun up against the tree." The old hands clasped together around an imaginary gun and lifted into the air.

"I saw Jake kneeling, blood dripping from his hatless head. Now, in all the stories I'd heard, the man to take out was the boss. So I aimed but closed my eyes as I squeezed the trigger.

"There was a yelp, and the fat one went down grabbing his knee.

"Made me mad I'd missed. So, I just started pulling the trigger. Jake was wrestling with the one with the knife, and Antonio ducked behind a tree and started firing back. Two shots. One just above me.

"Stupid. I'd emptied the gun before I knew it. God, I was inexperienced. And there we were. All three of us behind trees, the other two on the ground.

"'Kill the lights, Red,' Jake barked at me. 'Then go.'

"I ducked behind our car and around to the other black Studebaker. I fumbled for a moment, then found the switch, and shut off the lights to their car. Just then, a bullet whizzed past me, shattering the glass above my head. I slid from the seat to the ground and just sat there a minute. My legs wouldn't move.

"Another shot ran through the dark forest and another. I was so frightened. Tears were blurring my vision, and I ran for the Nooksack and didn't look back. It was cold as ice. The shock woke me from my stupor. I looked up and saw Antonio running down the edge of the river toward me. He fired at something behind me and stopped to reload, puffs of his cursing trailing behind him. A flash of white passed by me in the heavy current.

"I eased along the frigid water, being pulled under by its force now and then. I tried to find what I knew must be Jake's body. The river curved up ahead. I fought my way to a bend where a sand spit jutted out. Exhausted, I crawled onto the thick wet shelf when something grabbed me and pulled me back toward the water.

"'Not here,' Jake was yelling above the roar. 'Keep going.'

"'I can't.'

"'The hell you can't.' He never loosened his grip.

"I was too frozen to struggle. Everything about me felt numb. But I was back in the rough currents, holding onto Jake's shirt, bumping down the rocky flow. We passed a thick stand of trees. Then a drop. Scraped my leg badly. There was a wide turn up ahead. We worked our way to the shore. I don't remember much except the soft moss Jake pushed me onto before I went out like a light.

"Couldn't have been out for long because, when I woke up, it was still dark. A vision of the cigar illuminating Antonio's handsome, deadly face had startled me awake. I just lay there, trying to catch my breath, and looked up at those stars, bright and silver."

Her hat tilted back as Alex lifted her face to the sky. It was a powerful look she gave the heavens, as if her vision carried beyond the light blueness into the dark depths of that star-filled night long ago.

"Jake's arm was over me, and he started shaking. I pushed myself up, forcing my eyes to adjust to the darkness. My pretty little party dress was in shreds, as were Jake's clothes. Then I spotted the red that dripped across the white of his shirt. The coolness of the river had arrested most of the bleeding, but this was fresh.

"I worked his wet shirt off, rinsed it, and retied it around his waist, covering the wound. I stripped off his soaking trousers and hung them next to the remains of my chiffon shreds to dry. But it was cold and damp, and before long I was back next to Jake, pressed against his warmth, with his hot breath tracking down my back.

"I was restless and embarrassed. And I kept checking the spot for new blood. It didn't spread much, so I dozed off.

"The feeling that woke me later was one that I'd come to love and yearn for, the same one I'd had the first time Jake kissed me when Drummond had come aboard that night I was discovered as a stowaway by Jake and Stoney.

"My eyes opened onto soft streaks of light filtering between tall trees. There were so many shades of green. The long leaves of the ferns stretched out flat, close to the ground, from the recent rains and snow. Birds were singing in the morning, and the river in the daylight had lost its tremendous thunder.

"The warmth of Jake's hand was working its way lazily up my side. I closed my eyes and let that crazy sensation overpower my rising fear. But that was a good fear, you know."

The hat tilted, and her fingers found the water again. "I trusted him to be gentle my first time. And he was." Her chin went up with pride and moisture glistened in her eyes. "We had survived death.

Together. That makes you want to live and hold each other so close that you breathe life back into each other's soul.

"Well, the thick moss was soft underneath me, a soft green lace of growth hung from an old white birch branch above us, beyond that, the blue, blue sky. Jake started kissing my neck, and I rolled into his arms with eager lips and let his hand spread that tingling feeling all down my body. We never said a word. But the birds knew and the river. Our witnesses. The earth our bed."

There was a long pause during which Alex continued blinking away the tender tears of her memories. "It was March 14, 1927. A date I'll always remember. So, before I was twenty-one, I'd shot my first man and lost my virginity."

She smiled now. "Jake never traveled by road again. In the long run, I was glad it was Jake and I who lost the flip of that coin with Stoney. When we got back and I was with Jake, that wasn't what broke the three of us up, what ruined our trust."

Alex looked straight at me now. "Once someone has cut your trust in two, it takes a lot of little knots to tie it back together. If you can."

We sat motionless in the still water. I wasn't sure when I'd stopped working the oars, letting the power of the story draw all my strength down its trail.

"How'd Jake die?" I was certain someone other than I had asked. But, I'd observed, fish don't have lips. My hand grasped the sides of the boat, waiting for it to be tipped by the storm of her anger.

Her stride jolted, a fog settled in around her, and her vision focused across the sleek blue of water to the green knob of Barry Island.

"Heart. Before I knew it, he was gone. Didn't even get to sing "Happy Trails" to him. And I never found out if he …" She caught herself before continuing.

A crab scurried into the sea grass below us as I pondered how to backtrack to our topic.

"Pass me the thermos, Jean. All this long-winded talk makes me thirsty."

Chapter 10

Time drifted, as did we, in silence. My concentration bent on the oars as I struggled to master the balance of *Old Blue*. The calluses, already built on my hands, guarded against further damage. Every now and then, my back protested my labors. But I had discovered a new passion, a new challenge.

"Pull in over there. Harder on the right. That's it." She smiled at my appetite for precision, her voice filled with joy, "Boy, oh boy. If you haven't taken to rowing like a duck to water."

I glanced over my shoulder at the small, sandy cove.

"Bow first. It'll be easy with it so calm. You should try beaching in a storm. Have to catch a wave and hope for the best." She was intent on the shore as she spoke, "Nice and easy. Just before we hit bottom, give it one hard pull. More on the left."

I saw the sea grass rise closer to meet us from below, then the mucky bottom, and finally, drifts of small rocks.

"Pull now," she commanded. "Again. Harder."

With all my might, I bent into the oars, and we lurched to a stop with the nose of the boat plowed into the soft sand.

"Wonderful," she beamed. "Now, mind you don't try that in a larger boat unless you have your engine up and know your draw. That is," she added slyly, "unless you have to."

Her red toes were the first into the water as the back of the boat drifted toward shore. Placing both oars on board, I followed her. The water was refreshing. Imagining myself an old seafarer, I dunked my hands into the chilly water and splashed my face.

"Always tie your boat securely. You can get distracted by any number of things." She was wrapping the bowline around a large sun-bleached log, etched by artistic worms. It lay where the waters had tossed it, midway up the small inlet. The sand was finer here where Alex had finally stopped. Had there been a wind, it never would have found us, sequestered as we were with the deep gray rocks on either side.

The basket sat between us. Like a child on Christmas morn, I wanted to rip into the delicious surprise hidden in wrappings.

"Isn't this glorious?" She tossed small, warm grains of dry sand with a flip of her painted toes, burrowed them again under to cooler sand and sighed.

Across from us, the green mounds of Samish Bay's shore sat peaceful and idle. It was hard to imagine such wild dealings as the old weaver beside me boasted.

I sat categorizing my newly learned stories for our girls' pizza night. I could share some of these tales with them, I reasoned, without invoking more concern from Lissa. I hadn't told them about that New Year's Eve story with the Italian man who danced with her.

My body spun toward Alex, inadvertently flinging sand on her trousers. "Mrs. McKenzie," I shouted so suddenly I startled the woman next to me, "that was the same Antonio on New Year's Eve, right?"

She looked at me with something akin to disgust as she brushed the sand from her pants. "Yes, Jean." Her pants now free of sand, she turned towards the basket and opened it. "We had heard of him before we had the encounter at the river. He was trying to establish a territory for the crooks from back East. His mark was a slice down the face, like the scar he had from his ear to his chin. I'd see him around town, and he always tried to get close, but the boys wouldn't let him. He would watch me sometimes. I'd come out of a store, and he'd be there, watching me. He was persistent and dangerous. He'd made up his mind he wanted me, and it began to get under Jake's skin. Well," she unwrapped a thick, beef sandwich and offered me one, "at least I know you're paying attention."

She was the devil, I determined. I hated her smugness, her full life. I hated my boring, dullness.

Sensing my punctured ego, she began slowly, compassionately, to blend the two stories together, "Jean, when they made it against the law to sell booze, instead of getting better, as they promised, things got worse. The Mafia tried to take over out here, and we had to stop them. We ran clean. Oh, there were the hijackers, and they were dangerous. But if the Camorra had gotten established out here, there would have been more killings. Few were hurt before they arrived and riled everyone up. Why? Because people still drank. Good, honest, church-going men and women constantly broke the law. And not just here, all over the nation.

"South of Seattle, a very pious, plump, little old lady had her still blow up one day while she was in her rocking chair on the front porch. She had eight people working for her, dependent on her. You see, she used her money to help her church, family, and friends. Not all runners were bad like Antonio." She spit. "Sometimes just saying his name makes me sick. I wish he had never seen me at the river. He made up his mind to have me and made our life hell."

She slapped the breadcrumbs from her hands, her words as strong as her sentiment, "Teach this in your school. In the beginning, they cried, 'Save the children, outlaw booze,' because fathers were spending their pay at the bars. So, Prohibition. But then kids got involved in the running. Hell, if they weren't offloading cases, they were selling or drinking. Girls wore pantaloons with special pockets sewn in them to hold bottles. They'd carry it in milk cans to deliver the stuff. And then some of the poor children who were being used to run started to get caught in the crossfire between the law and the runners. People were crazy doing what they weren't supposed to. The law was in it too, the judges. There was no law. Women who hardly drank before this time now carried flasks. Why? We were told we couldn't. Then the depression hit, and the hope for more jobs and safer streets was in selling booze and making the profit. And the cry changed to, 'Save the children, bring back booze.'"

Alex bit into her sandwich, sad blue eyes focused on the water and the ghosts that played there.

<hr />

"You push us off." She lifted her long leg over the side.

I splashed us out as far by foot as possible, then, with an awkward rocking of the boat, climbed aboard, my launching not as accomplished as my landing.

Silently she let me struggle with the oars, having lost my rhythm to the roast beef sandwich, warm sand, and lazy sunshine.

"Head along the shore this time. This way."

I turned my course in the direction the arched appendage insisted. We began to zigzag our way along the deeply scarred boulders, where lush green trees clung to jagged outcroppings.

"Sometimes an inlet like that, or a shallow spit, saved a person. Jake knew every cove, rock, and the running of the tides. He had the sea rolled up in his sleeves."

A sleek Chris-Craft motored past us into the bay. "Bow in. Put your bow into the wake. Always take a wave head on, like life."

My uneven stroke tilted *Old Blue*, and the picnic basket squeaked as it slid across the planks.

"That damn Italian," she began, as if the sound had retuned her to our earlier conversation, "was bad blood. In '27, he brought some of his people out here from Lake Michigan or someplace back East to take over our business. They were Camorra and deadly. It seems he was part of a different Mafia from New York's Cosa Nostra and was trying to beat them out for this territory too. He learned which men in this area to take out so he could unite the riffraff. And Jake was high on his list. He thought he had it made that night on the Nooksack when we were coming in from Canada. But he didn't get the greeting he thought he would."

I wasn't watching the rocky cliffs or the blue waters. I was trans-fixed on the face below the brim, urging more words forth. When nothing came, I was breathless. "Why?"

"Because he didn't leave here alive," her stare reflected her words, hard and cold. "And that damn Drummond came and took my Jake away from me. Blamed him. But he didn't do it."

A heron, an eel dangling from its beak, stood motionless. His long, thin, legs solid on the jagged rock of the shore, he watched us closely.

"Quit eavesdropping," she ordered, splashing in his direction. "Go on. Shoo."

The grayish bird shifted his feet, slowly spread his large wings, flying low, taking his meal elsewhere.

She turned back toward me now, taking in my startled gaze.

"Look, Jean," her voice a whisper, "that's what I have to know. What I have to prove. Why I have to find it."

I didn't move. The only sound, the water dripping from the oars, suspended motionless in air.

Alex rushed on, "I need your help. You must help me find it."

Her voice weakened, breathless, "My God, child, before I die, I must know." A broken, desperate shell of a woman emerged under the big brim. A single tear slid down the sun-wrinkled cheek. "Please?"

"What is it we are looking for?"

Nothing moved but her lips. "No," she hissed. A light deep within her ignited. "Not until you promise that you're in, that you will tell no one. I mean no one until it's over."

"W-well," I stammered, my mind racing.

"I'll pay you well. But promise me. I loved Jake with every nerve and bone in my body. That's why I told you all those stories today. He loved me, and I loved him. We were one. But I have to know."

"Is it dangerous?" I really didn't care, but I hoped she would expose more of the game. I knew I could never outsmart this silver fox, but I had better learn to try. I waited.

"Old mysteries sometimes are."

"And the law?"

She wasn't budging, "They aren't interested. All this happened over fifty years ago. A lifetime. But I can't leave this life without knowing. I need to untangle this. To have peace."

From the distance of the other craft, this scene must have looked serene. Two women at opposite poles of the spectrum of life, one just stepping into her future, one preparing to depart. Heads bowed toward each other as they swayed gently in the current, adrift at sea.

Yet we were anything but tranquil. Storms raged inside us.

If I said yes, I would glide into a world unknown. Possibly dangerous. A soldier in an oblique war buried in time. But, an adventure of a lifetime.

If I said no, she would take her pieces of the puzzle and continue her search with someone else following her charge. For though she spoke of her quiet ending, this red-haired woman would trod the earth, snorting hell's fire in search of her Holy Grail. Of that, I was certain. In fact, at this point, it was my only certainty.

Hooked. Being pulled along by this undercurrent, I gave way to the lure of the hunt. "Yes," I ventured.

"And you won't tell a soul?"

I nodded. "Yes," my voice louder, stronger.

"Not your friends or even Mr. Chin?"

"Yes," echoed back from the rocks.

She extended her hand. I freed mine from the oar. She pulled hers back and spit in it, nodding for me to do likewise. I spat, and our hands met. It was a powerful grasp, linking lives, committed to spin time around, to walk backward to ease the future.

CHAPTER 11

"There. See over there?" Her arm was led by the waggling finger. "Whiskey Cove. That's where we had our stole-up hole. And that's where we're going. But not today."

I looked across at the islands in the distance. It was hard to tell from our boat at the mouth of the bay where "there" was. Mounds of green anchored in blue—trees and water against a pale blue sky— floated in the peaceful vision before me.

"I'll row for a while. I need to build up my muscles too."

We did the stooped dance of changing places in a small boat as *Blue* responded to our shifts of weight.

Behind Alex, the shoreline inched closer, every pull an even stroke. She relished her task.

The wind was picking up, adding to our speed as it nudged us along. The tide had worked its way up the beach, leaving a new water line, and was now heading back out.

With one last tug, she beached *Old Blue*, quickly snapping the oars from the oarlocks and plunging one into the soft sand. Alex held us fast against the undertow.

"Jump out and grab the rope."

I landed, the small grains oozing between my chilled toes, while the waves slapped against the backs of my knees.

"Pick up the bow and pull."

I lifted the nose of *Blue* while she pushed with the oar. The boat slid onto drier ground. Boating the oars, she stepped onto the seaweed as it crunched, sun dried and brittle, under her foot.

"Thank heavens we don't have to carry her far. These old arms have had it."

We left *Old Blue* as we'd found her, belly up, safe from the water's edge.

"Would you mind?" she held the basket toward me as we reached the base of the steps. Her hand grasped the rail, and she was off at an even, calculated pace.

Looking up, the flight of steep steps seemed insurmountable. Did someone add to them in our absence? I toiled behind, basket and thermos dangling from my now deadened limbs. I ached all over, legs, stomach, back, arms, and hands. The weight of my recent commitment hunched me further in my stride.

Mrs. McKenzie paused, breathing deeply.

I watched her closely, fearful the toil and heat would crumble this old statue.

Slowly, she began again.

What have I done? It must have been heat stroke that let me place my hand in hers, binding us.

We paused at the turn in the switchback. Fear pushed its way through my body. My arms began to tremble as I stepped between the short hedge onto the green grass. A breeze of salt air off the bay chilled the sweat on my face and that running down my back.

Alex slumped into a chair in the coolness of the kitchen. "Oh, it's nice in here."

The bird answered, running up and down his perch, a streak of yellow and noise.

"Hello, Pretty Boy. Miss Mama?" Her finger pointed toward the refrigerator.

I produced a pitcher, frosty and cold. We slurped down the water, forgetting to breathe.

"My heavens," she laughed struggling to her feet, "I need a lie down. I can barely move." Her voice trailed down the hall, and I heard the bathroom door shut.

I waited my turn and then disappeared into the sanctuary of porcelain and mirrors. I was a hopeless sight—red nosed, hair where not matted down with sweat sticking out in every direction possible. I couldn't imagine a man alive would find this object reflecting in the mirror at all attractive.

As I stepped back into the darkness of the passageway, I listened, trying to determine the whereabouts of my conspirator.

"In here, Jean." It was downright eerie how she could know my thoughts.

I found her reclining on the long couch across from the big windows with her beloved sea beyond.

"It's right there on the table."

I looked eagerly, hoping for a clue. I saw nothing but a stack of neatly piled magazines.

"Right there," she pointed aggressively.

I saw it then. It was my check.

"Well take it. You've earned it. But I must rest now. See you Monday. We'll find it and get me organized yet. And get some rest yourself."

I had been dismissed. I picked up the rectangular slip of paper with sailboats printed faintly in the background and headed for the door.

In the archway to the utility room, I stopped. The check was made out for $250, twenty-five more than the agreed price. I tiptoed back in and cleared my throat before beginning, "Uh, excuse me, Mrs. McKenzie, Alex. I, uh, I believe the check is supposed to be only $225."

"Well?" She blinked at me.

"Um, you've made it out for $250."

"Jean, you are such a nice girl," she shifted onto her side, her still damp hair flattened against the back of her head. "You're worth more. Buy some sunglasses and suntan lotion, for God's sake." Her arm barely lifted in farewell. "And stop and have a nice beer down at the Edison Tavern. It's legal now."

The seat in my car was scorching. The heat penetrated my clothing, warming and relaxing where it touched. I leaned into it and rested a moment. Life was bizarre. Nothing in my past had prepared me for the future I had just signed up for. My engine rattled to life, and a cloud of dust followed me down the driveway, only to linger at the pavement edge. Cruising the windy curves of the road, I watched a sea gull lift from the sloughs that snaked across the flats. In a dried-up jetty, the remains of a deserted, sun-bleached boat rose from the mud and tall brown grass. I turned onto the road toward Edison and slowed to pass through the small town.

My eyes lazed along the old homes. I had just reached the artists' galleries when the words of a sign shook my consciousness. Edison Tavern. The car followed my guide as I spun the wheel, heading back. I rolled to a stop, pausing across from the establishment. Now why would Alex suggest this unusual place? Was it just a coincidence, or was it another clue?

I pulled farther into the tall grass and left my car by a weathered sailboat named *Breeze*. She waited patiently on her trailer for her next journey on the sea.

It was dark and cold inside. As my eyes adjusted, they wandered from the neon beer signs to the stuffed goose on top of the shuffleboard. Deer horns, old saws, posters, and a jackalope adorned every inch of the wooden walls. I positioned myself at a small table far away from the bar, which had a big *E* hanging above its middle.

The woman behind the bar put down her cigarette, took a swig of diet coke, even though it was evident she'd abandoned her diet years before, and eyed me with some suspicion before budging. Obviously not one to misuse her time, she hovered at the end of the bar, caught in indecision, brows knitted. Unable to reach a conclusion, she shrugged and slowly slipped behind the wall, where a pheasant was suspended in the most unnatural pose, only to emerge again, a basket of fish and chips resting in the palm of one large hand.

The sight of the advancing food spurred on a nagging hunger, which had me considering wrestling her bulk to the ground, grabbing the basket, and devouring the feast. Hunger has an evil, dangerous side too. I smiled at the shuffling form in the hopes of lightening her step.

The young man in casual business attire nodded his thanks as she plopped the bountiful meal in front of him.

Her tennis shoes turned in my direction, the hems at the heels of her dull, dark, polyester pants were blackened with dirt from dragging on the floor.

"Whatelitbe?" was one practiced word.

"Those fish and chips look good." I was hoping for a smile or, at least, to entice her closer than the five-foot invisible line she had drawn between us.

"Menu's right there," her voice was flat, unenthusiastic. And to conserve energy there was only a slight nod of the tight brown curls in the direction she wanted me to look.

"Thanks."

She loomed, waiting.

"I'll try the fish and chips and a light beer. It's hot out there."

She grunted while she pivoted. I wasn't certain if it was the strain of the movement or an approval of my order. As I watched the shuffle of her hips, I noticed a chalkboard boasting of oyster shooters. How exotic for a bar. I picked up the Big E menu to see what other delicacies this eclectic establishment offered.

Steak, burgers, and fried oysters rounded out the suggested bill of fare. Hunger made me close the tan slip of paper, and I inserted it back behind the salt and pepper shakers in the bent iron holder. The photograph on the back cover caught my attention. Retrieving the menu, I studied the old snapshot of the first proprietor.

It wasn't my voice I heard as I read the small paragraph to myself, but the succinct diction of Alex McKenzie.

> The Edison Saloon survived Prohibition by operating as a soda fountain, card room, and pool hall. As the blue laws did not allow the use of the word "saloon," the establishment was licensed as Edison Inn and is more than likely one of Skagit Valley's oldest bars.

This is why she had sent me here. I studied the picture, taken around 1900, of John Bradley, the owner, with his bushy mustache and unmistakable pride in his business.

My head was shaking in amazement when the cold beer rocked the table. I looked up to see those tight curls and eyes, squinted, watching me.

"This is really interesting," I attempted to enlist conversation and waved the menu before her unflinching stare. "Are there any more pictures around like this?"

"I don't know," she mumbled, backing away and was off toward the security of the large wooden bar.

Sipping my beer, the massive, highly polished structure took on a new interest. The changes it had seen. The various hands that had leaned on its sturdy bulk, caressing, slapping, toying with its indestructible identity. Men's, women's and even children's elbows resting, spreading joy across its girth, or anger of the disagreement beaten into its timeless memory. Oh, to tap the conversations, the deals, the offers of love. I wanted to press my ear against its richness and listen for the shuffling sounds of lives and times gone by.

A thought caught me, and I laughed out loud. Was it possible they served rum flavored sodas?

⸻

The fish and chips now rested in my satisfied stomach. The crust had been crisp yet not heavy, the white fish meat tender and flavorful. And the abundant chips disappeared easily. So this explained why businessmen occupied so many tables. The age of the building did not reflect the quality of the food, fresh and delightful.

I folded one of the paper menus into my pocket. If the history didn't bring me back, the food would.

My waitress, sequestered behind her historic barrier, took another drag on her cigarette and watched me as I stood. I paused just inside the door to look at the photos that covered the entrance. There was no hint or further mention of this quaint, thirst-quenching parlor that had outlived many of its regulars.

The door opened behind me. I turned, blinking into the light. A silhouetted figure of a tall, slight man caught my eye as he entered, hesitating slightly before he disappeared into the dimness of the tavern.

I could understand his reason for pausing. I had felt much the same, being the only woman customer. He must have felt their eyes too, being Asian.

CHAPTER 12

"Hurry up. They're waiting," Lissa voiced her impatience as she sat on my bed, inspecting her neat, short-cropped nails. "Okay, let's go." I attempted to console her anxiety as I put the hand lotion down and continued to work the soothing, white cream into my calluses. We walked down the hall together and out into the night.

The ice cream parlor was packed. Barbara and Kitty had secured a small round table in the corner, and we headed in their direction.

"It's about time," Barbara blurted. "We thought we'd turn into cones before you arrived."

"Our historian here was trying to soften up her hands," Lissa said, sliding onto the pink-and-white striped cushion.

I took the last place left, facing the wall and the big-toothed smiles of the two perfectly tanned debutantes.

"Let's see," Kitty demanded, leaning forward. "Have they improved?" Her nails, fake and polished, led the way, grabbing my work-worn paw and flipping it over.

"Ouch!" she winced. "Is it hard work?"

"No," Lissa answered in my stead. "But she has a new sport. She's learning to row."

"Fun," quipped Barbara with a flip of her hair, dismissing the effort involved in the activity. "Will you take me some day? I bet I could get a real good tan on the water."

"Well, I'm not that good and ..."

Luckily, I wasn't given the opportunity to finish. Kitty and Barbie, ever searching for the perfect man to build their perfect dreams around, had spotted Nate entering with Jill. Chatter and speculation surrounded the couple before they even made it through the door.

Eventually, I turned to form my own opinion on the far too low-cut neckline of the absolutely wrong colored dress and that awful hair style on Jill and to determine if Nate really did look delicious.

My gaze and opinion were halted by a young man leaning against the windowsill, newspaper hiding his face. My movement had set him in motion, and he quickly turned from me, stuffing the paper under his arm. All I saw was jet black hair as he squeezed his slender frame past those coming in and slid out the door. I watched the window for another glimpse of the cat-like movement of the stranger, who seemed somehow familiar, but his route took him in the other direction.

"Jean," the low, controlled voice of Barbie was smothered with irritation.

I turned back to the austere faces across from me, questioning, "What?"

"Good God, they saw you staring."

I had broken a cardinal rule of social snoops.

"Is something the matter?" Lissa asked, watching me.

"No. I just thought I knew someone. That's all." I barely moved my head, fearful of another lecture.

"Who?" Lissa persisted, studying my profile.

"Never mind. I just thought I'd seen him before."

"Well, of course you've seen Nate Drummond before. He's the baseball captain," Barbie's voice dripped with disgust at my ignorance of Nate and his standing in the pool of available catches.

"Do you think they're going to Tom's tonight?" Kitty interrupted.

"I hope so. I don't know what he sees in that Jill. Oh, my God," Barbie's voice hit a higher octave, "he's looking this way." She assumed a pose she hoped would hold his attention.

Barbie and Kitty's hysteria got the better of me. This was one of the reasons I spent time with them, I reminded myself. They seemed to always create the excitement my life lacked, until I met Mrs. McKenzie. I pretended to drop my napkin and turned to see the topic of their admiration. Quickly, I ducked my head further under the table. The image of the green eyes watching me when he saved my book at the fountain outside of the library reignited a sense of interest and desire. Nate, the baseball captain, the pitcher. And he thought I was staring at him and not observing the man behind the newspaper! Great.

The coast cleared of the imposing Nate and his date, Jill. We took our cones with us into the warm summer evening. I looked up and down the street, hoping for another glimpse of the slim form holding the newspaper. But what I found was Lissa's eyes following my every move.

"What is it, Jean?"

"Just a feeling. That guy …"

"You mean the one who was watching you?"

"Really?"

"Yes, until you turned. Is he in one of your classes? I don't remember seeing him on campus or in the Library. Is he Japanese?"

"I don't know."

"Is everything all right? What class is he in?"

"It's no big deal. Just forget it," my statement forceful and loud.

The volume of my outburst stopped Kitty and Barbie. They spun in unison toward us, "Come on, you two," Barbie snapped. "I want to get to Tom's before the party's over."

———

Music blared, and brightly colored figures twisted, bumped, and gyrated to the ear-piercing sounds of Santana. Apparently, the party was a smashing success. Even I, with marred hands and peeling nose, had rocked to the beat from time to exhilarating time.

Hot and dripping after a particularly frenzied workout on the pseudo dance floor, I slipped to the back of the rim of onlookers.

I took another cold beer from the ice chest. It slid down my throat refreshing, enlivening, with its ability to deaden reality. What Prohibition must have been like! The excitement of walking a fine, lawless line, an illegal path binding the corrupt and honest together in the hazy veil of booze.

As I watched the energetic figures, my mind exchanged the now for then. Shorts and sun-dresses were replaced by satin and beads, jeans and madras shirts, for suits and polished shoes. Their deviant behavior, sipping of the forbidden hooch, spun them faster and deeper into wild and unchallenged hysteria.

Swept away by my vision, I didn't see him approach, "Weren't you at the ice cream parlor tonight?" He looked down at me, much taller than I remembered when only inches away.

"Uh, y-yeah," I stammered, instantly hating myself for my choice of words.

"I'm Nate," he shifted his beer to extend his large hand. His ruddy complexion, tan and freckles mixed, enhanced the smile. The collar of his ironed blue shirt almost touched his thick, sun-bleached, copper hair.

"Ah, yes, well hello." I began to back away, shoving my hands behind me, out of sight.

Somehow, I was certain all movement in the room had subsided.

"So, are you going to keep it a secret?" His smile broadened, white teeth filling my vision, and he casually withdrew his hand.

"What?" confused by the question, I backed up further into a long-legged wooded stand. A pile of magazines tumbled to the floor. I bent to pick them up, and my beer cascaded onto the perfectly painted face and bare shoulders of a cover girl, warping her image, and spreading onto the rug.

Nate squatted next to me. "Here," his one word stopped me, and I watched, fascinated, as with one quick motion, he had retrieved his handkerchief from his back pocket and was mopping up my mess before it penetrated the carpet.

Mesmerized by the sight of the plaid square he deftly used to soak up the smelly liquid, I watched in silence, embarrassed by my clumsiness.

"Don't worry. It was clean," he teased as he waved the wet cloth away from the now restacked pile of magazines.

"Come on," his voice was light as he took my elbow and led me out to the back door.

Over my shoulder, I could see three mouths drooped in disbelief. My friends stood motionless, gaping.

He stopped just outside, on a small porch with fading white paint. Above his head, a dusty light fixture held captive its cache of dead moths.

Slipping from his grasp into the comfort of the shadows, I clasped my calluses together behind my back.

"You haven't told me yet."

"Told you what?"

"Your name."

"Oh," I blushed, visibly relieved. "Jean."

"So, Jean, how is that stack of books you were reading?"

He remembered, and I blushed further. "Oh, yeah, thanks again." I shifted my weight, "I've finished."

"Impressive," his eyebrows shot up. "Are you in summer school?"

"No. I work to pay for my schooling. To graduate. Don't have much time," I dragged out the word "pay," watching his bright green eyes. I was slightly convinced his muscles received a scholarship his brains couldn't uphold.

"Yeah, me too."

My hands relaxed behind me, but my lips remained active, "Really? What?"

"Move furniture, paint, construction, anything I can get. How about you?"

"Same here. Right now I'm working in a garden."

"On campus or private?"

"For an older woman."

"They can be fountains of information, or a pain in the ass. How's yours?"

"A little of both," I laughed.

"Good, keeps things lively," he countered, folding his arms and leaning against the doorjamb. The smile reappeared.

Conversation turned to awkward stares.

"Hadn't we better get back? I mean, won't she be looking for you?"

He bent down to the ice chest and opened another beer, holding it out for me. "What are you studying?"

"I want to be a teacher. Music," I added getting used to my new identity. I took the beer and tried to relax.

"Noble profession."

My brow arched at his jest. Shifting, I prepared my departure.

"My grandmother, my mother, and my oldest brother all teach."

"Really?" I rocked back on my heels with a mixture of relief and excitement. "So that's who taught you to clean up and bought you the handkerchief?"

"Yes and no," his voice held a hint of laughter as he poked at the wet square on the ledge where he'd spread it to air out. "Handkerchief is from Grandpa. He was a huge Scot but always carried his kerchief. He taught me to be ready for any emergency, including spilt beer."

My blush was as deep a red as the stripes in the plaid print he was eyeing, attempting to determine what to do with it.

Suddenly he turned back toward me and changed the subject, nodding at my hand. "I have something for those calluses. An old family remedy. Let me see them."

I lifted my free hand, amazed at his attention.

"Must be some garden," his voice as gentle as the finger that pressed on the newly formed mound.

A shadow filled the doorway. Jill stood watching our smiling faces. "Here you are," she interrupted. Her nose wrinkled in distaste, and her voice slid higher. "What is that smell?" Her searching eyes fell on the plaid culprit, and she spat in its direction, "Yuck, throw that thing away."

I whispered, "Excuse me," hushed by the sight of the perfectly coifed hair, ratted and high, and the plunging neckline on Jill that started my feet in motion. "I was just on my way to the bathroom."

I shot past her, wishing I could agree with my friends. But, the truth was obvious,—Jill was beautiful.

"What did he say?"

"Did he ask you out?"

"Don't be a twit, Kitty. Nate's not going to ask Jean out."

Any attempt at comment was stifled by the rapid-fire questionings before the two dizzy debutantes were off on their own tangents, lost in dreams of unreachable enchantment.

When they had drifted away, I turned to Lissa, who had stood silently waiting for the tremor of excitement to pass.

"I don't know how you do it," she smiled sheepishly.

"I spilled my beer."

"Clever. I'll have to remember that one."

We both laughed, and I felt the tension slide from my body and dissipate into a whirl of youthful exuberance.

"Lissa, he's nice, and he comes from a family of mostly teachers."

"I know."

"What?" I looked at my friend as a new spring of information.

"Do you think we librarians only have knowledge about books?" She was playing with me, and I let her.

"Could I see your card file on him?"

"He just moved to his grandfather's house."

I gently nudged her to loosen her lips.

"He visits the library often."

"You're lying. You just want me to feel bad because I left that job at the library last year."

"Right now, he's reading Murray Morgan's *Skid Road*." She interpreted my blank stare and sighed with mock sarcasm. "It's a history book about Puget Sound, wonderful really. In fact, some schools in these parts recommend it to their students."

"History?" My thoughts and visions were still back with Nate and the new image of him, contentedly pursuing printed pages.

"Yes. He told me once he finds history 'a pool of information I like to dive into from time to time.'"

"He said that?"

Lissa nodded, her small figure bending with the force of her affirmation.

"Wait a minute," I leaned in closer to pose my question, eyes squinting. "Why didn't you tell me any of this before?"

"You were never interested before."

"Good point. And on that note, I think I'll head home." I put my beer in the trash can and started for the draft of cooler air, which led to the door.

"You should wait for us," she insisted, following me.

"It's only a few blocks. I'll be fine."

She studied me in her silent way. "All right. You do look tired. But slip a note under my door so I know you made it okay."

"Will do."

<hr />

The moon was playing hide-and-seek with me as it slid from white puffs to the blue-black of the open sky. The air held the warm smell of summer. People, enjoying the heat, sat on their porches, doors and windows open wide and inviting, as the lazy breeze surrounded them, carrying the lilt of their laughter into the calm night.

I moved slowly up High Street through the peacefulness, lost in the memory of my conversation with Nate. He wasn't my kind. Furthermore, I had no time for men in my life. But the sight of that crazy handkerchief and the fact that he uses his mind, as well as his bronzed "delicious" form, were twisting his smiling face before me. I would have to spend more time in the library.

The image of a sequestered rendezvous under the silent and reverent dome of the study room at the top of the well-worn stairs in the library, with stacks of books our only witness, made my feet light. Impulsively, I grabbed the trunk of a birch tree and spun around it, giddy.

Suddenly, I stopped, slipped behind the white bark, and peered behind me into the street. The moon, unwilling to help, stayed behind the clouds. Where I thought I had seen movement, I could find nothing. A chill ran through me, and I remained glued to the strong trunk.

Somewhere a woman laughed from safe within her home.

I waited, mind racing and pushing my heartbeat along with it. Finally, the cloud moved, and the filtered light became a full flood, momentarily illuminating the scene behind me.

Still nothing moved, and the brightness dispelled my fears. It must have been a shadow that crossed the moon, I reasoned. Sinking back against the rough surface of the birch, I took deep, soothing breaths.

"Silly," I scolded myself.

I looked down the line of trees in front of me, which led toward Nash Dorm, and stepped into the street, away from the shadows, to the full light of the middle of the road. Forcing myself to hum, I started down the two remaining blocks, wishing myself safely tucked under warm covers.

The first uneventful block gave encouragement for the second as the tranquility of the evening settled back around me, passing me gently along.

A car screeched around the corner behind me. I turned, this time seeing the dark figure as it slipped into the shadows. I began to run. The car slowing behind me, I ran faster, my legs attempting the pace of my heart. Fear propelled me. The car, only a few houses back, slithered in and out of the semi-darkness. A sinking sound met my ears. Mine were not the only feet hitting the pavement. Sweat dripped into my eyes as I reached the corner, jumped a short hedge, and dashed across the lawn.

The car stopped.

I felt for my keys, attempting to catch their weight in my fingers, as my small purse bounced on its strap at my side. The dorm door was just a few feet away when a thick figure stepped from the passenger side of the old Buick.

"Hey, baby. What's your rush?"

My keys, pressed between shaking fingers, worked toward the lock while my neck craned to keep the stranger in view.

"What's the matter?" he lurched forward, unsteady on his feet. "Afraid of the boogieman?" A heavy laugh sliced through the air. Amused by his own sick joke, he turned for encouragement from the faceless driver. Lifting his beer, he drank deep then burped long and loud before crawling back into the car. The empty can he tossed rolled to a stop at the curb.

Breathless, hot tears of relief now streaming down my cheeks, I pulled the door tight behind me and stepped back into the hallway. My trembling hand found the light switch and darkness surrounded me. Wiping my eyes, I crept to the long pathway of windows that created the dorm hallway overlooking Highland Drive and waited.

From nowhere he emerged, a fleeting slink of a figure. Like a shark, circling, just within peripheral vision, he traced my steps. He was slight of build, with quick, cat-like movements. Then, abandoning his hunt, he slid off into the night.

CHAPTER 13

The knock at my door was gentle, hesitant. Yet, I bolted up, startled by the brightness that filled my room.

Again the knock.

"Who is it?" my voice, filled with sleep, cracked in mid sentence.

"Me. Are you up yet?"

I slumped toward the door, pulling away the chair I had braced underneath the knob. It screeched across the cold, tiled floor, announcing its presence.

"What time is it?" I didn't bother with the politeness of a hello as I dragged my body back toward the warmth of my covers, snuggling under them.

"Eleven forty-five, sleeping beauty." She was working her way past my barriers of furniture and strewn clothes, scattered by my unruly mind, caught between exhaustion and fear.

"You didn't leave me a note." She paused. "Jean?"

"What?" my muffled voice was all but lost in the thick blanket.

"What is all this?" her gesture was toward the room.

"I'm redecorating."

"Better Homes and Gardens you're not." She sat on the side of my bed, her weight pulling me toward her.

"Well?" her expectant voice hovered above me.

"Well what?"

"What happened?"

"I don't know. I was walking home, and some drunken jerk followed me."

"What!" She snatched the covers from my face, I could feel her breath as she spoke, "Did you see who it was?"

"Naw." I struggled to pull the covers back, but her grip was firm.

"I think you should tell security about this."

"No," came quickly from my lips as I let loose the covers. I was none too eager, and she knew it. I didn't want to get security involved, not yet. My plan was to try to draw the shadow to the light, see his face, learn his game.

"Besides," I pushed a smile across my face, "what are they going to do?"

"Have a point there." Lissa returned the smile. "Come on. It's a beautiful day. Let's go have breakfast. You're going to need the energy to clean up this mess."

"Who all was there when you left?" I busied myself digging through a pile on the floor. I was fishing, and she knew it.

"He was still there when I left. But talking with some other guys."

My heart skipped a beat and fluttered with hope.

⟫•◦•⟪

Monday, and the sun-faded door was a comforting sight. I was thrilled to be standing amongst the neat lines of overturned earth. A soft coat of moisture from the salty mist sparkled over the grass, darkening the dirt. Spiders collected pearls on the delicate strings they had magically created between the rose bushes. The briny smell of morning filled my nostrils, spreading the sea scent down my lungs and throughout my body.

The fears of Friday night had eased from my mind over the slow, lazy weekend. The lurking image, brightened by the playful sun, no longer followed me. Rested, ghosts tucked securely away, I put on my new sunglasses and navy cap.

A fresh, new week lay before me like the expectant ground, supple, life giving. I looked forward to it with eager anticipation, certain soon I would work my way through the entanglements of Alex's life as much as I had the dried brown weeds of her garden. But as with any seed, caught by the wind or buried by hand, by squirrel, or by untamed nature, it would be impossible to foretell how the blooms of Mrs. McKenzie's story would unfold.

"Well, who do we have here?" the sing-songy voice greeted me in mock surprise.

I smiled at the tall, willowy figure, happy to see the wild red hair. A sense of relief shifted through me. I hadn't realized how anxious I had been to see her standing before me, to see the twinkling of life reflected in the soul of her blue eyes.

"Come on in, dear. What a week we have before us. I've been busy."

I could feel her excitement as I followed her into the turquoise kitchen. A pot of tea sat waiting.

"Say hello, Pretty Boy."

On command, the bird charged to and fro on his stick, twittering and trilling.

Like the gathering of old friends, warm and content, time moved between us in the laughter of the morning. She was filled with the news of the neighbor's catch of fish, crab, and with great pride produced a bucket of oysters.

Alex handed me an oyster-shucking knife, long, beveled on both sides. "Always come at 'em at three o'clock." She held an oyster with a hot pad and pointed her shucker at the side of the oyster. "Most people come in back here," she tapped the back of the shell, where it seemed to hinge, "but you can get a cleaner cut across the muscle at three o'clock." She demonstrated. Holding the oyster with the hinge away from her, she slid the shucker into the side, halfway down the length of the tightly sealed shell. The shell barely parted, and she expertly slid the blade under the top of the shell, slicing the muscles that held the treasure closed. Peeling the top off, she raised the juicy oyster to her lips and slid the morsel and seawater in all at once.

"Simply divine. Go on, give it a try." She nudged a glove and oyster my way, adding a warning, "Watch those barnacles."

I struggled, massacring my first attempt, unable to determine where the shells met in their wavy edges and barnacles. I had shell bits and seawater everywhere. Finally, it popped open. Not as brave as Alex, I simply put my opened delight down on the tray for future eating. Hopefully cooked.

Her gentle prattle continued as we worked the shells. She talked of everything but our quest. Somehow, it didn't matter.

Finally, the oysters neatly arranged on the tray, tea long gone, Mrs. McKenzie stood. I followed suit and drifted off to my work, amazed that one short week ago I had trembled at the thought of just such an encounter—how, at first, I'd backpedaled out of this very scene, anxious that Alex, in her loneliness, would drag me through her hollow memories and I would have to bear the burden of her repetitious boredom. And now, I had sat on the edge of my seat, longing for her tales to spill before me, like gleaming jewels before an awestruck child. But this morning, the treasure chest had remained sealed. In her caginess, she would drop her cache, gem by tantalizing gem, and I, the hunter, would gladly trip behind to collect and savor each shedding of the past.

By midafternoon, my toil bore fruit. The garden had become just that, a garden, complete with crisp edges, raked dirt, and a neatness bordering on compulsion.

I stood back to admire my handiwork. Strutting like a peacock down the drive past the roses to the square patch of soil, I pulled a wayward strand of weed here, smoothed there.

Whatever it was I was hired to find had not surfaced in my dredging. But the thought of that was far from me as I swayed from toe to heel in my Zen garden.

She had left me alone most of the day, and my job was now complete. That fact hit me suddenly. Like a snowball hits the side of an old barn, it splattered, rocked my soul, weakening my knees. If this job was complete, what had I committed to?

Fear is an unfriendly companion. It lurks just beyond reach, stalking your consciousness, controlling your life.

"Jean."

I jumped at Alex's voice, my peace shattered with anticipation.

"Jake would be proud." She stood on the small cement block that implied a back porch. Her eyes, soft with memories, scanned the yard.

My tension turned to pride as I watched her.

"All right," her voice was a whisper, as if she feared the slightest movement would break the spell and blow the white fairy drifts of bad seeds, recreating the tangled brown wreckage of last week.

Suddenly, the calm air was split with rage. "You miserable son of a shipwrecked sea witch. Where the hell is it?"

Her red face matched her hair. Eyes wild worked the ground.

I shivered, sensing the burnt trail left behind by her searing gaze. Paralyzed, wishing myself invisible to avoid her wrath, I waited.

Alex started through the yard, pacing, her stride measured by her anger. "Damn you, Jake. I just want to know. I have to know. I need to have things in order before …" She stopped, straightened her hunched and bent shoulders, and turned towards me. "Let's go. If it's not out there," she turned toward the sea, "then maybe I can rest."

She started at a good clip toward the front of her house. "Jesus, Mary, and Joseph. All I want is a little peace, to sleep through just one night." Her mumblings drifted off as we rounded the corner and faced the open bay. "God. I hoped we wouldn't have to do this. That it would be easy. But not my Jake. No, never."

We stood, the wind washing over us, listening to the gentle rushing of the waves. I watched as she lifted her chin, closed her eyes, and leaned into the breeze, breathing deep of the sea below. A calmness settled around her. For this strong vision of a woman, I prayed this very wind would guide us on our quest, that the murmuring sea gods would propel our pursuing craft swiftly and surely.

I was afraid to move, afraid I might give away my excitement at the prospect of our hunt and my complete selfishness in the thrill of my adventure. I felt it was out there, beckoning, whispering my name on the drifts of warm air. I waited. I wanted it. I shoved aside the stupidity of not even knowing what "it" was and replaced my misgivings with the assurance the journey would unravel the end.

Her arms began to swing, and her eyes opened. The steam within the widow was building again. I could see it in the agitation of her stance, the twitching of her fingers as she scoured the horizon.

"Jean," her finger tapped against the top of the long metal railing that snaked down beside the steep stairs.

"I only hope that someday you can understand and maybe forgive me." A deep groove of concern was wedged between forlorn eyes.

"It's all right," I eagerly attempted to lull her apprehensions.

"Well, I hope so. I sure hope so." Alex didn't move, but her hand reached out, found my forearm, and gave it a squeeze.

At that moment, there was so much I wanted to say. But the energy of the grip moved through me like a bolt of steel, riveting joint and jaw, stiff and still. All would be fine, my mind, the only limber part of me, insisted. I would make it so. Whatever it took, I would search until the object of her desire was found. There was nothing to fear, I reasoned, except for my questionable ability with the rowboat. And I vowed to work on that as I had never applied myself before.

"We'd better get started," before loosening her hold, she shook my arm slightly, the sound of her voice, like the gentle tinkling of a bell, rattled my nerves free.

"Yep," was the only response that tumbled from my lips.

Mrs. McKenzie flashed me a smile and donned her large brimmed hat before heading down the stairs.

I slapped my cap squarely on my head and followed.

Three-fourths of the way down, where the stairs jogged by the small, square cement shed, built into the hillside with the train-like tracks leading down to the water, she halted. There was a faint jingling as she pulled the long chain around her neck, boasting her accumulation of keys.

From behind, I watched her elbow twist several times in her attempt to free the lock. Alex grunted, a noise that hid a curse. With one more flick of her wrist, her struggles were rewarded.

"Aha!" Her shoulders lifted in conquest. Using her weight, she slightly lifted the door. It creaked open, emitting the dank, musty smell of time. A deep gouge in the floor finally halted the door's progress. Unlike its owner, weather and age had stripped the wood of its luster and agility. Mrs. McKenzie forged onward into the blackness.

I moved closer, sticking my head into the dark, breathing deeply of this airless crypt. I was about to edge through the archway when a square, material-covered object was thrust against my chest, preventing my progress. I jumped at the abruptness.

"Here, take this."

It was an order. An invisible line had been drawn, and I was not to cross it. Despite my piqued curiosity, I stepped back into the sunlight.

Alex did likewise, again slightly lifting the door out of its groove to close it squarely and firmly.

I had seen nothing, but there was no mistaking her movements. This shed and its contents were her private domain. Whereas, with the rest of the house, I had been eagerly welcomed to roam freely, here remained forbidden territory, a cement block, built to withstand the rage of storms in order to protect the secrets within.

"I know they aren't stylish," she said as she twirled her orange canvas life vest, drawing my attention away from the door and down the remaining steps to the bay. From her other hand dangled a square seat cushion like the one I held.

"But," her voice lured me in her direction, "we're going out far today. And whenever we're out of this bay, I'm wearing mine."

I was nervous at the thought. It had not occurred to me the sea would want to swallow my spirit. I had, in my innocence, sought the amusement of the sport, paying no heed to the depths of the danger. Knees slightly weakened by the prospect, I bent to follow.

Encouraging, the tide had rolled up the shore to make our departure an easy one.

"Let's see what you remember," she challenged me, lowering into the stern, the expectant passenger.

My shoes made a thud as I threw them into the bottom of the boat. Walking *Old Blue* out as far as possible, I slipped into the rocking skiff. Plunging an oar straight down into the muddy sea bottom, I used my weight against it to push us farther out. Working my oars into their oarlocks, I unwittingly dripped water all over my passenger.

"Sorry," I murmured, looking into the face of the speckled Alex.

"Good thing I'm not wearing silk, or one of my old furs."

"Furs?" It was a true test of my imagination to exchange the image of silk-and-fur-clad McKenzie for the one with faded orange life vest, overlarge brimmed hat, and sunglasses that occupied the seat across from me.

"Anyone with a nickel in her pockets and a sense for fashion wore furs." Still not satisfied with the expression on my face, she continued. "Oh, I know how they feel now about killing animals, but heck, they were warm, basic. And don't forget about Hollywood." Her finger chimed in. "Every star draped in this and that. Why, some studios had big connections with furriers. All their stars had to wear them. And what was that telling us? You know, I think Hollywood is partly to blame for our troubles. When you teach, teach that." She began to laugh at her own lecture. "Besides, a good fur did make you feel like a lady."

The crooked finger rose to waggle at me, then recoiled as she nestled farther against the transom, stretching her legs down the center of the boat. Occasionally, as we moved along, her pointer would lift and twirl through the warm air, indicating more pull needed here or too deep a stroke there.

In silence, we jerked, and sometimes slid, across the blue-green waters. Whereas my back relished the workout, my stomach muscles, undiscovered until last week's maiden voyage, spoke loudly of their discomforts. But I was gaining on my new activity. Determination to conquer lent new strength to my abilities.

A gull, screeching overhead, hovered, watching, mocking my inexperience. Checking my path over my shoulder, I saw a large circle of smooth, glassy surface. Undercurrents at work. I lay into the oars, fixed on streaking across this rippleless path of sea.

The hull nudged onto the flat water. To and fro my body worked, and like slow, deep breaths, we cruised along.

The bird, his head roving from side to side as he calculated my burst of activity, let out another cry before his wings propelled him away.

I laughed at my own triumph, watching the gray and white of the flapping wings grow smaller with distance. Feeling Alex's eyes on me, I lowered mine. I knew the old bird was still watching closely, scrutinizing my actions.

"It's easy in here." The arm waved, indicating the bay. "Wait until you get out there." The hand led the direction. "What if it starts to blow? Or the rains sweep in? Promise me you'll never try this alone."

The thought had never occurred to me. I started to shrug my shoulders, but the icy, menacing tone of her voice froze my movements.

"I mean it, Jean. Promise me you'll never, under any circumstances, go outside this bay alone."

We drifted, oars poised above the water, the only sound the tear-shaped drops from the wet wood splashing back into the sea.

"I just couldn't take on the responsibility if something happened to you too."

"All right." It was a casual, off-the-cuff reply. As far as I was concerned, it was just more of her exaggerations. I couldn't fathom why I would ever attempt such a journey.

The distancing mood her demand had put over us was lifted as we reached the mouth of the inlet and edged out into the channel. Vessels, large and small, dotted the horizon. The waters, choppier from the stronger currents and turbulence, made our progress slower and tougher.

"Now you'll get your workout," she proclaimed with a somewhat wicked smile. "You're doing a great job. I just wanted us to stick our nose out a little so you can get a feel for this deep stuff. My, what a glorious sight. I haven't done this in years."

Her exhilaration carried me along. Fearlessly, we charged forward over the crests of small waves.

Mrs. McKenzie waved. I turned to see the object of her favors and saw a thirty-six-foot Grand Banks plowing through the waters, hugging the shore. In the custom of all seafarers, the distant figures on deck waved back, smiling

I hadn't seen the craft approach, nor had I heard its engine. A chill ran through me as I remembered her story of the thick fog and the small rowboat that was crushed. In silence, I strengthened my vow never to attempt the open channel alone.

"Now. Get ready to put your bow into their wake." The sound of her voice snapped life back into me. "No, the other side. Hurry. Hold it."

Like a roller coaster, the large waves approached, bouncing us up and down, nose first. She was laughing now, enjoying the ride. Watching her cheerfulness released my tension onto the undulating water.

"There," she pointed, "that's where we are going."

In the distance rose a small emerald amongst the blue. My arms already screeched of pain, but my desire would not release the oars. The open waterways pushed and pulled us along as we slowly inched toward our destination.

"Isn't this grand?"

I didn't feel grand. I knew I didn't smell grand, yet I didn't have breath to relay this obvious fact. Sweat moistened my cap. It felt cool and clammy where it pressed against my forehead in the breeze, and my shirt clung to my back like glue, the effects of my toil.

"Pull in over there."

We were here, finally. Hunting down the lost object. The thought moved the boat, sucking it towards the shore. I headed in the direction of a gently curved beach. The cove was nestled between two sheer rocks like bookends, guarding the small drift of sand. The island stretched modestly before us. Small in comparison to its neighbors, it sprouted lush and green on gray rock anchored in blue.

"These islands were made for plunder," her words encouraged me. "There are nooks and crannies, caves, old dead stumps, you name it. Jake picked this spot, Whiskey Cove, for his private cache because it was close to Samish. Also, it was in the open, in a way. He could be sure if someone was snooping around. But Jake liked the open too, in case of real trouble, like those damn pirates."

I remembered staying in the open on Friday night when I was being followed. I was beginning to understand Jake and like him even more. How I wish I had met him.

"It's expected that you will keep an eye out in these parts. For the most part, those who choose to live by the sea are good people looking out for the other. Like those dang foolish kids a few years back, about your age. They were leaving Roche Harbor to go to a party on John's Island in a Boston Whaler. But they had loaded her down with thirty pounds of chicken and a keg. Youth. And in the fall too. Well, they got out into the open channel, crossing toward Spieden, with all that weight. The wind was up, pushing the waves, and over they went. The keg, the chicken, all gone. And those young fools clung to the upturned belly of that boat. But they were lucky, see. Someone on Stuart Island had been watching them through his binoculars, rushed out, and saved three lives. You don't have long in these waters, you know."

She lazed her fingers in the chilly water, sprinkling icy drops on my bare legs.

"But Old Tarte, he has a different story about binoculars."

The story had carried us in, and my oars registered my carelessness by vibrating against my calluses as they stuck bottom. My strained muscles made pulling the oars aboard a challenge as they resisted my limp limbs with their seemingly preposterous weight.

I stepped into the shocking water, and life, tingling and fresh, spread through me. I could not imagine spending great amounts of time in this biting sea.

Alex didn't wait for my shuffling feet to reach the warm sand. She crawled to the bow, plopped through the water to the shore, dragging the nose of *Old Blue* deeper into the sand.

Thrilled to be on familiar turf, Mrs. McKenzie set off across the beach to the base of the cliff. She secured the bowline around a log wedged deep into the rocks, which skirted the base of a dirt slope, dotted with trees. Unbuckling her life vest, she stretched her long legs in my direction and stood over me.

Contrary to her vigor, I had collapsed on the shore. Exhaustion brought giggles as my imagination conjured up a passerby's view from his perch with the added gift of sight through binoculars: The hare and the tortoise mount the beach.

I fell back into the cooling sand.

"Oh, my," she shuddered, great concern holding her voice above me. "I've made a huge mistake. I didn't bring along water. Damn my temper."

I eyed the rolling blue channel and laughed even harder.

"Jean, get up this instant and take off your shorts and jump into the water."

"What?" I tried to roll myself up, the sand adhering to my moist shirt.

"Go on," she commanded, pulling at me.

"What?" I laughed at her.

"Jean," she bent down, smiling and controlled, "come on. You need a cool, refreshing dip." Her long fingers wrapped around my arm, gripping. As she stood, her weight pulled against my limb, but it dangled, limp and useless.

For some reason I found this scene to be extremely entertaining.

"Come on." Her voice became edgy above my guffaw. She dropped my arm and moved behind me. Snapping my cap off my head, she began to fan me.

"Come on now, Jean. We have to get moving. Get up and strip off those britches and wade a little."

I remained hunched forward in my hilarity, an exhausted rag doll. I saw the blue veins on her ankles flick past me in the sand and heard the splashing as they entered the water. Within seconds, her wet tennis shoes were before me again, soaked through. A burst of shocking, cold water poured over my head. I bolted up, kicking sand in my hurry. Mrs. McKenzie stood before me, a twinkle in her eye and my wet and deformed navy cap in her hand.

"Now, don't be shy. Get in there. You'll feel wonderful. I love to swim in this water. Used to do it every day. May again." She was nudging me towards the water's edge.

Enticed by the refreshing water, I slipped off my shorts and stepped into the salt chuck. The chill grew with each step on the giving sand. I was just past my knees when her words prompted me on.

"Just dunk. Don't go slow. That's torture. In this water, it's dive or dunk."

I stood in the clear water, watching, fascinated by my toes and how they sank into the sand. I didn't hear her coming, but suddenly, I was flying forward into the chilled water from her push. My shirt filled with air, ballooned up, hiding my face, and I yelped in terror. I shot up, and my shirt, wet and transparent, clung to me like new skin. My laughter this time was one of satisfaction. The shock gone, I slid back under the water, grateful for its coolness. I could feel the dissipation of searing heat. My head felt light as I struggled to regain my calm.

I splashed, twisted and turned, amazed at the glorious feeling of the icy liquid. The heavy pressure of the heat inside my head was now oozing into refreshing sobriety. Life was so full of the unexpected. None of the landlubbers from back home would have imagined this. I was floating off a small island in the San Juans on a hunt for buried treasures and loving every minute.

"Well, you are a fish." She had squatted where the white lacy edge of tide played tag along the shore. The water dripped through her fingers and glistened on her cheeks. "I used to love to swim naked, nothing like it."

"I used to swim all the time. But in a pool."

I watched her as the waves gently built up courage to rush the shore at her feet. She looked peaceful as the rivulets of water reflected slivers of light across her face. Timeless and strong, she was like the two great stones behind her.

Resembling the great pull of the oceans, my feeling for her had grown deep. I wanted to be her, to inspire, even when the sands of time have eroded figure or limb, to still possess the fortitude to encourage and guide. Silently, I restated my promise to help her. I could feel the tug of my growing love with each wave that washed over me, rushed to her feet, and slid back into the depths of the sea.

Rising from the water, hair slicked straight against my head, I pulled at my shirt, prying it from my body with a loud sucking noise.

Dropping the pink scallop shell she had been idly digging with, Alex stood and brushed the bits of lingering sand off her pants.

"I've been making a plan," she half whispered as she fell in beside me and stood as I pulled my dry pants over wet skin. "We'll climb up there and see the old tree and all before we check out the cave. It's always best to know the lay of the land in case we need to beat a hasty escape."

My skin pricked against the breeze, and I shivered. It wasn't the warm wind that had solicited my response but her words. Why did she keep insisting there might be a need to escape?

The treasure must be of great value I reckoned as I wrung out the edges of my dripping shirt. I stopped. "The cave?"

She frowned, hushing me. I could feel the excitement growing. It was here, not far away, and I was as determined as the red-haired widow to find it.

She led the way to the base of the rocks and searched the hill. I followed like the puppy that stays in the shadow of its master.

"There used to be a path here. Change is everywhere." She straightened with her resolution. "Well, we'll just have to make one."

Alex leaned into her task, griping the earth with long fingers, stomping down a bit of grass to form a foothold, working her way up the rocks that led up the embankment.

My reach was not as long so I created my own trail, mimicking her, stomping here, checking for a hold there. On a small ledge, I took the lead. Within minutes, I crawled over the crest, where the shifting dirt met its grassy lid. Extending my hand down to Mrs. McKenzie, I helped her breathless frame over the edge.

"My God." Her tired lungs heaved with the efforts of her speech. "First a fish, now a mountain goat. I knew Jake sent you to help me."

Inspired, feeling the scent of the trail, I stood to survey the land. The ground was flat on the bluff before it eased further up over an exposed rock slope, topped with dense bushes and a smattering of tall evergreens.

My feet itched to begin, to tramp down the tall, sun-dried, yellow grass and disappear up the hill. I was torn between my desire for flight and Alex's heaving form, struggling to collect herself.

"My," she sputtered. "I'll be fine. Just too much too fast." She was on her knees pushing herself to her feet.

Retracing my impatient steps, I extended my hand, and she gripped mine securely. Instantly, I felt my mistake as her weight pulled against my tired muscles. I said nothing as her flushed face lifted past mine.

"There now. That's better."

Stymied by her dwindling energy, I marched on, intent on streaking a new path.

"Ohmygod," came as one word from behind me.

I turned to see her hands gripping her chest, ripples of shirt gathered between clenched fingers.

Her heart?

"What is it?" Concern carried me back.

"Isn't it beautiful?" Like a young maiden in love, her hands floated to her side as she looked off to the horizon.

"What?" my tone was undisguised frustration.

"The Two Lovers."

I searched on shifting feet and found no one.

Her pointer drifted in reverence in the direction she wanted me to look, "The trees."

I saw it then, a tall pine, unique in its growth. Just above the base, the tree had split, with two shoots sprouting up, embracing, the limbs woven together like lovers holding each other in their arms. The wind, providing a command performance, danced through the branches, lifting and embroidering their fine greenery. Two as one.

Yes, it was a wondrous sight. But we were not here to admire nature. We had a task. My arms folded across my chest as I glared at the intruding tree.

"Come on. I'll show you." She began to follow an unmarked trail, a path of the senses.

I hesitated, fearful. Her ability to read me was far too heady. When her figure disappeared behind limbs of green, I released the tension in my step.

We crackled and crunched on the dry leaves and twigs, mindless of a world outside of these restful surroundings. Peace took hold and led us. The island flattened, and the trees thinned. The blue water sparkled below. We passed an old wood cabin, its sides bowed with age.

Alex nodded at the old stone chimney, smiling with her private memories of island lust. Suddenly her blissful mood was shaken, and she turned, frantic, in my direction.

"What's that noise?"

I listened motionless. There was the droning of an engine.

"That's not a boat. Something's not right." The urgency of her words matched her pace. My shorter legs worked harder to keep up with her. She was a regular steam engine again, whizzing past brush, irreverent of bush, eyes ever fixed on the Two Lovers. We charged through the light woods to where the bushes stopped, suddenly and violently. A sea of brown earth, excavated, ripped, and jagged, spread lifeless before us.

"Oh, no." She jumped back into the shadows of a low-hanging branch. "What the hell are they doing? Can you see?"

Silence had once again taken the lead as I looked across the rough edges of sloppy earth to the patch of standing green where the trunk of the Two Lovers boldly remained, a vestige of time refusing to be forgotten. Along the crest of the cliff, the earth was worked and loose. My gaze was drawn up the hill to where three men, wearing the armor of their occupation, tool belts filled with hammers and such, were busy discussing the plans as they walked from one framed room to the next. The shell of their labors boasted of a veritable palace. "The Joneses" were building, intent on displaying their opulence, visible from miles off. A castle to honor themselves, this was no mere summer home designed to fit the surroundings, to complement and encourage nature. This was the city slicker conquering and seducing.

Instantly I hated them. They had raped the land.

"Isn't this a pile of you-know-what?" her voice was strong, but her hurt was deep. "Oh, my," her pity poured out, "they've cut down the snag."

"The what?"

"The old snag," she could barely lift her arm to point. "The eagles just loved to perch in that old thing. Down with the old. Up with the new."

In the distance, there was a loud burst of laughter from the three men, followed by the splitting sound of hammers hitting their mark.

She grabbed my arm and spoke above the sound of the hammers, "Go see." She pointed toward the shrubs that hugged the base of the tall tree from whence the two green tops split, shivering. "See if that's a fluorescent orange cord around the Two Lovers."

"A what?"

"A marker. A marker to cut them down."

"To cut …"

I left her there, propelled by my rage as I headed off across the uneven earth, eyes concentrating on the thin piece of bright cord, a marker, which was barely visible behind the bushes.

The shrill screech of a chain saw roaring to life drew my attention up the hill. I had forgotten I was in the open. Luckily, all three figures were bent at their task. Impossible to become invisible, I quickened my step, hunching my shoulders forward, casting an eye up the hill every other stop.

I was just a few feet from the end of the upturned earth, close enough to see the tape, its bright fluorescence tolling death, when the hum of the saw stopped. From the corner of my eye, I saw the stillness of a tall figure. I continued, knowing I was being watched.

The saw again shattered the silence, and I jumped, turning toward my observer, breaths coming in shallow pants.

He was walking, coming toward me, broad shoulders and muscular tan legs working in determined steps. Nonchalantly, he slid his hammer into his work belt.

I ran.

Mrs. McKenzie, seeing the terror in my eyes, turned and began moving back toward our boat.

He moved to head me off. We would reach the edge of the bushes at the same time.

I saw his look of recognition and wanted to crawl into a hole.

"Hey, hi." His smile was welcoming.

"Hi," I muttered, storming past him and into the bushes, leaving the flabbergasted Nate behind.

Anger carried me down the slope. I hated Mrs. McKenzie. All she did was lead me around by the nose and get me into embarrassing predicaments.

Nate, bronzed by nature, his reddish hair sun streaked and his freckled complexion smoothed over with a tan, every part a Greek god. And I looked an unquestionable mess—hair wet, dripping and clinging dirty clothes, a real fashion plate.

Alex was up ahead, perched on a leech-covered rock. "That's my girl. I knew you could handle yourself."

I didn't answer but stomped past her and started down the rock-face to the water. I heard her tittering, and my hatred deepened as I glared in her direction.

Seeing the look of mortification on my face, my employer attempted sobriety. But I heard the peal of her laughter when my head disappeared down the bank.

"Well?" she was standing at the edge now, looking down at me.

I answered her with my back, facing home, certain I could walk the distance on the water. The steam from my overheated temper would allow me the rights vested only in Jesus.

"Well?" her voice was demanding. "Was the marker for the trees?"

"I don't know," my voice cracked, near tears.

"What?" she hollered at me.

I spun around. "I don't think so," the force of my words bouncing off the rocks, resounding across the waters. "I'm tired of this stupid game. Can we go now?"

CHAPTER 14

Alex stood a moment before beginning her descent. Carefully and slowly, she worked her way past the rocks and down the sandy face of the embankment, sliding the last few feet. Dusting off her bottom, she headed for the boat and rummaged around before pocketing a long object.

A sense of relief mixed with greed flooded me as I watched her. Guilt pushed me forward.

"I'm sorry but …" my words ended because my thought would not form.

"That's fine." Her head was high. "I just thought you would like to learn a little history and to see the cave."

"But we didn't go to the cave," I protested.

"But we're here." She looked at me, and I realized she had, for the first time, passed on valuable information.

"You mean it's up at the tree?"

"No, that was a stakeout or signal hold," she answered me straight. "Besides being a thing of exquisite beauty, that damn tree was very helpful to man and creature. I told you we were going to check our surroundings. Know who's prowling around and why." She paused to let the full intent of her modus operandi sink in. "Besides, in some ways, that tree is more valuable than all of this. But, you're right. We can't worry about that right now. We'll leave that project for another day." She smiled and started toward the rocks again, "Are you with me?"

"Well, at least I don't think Nate followed us."

She spun toward me. "Nate who?"

"Nate Drummond. He saw me."

A cloud covered her eyes. "How do you know the Drummond pup?"

"I met him once at a party at school. He's captain of the baseball team or something."

She eyed me, the heat of her expression chilling me. "Have you talked to him much?"

"I never see him. What's the matter with Nate? What did he do?"

She didn't answer immediately but began to pace. "We'll have to work fast now. Cut it short today. And take my advice," her feet had brought her to me, "stay away from any Drummond."

I watched her as she started off toward the large rock on the south side. Lifting low-hanging branches, she disappeared behind the monolithic rock. Directly above the rock, a madrona trunk, its red bark peeling, held the earth in its knotty roots.

Intrigued, curious about her comment regarding Nate, I followed. I found her just on the other side of the rock, sliding her hand along the cliff's edge. She bent down, following her hand to just above the sand.

"There's been some erosion." She wasn't talking to me. It was a statement to time. Like a doctor, she prodded and poked. "Come in, Jean." She hadn't turned toward me but kept her concentration on the earth before her.

I squeezed into the small opening, past the large stone, our guard from the sea. It was cold with no sun hitting us as we stood in the shadows of the tall rocks.

With her hands, she dug at the earth, and a small hole quickly formed, the sand from above dripping into the hollow.

"Good, it's still loose dirt. This won't take long. I was afraid Jake might have …" her voice trailed off into her efforts.

I maneuvered around her to the other side, and within moments, we had removed the soft mud, creating a small opening. We dug like children at play, content with our creation. Soon, we both knelt before a low arch that opened into darkness.

"The fox's den," she whispered, thrilled by our progress. "Here, Jean, see if you can fit through there."

My eyes fixed on her with newfound horror.

"Don't worry," she cooed. "There's a lovely cave just through that tunnel. I'm sure it's still there. But if they cut down the madrona tree, the cave will go too."

The sandy soil had moved easily. Anything was possible. I looked up at the madrona and was grateful for its strength. Taking a long driftwood stick, I thrust it into the opening, stalling, checking. The length disappeared. The tunnel was still there.

"But there's no light," I whimpered.

Alex worked a layer of sand from her hands then slid the long object from her pocket. A flashlight. "Take this. Just go in far enough to tell me what we'll need next trip."

My excitement overcame my fear. I was to be the first one inside. On all fours, I snaked into the opening. A few feet inside, I felt cool air above me. The small light confirmed my suspicions. The ceiling followed the edge of the cliff outside. I stood under the heavy roots of the madrona. It was cold and dark and damp. Chilling, dank earth and rocks surrounded me. The cave did not appear to be large but rather angular and jagged.

I could see nothing and didn't know what I was searching for. Fear controlled the small beam of light as it flickered on the rock-face across from me. Crouching, afraid to blink, I abandoned the darkness. Like a crab, I backed out into the half circle of light.

Her blue eyes glistened, wide with anticipation while mine adjusted to the glare. The thick, musty smell of the cave lingered in my nostrils as I stood.

"What did you see?"

"It's really dark, and I couldn't see much."

"Was there a slide inside?"

"It didn't look like it, but I don't know really. A lot of dirt."

"Did you walk around the big rock and see the mother cave?"

"No, you didn't tell me that."

The rapid fire of her questions and my slow, labored answers made for an uncomfortable seesaw. Finally, abandoning the frustration of our discussion, we fell into silence in the small rock cove.

"All right." She began to pile the dirt haphazardly back into the opening. "We'll be back, and then we'll take a good look. Go on. I'll meet you out there. And make sure no one is watching."

The warm sunshine felt good against my chilled body. I hadn't realized how cold I was until I stepped into the heat of the light. My shivering brought my arms closer to my body when suddenly I jumped, pulling my damp shirt from me. A reddish-brown, multi-legged creature was marching across my belly, its many legs rising and falling against my skin in syncopated rhythm. I plucked him from me and ran for the shore. Bits of mud and green slime streaked my arms, legs, and clothing.

Whereas earlier the water had been inviting, refreshing, now its frigidity turned my skin to ice. But I did not stop for fear other centipedes, or worse, lingered on my back or in my hair. I plunged into the salt water, dunking my head. I hated what I had gotten myself into. Bugs.

"Jean," her voice was sharp, "you'll freeze on the way home. Come out of that water. We have to go."

I shot an icy glare at the reason for my torture as she worked the knot on *Old Blue*. Drifting from the shore, exhausted, I fingered my cap. I felt I had aged as much as my hat had on this day. I had seen the cave. It did exist. But was it worth all of this?

Silently we carried the boat as we did our private thoughts. Coldness stripping what little strength I had left, I placed the oars in their locks and attempted to row. Every movement cried a new pain. I no longer attempted to keep my face separate from my anguish.

Mrs. McKenzie watched me, and I saw my laboring reflected in her eyes. Suddenly she smiled.

"Well, it's a good thing no one has binoculars on us right about now." Her laughter started deep and grew to a shaking howl as her eyes fell on me from time to time, bringing new bursts of laughter.

The oars hung over the water, and my lip was held tight by my teeth as I considered her source of humor. Her pants had mud splattered on them, dirty fingernails were crusted with soil, and wild red hair refused to be restrained beneath her hat.

Taking note of my own state, wet hair, and clothes, smelling of salt water and dank earth, cap pulled down, it was hard to imagine a more hopeless looking duo. I couldn't help but join in her gaiety. We roared, exhaustion tumbling out as joy.

Suddenly all was funny—my sneaking across the plowed earth hoping to go unnoticed; Nate, chiseled and muscular saying 'Hi' as I brushed past him; the black cave; the creepy crawlers. It was far too crazy to comprehend.

Regaining control, wiping the tears from my cheeks, I set back about my task.

"I suppose we're lucky that we don't know if anyone's watching."

"Oh, but if you're lucky, you do know. Remember Old Man Tarte?"

"No."

"But I just told you about him."

"No, you told me about the kids off John's Island."

"Oh, my mind is playing tricks." She looked away, but I saw her concern, felt her shift as she struggled to remember. "That's right. I was about to tell you." Her face brightened at her memory, and she leaned into her tale.

"You see, rumor had it that Old Man Tarte was running liquor into this island. He's had a place over there by Wasp Island for years. One of the Tartes later bought Roche Harbor."

I was too tired to turn toward her pointer but nodded.

"One day, he was lying there on his cliff, contemplating life, when he saw a strange flash from across on Cliff Island, part of what we call the 'rock pile.' So, anyway, he snuck back to his cabin and got his binoculars, then back to the cliff. And what did he see? Following the funny reflection, he discovered two Feds, watching his island. The sun was shining off their binoculars.

"Well, Tarte was never one to let a dog lie. Story goes he went to his stash, dug up a few bottles, and hid them in pear crates, putting some of his fruit on top. Then, in full view, the old codger loaded the crates into this rowboat, put in his fishing gear, and positioned himself right in front of those Feds. So, after he'd pulled in a couple of nice fish, he rowed over to his big boat. He loaded his fish and crates of pear-covered booze and headed for Bellingham. Sold all of it. Then he came home.

"After a few days of this show, Tarte got so disgusted with his neighboring spies that he just sat on his island. Finally, the Feds gave up and left. But if it wasn't for that sun shining just right to catch the reflection, old Tarte might not have been so careful in hiding his booze and could have been in some trouble."

I pulled against the wood oar as I considered the story. It was getting a little difficult to visualize the various weaving of the tales she could string together.

Feeling had left me entirely. Forward and back, my body moved in no particular rhythm. It just moved with no one controlling it. Deadened, wet noodles had more life. I was lost in a haze.

"Here." Her body bent low, preparing to move. "My turn."

I slumped against the transom, arms dangling limp at my side.

Her stroke brought us to the mouth of the bay, and we slid inside, gliding across the smooth waters. I relaxed into the warmth of the stern, as the sun hit my limp body. The gentle curve of the shoreline faced me. I watched the cliff draw closer and let my gaze work across the row of houses, then follow the slope, which eased around to where the large gray rocks met the channel.

Suddenly, something flashed just above Alex's shoulder. I sat up. There it was again, coming from deep within the jagged rocks. Looking back over my shoulder, I saw the sun hovering above the islands behind us in the west.

Mrs. McKenzie hadn't noticed, so I kept my gaze calm as I attempted to memorize the sharp point of the rock that hid everything but the reflection of sun on glass. It was a coincidence. But someone was watching us from behind the rocks. Fear crawled up my spine.

"You cold? You'll have to get out of those wet things before you head home."

"No. I'll be fine." I flashed a smile to assure her.

I had no time to waste. If my shadow had left the night and was walking in daylight, I wanted to look at him.

I willed the oars to a faster pace, trying not to stare at the spot of the reflection. *Please let my suspicions be wrong.* That, once again, my over-tired body had pushed my overactive imagination and the reflection was of no concern.

There was no reflection as we carried the boat the short distance across dried seaweed to the safety of high land.

The scent of the chase carried me up the long stairs in protest to my tired limbs.

"We'll both be in great shape by the end of all this." Her hands found the base of her back as she straightened.

"Come on, Jean. Let's have some tea and a quick bite to eat."

"No, thanks. I've got to hurry."

"Are you sure?" she handed me a glass of cold water and drank one herself.

I was nodding and drinking at the same time.

"Always in a hurry. All right. But I have cake."

"Save it for tomorrow."

"Oh, that reminds me," she paused, the teakettle suspended in midair above the burner, "tomorrow we start late. I've planned a little surprise for you. So come around two thirty or so and plan to stay late. We're having a very special dinner, and you'll learn a lot." She slumped into the chair, slapping her hat on the blue turquoise counter, encouraging Pretty Boy's chattering. "Be prepared to stay late. And bring a note pad. Tomorrow you'll learn more than you can imagine."

"Great," my excitement spilled into the room as I kept up the hunt for my keys.

She wasn't about to tell me more. I knew that by now. Besides, tomorrow was a long way away. My immediate concern was with the rocks and who was hiding in them.

My keys were there on the counter. But something wasn't right. I could feel it. Disregarding my inner suspicions, I snatched them up and quickly said my good-bye.

My Volkswagen Bug sat where I'd left it, only now, it was in partial shade from the shed. I fired it up and started off down the driveway when my glove compartment sprang open. Remembering the keys on the counter, I hit the brakes, checked the back seat, and breathed again, finding no one. Leaning over, I saw that everything was still in place, but someone had gone through my car. My glove box, possessing a mind of its own, was very tricky to shut. It would stay closed only if wedged by a small corner of a matchbook. I checked the floor, and there, quietly waiting as evidence of the search, lay the innocuous green and white corner.

Driven by rage and terror, I raced around the sloping curve of road that led away from town. The houses ended along the short stretch, and the cement trail sloped up slightly to a stand of tall trees and a large wood plaque marking this small "Samish Park." I pulled off, and my glove box bounced open at the sudden stop. There was only a new, bright red Jeep claiming a spot under the trees. I worked my way along the edge, eyeing the rock from above where the bush allowed. There was no movement.

The brush opened before me, and a dirt path led to steep steps. I clanked down them, gripping the railing when a tired knee faltered from overuse. My feet sank into the sand as I hurried along, tracking back towards the jagged point of gray slate. Climbing high on the bank, I saw no one. Carefully, I picked my way along the crest of the massive mounds of solid rock, encouraged by my lack of discovery. There had been no one. Relief flooding me, returning my breath, I sat to rest. Then I saw it. Wedged between two rocks, twinkling in the light, was the silver foil of a gum wrapper.

It was blown here, I reasoned. My fingers slid between the damp moss-covered rocks and lifted the foil. Below it, further down, rolled into a tight ball, was the light green cover of Wrigley's. Instinct brought the foil to my nose, and the minty scent filled my nostrils, reviving my dark thoughts. Someone had been here recently and left his hallmark.

The red Jeep.

I crawled across the rock's surface and splashed into the moist sand. Why hadn't I looked inside? Pulling with tired arms, pushing with exhausted legs, I climbed the stairs.

An engine sputtered to life as I stepped onto the dirt trail. Racing forward, I cleared the bushes as the Jeep started off down the road.

My door was still open as I turned the key, released the brake, and was off in mad pursuit. My prey appeared and disappeared with each new bend in the road. I was gaining on him, but at any moment, I could lose him as the pavement led down onto the flat slough where it zigzagged back and forth, as if uncertain as to where it would end. The Jeep was ahead on my right then on my left.

I pressed my old VW on as we reached a straightaway before a stop sign. I was right behind him now, and not knowing what to do, I honked. He started to pull out fast. I honked again and followed closer this time.

He slowed and eased onto the shoulder. I circled in front of him. Still without a plan, I blocked his car. Gathering strength and courage, I dashed from my Volkswagen Bug, heart pounding, as I stood, red faced and trembling, outside his door.

The window slid down, and I stepped back.

A girl's head popped out, accompanied by blaring music. "Are you lost?"

"Ah, no," I stammered. "I was just wondering, were you back there at the park?"

"Why?" She snapped the music off and leaned farther out the window. "Did you see me?"

"Yeah. You were hiding in the rock, watching me."

"That wasn't me. That was some guy."

"What guy? What did he look like? Did you see his car?"

"I don't know. That's why we left. We thought he was weird. Only saw his back and the binoculars. He went out the other way, along the rocks."

"Who's 'we'?"

"A friend." Her tone was defensive now, protecting.

"Well, did he see him?"

Her short hair swung as she confirmed my fears. My shadow remained faceless. "Naw, Jimmy was the one who wanted to leave." She looked at me hard. "Boy, it sounds like you're in some real bad trouble. People watching you and all."

"It's nothing." I backed away from the car kicking at a rock. "How about you?"

"Naw, just my dad. He can't stand Jimmy."

In unison, we both smiled, nodding in female understanding. She waved as she pulled away, taking with her what little remained of my sense of peace.

CHAPTER 15

My clothes, damp and reeking with the lingering sea smell, were piled on the floor just inside my door. The soft towel my mother had insisted I take to college, felt warm and soothing as I wrapped it around my aching head. The hot bath had loosened the muscles but not eased the mind, which spun wildly with worry. My excitement with tomorrow's rendezvous was overshadowed by the figure that had followed me.

For what seemed like the three-hundredth time, I checked outside my window without moving the blinds. Nothing. The street below was empty. Even Bellingham Harbor offered little activity.

It was 7:10 p.m., and I felt trapped. I needed to find out who he was. But how?

I sat on my bed to collect my thoughts and pushed aside the anticipation of tomorrow night. Quickly, I retrieved that thought. The dark of night was the best cloak for spying with its underlying danger. I needed to flush him out now.

"It's me" accompanied the rap on the door, which had sent my heart racing.

I attempted to undo the locks quietly so she would not discover my growing fear.

Lissa stepped over the pile of clothes and wrinkled her nose, "A new perfume? Eau de Mer?"

"I went for a swim." I was becoming masterful at plastering a reassuring smile on my face.

"I thought you worked all day."

"I took a break."

"Oh, so now you like to swim?"

This time, not forced, I beamed with the thought of how Lissa would have interpreted my dip in the "mer."

"Well," she bubbled into the chair at my desk, attempting to hold her excitement in check. "Do I have news!"

"What?"

"Get dressed. We're being taken out."

"No," I blurted, unable to hide my terror. I couldn't involve this frail friend. I pulled my bathrobe tighter.

"Jean, what's the matter with you?"

"Sorry, I'm just tired." I sank back onto my bed.

"You won't be when you hear who wants to buy us a drink."

"No way." I hid my eyes with the towel.

"I guess," she sighed, overacting her part, "I'll just have to tell Nathan Drummond you're busy."

The towel flipped back, "Nathan? Nate?" I was stunned, but not thrilled.

"The one and only."

"Where'd you see him?"

"He came into the library tonight, and he asked about you."

"Me?" I shot up. "What did he say?"

"He just wanted to know if you would join us and come out for a drink."

"Anything else?"

"Pizza." Her eyes twinkled. "Oh," she dragged on, fingering my desk, "he did ask if you were still working."

My feet hit the floor with a thud, and the towel slid, covering my bare ankles as I leaned into her, "What did you tell him?"

Lissa straightened at my inquest. "'Of course, she works very hard,' I told him. 'And she's learning to row.'"

"You told him that?" I began to pace, kicking the towel across the linoleum flooring.

"Don't be such a dope. He was all smiles. I think he likes you. So come on. Stop pacing and get dressed."

I wanted to tell her the fox was all smiles because she had told him too much. But, the lamb would meet the fox.

I grabbed the closest thing around, some old jeans. But Lissa had opened my closet and pulled out a madras shift.

"No, no, no," she waved the dress before me, "this."

"Oh, all right." It was on in a wink.

"Oh, geeze." I ran a quick comb and picked up sandals as I ushered Lissa out the door. "I forgot something. Why don't you go on, and I'll meet you there?"

"No. I told him we'd come together. Besides, you've been so spacey lately you'd probably forget where Bullies is."

"Okay," I relented with trepidation, "meet me at the door."

Once I saw her trailing safely down the hall, I slipped back inside my room and checked the street outside. Empty. But I had learned that was far from reassuring.

I had seen no one beyond the glassed-in entrance and took the lead down the stairs, past the hedge, to the parking lot, trying not to show concern as I memorized every bit of the surroundings. Nothing looked out of place, just the general hubbub of a campus area.

We got into my Bug, and I reset the mirror, attempting calmness as I asked, "Think, Lissa. I want to hear every word he said."

My matchmaker purred at my interest as she repeated the conversation with no new information.

Nate was sitting at a table near the front and stood when we entered. I jockeyed for the chair that would give me an overview of window and door.

"Long time, no see." He winked at me as I checked my sight lines above the half-curtained dividers of our booth.

"Have you ordered yet?" I looked straight at him. It was a warning. I had changed the subject, and it would stay changed.

He thought for a moment as he leaned back in his chair. "Only this pitcher of beer." He eyed me intently and then broke into a wide smile as he leaned forward. "Here," he offered, filling our waiting glasses.

"So," Lissa ventured, not understanding the exchange, but sensing the relief, "thank you for the invitation." She kicked me under the table.

"I was just doing a little research." His stare was on me, watching, as I, in turn, remained intent on the white foamy brew.

"I know," Lissa wrapped her small hand around her glass before she innocently dropped the bomb, "Prohibition."

My reaction was instant and intense. I looked up from my glass but could read nothing in his calm green eyes. His blend of tan and freckles gave him an all-American appearance. But my head buzzed with alarm.

"Whodoyouworkfor?" came out in a rush as one word as I blundered for an avenue of knowledge.

"Henry and his dad. Mr. Campbell is a builder. But you know that part." His lips formed a sly smile.

"How do you get to work?"

Lissa was gawking at me with unabashed embarrassment as if I'd gone mad.

He stretched, lazing into his answer, "Henry's boat. It has a motor on it. He dragged out the key word, motor, before sipping deep of his beer, his auburn, long hair swaying slightly with the motion of his head.

I sat frozen. I needed time to sort out the pieces. The bubbles that gathered at the surface in the light brown liquid held my dazed attention.

"I'm starving," broke the chill, which had fallen around the table. My friend blushed at her own outburst.

Nate pushed away from the table, stretching to his full height, taking the cue. "I'll order. How about the house special?"

"Great." It was Lissa's turn to force a smile.

He wasn't out of earshot when my friend began, "What's up? You could cut it with a knife."

"How long has he been interested in Prohibition, and why didn't you tell me?"

"Get off it. His grandfather was the sheriff up here or something like that. He's a history major."

"Did you tell him about me?" I tried not to show my anger.

"What?"

"About Prohibition?"

"Just a casual—"

"What did you tell him exactly?" My words were even, gauged and forceful.

"What is wrong?"

I didn't answer, but I didn't move.

"I think I mentioned you had checked out a particular book and you were working for someone who claimed she'd been a rum runner."

I sank further into my chair. It was too fast, too much.

"Have I done something wrong?" her distress was a whisper. "I thought you liked him, and he sure seems to like you."

"No, it's all right," slid from the depths of my exhaustion. In an attempt to quell her injured pride, I added, "I do like him."

"Okay," Nate broke in as he breezily regained his place. "What are you two talking about?"

The stilted conversation twisted around subjects, never through them: favorite teachers, music, areas of interest, dipping into baseball and his team briefly as the pizza arrived.

Listening to the now gentle banter while munching on thick slices of crusts festooned with oozing cheese, olives, onions, fresh tomatoes, peppers, and globs of meat settled my nerves.

As it turned out, Nate was more than attractive. He was also smart and funny. But was he an enemy? I was losing my edge and, for a brief moment, let it go entirely.

Lissa stood, "Excuse me. I'll be right back." A sheepish grin formed as she started off toward the back of the restaurant.

I watched her go with trepidation, feeling like a child whose security blanket was suddenly wrestled from between tightly clenched fingers.

"What's up?"

I jumped at the sound of his sincere voice. "Nothing."

"Relax," his voice was low, calm as he leaned forward to fill my glass again. "How are you liking your job?"

"Fine."

"She seems to work you hard." He smiled as he continued to tease, "But work is good for you. Besides, the sun agrees with you."

My emotions were getting confused. I wanted to fold into the comfort of his presence.

"Here, let me see those hands."

Before I could move my battered mitts away from his reach, he had secured my left hand in his and began to examine and press against the newly formed, hardened layers of skin.

"They're not bad. Shows you do honest work." His eyes lifted from my palm and met mine. "I'll get you that cream to put on them at night. It'll help. You have pretty little hands."

I could feel the blush, which accompanied the other tingling sensation, as his large hand gently worked across mine, warm and reassuring. I quickly fixed my other appendage around my chilled glass, to cool me, to give me an anchor.

"So, you're researching the 'Noble Experiment' too?"

My hand jerked, but he held it.

"I just find it the most fascinating time in recent history. Don't you? I mean, as we're sitting here sipping our beer, proof the experiment didn't work." He was searching my face for my reaction.

Frozen, I nodded.

"In fact, my—"

The loud badgering of approaching voices halted his next words. I leaned forward to try to encourage him on.

"Hi, Nate."

My head snapped up in disbelief. There, flanking Lissa, were the two society queens, Barbie and Kitty.

Lissa offered a weak smile before announcing, "Look who I ran into."

Small towns do have their disadvantages. Everyone knows everyone and everyone's business.

"Hi, Nate. Jean, your poor hands!" Barbie's dig was not lost as she glared at my hand in Nate's.

Nate did not blink as he released my calluses.

Lissa stood statue-still while the two bubbled at her side, flirting reaching new heights.

"Shall we go?" Lissa took command of the gushing forms. "They've asked me to go with them to that movie. You know the one I've been dying to see. You don't mind, do you?"

The question was addressed to me, but Nate answered, "Not at all."

"See you later." Lissa impishly turned to leave.

"Have fun," Kitty added, and then forgetting her exit cue, continued to drool at Nate.

Barbie snapped Kitty around to push her toward the door.

As my traitor disappeared, I sat nervously with the object of those plastered smiles. We said nothing as both minds assessed the new situation. If he was following me, I was right where he wanted me.

"You haven't finished your beer." He was making a statement, not a demand.

"No, I'm full."

"How about a walk?"

"I really should be going." I wasn't convincing.

"I have an early morning too." He suddenly looked tired, his shoulders slumped as his thoughts drew him farther into his chair.

Something tugged inside me. This slight slip of his mood had pulled me along with it. I wanted to know what he was thinking, what had made his brows knit as his mind worked the puzzle.

Feeling my stare, he shifted. An embarrassed half smile brought him to his feet. "Shall we go? I could use some fresh air."

Outside the summer night was fighting a cool breeze, which brushed passed us in drifts. The streets were quiet, lulled in the later evening sun of the north.

We reached my car, and he leaned up against it, stretching his long legs, blocking the driver's door.

I stopped, my breath caught. "How did you know this is my car?"

One leg crossed the other as he relaxed into his pose. "I've seen you drive it. Small town, remember?"

Where and when were questions I did not dare ask yet. My nerves were rattled. I dug into my purse for my keys as another thought struck me. "Oh, I can't find my gum. Do you have any?" I surprised myself with my coyness.

"Sorry, can't help you there."

"I like spearmint."

"Don't touch the stuff."

I was not relieved. I was frantic. I kept my eyes riveted on my shaking hands, searching in vain for nothing.

The shadow of his hand reached me before the warmth of his touch. "Can I help you?"

I looked up. How could his concern appear so honest?

"Come on." His grip tightened around my arm. "Let's walk awhile."

It felt good to be moving. The energy of fear hastened my stride as I kept pace with his. Somehow, it seemed being closer to the suspect gave me some assurance. Heading down hill toward the bay, we veered off the main road for a small hill. A smattering of trees enclosed a grassy knoll overlooking the lagoon, which emptied into the bay. Reaching the middle of the opening, Nate plopped down on the dry grass.

"My grandfather used to like to sit and watch the clouds," he began in a low voice, not suggesting I join him but drawing me toward him with his story.

I lowered myself onto a rock across from him, "Does all of your family still live around here?"

"Gram is in a nursing home. She fell and broke her hip recently, and now they're afraid she can't live alone."

"I'm sorry." I had never known my grandparents, so I could not appreciate the potential loss. But I could not envision losing Mrs. McKenzie. I smothered my fear with the knowledge something that tough never dies.

"Do you visit her often?"

"I swing by a few times a week. She was a very beautiful woman."

"Was she the one who was married to the Scot?"

"Oh yes, and he was an ornery one. He was the sheriff around here, as I'm sure you've heard. He had a lot of friends and a lot of enemies."

"Why?"

"The times."

"You mean Prohibition?"

"Yes. The Eighteenth Amendment was an interesting concept. Made for tumultuous times. Even President Wilson vetoed the Volstead Act that Congress passed in response, most would agree, to the cries of women, like Carrie Nation, to clean up society. My God, Carrie Nation was six feet tall and one hundred and eighty pounds. I would have run, too, if I saw her coming at my saloon with an axe."

I was impressed he knew his history and felt the need to contribute my findings. "Well, part of that was because of the war and the need to save grain for food. But the Great Depression helped bring about the end to the Noble Experiment, besides the fact that women were now enjoying booze."

"That's right." He screwed his lips up considering his next question, "How do you like working for Mrs. McKenzie?"

Again, my tension was electrified. "How do you know so much?" My body slipped toward the edge of the rock. I was ready to spring down the hill.

He rolled onto his side, faced me full on, pulled a cloverleaf, and spun it between his fingers. "Some things interest me more than others."

"What do you want from me?" my voice cracked with alarm.

His eyes fell onto the small green leaf as he calculated his next words. "Nothing."

He was not a good liar. The brows and eyes, the sinking of the shoulders, all spoke what his words did not.

"Why are you following me?" My words came in shaking, low tones.

His head shot up, a growl of defiance followed his words, "I'm not following you."

"Then how do you know who I work for?"

"I have eyes. The two of you were on the island together. And what were you doing there, anyway?"

"She was worried about the trees being cut down." I rushed to cover our exposed tracks. "What about my car?"

"I saw you drive up with Lissa."

It was so simple it was startling. Embarrassed and uncertain, I wanted to be under the rock, not on top of it.

"Is that why you were so nervous?" He began to laugh. "I thought it was because …" He caught himself, flashing his own awkwardness. "Never mind," he recovered.

My flushed cheeks gave way to a grin, followed by giggles as the tension spilled forward into the air. The pink and blues of the night sky were our backdrop as we shifted and began to rummage through memories, changing places and positions, embellishing childhood tales.

We sat close now, the darkness, which had crept around us, making it necessary. The North Star, a bright beacon, glittered above us. I didn't want to move. I wanted time to stand still and let me rest in the circle of trees with the stars moving through the heavens overhead.

"Do you have any idea how late it is?" the realist in me asked.

"How late do you want it to be?" A dimple appeared as he grinned.

"Tonight, I don't care." I squeezed my knees tighter, rocked back and forth, enjoying for the first time in days the calmness of the night.

Nate didn't say anything. He just sat quietly.

Suddenly, our silence was shattered by the creak of a breaking twig.

My arms shot out as I prepared to stand. Nate grabbed them and motioned for me to be silent while he listened intently before sighing, "It was only the wind."

"The wind doesn't snap twigs."

"Why do you think someone is following you?"

"I don't know, but he is. I've seen him." I was thankful for the semi-darkness. He could see fear in my eyes but not the redness in my cheeks as I became shy. I sounded frantic, lost.

The hush was filled with tension, bouncing between us. Nate sat frozen, yet his eyes searched dark shadows before they found me.

"Probably just a dog." Nate attempted to sound nonchalant. He smiled, standing to brush the pine needles from his back and legs. I reached for the twig caught in his long hair, and he smiled.

His reassurance did not spread to me. Fear gripped my limbs, holding them. I suddenly felt overwhelmed. Who was out there?

"Let's go," he looked down at me, concern carrying his voice through the darkness.

I couldn't move. I knew I appeared pitiful, and it was unsettling, but I felt drained, limp. The beer, the long day, the chilling reality of being watched. I fought back tears wanting to leave their hot trail down my cheeks.

His hand stretched down towards me, but I couldn't take it. He squatted down, his tone soft, controlled. Like the key unlocking a door, his words were soothing, loosening the tightness and a smile. "Come on. I'm going to see you get home okay."

"You're right. I'm tired." His strength pulled me to my feet, and we stood inches apart. I could feel his breath, and it affected mine, drawing me closer into safety.

"It's a beautiful night. I hate to go." His head bent back toward the wide sky, the line of his jaw caught by the light of the half-moon.

All was calm, warm, inviting. I wanted to linger, to nudge forward into his arms. "Yes, it is beautiful."

We started off down the hill toward my car. The stars were gaining their brilliance, beacons to lovers. Even the streets seemed peaceful now. A car slowly eased down the road past my Bug as we reached it.

"I'll ride back with you then walk from there."

We were on the passenger side of my Volkswagen. Lifting my purse away from my shadow into the streetlight, I dug once more for my keys. Something caught my eye, and I lost track of the conversation while I attempted to convince myself the shiny new gum wrapper at my feet had been there all along.

"I'll come with you back to your place," came through louder, as if he were speaking to deaf ears.

"Fine," the taffy pull of emotions making me putty.

He folded his large frame into my car as I got behind the wheel and mindlessly pulled away from the curb.

Nate huddled next to me, bent knees protruding above the seat level. "So, you have to be at work early?"

Conversation was beyond my abilities. I nodded, feeling removed from all things, including the steering wheel. My car propelled itself as my foggy mind struggled. Nate's silence made him invisible to my aching mind. An element was missing, and it wasn't emerging to the surface.

We pulled into a parking space just down from Nash Dorm. I didn't notice when Nate stretched out into the street and found the handle on my side of the car.

"Come on, sleeping beauty."

I didn't respond but, in the distance, felt my body going through the motions of getting out of the car and locking it.

As we reached the door, Nate's voice broke through my daze. His voice was forceful, urgent. "Get inside your room. Lock the door and stay there."

I felt his hand pushing the door shut behind me. Like a slow machine, I trudged past the hallway windows. Nate was gone.

A shriek of tires brought me back to the windows. In the street, half in shadow, a figure was pushing up from the pavement. He brushed his hands and bent to dust his pants. His hand went to his forehead and then lowered to eye level, examining it.

I ducked from the window. I didn't know what had happened or why Nate had been on the ground. I hurried off to my room and locked the doors before collapsing onto my bed.

CHAPTER 16

The steam of the coffee had long died away, and still the fog in my mind had not parted. As I toyed with the cool liquid I realized I had slept though breakfast and was reluctant to leave the security of the building. Caged in and lonely, I sat in my room, hoping this evening with Mrs. McKenzie would unravel the mystery and release me from my present isolation. I thought of Pretty Boy and how he paced back and forth on his stick. The urge to set him free was suddenly great.

I was restless with nowhere to go. Lissa was arduously working. The halls were empty. I'd even called the always entertaining Barbie and Kitty, but they were at the beach for the day.

I sank back onto my covers, closing my eyes to envision the stars, feel the warm air, and gaze at the slip of the moon of last night. My mind idled through the tales Nate and I had shared as we glimpsed each other's past. I tingled with the thought of his breath on my neck, his hands taking mine.

"Back to your dorm," the hush of his voice sounded in my mind. I shot up, almost knocking my coffee to the harsh linoleum floor. Dorm? How did he know where I lived? Had he lied to me? Had he followed me before or just guessed?

My feet paced the fine line of the seam in the floor. Like Pretty Boy, feathers in a twit, I traversed my confinement, building steam with each turn.

I would have to meet my shadow.

Grabbing my note pad, I prepared for the night's work. Gloves, hat, flashlight, sunglasses, even my dark blue bandana, an afterthought, were stuffed into my small daypack. Two hours remained before I was to be at McKenzie's. I would head out, stay in the open, draw him into the light.

The morning had passed without my noticing it. The sun was high when I pulled out into the street. Its warmth flooded through my front window, at times blinding my vision. The heat was a comfort, encouragement. I went slowly, with no destination, aimlessly traveling the streets.

My car found Fairhaven, and I parked across from Tiny's Coffee. Inside, the aromas of dark beans and bakery goods diverted my mission. I juggled my cinnamon bun and cup to a round table just in front of the red double-decker bus that occupied the corner, the hallmark of this establishment's outdoor patio. Facing the street, I attempted nonchalance.

It was not easy because I didn't know whom I was watching for. Twice I had noticed a young Asian student, but that could have been nothing. Last night, I hadn't gotten a glimpse of a face, and the gum told me nothing.

An old rusty red Chevy, with white-wall tires crusted with dirt, slowed as it passed. A young man ducked his head so he could get a better look at me.

I stood, hesitating, when his concentration moved back to the street and he rolled on.

Edgy, I sat back down for another bit of the gooey bun. An old woman, bent with age, struggled with her heavy load as she shuffled across the street. A young mother, tan legs and arms, squatted before her child's stroller. It was a slow, lazy afternoon in the summer sun.

The rusty red truck, like a shark, cruised by again, the head of the driver bobbing from side to side, searching. I stood again and ran toward the vehicle. The car stopped. I had reached the curb when, from up the street, a brunette emerged from the pharmacy. I halted as she waved, approaching the beat-up vehicle.

Feeling a combination of relief and embarrassment, I turned toward my Bug. Need was creating desperation.

Wilson Library was cool in the afternoon heat. The silence of the old building and the high leaded-glass windows gave a mystic aura. I had not been followed, even though I went obviously through town, turning on blinkers far in advance, drifting around corners. Defeated and deflated, I sought the solace of silence and a friend. I wasn't in a hurry as I wandered past the stacks of books and up to the front desk. No one was in sight. I backed away from the counter and poked my head down the aisles, looking for Lissa's familiar slimness. I found only a few students, their concentration riveted on the rows of titles.

The chair at the research desk was occupied now by a middle-aged man, his glasses and round form unfamiliar. He looked up at me with a scowl, forcing me to step away. He lowered his head, eyes watching me above his glasses, an acquired glare, which created distance.

Feeling further foiled by not finding my friend, I turned to climb the immense Chuckanut sandstone steps, past the banister knob of acorns and leaves, to the top floor and my favorite room. The leather doors with the brass-hammered studs, creating a linear design, spoke of old craftsmanship. Tranquility passed over me as my eye moved down the long silent room. The soft light filtered through the purple and gold leaded-glass windows, steeped with the dust of knowledge, and fell upon the rows of old oak desks, surrounded by shelves of books, quiet, peaceful, and safe. I lingered under the tall dome-shaped windows, each boasting unique cut-glass squares of rose and purples. The tops of green trees swayed beyond. But it was the ceiling that will remain embossed permanently in my memory, the beams festooned with intricate patterns of golden browns, greens, silver, and blues. One portion of the design resembled several zigzagging arrows, their tips pointing this way and that.

I waited, but no one came to disturb this meditative room. Lissa was nowhere to be found.

Outside in the sunshine, a noisy contraption was moving across the green lawn, cutting, clipping, manicuring around an old gnarly maple tree. The operator worked the machine close to the sidewalk, then turned, oblivious with his earmuffs to the level of intrusive noise he spewed in his wake.

I skirted his loudness to head down the Alumni Memory Walk, playing tag with the white, marble steppingstones that bore the name of each graduating year from 1912 forward. Underneath each stone was buried a white box, which held one treasure of each graduate. Placing your chosen item in the box to be buried was one of those traditional moments, those glimmers of the past, still employed in the present. A moment of arrival.

I had thought often of what I would drop into the box as my class, wearing caps and gowns, strutted down this walk, entrusting to eternity our brief passing.

The large cedar trees, which claimed the top of a small knoll, hid the street from me momentarily, but still no one was about. I reached my car and slid in on the warm seat. All parked cars were empty. My car sputtered to life, and I headed toward Fairhaven again. The traffic was a gentle roll as I entered the slow wave of motion onto Chucka-nut Drive. Just past Larabee Park, I pulled into a lookout point and watched the green-blue waters below. Had anyone been following, he would have been forced to pass me on the tight two-lane road with chiseled rock on one side and a steep, sheer cliff, where trees had trouble clinging to the slick surface, on the other side.

My spirits rose as I entered Edison and fell in behind pointing tourists. I inched past an old gabled house, the sharp bend at the Saloon, and the block of what was Edison. Finally heading across the flats, birds rising from the grasses, my mind edged forward toward the evening. I was thrilled, confident the culmination of our search would unravel itself by the evening's end. But I also felt a tug of sad-ness as well as great relief in knowing the finish line was indeed in sight, that is, if we reached it safely.

Winding along the crest of the island, I observed the water below looked smooth and inviting. There was still the matter of forty-five minutes to waste. I drove past the short lane that led to Alex's house, and skirted the ridge of land toward Samish Park. My feet guided me down the wooded trail to the top of the stairs. Within minutes, the sand gave way under my step. I plopped down, the heat burning my bare legs and warming my shorts and shirt. Kicking off my tennis shoes, I buried my toes until they touched the coolness of the unexposed sand.

I closed my eyes and cleared my mind. Alex and I might be followed tonight. I would have to be extremely cautious.

The sound of an engine drawing nearer stirred my meditative mood. I opened my eyes. Clipping along close to shore, a red-hulled craft headed for the bay. The driver stood, cap and glasses partially masking his identity. I watched his image bounce across the waves. It would be easy to mistake one person for another.

Brushing the sand from my legs, I hugged my knees. Excitement was building, and I pushed myself up, stretching in the sunlight. A burst of energy led me back to the rocks where I'd seen the reflection the day before. Scaling the stones, I stood scanning the inlet. Tiny rivulets fanned across the surface. The row would be easy, smooth.

The bow of the motor boat parted the stillness. Movement on the cliff caught my eye. The figure was small in the distance, but I could make out the brim of the hat, large and telling. From her perch, Mrs. McKenzie waved to the now beached powerboat. The figure pulled up his engine, threw a rope forward, and plopped into the water. He tied off before pulling something from his boat and carrying his load up the steps.

A shard of fear, jagged and deep, seared though me. Was she having me followed? Was the spider knitting this dangerous web of deceit?

I could not answer, but for now, this fly, glued to her destiny, mounted the steps towards her car.

CHAPTER 17

The house seemed quiet, restful in the afternoon sun, as I pointed my car down the drive and stopped halfway. The drifts of salt sea air were welcome and refreshing.

The back door flew open. Alex, her bib apron covering her like a dress, waved her dishtowel at me. "All the way," she instructed, beckoning me forward, "pull down all the way."

My car kicked back to life and rolled down the drive to where her guiding finger bent with instruction.

"Thank God, you're here. I'm running behind. Let's get the table out right away."

She had started across the lawn, whipping the dishtowel over her shoulder to free her hands.

Keys jingled as she pulled them out and deftly opened the garage door. "We'll need the benches and about three chairs. Don't bring that old lounge chair." She waved into the half-dark corner where a stack of folding chairs waited to breathe the fresh sea air. "The last time Josie sat in this chair and leaned back with her drink, she just kept on going. Right over." Her hand demonstrated the action before it slapped her thigh as she exploded into laughter. "Legs straight up, skirt sliding down over her rolled-up hose at her knees. But, damn if she didn't save her drink. Didn't spill a drop!"

She turned straight toward me, eyes blinking tears, which wanted to spill forward with her joy. "What a vision. I nearly burst my britches. Well, you'll meet her today. Here's the table."

She left me standing as her long, determined stride took her across the cool cement floor. *Meet her today?*

"Here, get that end." She had removed the few pieces cluttering the tabletop, leaving in their absence a faint outline in dust.

Puzzled, on guard, I moved to the far side of the slatted wooden picnic table. Together we hoisted it up and guided it out the door into the bright light.

"After you bring out the benches and the chairs, just take the hose and rinse them off." She was brushing her hands together, working free the grime, which had settled there. "Then come inside. We've got a lot to do."

She charged for the back door and was swallowed by it.

I stomped back into the cool building. Now what? I thought this was supposed to be a secret.

My anger was released into my work as I dragged chairs and benches out into the open. What a fool I continued to be. It was amazing. I stepped back inside the shed to scan for anything else I might need. With *Old Blue* gone, the rafters seemed higher. My eyes followed the neat compilation of tools and then stopped short. The shovel was still in its place. She would have thought of taking it. We weren't going anywhere today.

"Okay, that's good." It was her shrill voice, warning, commanding. "The hose is over here."

I knew where I'd find her and stormed into the sunlight in her direction.

"Here's the tablecloth for after you've hosed it off." Her tone was now innocent, sweet. The queen of manipulation.

"Tablecloth?" I stopped to face her now.

Having neatly placed the floral print tablecloth on the back steps, away from the spray of water, she stood watching me. The blue eyes sparkled. "For the party I'm throwing for you. You'll see."

She was gone, but the lump in my throat remained. For me? I was glad she had left. Mistrust and disbelief were spiraling, vibrating my hands with the shock waves. Mindlessly, I turned the hose onto the dust-covered furniture. The drops sparkled in the sun, cleaning, clearing, making new the old.

With particular attention, I made certain the plastic-coated, turquoise-and-green-floral covering draped equally over all edges of the old table. The different colors of the weave on the folding chairs made a bright, festive semi-circle, enclosing the spot of lawn that stretched between the drive and the square patch of freshly worked garden. It looked neat, inviting, in an eclectic fashion.

"That's just grand, Jean." Her eyes shown as she worked her hands on the edge of the striped apron, lifting it, exposing light-blue slacks.

I felt proud and embarrassed. Confusion made me shift and my hands awkwardly seek the pockets of my shorts.

"Now," she turned into the threshold, her voice drifting in the shadows as she streamed down the passageway, "come on in here. We've got plenty to do."

I stepped into the hallway and instantly felt a twinge of hunger. The aromas drew me into the kitchen. Fresh bread was cooling on a rack. A whole cooked chicken sat in a large bowl, cooling. But it was the large pot on the stove that held Alex's attention. As the redhead lifted the lid, steam poured out, billowing a garlic-and-herbs cloud of flavor, which hung, enticing and rich, above the broth.

"This is my specialty." She maneuvered the wooden spoon in the deep, speckled pot, speaking more to the pot than to me. "I like to start with fresh chicken broth. Save the chicken for sandwiches. Then I do add some clam nectar, whole tomatoes, celery, a little onion, parsley, fresh herbs when I can get them, and I always add a little vermouth. That's the kicker. I put this on last night. I like my broth to simmer awhile." Her fingers moved above her concoction on the word "simmer" as if their movement enhanced the zest.

Yet, from where I stood, nothing was needed to add to the succulence except my immediate possession of a bowl and spoon.

Observing me, she saw the hunger in my eyes. "Oh, heavens, child, I'll fix you a little something now because we aren't eating for a while. Honey, this is just the stock. I have to add all of this yet."

Her hand led the way to the sink. The strainer was overflowing with shining blue-black shells of mussels. Next to them, in a bowl of salt water, were small, creamy gray butter clams. Oysters still in their tough shells, dotted with barnacles, were a great contrast on the turquoise counter.

"I've debearded the mussels, rinsed the shrimp, and cut the halibut and cod into chunks. I'm just about to shake the crab. But these won't go in until just before we eat. And it's the order and timing that are the most important. Grab that shucking knife and get started on the oysters, will you?"

I picked up the long blade that was beveled and rounded at the point. Mrs. McKenzie handed me a glove and old Christmas kitchen mitt.

"Remember to come at 'em at three o'clock. Right here."

"Three o'clock," I repeated and tried to pry the blade between what appeared to be seamless edges. The shucking knife slid in and across. Bits of shell floated in the salt water that occupied space with the oyster, and some of the white muscle still clung to the top, but I was proud of my accomplishment.

"Not bad," she encouraged me. "Now, keep at it and watch that blade and those barnacles. We still have a lot to do."

Mrs. McKenzie wasn't letting out any more information. I peeked at the stack of dishes she had set out and tried to imagine whom they were for. Without trying to be obvious, I couldn't tell if there were six or eight.

She put a sandwich on the far counter, placing my oysters and me out of her way as she busied around her kitchen. "After you're through, why don't you go on down and take *Old Blue* out for a spell by yourself. Tide's just about right."

I nearly choked on the rich chicken, mayonnaise, and lettuce on sourdough.

"You need to keep your strength up, and your skills."

Mine were the only steps echoing down the long set of stairs. I jumped, landing on both feet, sinking into the sand, feeling the freedom of a small child. My light feeling soon was anchored by the realization my employer had obviously overlooked one major problem. *Old Blue* was upside down, clearly fifteen feet from the water's edge.

I looked back up the cliff where the top of the house was hidden behind the small hedge. "Damn you," I kicked a rock toward the inanimate staircase. She got me again.

Determined, fired by my temper and guilt, I hoisted the edge of my vessel up over my head. Her weight, threatening the delicate balance, took hold, and *Blue* demonstrated her strength. She flipped onto her back, smashing into the sand, rocking to a standstill.

That felt good. Encouraged by my progress, I placed the oars inside, grabbed the bow, lifting her slightly, and began to drag her toward the water. After three feet of straining, *Blue* begrudgingly began to slide down the small drift of sand, across the seaweed line, onto the mud of the shore. I had to pause frequently, my hands indented from the weight. I shook them while I checked the horizon for any unsuspecting passerby who could be enlisted for service.

I was alone in the afternoon sun with the tide inching toward me, mocking my toils. The lazy breeze was cooling as I stooped back into my task. Like a snail towing an overlarge shell, I left a deep groove in the sand as I reached the water's edge.

The lightness of *Old Blue* as she slid into the water was welcomed by my tired limbs. I lifted my dripping legs over the side, adjusting my position. Immediately, I felt the difference of my solo journey. She sat higher in the water, responding easier to the oars without the added weight of any passenger, and this encouraged me as I put the oars to work.

The waves were gentle, so I swiftly moved along the shore, enjoying the pull, exploring my abilities. My arms and stomach muscles echoed the sensation, which ran down my back. It was exhilarating, being alone with the water and the sky. I rested briefly, bobbing on the lulling drifts of current. My mind, loosened by the expansion of my horizon, traveled on the water's surface towards the small black cave and up the hill to where Nate was working. Was he watching me now? Or was someone else? How was it Mrs. McKenzie could be so certain her treasure was tucked inside that cavern?

As the current lifted my boat on its tidal course, drawing me along, I felt the tug of the widow's current, running deep, sweeping several years, hiding a dangerous undercurrent perhaps. But as all wise men will warn you, when caught in a drift, don't try to swim against it. Go with the flow until it loses its power, and then make your way to the safety of the shore.

Closing my eyes, I drew in the oars to let the drifts move me at their will. My head went back, face full to the sun. The warmth reminded me of Nate's touch, relaxing and thrilling at the same time. My mind toyed with our next meeting.

The cry of a bird turned to that of the familiar, shrill whistle. I searched the crest of the bluff. There, perched amid the hedge of her domain, stood Mrs. McKenzie flanked by two figures.

Her hat waved, briefly covering the face of the tall gentleman who loomed just behind her right side. The big brim then dipped to hide the other man who leaned on a stick to her left.

It was my signal to return. My guests, faceless and unknown, had arrived. I flashed my cap back at her and then picked up my oars. Strengthened by my audience, and a bit taken with my own progress, I pulled, working my stroke to it fullest. Checking my position briefly over my shoulder, I saw her point toward me and the two heads nodding in agreement.

Pride pushed me. Sweat dripped from below my brim. My heart thumped to my new beat. The race to nowhere was on.

Gliding over the seaweed, my oars dipped deep. The sea floor was rising to greet me, coaxing my efforts. Pull. Seaweed gave way to mud with scattered large rocks, speckled with white barnacles. Pull. Then came the fine sand of the shore. Pull. With one final great thrust, the bow sank into the dry sand, which the water was reclaiming with its incoming tide. Mercifully, the salt water had inched farther up the beach. I jumped from the boat, catching the bow in one swift move and sallied forward. *Old Blue* slid the short distance, as if proud of her display. Rocking her into motion, I lifted her side and gentled her down, leaving her as I had found her, crablike, hidden under her blue shell.

I stood, brushing sand and sweat. From the base of the stairs, I saw the trio smiling before they waved and turned to go. The show had ended.

My breath was still laboring for an even pace when my foot hit the bottom step. The surge of confidence lightened my feet as I began heading up the stairs. At the top, I sailed between the bushes, hot, breathless. Self-importance had undone my calm. I leaned forward, arms seeking my knees for support.

From this bent position, it was his black cloth shoes I saw first. I followed the dark brown pants to the edge of his Chinese jacket and the glass of iced lemon water.

"Mrs. Alex thinks perhaps you are thirsty."

I laughed as I pushed myself up straight.

The deep creases around his eyes were in contrast with the smooth tan of his high cheeks as he smiled across at me.

"A desert." I licked my dry lips at the sight of the moisture dripping down the side of the glass.

"She is very proud of you." He leaned forward, confidently, but the beverage moved further away in his iron grip. "You found it then, yes? That is why we gather?" His smiling eyes and face were eager for my reply.

"Well," I panted, licking my lips again to clear way for speech. "We did find—"

"Jean."

I jumped as the big brimmed hat swooped toward us. The single word still rang in my ears, sharp, commanding, cautioning. I froze.

"Drink your water, dear," she cooed. A smile forced its way across her face, but her eyes held me in suspicion. "And then come meet the rest of our guests."

Her arm went around me.

Mr. Chin, ever convivial, muttered, "Yes. Drink the cool water," as he placed the tantalizing liquid in my hand.

I gladly took a deep gulp before I was rushed off around the corner to the backyard.

Two of the chairs were occupied, and the figures rose as we three approached.

"Stew," her voice tinkled with delight, "this is Jean."

Stewart straightened to his full height, looking down at me with a half squint, chin lifted slightly, a frightening gaze from an aging giant. He held me for a while with his penetrating dark stare before the silent, chiseled face cracked into a smile as he extended his hand. It, too, was large, fingers thick as sausages, bent and twisted with time. The skin felt rough against mine, a toughness that accumulates with hard work.

"Welcome aboard," his voice bellowed gravelly, matching his rocky exterior. His white hair was cropped close under his dark cap that boasted in bright red letters, "I fish, therefore I am."

Fitting, I mused, for he was the personification of the sea-jagged, briny old codger with an assuredness and gruffness that lures you to like him.

"Don't mind him. He's harmless." The voice, distorted by age and smoking, was low and comforting, matching the jolly round figure of the man who had maneuvered next to Stew.

"I was wondering how long it would take you to get over here." Stew lifted his chin in mock chastisement. "You can always count on Charles here to get a move on if there's a pretty girl around. Fast Charlie, that's what we call him."

"Like I said," the low voice took the lead, "don't believe anything he says." He smiled brightly, blue eyes clear and happy. "How do you do? I'm Charles Winger. Nice to meet you."

I took the round, calloused hand he extended toward me. His index finger was cut off at the knuckle. I smiled back, ignoring it.

The two roosters continued their friendly competition, bantering on while I watched and listened. Together they were almost comical, the most unlikely of bookends. Where Stew was tall, Charlie was short. Where Stew was dark with thick bushy brows, Charlie was fair, freckled with a thin layer of hair resting on top, cascading onto thicker sides. Yet you could tell, for all their exterior differences, they held much in common.

"Well, don't just stand there. Let's sit down you big galoots and have a cool drink of tea." It was apparent from the way they jumped to her command Alex had barked orders at these two before.

"Jean, will you help me a minute?"

I followed her into the cooling shade of the kitchen, thankful for the break. I ducked down the hall and into the bathroom to rinse off the salty sweat from my row.

Back in the kitchen, I didn't have time for my thoughts. Alex was rambling on about the ice melting and Josie always being late. She hadn't mentioned Mr. Chin, but I felt her eyes on me constantly.

We served the iced tea in a buzz of chatter. I watched the four old compadres hurl playful accusations and teasing across the small stretch of green lawn, as if they were playing croquet. Stew and Alex took the lead while Charles and Mr. Chin only chimed in with occasional zingers.

The topic gravitated back to the tardy guest who was to occupy the last empty chair.

"Josie's doing fine but doesn't get out much now that Victor is gone … Too bad about her son … Yes, her grandson is trying to keep the restaurant going … How was she getting here?"

As if on cue, a new, shiny black Cadillac turned down the driveway, honking a cheerful beep, beep, beep.

"What in blue blazes?" Alex muttered, standing to confront the intruder.

"Who the hell …?" Stew followed suit with the other two popping up like corks in water.

I was forced to stand to see what all the excitement was about. I went to the end of the line of the well-aged group just in time to see the car door pushed open.

"It's me. I'm here now," came an excited squeak before the owner of the voice groaned as she shifted her weight. A short round leg struggled for the ground, skirt hiked up, exposing the nylons which where seriously secured just below the knee. A plump hand, speckled with dots of aging and sporting rings encrusted with diamonds, gripped the top of the door. She shuffled and grunted her way to the edge of the seat and then plopped both feet squarely on the ground. With great triumph, she closed the door and then turned her floral dress in our direction.

"Here I am," she threw both arms up, standing like a round exclamation point in the sun. "Let the party begin."

"Josie," Alex started toward her, "where on God's green earth did you get that?" Alex's pointer jabbed at the Cadillac.

"I bought it," she proclaimed as she primped by running her fingers past the edge of gray hair to where the black dye set in and finished up in a smooth, small knot at the top of her head.

"But you don't have a license, for Christ's sake," Stew protested.

"I do now," she beamed. "Come on. Take a look." Her arms spoke as she did, beckoning, "I've decided Vic would have wanted me to have it." She made the sign of the cross, her private pact with the dead.

All heads bobbed in confirmation at the silent conversations one has with his or her beloved deceased.

They stood, gaping in disbelief at the large black car. Charles spoke first, "It's beautiful, Josie. I'm happy for you."

"Thanks, Charlie. Want to go for a ride?"

In unison, everyone stepped back. "No ... no, thanks, maybe later."

Alex didn't allow Josie time to be disappointed, hurrying to interject, "Come on, Jo. I've got a surprise for you too."

"What?" her large brown eyes grew behind her glasses like those of a child.

"A little later."

"You won't beat this," her thumb indicated the large beast of a car. Her hands rose into the air again as she moved toward her old friend, arms wide, laughing.

The unruly red hair bent into the welcoming embrace as the two women hugged their greeting, holding each other tight, two solid rocks against the merciless winds of time.

As they parted, the warmth lingered. "You look well, Al. You seeing a man or something?"

"Nope. Just a little exercise."

"Hey," Stew broke in. "For Christ's sake, would you two stop yappin' so I can get my kiss?"

Josie's hand went to her lips. Like an embarrassed bride, she sidled up to him. "Ah," she purred, offering her ample cheek, which he readily bent to kiss.

"I'm sorry about your son," his tone was soft, comforting as was the hand he gently rested on her shoulder.

"It's okay. He moved too fast. Too much. We need to live life now."

Charlie cleared his throat, drawing Josie's attention before speaking, "What about me, princess?"

"Charlie," she squealed with delight, throwing her arms up again. "How are you doing darlin'? Miss me?"

"Every minute." They snuggled into an embrace.

"How's the family, Mr. Chin? And the shop?" she added, folding her hands over his.

"Very fine." His eyes were almost lost behind the pull of his cheeks as he offered her a broad smile.

"It's so good to see you all. I could cry." She pushed her oversized, thick, gray-tinted glasses farther up on her nose and wiped a tear, which had slid from under the rim.

"No time for tears. This is Jean." The pointer finger, bent in my direction.

I smiled and waved, "Hi."

"She's so young and pretty. Charlie you behave." Her hand swung at him, giving him a friendly reprimand.

"Come on, Josie. Let's sit." Alex gave the ringed hand a pat as they walked together to their seats.

I stood behind, watching the parade. Stew's long legs slowed behind the two women. For the first time, I notice Charles's limp. The jolly man swung his stick and leg as he gimped to his chair.

"Jean, how about more tea?"

She didn't turn in my direction, but her voice was happy.

Sparked into motion, I ducked into the aromas of the kitchen and reluctantly emerged with the tea. They sat in their half circle, waiting, like five pillars, proud, strong.

Josie, her hand constantly in motion with her words, was telling of her grandson's success with the restaurants. Each, in turn, took a few moments recounting tidbits of their lives since their last gathering.

They were a wonderful group, I decided, full of life, still living for today, not the past. The sun, well into its slide towards the islands on the far side of the house, cast a long shadow as it inched towards its bed.

In a brief lull, while pouring Josie more tea, she whispered to me in the fake whisper all can listen to, "Alex tells me you plan to be a teacher. And that you wanted to hear some of our stories."

I tried not to blink at having my future planned and orchestrated for me by a woman I'd known less than two weeks.

"You ask Charlie. He'll tell you," she winked. "Ask Winger."

"What are you two talking about over there?" The man blushed at the mention of his name.

"Go on." She all but pushed me in his direction, "Ask. Ask about the Noble Experiment."

Unsure, I passed the nodding redhead.

Stew tucked his long legs closer to his body, opening a path, and put in his comment. "You might as well sit down, kid. Once Charlie starts, there's no telling when he'll stop."

Josie slapped her knee as the others guffawed at the jab.

"That's not entirely true," Charlie's eyes glistened, "but sit over here close to me."

"Oh my God," Stew shifted. "Here we go."

Still holding the pitcher, I lowered onto the picnic bench.

"What these rascals are referring to I couldn't tell you. But what I can tell you is that Stew here is just plain jealous. You see, Stew was the second born at the new Swedish Hospital in Seattle, just seconds behind that Johnson baby. That other baby was unanimously voted an honorary board member of Swedish Hospital for life. And Stew's been in knots about it ever since."

Stew adjusted his cap to the roar of laughter around him. "Get on with the part about you, you dope. He was Jake's counter. Tell her about the pirates."

Charlie's face took on a sly angle as he began, "We gave 'em a run for the money, didn't we?" He looked straight at me now continuing, "I was Jake's accountant. I handled all his money. And for a while there was plenty."

He sneaked a consoling glance at my employer. She raised her glass, "Easy come, easy go."

"Hell, Jake shouldn't have given so damn much of it away. And what that damn lawyer took—"

"Stewart." Alex cut off the gruff mumblings.

"He tried," put in Josie. Then forgetting her composure, burst out, "I hated that Antonio Vitrona," She spit on the ground, emphasizing her point. "Part of Camorra. I wish I'd killed him myself."

"Jake didn't kill Antonio." Alex's voice was even as her eyes concentrated on the ice cube and bit of lemon fighting for space at the top of the brown liquid.

"Hell, we know that, Al," Stew reassured, stiffening.

"No. Not Jake," Mr. Chin agreed.

"Of course he didn't." Josie accentuated the consensus.

"I think it was those damn cops themselves who killed him. Hell, they would confiscate our booze, call in the Ladies Society, and pour our good liquor down the drain, right in front of the clapping society queens and the newspapers. What those damn fool ladies didn't know was that sink they were pouring the booze in at the police station went straight down to a couple of cops with barrels catching the liquor so they'd have it to drink later."

Everyone nodded in agreement at my amazement.

"No. I think it was the Cosa Nostra because he was trying to take over out here and they wanted this territory." Josie, the Italian, rolled her r's with vengeance at the mention of the Mafia names.

Charles's voice, smooth and clear, removed the awkwardness of the topic, "I'll have a little more, dear." He extended his glass in my direction. "Then perhaps my friends will let me tell about the pirates?"

There was snorting and shifting as the silence fell, allowing space for Charlie to proceed.

It took a second for my mind to catch up with the fast-paced banter, but the almost-empty glass was my cue.

"Oh." I rocketed back to reality and almost spilled the entire pitcher in my effort to comply. Not wanting to disrupt the untangling story, I said no more but waited to hear who the killer was.

"It was a dark, dark night," Charlie began again as I poured his tea. "Windy and thick rain. The best for running in because no one else liked to be out in it. We'd brought a load ashore to meet the truck. And I'm here to tell you, I'm lucky Jake listened to Alex here."

"We had a new driver, see. And Al did not trust that boy from the get go."

All eyes riveted on Jake's widow. She shrugged her shoulders.

"A woman knows," Josie answered for her.

"We hired kids to run the cases of booze from the boat to the truck. We clocked them, how many crates they could run in what time. The fastest were asked back. But this one kid, the Baily boy, was greedy, wanted more and made a stink. Alex didn't trust that boy, a woman's intuition. But Jake kept the Baily kid on for one more run, anyway."

The storyteller paused for a sip of tea before continuing. "Jake sent us off alone that night, unarmed. See, Jake didn't like us to carry guns. Not at first. So when those thugs jumped out of the bushes armed and trigger-happy, well, we knew we'd been had. Those pirates were mean SOBs. This big ape," his thumb jabbed in Stew's direction, "started giving them lip and got himself smacked."

Stew proudly crossed his long legs, his hand working his jaw with the memory of the blow.

"The Baily kid was in with them and wanted to kill us. He got behind those pirates and was telling them, 'Shoot, shoot.' They probably would have too. They told us to start for the woods. We thought we were done for. We didn't get very far before someone else came at us from the brush." Charlie started laughing, anticipating the rest of his own story.

"Yeah," Stew, seeing a hole took it, "and you should have seen this jackrabbit run. Nearly knocked Jake over."

Charlie nodded, eyes wide. "Jake just shot up in front of me. Scared me to death. He was wearing this long trench coat like an agent and a different hat and all. I didn't recognize him at first. 'You boys wait here.' Now, I'd never seen Jake look so mean. He and Stoney started out like hounds on a hunt. Only this time, they pulled out guns.

"Jake shot three rounds above their heads and called out into the darkness, 'United States Federal Agents Standard and Todd. Put down your guns.'

"Those fool pirates ran off into the brush, firing back at Jake and Stoney who were just sitting behind rocks, firing into the air to make noise. Then, once the firing had stopped, Jake started toward the truck.

"The Baily kid had hidden behind the truck, and when he saw Jake, that kid changed his tune as if he had tried to warn us and all. Jake just stormed right past him to where the pirates' boat was waiting and started shooting at it just below the water line. Well, when Jake turned his back, that damn kid slipped into the truck and started up the hill with our load and all.

"I heard it coming and ran to meet it, thinking it was Jake and Stoney. Then suddenly, I heard Jake's voice booming from behind me. I jumped up on the running board, and the kid panicked and started going faster. It was a nasty trail, so it wasn't easy. But the kid pulled a gun and shot. I ducked. The window shattered, and before he had time to realize his bad aim, I punched him in the jaw. The truck veered and rammed a tree."

Charlie smiled at me now as I sat trying to digest the entirety of the story.

Stew sat forward, breaking into the story, "You left out something."

Alex filled the void, "Everyone leaves out something. The truck pinched Charlie's leg, crushing it."

"Aw," Charlie sat back, "it didn't hurt me as much as it did Jake seeing my injury. Made him sick he hadn't trusted Alex's intuition and that I was hurt because of it. He couldn't tolerate turncoats. Besides, I got a new desk job, promoted to accountant."

"What happened to the Baily kid?" I wanted to live every detail.

"Jake and Stoney put the kid and me in the back of the truck, filling me with Canadian Club. The kid was scared, all right, with Stoney sitting there, watching him. And all of a sudden, he just leapt out of the back as we were heading down the road. Heard he got killed a little while later in a knife fight down in Skykomish.

"But the best part was me at the hospital doors. Jake carried me in, and Stoney followed behind, handing out bottles. The waters parted. We sure had fun. I've never seen such beautiful nurses. Even old Stew, here, would drop by on a regular basis."

"Damn right." They both laughed, their memories spilling, becoming one. "'The water of life,' our Canadian whisky, brought out the best nurses and doctors."

"Drove those nuns crazy at St. Joseph's when they couldn't figure out where you kept your stash in the hospital," Alex put in lightly.

"God bless Josie for bringing me my very own statue of the Virgin Mary." Charlie raised his glass in salute.

"Good for the soul," Josie supported his toast. Raising her glass, she tapped Charlie's, and they both drank.

Stew answered my look of confusion. "The statue of the Blessed Virgin, beautifully painted in blue and white, was hollow with just enough room for a bottle. So we'd sneak in booze and hide it in the hollowed-out statue of the Virgin Mary. The nuns would come in and find Charlie's empty bottle but couldn't figure out where he was hiding his hooch. One small, round nun kept telling Charlie he needed to pray to the Virgin Mary for his sins. He dutifully took her up on that, and the two would pray together to the statue. Hail, Mary, full of grace." His glass went in the air before he sipped.

"After that sham battle, things changed," Charlie picked the story up again, "Jake didn't like it that he'd let a traitor in the ranks. He didn't like the guns and suspected more trouble was up ahead. But life has a way of taking hold of you and propelling you forward. Jake never wanted to see Antonio again, but he wouldn't have just gone after him like the police claimed. He was just protecting us."

"Hell, yes," Stew's big booming voice shot out in backup defense. "For a while there, it was war."

"Jake ran clean. Brought in only the best bonded Canadian whisky. Some people made their own, like Vic. Tarnation, he made the greatest wine." Charlie bent in Josie's direction.

Mr. Chin nodded. "To Victor."

"That's right," Josie puffed up. "Because he used buckwheat paste around his seal on the cap of that old still. The heat would bake the paste on and seal it good and tight. And it was Franco's prunes. That was his secret." She winked her knowledge at me. "We had to have wine for our restaurant, just for special people." She slapped her thigh at her memory. "But remember the old codger down south?"

"The crows gave him away by circling the run-off?" Mr. Chin looked confused.

"No. The bees," Josie insisted, gently patting his hand, covering his gold ring with her plump fingers encrusted with jewels.

"You believe that?" Stew scolded in his gruff manner.

"Yes. The bees got into the mash, that's the fruit stock," she looked at me, "and got drunk. Someone caught one of the bees as it was circling slowly and kind of lopsided, and that little thing acted so strange they took him to the University of Washington to be examined. Well, they discovered that little bee was drunk and called the locals. They took the bee back to the river and followed him right back to the still."

Josie stayed proud, straight faced, while I tried to hold back my giggling at the incredulous story.

"Go on. Laugh." She shook her finger at her friends' gaiety. "It's true. I know it." She folded her arms across her large bosom.

Charlie had contained himself and now added, taking back his role as storyteller, "Oh, there are stories. Remember the log runner?"

"Christ," Stew lit up, "that fellow would fell his trees, grease them with dogfish oil to slide them to the water, hollow them out, stuff 'em with hay and booze, then just slip past the rum chasers in broad day light."

"There was no real law then," Mr. Chin spoke in sincerity.

"You know," Stew leaned forward, putting his weight on the arms of the chair, "it was hard times for everyone. Even for those that didn't drink. Remember Vince Procter?"

He rearranged his cap, chuckling with the others over the upcoming tale. Even Chin's face lost its dour frontage in lieu of a grin.

"Poor Vince," Charlie sighed, catching his breath. "He never touched a drop, but his every move was dogged by blue shirts from state to state."

"You see," Stew took the story back, "there was much to do before the big day hit, before Prohibition set in."

Josie broke in, "I remember it well because Vic was in such a hurry to move his winery, his grape juicers, as he called them. Put them in an old barn."

"So, knowing Prohibition was coming," Stew continued a little louder, "some people filled their closets, built fake walls, anything. But someone else came up with the bright idea of storing some booze in Procter's attic. No one would check there because he didn't drink. Procter agreed, and up went the stash.

"Now his sons thought this was pretty handy, see. So they'd wait until the old man was on the road with his job. Then they'd pop a few corks and have a shindig. Pretty soon, the kids got busted, but this cop was thrilled—he'd discovered a gold mine. The cop decided to keep this his secret and have his own parties. He'd get on the phone and call his cop friends all up and down the coast, and they got this network going on poor Procter. They'd call from Vegas, 'Procter just left the Silver Dollar on his way north.' That way they knew when to stop the parties. But the worst part of it was, for years, his kids used the information from the police on where their dad had been hanging his hat, if you catch my drift. Every time Vince would start in on one of the boys being caught doing this or that, those kids would come right back with what Vince had been up to. Nearly drove Vince to take up drinking."

The air filled with laughter and then silence.

Alex stretched out of her seat. "All this reminiscing is stirring up my appetite. How about some chow?"

"By golly, I never thought you'd say that." Charlie smiled up at her, his eyes twinkling in anticipation.

CHAPTER 18

I stood before Josie and Chin. It seemed there was a definite order as to who was allowed into the inner sanctum of the hearth, established lifetimes ago, unchanging, among friends.

The kitchen bustled with the last-minute preparations. We were well orchestrated under the watchful eye of Mrs. McKenzie and her feisty bird. Josie sampled the broth as Alex fed in the various fish and crustaceans in her own divine order. Chin put his farm-fresh corn into boiling water, and Alex added a pinch of sugar, just to keep it sweet. I cut the bread into hefty chunks, having been shown exactly how thick by both women.

Charlie and Stew loomed in the doorway, encouraging us from their viewpoint with their longing stares. Alex, enjoying her role, put them to work carrying bowls and more glasses. The anticipation of the rich seafood soup wafted in the air.

Finally, we all sat at the table, eyeing the steaming corn, fresh bread, oysters, and large pot of soup. Like good children, we waited for the signal.

"Before we begin," Alex was up once more, having already checked butter, salt, pepper, "I have a little surprise."

She whisked away to the mumblings at the table and returned with her hands behind her back.

"Al, always the show." Josie straightened her napkin in mock criticism. "What are you up to?"

The redhead smiled as she pulled the object from behind her back. "This," a shocked silence fell as she held it high in plain view, "is a special treasure."

"Oh, my God," Josie's hands went to her heart. "Is it?"

"In honor," Mrs. McKenzie started up again, "of days gone by, I can think of no other friends I would like to share this with. Here, Josie."

Alex placed the bottle in her old friend's shaking hands. A little dirt still clung to the label, which now hung forward, caught on the glass by just the corner. Through the layer of stain on the old label, part of Josie's family crest was visible.

"Well, I'll be damned," Stew's voice was soft, reverent.

Josie's eyes were wide with wonder behind her thick glasses. "Look, everybody," she displayed the bottle to the others, "it's my Victor's."

Her excitement caught in her throat as she now pulled the bottle close to her bosom, as if the long cylinder held her beloved husband. A single tear, filled with their years of separation, slid from under the dark frames and rolled down her full, round cheek.

"I can't ..." Emotion held Josie's speech.

We waited for the receding tide.

She blinked. "Where did you find it?"

"I didn't." Alex folded her hand over her soup bowl, waiting before she spoke again, ensuring her audience's full attention. "Jean did."

I shot straight up at the mention of my name. All eyes were fixed on me.

"She cleaned the garden and dug this up."

I realized now the object leaving speckles of dirt on Josie's blouse was the mud-encrusted object I had pulled from the earth on my first day of digging.

"Then she'll have the first glass." Josie was up now and had taken her prize to Stew to open.

He held the bottle, inspecting it with both reverence and skepticism. "So you think it's good?"

The Italian's hand found the back of Stew's now hatless head as she ranted on about the qualities of her deceased Vic's vineyard.

The table exploded into laughter as Stew docilely complied with her commands. Then a silence of anticipation fell as the cork popped with the unmistakable sound of hearty wine. The cork was dry and smelled of rich fruit. Cheering followed as Josie snatched the dark brown container and marched around the table until she stood next to me.

The brilliant red liquid splashed into my glass. Josie signaled for me to taste the drink, then waited like a well-trained wine steward.

My nose was filled with the enticing scent of strong Chianti. It slid down my throat, warming it. The liquor was chewable, delicious.

"That's great." I had the words ready before I'd tasted it, not wanting to puncture her memories. But I was able to deliver my line with undisguised authority, for it was truly delightful.

Proudly, gripping her bottle in both hands, rounding the table, she poured each glass before she came to Charles.

"I'll take two fingers, Josie. For old times' sake."

From the nods and shrugging shoulders accompanying Charlie's declaration, it was clear his tasting of wine was out of the ordinary.

Ceremoniously, she returned to her seat and maneuvered her plumpness onto the bench.

Alex held up her hand, and the shifting settled. "Let's take a moment to remember those who used to share this table and are no longer with us."

Heads bowed. Eyes sparkled with moisture in the now somber stillness. The moment, awash with the spirits of friends and family, passed, leaving dusty love covering the small group.

Softly, voices recalled the names, barely audible, "Jake, Victor, Stoney, Gin Dillard …"

"And now," Alex grabbed her glass, "to the living!"

The sun, catching the ruby red glasses held high, gave them a spiritual appearance. Lowered, the cordial liquid met willing lips.

"Well, I'll be damned if this isn't something," Stew's voice reverent, eyes were fixed on his drink.

"Very nice," Chin bowed.

"Mighty fine," Charles found space for his acknowledgement.

"I'm tickled pink," Josie fluttered.

"Let's eat." Alex stood, lifting the lid from the large pot. A cloud of succulent steam lingered above the broth, drawing us near.

My wedge of bread dissolved in the exquisite soup as I listened to the moans, the songs of the soul, acclaiming this to be food fit for gods.

A second bottle of wine found the table, startling in contrast with its shiny exterior.

"Stew," Charlie started slow, calculating his words, "I bet you can't remember all of your favorite toast."

Stew, ever willing to expound and egged on by his sidekick, stood. "You bet your bottom dollar I remember it. I'll dedicate this ditty to Roosevelt and the Twenty-first Amendment for repealing the damn Eighteenth Amendment." He cleared his throat in anticipation.

> The horse and mule live thirty years
> Yet know nothing of wines and beers.
>
> Most goats and sheep at twenty die,
> And have never tasted scotch or rye.
>
> A cow drinks water by the ton
> So at eighteen is mostly done.
>
> The dog in milk and water soaks,
> And then in twelve short years, he croaks.
>
> Your modest, sober, bone-dry hen
> Lays eggs for noggs, then dies at ten.
>
> All animals are strictly dry.
> They sinless live and swiftly die.
>
> But sinful, ginful, rum-soaked men
> Survive three-score years and ten.
>
> While some of us, though mighty few,
> Stay sizzled till we're ninety-two.

I clapped heartily along with the others, amazed at the memory of the man with the close-cropped, white hair, who bowed before us. Charles was pounding his back as Stew, satisfied with his brilliance, eased back into his seat.

Josie was still chortling. "Oh, I'm drunk," she covered her face, peering over her hands, blushing.

Shaking her head, Alex stood to clear the table. I was following her lead when Josie caught my arm.

"Thank you for helping, Alex. She's so alone out here. She never goes out anymore. My, she used to get all dolled up—furs, jewels. I remember the night when Jake gave her that beautiful engagement brooch."

"Oh," I beamed, "the one that looks like the half-moon?"

"You've seen it?' Her eyes widened.

"She told me about it."

"Oh," her eyes dulled. "I thought maybe she'd …" Josie's voice faded as Alex sat back down at the table. The old hand, laden with rings, patted my arm, dismissing me.

I carried the last load of dishes to the kitchen and stood in the doorway, watching the candlelight flicker over their faces.

"Damn, if I don't feel like a wild cat tonight."

"Keep your britches on, Stew," Alex shot at him across the table, then stood looking at Josie's new car. "I have yet another little adventure in mind. Josie. Want to give us a lift?"

Josie clapped her hands together, "You bet."

The two men exchanged looks of horror, afraid to get in the car, yet afraid to tell Alex no.

"Come on, boys. I've cooked up a little something you won't want to miss." She started toward the car. Feeling their hesitancy, she threw back over her shoulder, "We're just going around the bend." Her crooked finger lifted, pointing down the cliff towards her neighbors' homes.

I followed behind the two men, shaking their heads in uncertainty as they ambled toward the long, black Cadillac.

"Come on, everybody," Josie encouraged, beaming as she worked her round frame in behind the wheel and honked her own beep, beep, beep. "Let's hit the road."

We packed in. Mr. Chin took the center of the front seat with Stew's long legs stretching next to him as he grumbled, "Christ, this may be the last trip I make."

"Don't make her nervous," Charles voice was quiet as he leaned back, his view partially blocked by the black cap of his friend.

I sat in the middle with Mrs. McKenzie on my left.

"Watch this," Josie caught everyone's attention as she pushed buttons. The dash, resembling a streamlined airplane cockpit, chimed and glowed to a variety of commands. Suddenly, she threw the gears into reverse, adjusted the pillow, which added height for vision, and turned to see out the back. She stretched her neck higher, only to find the bodies in the back seat blocking her view.

"Get down," she commanded.

I immediately slid down as all the others craned in the same direction as the small head with the tight knot of hair. From below, I listened to the confusion as each passenger joined the cacophony of directions, urging the driver backwards along the path to the street.

"Okay. Okay," Josie was waggling her hand to quiet the noise. "I got it. I got it."

I eased back up the seat in the silence. Stone faces riveted on the cement stretch as we crawled along.

"The third house on the left. Pull in the driveway." Al was regaining command.

We pulled into the turnaround driveway, and everyone relaxed.

"There now. Wasn't that somethin'?" Josie smiled into the rear-view mirror.

The doors flew open before the mouths answered and "Great …. Just fine … Glad we made it" tumbled into the open air.

Mrs. McKenzie patted her friend's shoulder before she stepped into the neighbor's yard.

A man in his fifties emerged from his house, waving. "Hi there," he greeted the group, dusting his hands on his trousers. "I thought you'd just walk over."

"Changed our minds," Alex replied casually. "This is Jimmy White. Come on, Jimmy. Let's show 'em what you've got."

He smiled sheepishly and then cocked his hat further back on his head, taking note of the ancient ruins, which stood before him. His eyes drifted across the lineup as Alex ran out our names, Stew, Chin, Josie, Charlie, and the obvious misfit, me.

"I've heard a lot about you."

Suddenly, I was jealous, knowing that comment was reserved for those who had accomplished more than a lifetime in just a brief segment of their span. Like rogue waves, they had surged and consumed and then withdrawn to lap gently against other shores.

Jimmy turned to lead us around the side of his house toward the water. There was a carport, or cover, over what appeared to be a small, square trolley. It was used to haul people, and things, up and down the steep slope to the dock below.

"Holy mother of God, would you just look at that," Stew whistled. "Isn't she beautiful?"

Truly, I was fascinated by this small boxcar, but I did not see her beauty.

"Just like the *Old Moon Beam*." Charles voice cooed like a proud parent.

I turned to look back at them and discovered the reason for their admiration. Below, lolling in the gentle waters, was an older wooden boat, polished and spit shined.

"A Blanchard," Stew's voice was soft with reverence as he blinked his watering eyes. "Damn if that's not the most beautiful sight I've seen in years. Come on, Charlie. Let's take a peek."

Quickly it was decided Josie and Charlie would ride the contraption down with Jimmy. The rest of us, single file, with Stew in the lead, charged down the zigzag stairs to the landing.

Stew shifted and squirmed as he waited for the tram. Like a child on Christmas morn, his eyes were as bright as stars. Jimmy, flanked by his new admirers, Stew and Charlie, led the entourage down the short distance of the dock, attempting to answer a rapid fire of questions.

Stew leapt aboard full of questions, "She was down in San Fran?"

"Yep," Jimmy casually answered as the two men helped us aboard. "Had to strip her all the way down. New engine. The works."

"Damned expensive mistress." Stew was off, exploring, as we were all safe on board. Like kids trespassing in some long-forsaken pirates' den, the two old codgers moved from side to side, inspecting and inhaling the intoxicating fumes of new varnish, diesel, and seawater.

Charles ran his old, gnarled, four-fingered paw along the smooth, polished teak. "My, my," he repeated time and time again as if greeting an old friend.

Josie was a little unsure and, once through the cabin door, plopped down on the long, built-in seat by the table in the shining galley.

"Well," Alex's statement was filled with anticipation. She leaned against the deep wood, where the rivulets of light reflecting off the water moved across her face, lighting her eyes. "Shall we take her for a spin?"

The new crew, like well-trained soldiers, took their posts. To avoid the bustle and being a total novice, I stationed myself on the starboard, facing Chin and Josie. Through the long windows above my seat, I watched as Stew helped with the lines. Charles's offer to man the wheel had been met with a nod until Jimmy returned to guide his girl away from his dock and out into the bay.

"I've only had her home here about one year," Jimmy was explaining.

"All travelers come home to rest," Alex's voice held the melancholy of her thought.

I felt eyes on me. Following the pull of the sensation, I turned to see Mr. Chin was watching me, motionless, still, ever-present.

"She's beautiful," I said to no one in particular, nerves talking.

Alex left the scenery to question me, "Do you feel it Jean? The excitement of dashing across waterways in a powerful boat like this?"

We had reached the edge of Barry Island, and I turned my attention to the windows, studying the land from this vantage point. We clipped past the little cove with the two giant rocks acting as pillars, flanking the beach. Past the big madrona, whose long, ostrich-necked trunk swooped down the side of the bank before its branches reached back up high into the sky. Beyond this point, it was all new for me, and my interest was apparent.

"There they are," hooted Stew.

Alex had shifted sides, kneeling close to me to better her view from the window, then signaled as she spoke, "Take it down, Jimmy."

We slowed, the waves of our speed catching us, a white foamy wake on deep icy green.

Josie and Chin rose to join us. I was surrounded by the admirers as in silence they stood, eyes and hearts riveted on the rocky shoreline of Barry. Ahead, waving their eternal flag of green branches, the Two Lovers billowed in pink hues of the setting sun.

"Aren't they splendid?" Josie's' voice caught in her throat as her memories carried her far from us.

"I'm glad no damn fool has cut those two down." Stew shoved his hands deep inside his pockets.

I waited but Mrs. McKenzie said nothing. I remembered our pact to tell no one. Not even Chin. It hit me then. Not even Chin. So when he spoke, even though it was soft, I felt a chill run down my back.

"Two lovers clinging always until death."

The others nodded in unison. The slight twitch in Alex caught my eye. What did Chin know of our doing? Was he having me followed?

"What in blue blazes is that?" Stew's hands jerked from his pockets as he made his way to the starboard passageway. Everyone filed out behind him while Jimmy instinctively pulled the throttle into neutral.

We stood, lined up against the wood railings like birds on a wire, fingers pointed. The voices rose, and speculation shattered the calm as we vehemently chastised the destruction of the uneven earth and the large hollow shell of new construction.

I bit my tongue as I noticed my boss did very little talking, acting surprised and outraged by the sight, never letting on we'd just explored the terrain the day before. She was more a master at the game than I had expected.

Pretending to be following the long stream of bull kelp floating past, I saw, out of the corner of my eye what I had suspected. Mr. Chin's small, dark eyes were watching me as I had been watching Alex. I tried to remember if any of my actions had given us away. Had I studied too closely the two rocks at the entrance to the cave when we passed? Had I blinked? Shifted? In an effort to throw the hound off the scent, I furthered my career in acting by taking a deep interest in a different inlet on the far side of the famous trees.

Josie was the first to leave the railing, sadly acknowledging, "It'll all be gone someday." She struggled her sweater together over her chest.

Charles followed her lead. Next Stew ducked to reenter the cabin.

"Jean," Alex worked her way next to me, "why don't you sit with me on the bow for a while?"

I followed her along the railing until she sat on the rise, which formed the forward cabin below. With one hand gripping the inch-high wooden railing flowing along the ridge of the mound of decking, she signaled to Jimmy. "Hit it." She leaned into the wind as we gathered speed.

"Keep your eyes peeled for whales," she half-shouted above the engine.

We bounced across the water, hair slicked back by the force of the wind. I didn't really have a clue what I was searching for, but I searched, eyes squinted, across the blue-green waters.

"Deadhead." Alex's arm went up to warn and motion the boat away from the log drifting in and out of view in the waters to the port side.

"Those floating logs are the most dangerous at high speed." She leaned closer to continue her teachings, "Hit your propeller, put a hole in the bow, could send you straight away."

A bed of seaweed, thick and tangled, floated on the surface like the long hair of a maiden. Again, the arm of the pointer next to me went up in warning.

"You ever see a whale?"

I shook my head, no, watching her break into a smile.

"They're truly a wonder. They can live to be seventy-five years old, and the son stays with the mother for life. But it's the females that lead the pod." She winked at me. "Smart bunch."

"A long time ago on a night like this, Jake and I were on the far side of Stuart Island, looking back at Canada. There wasn't another boat on the horizon. The sun was sneaking behind the mountain peaks, casting a gold light over the water and the cliffs. It was the most majestic afterglow I'd ever seen. And that's when we saw them. A whole pod, dipping and diving their way up north.

"Well, the sight of those beautiful fins with their black and white markings just got to me. And I started making this sound I'd heard some of Old Roaring Thunder's family chant, like this, 'Hi yah hay, hi yah hay, hi yah hay, hay, hay.'"

I watched, transfixed as Alex threw back her head and let out a rhythmic sound from deep inside, a chant of her spirit calling and encouraging the wild within, drawing the wild out. Her free hand beat against the teak, keeping time, like one large vibrating drum, sending out waves over waves.

"Hi yah hay, hi yah hay …"

Fascination glued me to her. I studied her concentration.

"Hi yah hay." The sound died to a whisper, leaving the wind and the engine to fill the surroundings.

"Suddenly," her eyes opened again, and her hand joined her speech, "they turned toward us. About fifteen of the pod came at us from out of the strait. Dead on they came, leaping, diving, black and white, black and white on golden tipped waves. They reached the *Moon Beam* and circled her. Jake cut back to a drift—something I'd never seen him do with a full load. But we both felt it in the air—the spirits, the force of those creatures of the sea. I went forward to the bow, right up there, and leaned over making my sound, 'Hi yah hay.'"

Her cry was louder now, clearer, the force of her tale exploding in her throat, accompanying the beat of her hand.

"They dove below the bow, playing tag with us. The sun had fallen, the sky had lost its pink and blue to those rare amber hues, and the water was now an emerald green. The white markings on the killer whales were now green under the surface of the water. Emerald and black, they dove beneath me at the bow. I could feel their breath."

Her waving hand continued the story, sweeping up and down, cutting the air, following the path of the large mammals.

"They stayed and played like that for some time. It was so spiritual. I hated to see them go. Jake knew it, too. He came up behind me and helped me off the bow. 'Come on Red. We've got to move on.' But we didn't go right away, you know. He held me tight, close as if we were one, while those beautiful and powerful whales circled us with their unearthly show."

I could see it. She had worked the paintbrush well, and I could see them clinging to each other, riding emerald waves through eternity, led by the creatures of the sea.

Her hand rested on my knee, holding me in her pause. "I cried a little when they left us to join the others heading up the channel. There are times that run deep in the rivers of your soul, times you know will never happen again. And they stir whirlpools of emotions you didn't even think existed because you keep your surface calm, free of bumpy waves. But those undercurrents catch up with you from time to time, and like any strong flow, it's best just to ride with it. Otherwise, you exhaust yourself in your own struggle and drown."

The power of her story spread down her hand to my leg, immobilizing, numbing it. Even when she lifted her hand into the air, the sensation lingered.

"Come on, Jean," she said closing her eyes to the passing sailboat lowering its sails with the setting sun. "Let's call up some whales." Her head went back as her throat worked the sounds, "Hi yah hay, hi yah hay."

"Hi yah hay," I stumbled through my novice attempt at the ancient words and rhythm.

Her cry became louder, encouraging. I closed my eyes and joined her. Together, as one tone, we sent our call upon the wind and sea.

A gull, riding the waves on the log adrift in deepening blue waters, turned his back to us, then craned his neck, keeping an ever-watchful eye on the two women on the bow.

"Hi yah hay ..."

We skipped across the fading light.

CHAPTER 19

"Al," Stew boomed as he held her hand, steadying her landing on the dock, "I can't think of anything in years that would top this."

"Some grand time we had." She let him put his arm around her as they fell in behind the others.

Jimmy checked the lines on his beautiful old craft as she swayed peacefully in her slip. Then he joined the group, which huddled, chattering, at the base of the stairs.

Charles, starting low, hummed a few bars and was joined by Josie. Soon the soft moonlit bay was filled with the familiar words. "By the light of the silvery moon …"

As their tribute to days gone by lilted across the water, we slowly worked our way up the side of the cliff, drawing with each step the flood of memories this evening with its eddies and tides had replayed before old eyes, hungry to reclaim those sparkling moments.

The small trolley car clicked to a stop on the top of the slope. The bay below was peaceful now. The singing having died out due to the journey's end, we stood, a ribbon of souls looking across at the slip of moon and stars, a sight which some of this small gathering would never return to share.

The thought hit me with sheer force, almost knocking me back down the brown-grass face of the hill to the cold water below.

Charles, mistaking my sudden change, tried to console me, "Don't worry, Jean. We'll see a whale on our next trip."

Our next trip? How could he so lightly speak of the improbable? I looked down the line of old friends, while pain tore at my heart. I could not lose them. I wanted to grab each one and hold them fast, giving of my youth to fortify the old. I fought back tears. How do you stop time?

They were peaceful, content as they faced the few remaining steps of the long full trail of their lives.

"Well, kiss her good-bye, boys." Alex's words shook the silence. "Tomorrow is another day. How about some pie? Join us Jimmy?"

"You've worn me out," he laughed. "I'll swing around tomorrow."

"Suit yourself. Come on. These old bones need a rest." She put her arm around Josie and started for the shiny black car.

"Thanks, Al," Stew tipped his hat back, "but we'll walk."

She waved her acceptance to their proposal over her shoulder.

I stood torn between my choices when my boss decided for me. "Come on, Jean. Let's let those scalawags walk."

Chin had been holding back, undecided, watching. He started for the car as I did but was signaled away by Alex.

"Thanks again, Jimmy," the voices rang out, seeming to unite and become one.

Our host tipped his hat and stood watching the exodus.

———◦◦◦———

The pie disappeared with the tea, which Mr. Chin prepared. We sat in darkness in the living room, watching the evening through the large glass windows. The quietude of the calming liquid gentled in around us as we sat, captivated by the reflection of the moon on the bay.

"Well," Stew stretched, "we'd better shove off before Chin slips us some of his damn magic and we sleep right here."

The laughter told the truth. Chin was capable of Stew's suggestion. I remembered the needle I had seen that day when I bumped the magazine. What was he giving to Mrs. McKenzie that was in that red box with the dragon?

Charles grunted as he pushed himself up from his chair. "Better go before I get too stiff to move." His movements were slow, calculated.

Chin stood and gathered the cups, hustling them to the kitchen. "Many thanks. It has been a remarkable evening."

I tried to stand but couldn't, exhaustion of my thinly stretched emotions anchoring me to my seat.

Alex eyed Josie, who had drifted off, snoring in the midst of the shuffling.

"Leave her," Alex warned softly. "I'll call her grandson. She can stay here."

Josie gave off a deep snort, confirming the decision.

Following my boss, I struggled from my chair, the cool evening air reviving my body but not my spirits. A deep feeling of loss ran through me as we said our good-byes.

"I'm glad you're here to help Al," Stew bellowed and slapped my back, the acceptance ritual. "It was nice meetin' you." He tipped the black cap before slipping into his car.

Charles, extending his hand, gripped mine. "I hope you liked our stories. We're always willing to talk about Jake and Stoney. And Al is the greatest. If you ever need anything, call me."

"Thanks." I hated to let go our grip, to let go of this fragile life, which for this brief time had spilled into mine, knowing soon it might be gone forever.

His hand gave me one final shake before he turned to maneuver his leg to the far side of Stew's car.

"Happy trails to you," Charlie started to sing, and Stew followed, the formal good-bye of their own private tribe.

Alex choked beside me, then caught up with them, "Until we meet again."

Jake's song. She had told me of this parting ritual, and now hearing it brought chills and a sense of unearthly beings among us. I turned my gaze to the sky, thanking the heavens for this evening and these incredible survivors of time.

The car pulled from the drive, and the lights disappeared.

"Well that's it," Alex sounded tired. Her hand was on my shoulder, and she leaned on me slightly. "We have much to do tomorrow. Get some rest, and I'll see you around nine on the tide."

We headed for my car. "Thanks again for all your help."

She waved as I guided my Bug onto the street. The ride home was lost in the many journeys of the evening. Already much of what was said was becoming jumbled, blending. I was now angry with myself for not taking notes, using the pad and pen sill remaining within my daypack. I vowed to jot down the stories as soon as I was in my room.

The half-moon was beginning its downward slide when I pulled my car over on the street just past Nash Dorm. The pleasantness of the evening had erased my tension. I headed for the door and down the hall. I was halfway up the stairs when I heard footsteps. Some-one was running down the hallway below. I began to run, taking the stairs two at a time. I was at my door, trembling with my key, when I realized the running had stopped. Silence filled the halls as I closed the door behind me. Inside, heart pounding, I checked my room and the street below. Nothing.

Plugging in my kettle, I placed myself at my desk, bent on recap-turing the evening. I began an outline—Mrs. McKenzie, Stew, Charles, Josie, Mr. Chin, Jimmy's boat, cave—when there was a familiar rap at my door.

"Lis, is that you?"

"Are you dressed?" she answered.

I opened the door and stood back. There, looming in the shadows behind my small friend, was Nate.

I smiled, glad at first to see him, then blushed with confusion. "What's up?"

They stepped inside my small room, filling it.

"Nate just wanted to say hi." She was lying and terrible at it.

"Have a seat." I waved them inside, grateful I had straightened up that morning. Nate took the chair by my desk, and I hurried to cover my notes.

The silence rang of something far deeper than a simple visit at this hour. I sat on the edge of my bed, arms folded. My shield was up.

"How was work?" Lissa twitched in her uncomfortable role.

"Fine." I wanted to scream. Why the interrogation?

Nate took the lead. "Look," his fingers meshed together as he prepared his speech, "I don't know how to tell you this, but I do think you're right. Someone is following you."

My arms tightened as did my lips. The acknowledgement others were aware of my situation was somehow not a relief. The cords of my nerves were vibrating.

"We're worried," Lissa added, trying to appease me. "We want to help."

My head shook no. "I'm fine."

They exchanged looks, and then Nate tried again. "Jean, last night someone almost ran me down."

My heart was thudding in my ears.

"Tonight, again, someone was waiting for you outside. I tried to cut him off around back but missed him."

The footsteps in my hall ... My brain was short-circuiting. I was losing focus.

"Do you have any idea why?" Nate's voice was even.

My jaw was locked.

"I'm calling the police." Lissa sprang from the chair.

"No," I shot up too, my hand firmly on the phone, my voice strong and steady. "I'm fine. Maybe it's you. Maybe someone is after you." I didn't mean to lash out at Nate, but I needed time, and I needed to do this alone.

My accusation slid past him. His words were even, chosen to make an impact, "It has something to do with your job."

"No."

"Please, Jean. Stop all this and let us help," Lissa voice was an octave higher.

"Tomorrow is my last day. Everything is fine."

"You promise?" Her small frame was determined.

"Yes. Tonight we had a party because tomorrow it's all over with." I was trembling in my performance. "I'm tired. I need to sleep." My hand shook as I opened the door.

Lissa hurried out while Nate lingered just inside the door. He turned to watch me as I prepared my bed. "Jean, here's that salve for your hands I promised." He held out a small container.

I reached for it, and he took my hand, holding it firmly. "I want to help you. There's more here than you know. I'll check with you tomorrow. Now lock the door."

He placed the object in my hand and shut the door softly, leaving me as I crumpled onto my bed with the warm sensation of his touch.

<hr/>

A noise woke me early. I sat up, heart pumping, listening. Outside the wind was blowing. The trees were squeaking as they bent with the force, brushing from time to time against the back of the building. Convinced of my safety, I eased back down only to be startled awake again.

There was a tapping at my door. "Jean," the voice whispered, "Jean, it's me. Can I come in?"

"Do you have my bodyguard with you?"

"No."

I opened the door to Lissa, who held two cups of coffee.

"Forgive me?" she extended her offering.

Fixing a stern look on my face, I nodded, accepting the cup. I opened the blinds. The tall firs were a mellow green against the gray sky. The sun was hidden behind dark-rimmed clouds. A soft, filtered light filled the room. Whitecaps brushed the bay below.

Lissa took up the chair, facing me, not knowing where to begin. "Are you mad at me?"

"No, you were only trying to help." The deep, rich coffee was a welcome treat.

"Aren't you excited?" She leaned forward, eyes wide.

"About what?" I blurted against the trap.

"How much Nate likes you." She appeared shocked by my oversight.

I weighed the comment, not 100-percent convinced I was the sole object of his attentiveness. He knew something more. That was clear. I'd have to find out what he wanted with me and where I fit in. Remembering his touch, I hoped Lissa was right in her assessment of his attentions.

"Why didn't you tell me he was so interested in Prohibition?"

"He's interested in several things. He's always checking out books." She straightened, defending his charms.

"Can you get me a list of all the books on Prohibition, and that time period, he's checked out?" I surprised myself with the idea. "I mean, you have a list somewhere, don't you?"

Her head nodded slowly, watching me as she spoke, "I thought this job was over today."

"Well, it is." I fingered the rim of the cup. "But, I've decided I might want a history minor. And I'd like to know more. Wait until I tell you about what Mrs. McKenzie's been saying and her friends. Get me the list, and we'll talk tonight"

"Okay," she took my bait and stood. "I suppose you want the books too?"

I smiled at her brilliance.

CHAPTER 20

The drive was subdued like the day, held in a gray shroud, which is truly the Northwest.

The house sat in the dense mist, appearing lifeless, damp, and uncomfortable. I rapped at the peeling paint of the back door. There was no movement inside. Not even the tittering of the parakeet. I knocked again, checking my watch. Maybe Alex was at the neighbors.

Stepping back into the yard, I looked along the cliff. Nothing moved. All homes were shut tight against the impending rains. I checked another source, but no footprints showed in the green, dew-covered grass. She was still in the house.

Hearing the door give way, I started for it. It was opened only about two inches. Through the crack in the door, I could see tuffs of red hair and one blue eye.

"There you are, Jean," her voice broke mid sentence as she opened the door wide, "come on in."

Her nightgown trailed below her baby blue, chemise robe.

"I'm moving a little slow this morning." Her form ratified her statement. She leaned on the turquoise counter as she passed by. "Fix yourself a cup of tea if you want."

I followed her shuffle into the room with the big windows. The dullness from outside filtered through the house, bringing with it a gloomy mood.

The old widow pulled the crocheted, granny-patch blanket over her feet and lap. Her gaze was held by the nothingness outside the large glass openings. Through the mist, the waves below formed whitecaps as the wind pushed them, high and rolling, to the shore.

"Pilchuck Julie would have warned me about today," she sat motionless, speaking to the window.

"Pilchuck Julie?" I realized I needed to nudge the story along.

"She was a seer. Born on the Tulalip Indian Reservation with strong magic. Jake would go to her for the weather and other things from time to time."

Her mind drifted back out the window.

Having never seen her like this, I was somewhat confused as to what to expect. Mrs. McKenzie appeared small in the lifeless room. The dark beams and empty fireplace added a lonely, tired feeling.

"Would you like some tea?" It was difficult to watch her in this state.

"Had some when I got Josie off. I couldn't sleep last night." She drew the blanket closer, her words spilling out laced with edginess, "My mind got all riled up. I could feel Jake and Stoney sitting with us last night, and I missed them so. I wanted to travel back down that road and change things. I wanted to change that ni …" Her voice cracked, fading into the hollow-sounding room.

Uncertain, I sat as still as Alex.

"You know, Jean, all paths have sunshine and shadows. But some shadows grow with time. They cling to you and grab at you, choking life. My poor Jake was innocent. Lots of people wanted that Antonio dead, including the police. There were those that said Drummond shot him himself. But if I could only find it, then I'd know." Her hand found her eyes, now filled with tears.

I watched her pain, feeling it transfer to me.

"Maybe," I began timidly, "if I knew what we were looking for, I could be of more help."

She pulled a flower-patterned handkerchief out of her nightgown sleeve to dab at her eyes.

"Well, I knew this would have to come out. Go into my office and get the photo album on top of the stack to the right."

I didn't realize how tense I'd been until I stood and started down the dark hall. My body demanded a stretch. I paused for a moment, raising my arms, reaching for nothing.

"Did you find it?" her voice came at me down the hall, pushing me on. Pretty Boy echoed her concern with his trill.

As usual, the room was dark.

Things had changed from my first viewing of her private room. The stacks were smaller, more compressed, and organized. Alex had spent some time sorting and rearranging the room she had called her secret place. She was trying to bring the order to her life she had so desperately mentioned several times. The photo album was just where she said it would be.

I picked up the rich, leather-bound book. It was dense and heavy. Excitement replaced my tension. I wasn't certain what I was to hear, but this time I would ask for more details, more clues. Too many gaps needed filling.

"Atta girl." Her hands stretched out, anxious to hold the memories. Like a mother accepting her child into her arms, she cradled the book momentarily before patting the couch, indicating my seat. The bird silently walked to the edge of his cage and watched us with one eye.

"Do you like to look at pictures?"

I positioned myself next to her, hoping my answer would comfort her a little. "I love it." Little did she realize I wanted to snatch the leather-bound book back to begin my own journey through the pages of time.

"Well, you're in for a treat." Ceremoniously, she flipped back the first page.

"There we were in our heyday with the wind at our backs and calm seas ahead."

I was drawn to where her bent finger arched before it tapped a picture of the three young partners. All the words used to describe her husband did not do him justice. He was tall, sandy blond, broad shouldered, and just plain handsome. The smile was warm, confident, and definitely alluring.

A young Alex stood in the middle, indeed a striking woman, all dolled up, ready for the world. While Stoney Black was the opposite of Jake in coloring, his wavy black hair slicked back in perfection, their frames were similar. His smile less broad, he had a caution, almost shyness that, of itself, was captivating. His eyes shone pure joy of living. It was easy to imagine the stir this trio created when they entered a room together.

"We were like the three musketeers." Pride smothered the sorrow in the room. "We'd walk down the street, and heads would nod. It was grand." Her chin lifted with the vision.

She turned the page in concentrated silence. Then her finger fell again. "This was the party at the Del Mar Hotel in Seattle. There was a fountain with a long pond in the courtyard. It was gorgeous. Big staircases, chandeliers, Tiffany glass. Downstairs was a beautiful ballroom with separate entrances for men and women. It was a party for all the runners who were attending the big convention in June of '31.

"And we must have made some sort of impression because the next thing you knew, within a few days, the Feds were busting up places all over town. It broke my heart when they busted up the Rose Room in the Butler Hotel. The Butler Hotel was stunning and full of high society. Part of the excitement for those folks was having the Feds swoop in, collect a few half-empty containers of hooch, and take away a waiter or two. The crowd would all sling insults and boo. We went one night to hear this new talent, Bing Crosby. They didn't ask him back, didn't think he had enough experience for them." She was chuckling and catching her breath before adding, "Ah, heck, you could go to some of the fine downtown hotels or pool halls and buy a milk bottle filled with bathtub gin. But, remember, we ran the good, bonded stuff."

"Only the best," I echoed and encouraged.

"Anyway, it was one night things started to heat up. This convention was right after that sham battle where Charlie got hurt. People were buzzin' with apprehension. Antonio was leaving his mark. Bodies were showing up with long cuts from the lip to the cheek, just like Antonio's scar. He was making it clear he wanted the northwest territory, that we should just give it to him. Well, we'd do nothing of the sort. So that son of a gun went after the pirates, gave them guns, offered a better deal on the Canadian side, or so he claimed.

"But when Antonio just walked on into the ballroom that night at the Del Mar, it was as if the waters parted. He had on this long black coat that almost touched the ground. Just draped over his shoulders, spats, gloves. Really putting on the hog."

The life of the story perked Alex up, and her eyes began to burn with anger. "Do you know, he just stood there, handed his coat to his goon, the short fat one, and said in that slimly accent of his, 'What's this? A convention without me?'"

Her hand and shoulder lifted through the air in mock Italian style. Josie couldn't have done it better.

"Our host told him he'd better keep moving, that this was a private party."

"That damn, dark Italian. His monkey lit his cigar. He took a deep drag on it, then smiled, before saying, "But I'm here to help you. You need me. So, what is it you want from me?'

"Stoney couldn't hold Jake back, and my Jake went right up to him and said, 'The space you're taking up in this room.'

"Everybody took a step back. But Jake just stood there. Well, once that bugger saw Jake, he must have figured I wasn't far behind. Smoking his cigar like a king, he circled around Jake, eyeing the crowd until he saw Stoney. I was hiding behind him, see, peeking around. And Stoney was a rock. Wouldn't let him near me until he saw his goons pull their guns, and Jake signaled him to be still.

"Then that Antonio leaned in close to me. His breath held the taste of cigar. He took my hand and bent to kiss it. He had a way of whispering that could make your blood run cold. "My beautiful firebird. So lovely to see you again. And for once, both shoes on?"

My eyes were wide with the excitement of Alex's tale. "What did you do?"

"The only thing any decent girl should have done. I spit in his face."

"Jake started laughing and caught the pudgy one, Ceiro or something like that, off guard. Slugged him so hard he disappeared into the crowd. Stoney was right behind Jake. Then others joined in. One bullet went off into the nice wood ceiling, but that was all."

She began to turn the page as if she had unfolded a breezy story of summer lust.

"Well? What happened?" I bounced on the couch.

"They were escorted out the door."

"Did it scare you?"

She paused before giving me her answer. "Yes, because right before they pushed Antonio out the door he turned toward me and in a clear voice claimed, 'I'll be back for you,' and he wiped away my spit still on his face. That's when I got scared. Deep down, bone scared. Because I knew he would."

She coughed once, and Pretty Boy sputtered and chirped from his perch.

"Why don't you make us some tea?"

Chapter 21

I was to be allowed alone in the queen's kitchen. *She must be very sick or tired.* The thought of this, the mere inference that Mrs. McKenzie, the supreme battleship, weathering all storms, was listing, made my heart race with an undeniable fear.

Nothing must happen to her, I swore repeatedly as I put the kettle on and dug into the old canister marked "tea."

She hadn't moved when I returned with the tray holding the steaming brew. Her eyes were fixed on the drizzle that was now falling soundlessly outside.

"We'll never find it," she muttered as I placed the tea on the table in front of her. "And then I'll never know and never rest."

"Yes, we will," I heard myself assure her. "But it would help if I knew what 'it' is."

She chuckled, "You poor thing. I haven't been fair. All right. Let's keep going." She patted the couch again and flipped that page of her scrapbook.

A picture of three young girls, arm in arm, smiling straight at the camera, slid from the book to the floor.

I picked up the old black-and-white snapshot and drew it closer for a better look. All three of the girls had large bows in their short hair and matching dresses. I recognized Alex by the unruly curls, her legs longer than the others, her stance defiant.

"That's nothing. Let's just put it back."

I placed the photo in her extended hand, and she deftly put it in the back of the scrapbook.

She flipped the book back to the other page and tapped next to a picture. "There she is. My little beauty. That's my Diesel Rose."

The ragamuffin dog she held in her arms was hardly a beauty. Mischievous and happy would be a better description. Eyes partially hidden behind coarse-looking hair, with a nose a bit longer than most, she was a mutt through and through. "That was the damn smartest dog in the world. Saved my life. But I couldn't save hers.

"See, after that scene at the ballroom with Antonio and his crew of nasty men getting stronger, Jake kept a close eye on me. I felt like Pretty Boy. I couldn't go anywhere alone. Not even to have my hair done. It was driving me crazy."

I was studying the picture of Alex and Diesel Rose and noticed she wore the same half-moon pin on all her dresses.

"That's a pretty pin." I was digging for clues, certain it was the one she had mentioned before.

I could feel the cold emitting from her. "Yes. That was my engagement pin. I loved it. Pearls and three small rubies in the shape of a half-moon." Her words stopped, but the chill remained.

I looked at her in great anticipation. Was the pin what we were searching for? Something deep down kept the words from sliding past my lips.

She closed her eyes and drew me back to her pace. "For two months, I felt trapped. A prisoner. Until one night, I demanded we go out. It was a birthday for one of my old friends, Lucy. And I insisted we take her and her husband, Frank, out dancing. There was a speakeasy on Flynn's houseboat, great music and dancing. Owned by an ex-policeman so it was usually not bothered, and you could get a decent drink. Dusty was singing with her deep blues voice that night, and Stoney had a soft spot for her, so he was raring to go too.

"It was a warm August night. A slip of a moon and stars twinkling. We had stars back then. Thousands of them. And shooting stars, leaving trails across deep, blue-black skies. I was so restless. I made Jake take me out when he knew it wasn't safe. But I was mean, angry and bound to have my way. So, I put on my nice summer dress, my sandals with heels, red lips, grabbed Diesel, and stormed out the door. That sweet dog went with me everywhere. But this was her last trip with me." She sighed heavily before continuing.

"Jake and Stoney didn't put up much of a fight. They grabbed their hats and came a-running after me. If I'd known better, I would have stayed put. But no. I made him take me to Flynn's joint, down there in the old Fairhaven area.

"We stopped along the way so Jake could make a call. I knew what he was up to, and sure enough, by the time we arrived, there were two of his boats sitting there. And some of the men too. My own private army.

"Well, we went inside, and Lucy and I were dancing with whoever would walk by. Dusty was giving it her all with Stoney there. I just needed to shake a leg. But even that wasn't enough. I was still restless. So I picked up my Diesel Rose and went out onto the deck running along the houseboat. I took off my shoes and sat on the edge. I remember the light from the window made a pattern across the deck so I shifted into the darkness so I could see the stars. That's probably why I didn't see them coming.

"I lit my cigarette and put the pack back in my bosom so Diesel wouldn't try to snatch them. That little rascal. Then I lay back onto the dock to watch the show in the heavens, my feet dipping in the water.

"I felt safe. Stoney was at the window watching. But there was this young floozy, new to town. She had come in, and someone had bought her a drink, and then she left. She came back later and was all over Stoney, and we didn't think anything of it then. But when we saw her later with one of Antonio's men, we put it together. Served her right she got with child, and he just left her, high and dry.

"So, I was sitting there watching those stars when Diesel's ears went up and she growled. I didn't pay much attention. I was being too selfish, didn't want anything disturbing my night out.

"I didn't see the boat moving. They had the engine off and were just hand-pulling it along the dock. The next thing I knew there was a blanket over me, and I was being handed into a damn boat. I could hear Diesel yelp as she got kicked. But that precious dog just kept on. Jumped right on their boat. They threw the two of us below.

"Jake, Stoney, and the others heard the commotion and came running out. All they saw were my shoes and the wake of the boat in the moonlight. The crew was throwing off the lines just in time as Jake and Stoney took off in two of our boats.

"Oh, that black devil had hired himself a good driver all right, Thompson. Straight from the police payroll to the Camorra gang. It was that short, wild-eyed character who used to work for Drummond, the one with Drummond when they stopped us the first night out. He'd gone to the other side for money.

"But he wasn't a match for Jake. See, Jake ran a tight ship and was always making plans, 'just in case plans' he used to call them. So that night, he'd had one of the boys bring out the sea sled, fastest boat around in the right conditions, and that's what my Jake was skippering.

"We'd raced across the strait, cutting up to the north tip of Lummi. Jake was scared to death Antonio was going to get me across into Canada. That would have been big trouble. So he and Stoney kept to the starboard as they tried to corral Antonio's boat into the islands.

"Calls had gone out, and others were getting their boats out to join the search. Jake would signal them with his light, their own private code. He'd been afraid something might happen so he had men ready all up and down the bay, and when he made the call, he sent out his sleds and the blacks, his fastest fleet of boats, just off the west bank of Sucia.

"It worked. Stew charged at Antonio's boat, forced him down Presidents Channel. We rounded Point Disney and flew past White Rock.

"Jake and Stoney split to go around Flattop. Jake ducked into a clump of rocks just off Spieden and killed the engine to wait for the boats to pass.

"You had to get up pretty early to outfox Jake. See, I could hear the engines roaring around out there, and I could tell when the sound became just one boat. Jake was lying low, waiting, while Stoney was making noise, which disappeared into the distance.

"When it had been silent for a while, the hatch opened, and Antonio and his fat gorilla, Ceiro, came below, and my Diesel started to growl.

"If the dog makes any noise kill it." Antonio spoke the words as easily as if he'd just ordered a piece of apple pie.

"Thompson, that two-faced good-for-nothing, agreed Diesel should be killed. He didn't like having a dog aboard. Some people are very superstitious—never mention a four-legged animal on board, a knife in a mast means trouble, or a hatch cover upside down is bad.

"There I was trying to keep Diesel quiet. I was so afraid for her. I wasn't even thinking about myself. But you know," her finger touched my shoulder, "those goons stayed away from her.

"I didn't know what to do. I had to signal Jake, and I guess fate just took over for me. Antonio offered me a cigarette, and I shook my head no. I wasn't taking anything from him. I was shaking when I put Diesel Rose on the bunk behind me. I didn't know what I was doing. Antonio lit his cigarette and was just standing there drooling at me.

"'I finally have you, my firebird. I knew I would.'

"I hated him so much I could have killed him myself then and there. He disgusted me. Then he put his cigarette in the ashtray on the table and came towards me. I backed away from him, heading for the hatch. I was trying to draw him away from Diesel Rose.

"And that's when it happened. Diesel saw that cigarette, jumped right up onto the table and grabbed it, and shot past me onto the deck. Then all hell broke loose.

"I threw myself in the gangway to try and stop Antonio from reaching Diesel, but he just pushed me aside. Up on deck I could hear them begin to chase her, but she was fast and not afraid."

"Jake heard the noise, of course, because with the islands on either side of us that sound just carried across the water. So he followed the sound until he saw that little light bouncing around the boat and knew what had happened. He signaled Stoney and came at us alone.

"We were a sight. I was yelling for Diesel Rose to come to me, and I was trying to get to her. But his disgusting gorilla got her first," her voice seethed with hatred as her hands once more joined the story. "With one quick snap he broke my little baby's neck and tossed her poor little body into the dark, cold water. And I went right in after her."

Alex gave a little shrug, as if apologizing, "I just kept diving for her. But it was so dark."

"Was Jake there yet?" I wanted to help her, take the darkness and give it light.

"Yes. He started firing at them, shining a big light right in their faces so they couldn't see me, and Thompson took off. Jake put our boat between me and that damn boat of theirs and was trying to get me out of the water. He was hopping mad because he had to cut the engine to get me aboard. There was shouting, and the boat came around toward us.

"'Al,' Jake kept hollering, 'get in the damn boat.' I was so upset I took one more dive. We barely got out of there. We were taking on water. But Jake had his plan. We scooted straight across to John's Island. Ran the boat right up onto the beach next to the rocks. Then we started running. He was draggin' me. I wanted my baby, Diesel Rose. We got to an old log cabin before the fern field, and Jake pushed me on ahead.

"'Get going.' I could barely see his eyes, but I knew he meant it. I knew he loved me, and that was all that mattered. 'And keep low, Alexandria. Stoney's there waiting.'

"I didn't want Stoney. I wanted my Jake. I'd just lost Diesel, and I couldn't lose Jake too. I hated that run across the fern field. I was wet, cold, scared. Numbed by the loss of my little darling, I think I wandered until I heard shots. I was about halfway across and knew I couldn't stop. Somehow, my legs took over, and I stumbled to the other side, to an inlet.

"I jumped down the small embankment and a hand grabbed me.

"'You okay, Al?' Stoney never could really whisper. 'Where's Jake?'

"Just then, there was an explosion, and I jerked in the direction, but Stoney had a firm grip on me. He scooped me up, and I was giving him a fight too, and he carried me into the water and put me over the side. I remember I sort of crumbled onto the deck. I just lay there, afraid to move, afraid that if I stirred I might wake up out of that horrible dream, and there would be no Jake. I couldn't believe my selfishness had brought that on us.

"Stoney was torn. He wanted to go after Jake, but he knew the routine, and he knew he couldn't leave me. He was a man caught in his duty, like salmon whose duty it is to swim to the place of their birth to lay their eggs, but they get caught in nets along the way. The net held us in the silent bay.

"Finally, I couldn't stand it anymore. I pulled myself up and was looking over the rail. The waves were lapping gently along the shore. Peace surrounded our turmoil. Stoney reached out to start the engine.

"Not yet," I hissed at him.

"He didn't argue, and we sat there for what seemed like an eternity, listening to nothing. The sea of sorrow was rising to swallow me as I looked into the black night. The clouds rolled across the sky, and the little moon came out to join our search.

"Then there was a faint rustle of the ferns and panting. I saw his belt buckle flicker in the light as he landed in the sand. He was in the water, and we were off before the other figures became visible on the shore.

"'Are you okay?' Jake's eyes were taking inventory. Then he grabbed me and held me close. It was a fierce hug. I wanted to crawl inside of him and make everything all right. But I knew over my shoulder those two men were looking at each other and, without words, were making their plans.

"We cleared the bay, ran along the cliffs, headed south past Spieden and into San Juan Channel.

"When he finally released me, I fell apart. I started whimpering, 'Jake, my baby. I want my Diesel Rose.'

"He just let me cry for a while on his shoulder. You see, dear," she turned toward me now, her utterance coming from far away, a speech repeated several times but not accepted, "we couldn't have children. I was Rh-negative. Back then, they hadn't quite figured it out as they have today. I just lost them all. So Diesel Rose had been my baby, and now she was floating somewhere in that dark, cold water."

"Couldn't you adopt?" my eyes were blinking like butterfly wings, trying to hold back the tears.

She looked down at her hands where blue veins mapped across the thin, freckled skin. "Who's going to let rum runners have their baby? Especially after the trial. No, between us and God, we made a mess of things."

They moved freely now, rushing down my cheeks, the tiny drops of misery checked only by the back of my hand. I wanted to reach out and hold her, to tell her everything was going to be all right or that her life was so full and beautiful without children. But, I couldn't. Her pain was far too real.

"Oh, dear," she was watching me now, concern covering her emotions. "I've upset you. I'll stop."

Chapter 22

"No!" I nearly jumped at her. "No, please don't stop. It's so wonderful—how much Jake loved you and all you did together."

"You think so? You think Jake loved me?" She was the frightened child again, needing the tenderness of reassurance.

"Of course he did," it was my turn to be harsh.

"But what I did," her eyes were wildly blue and imploring, "it was horrible."

"No, it wasn't. You didn't know." I struggled for words to heal hidden wounds.

"No, I didn't know. But …" Her frame sank with the weight of her memories.

"What was the explosion on the island?" I wasn't sure if my interest was the correct course at that moment or maybe a diversion.

She straightened before answering, "Jake had doubled back, lured them off their boats, waited until they were ashore, then set their boat on fire. We were at war." Her arm reached for the tea, but her hand was shaking, so she retracted it.

Taking charge, I poured her a cup. She waved the scrapbook away as I took the memories and replaced them with warm liquid.

I couldn't let her stop now. I encouraged her along. "How did they get off the island?"

"Someone called the rum patrol." She smiled bleakly before continuing, "But the police were all up in arms. Old Sheriff Drummond was furious. This was just what everyone didn't want. So he kept an eye on us, for our own good, he kept saying. From that night on, we had two damn fools parked outside of our house twenty-four hours a day. Drove me crazy.

"Jake stayed real low. Boy, it was bad. It's hard to watch someone you love turn on himself before your eyes. But there wasn't anything we could do about it. Oh, he was crazy restless like I had been. Then we got word one of our men had been shot at on his way home, wasn't hurt bad, but still. We knew who had done it, and the police had nothing on them. Something snapped inside of Jake, and he became real calm. And I knew it wouldn't be long before I'd wake up one morning, and he'd be gone.

"I was right. About one week later, he left without saying a word. Chin came and stayed with Stoney and me. The guys outside didn't know Jake had slipped past them, and they didn't suspect anything. So there we sat. I had guards outside and in. After two days of this, I went crazy too. Stoney wasn't talking, and I thought Jake was dead. It was hell.

"On the second night, I was nothing but nerves. There was a storm outside, the kind runners live for, winds, rain. No one in his right mind would be out in it. Trouble was brewing. You could feel its electricity.

"About six o'clock, there was a knock at our front door. No one ever used that door, not even our watchdogs, so we knew something was up. Stoney checked, and the two cops were standing outside of their car in the rain. Another car was parked behind them. Stoney opened the door with his gun drawn.

"This kid was standing there, scared to death, with a dozen red roses. Stoney pulled him inside and checked him. Poor thing was frozen, bulging eyes and stuttering.

202

WHISKEY COVE

"I grabbed the roses before Stoney could. A small note was attached, and I read it quickly, then shoved it into my bra. I don't know how, but I smiled at Stoney. My voice was as nonchalant as I could muster without having it shake, 'It's okay. Let him go.'

"Stoney looked at me hard, but I was cradling and smelling the roses. He opened the door, and that kid ran like a scared rabbit.

"'Jake's on his way home. Just wanted to let me know he's fine.'"

"But Stoney was just lookin' at me. He didn't believe a word of it. 'What'd he say exactly, Al?'

"I started for the kitchen. 'He's fine. Be home soon. Love me. Hi to both of you.' But Stoney just followed after me, so I just kept on talking. 'Let's celebrate. How about steak?'

"I threw that in and began to holler for Chin, scared stiff Stoney was going to catch on. 'Chin, let's get some steaks ready. How about your special vegetables and your rice?'

"Stoney was just watching the show, still not convinced. He could read me too well.

"Chin was staring at me. He knew, too, what was going on. But he came to my aid. 'We have no beef.'

"'Well, someone will have to go get some.' I looked at Stoney now, and he was measuring the situation. I kept busy putting the roses in a vase Jake had given me. I hated putting those damn flowers in that beautiful cut glass. I hated the roses. I hated what I was about to do. I carried those flowers to the place of honor on the piano, 'Shall I go?'

"Stony was caught, but he didn't want to upset me anymore, either. 'I'll do it.'

"'The big fat, juicy ones. A real celebration' I hurried him toward the door, promising not to move. I was going to take a long, hot bath. I watched as the two police asked Stoney a few questions. Then the minute he pulled away, I was in the kitchen pleading with Chin.

"'Chin, they've got Jake. They told me to come alone, or they'd kill him. You've got to help me get past those two watchdogs.'

"Chin's eyes almost shut as he considered the situation. 'Too dangerous.' He went back to chopping his onions.

"I grabbed his hand. 'Chin, I don't want to live without Jake.'

"At first, I didn't think he'd help, but then he nodded and put down the cleaver and brought out the bag he carried with him. It was a satchel he kept herbs in. His medicine bag, we called it. I stopped at the door and looked back at him as he pulled small bottles from his sack. 'Chin, don't kill them.'

"'No,' he was smiling now, 'just sleep very soon.'

"I ran upstairs, changed my shoes, and got a gun from the bedside stand. From the back bedroom window, I watched Chin take two cups of hot coffee to those poor fools on stakeout.

"Within minutes, those two cops were laughing and nodding off. I got past them and took Chin's car and went to where I was told, in front of the Leopold on Cornwall. My God, I was stupid. I didn't even think of anyone seeing me driving through Bellingham." The cup rattled as she clanked it onto the table. Drawing the covers up around her neck, she continued in a stilted, remorseful manner. "I didn't want anyone hurt. I just wanted Jake back."

She brooded in her silence. It was disturbing, unsettling. Even though I tapped my cup against the table, she didn't budge.

There was much more to the story. It hung in the air, evasive, not allowing itself out.

"Was he there?" Unable to control my growing impatience, I broke the deafening stillness.

"No," she whimpered. "I didn't know what to do. I didn't have a plan. No one knew where I was, and I was scared beyond belief. I drove through the turnaround and then parked across the street. I got out of the Studebaker and lit a cigarette. Just then, this Ford pulls up, all shiny. The goons. That fat Ceiro told me to get into the car, but I had my gun out before he finished the sentence.

"They must have had orders not to hurt me because they finally let me have my way. I followed them in Chin's car.

"Hell, I didn't know what I was doing. I was trying to act like Jake would, tough, sure of myself. Well, we pulled up in front of this big castle-looking house on Knox Avenue. I parked across the street and followed them with my gun drawn inside my purse. I couldn't have hit the broad side of a barn I was shaking so much. I followed them up the front steps past these two big life-sized figures and past the iron gate. I stood on the porch and looked inside. Across the hall was a large room with a fire going. They stood back and let me cross into the room. Then they shut the doors—those big ones that pull out of the wall—and I was alone. I checked all the windows but saw nothing. The other set of sliding doors was locked. Even though the room was lavish and the fire was going, it had a cold feeling.

"Finally, the big doors slid open, and Antonio sauntered in, impeccably dressed in his fine suit and all. I could tell immediately I had made the mistake of a lifetime. It was in his eyes and spilled across his face. He had me. I was the bait, and I'd walked right into his arms. I was just about ready to shoot him and then myself when I realized he had to know something about Jake or he wouldn't have sent flowers.

"'Where's Jake?'

"'In due time, firebird. Would you like a drink?'

"'No. I want my husband.'

"He laughed at me as he started toward me. I've never hated anyone so much. I pulled my gun out of my purse, and he just shrugged his shoulders.

"'You won't shoot me because if you kill me, my men kill your man.'

"I was like a piece of glass that had been shattered into a million pieces.

"'I want to see Jake.'

"His eyes got darker as his anger passed over his face, dangerous and menacing. He mumbled something in Italian and took a step toward me. But I just lifted my chin and my gun.

"He turned without a word and headed out of the door. I walked behind him up the stairs and down a hall. There were two men outside a door at the end of the hall we were headed for. They stepped aside when they saw my gun, which I now pressed against Antonio's back. I could smell his thick aftershave, and it was making me sick.

"I backed in the open door, but there were no lights on. Something was wrong—I could tell in an instant—and when he flicked the switch, I knew what it was. The room was empty, except for a chest of drawers, vanity, and bed. There was another door on my left. I ran to it. A closet. Then I tried the one across the room. A bath, but no Jake.

"'Where is he?'

"He held up an object I hadn't noticed before, Jake's hat. I stared at it in disbelief. Then he threw it at me, and the gun went off, and he grabbed the gun from me before I could move.

"I wanted to die rather than have him touch me. All I could think of was if Jake found out, if he wasn't dead already, this would kill him. I struggled like a wild cat. But the more I fought, the more he wanted me."

She began to quiver. "What could I do?" Her eyes were magnified by the liquid wanting to spill from them. "I'd gone right to him. What would Jake think?"

"'Nothing,'" I spoke gently to ease her pain, the tragedy of her story flattening my voice. "You did what you could."

She patted my hand as the tears tumbled, splashing on her blanket. "You are so sweet, Jean."

As she pulled a tissue from her nightgown sleeve, I filled her teacup. She drank it down to the last drop.

"Did Jake come and get you?"

"No." She twisted with fright. "No. Jake could never find out what I'd done, how stupid I'd been. I lived each day with the fear he would find out."

I was frozen by her words. It was clear from that night on, fear had been her partner. It was a dark secret, which must never find the light of truth. Jake could never know.

"After a while, there was a knock at the door, and Antonio got up to answer it. I could tell by their voices that it was important. He stepped out into the hall. I ran to the door and listened. It was easy to hear because he was mad as a bull, yelling. I heard Jake's name and knew Jake was alive, and he'd gotten away from them. Feet were running every which way when the door slammed open. Antonio came hustling, pulling up his suspenders, and he wasn't paying attention to me. All I knew was Jake was alive, and I had to get home before he found out what I'd done. I grabbed onto a lamp by the bed as he sat to put on his shoes. He was saying he would return soon for more fun when I hit him on the head ...”

Her hands and face told the rest of the story.

I was panting beside her. I wanted him dead.

“I grabbed my things and got out of there fast, knowing that devil would come around soon. Since most of his men were out chasing Jake, it wasn’t hard. I made it home and past the two guards, who were still lethargic. Stoney was wild mad at me. I ran upstairs barely giving him time to talk. Told him Sally Swanson’s child was sick and I took them some bourbon and I had to hurry because Jake was coming home. I drew a bath and scrubbed and scrubbed. I could smell Antonio’s aftershave on me and it made me sick.” She pulled the blanket back up around her.

“When I came back downstairs later, Stoney didn’t say another word to me. I took those roses and threw them on the fire. Chin brought me some dinner, but I couldn’t eat. It was late. About two-thirty, Jake appeared at the back door. I was just sitting there, watching those blue-tipped flames of the fire. I felt dead. For the first time, I had a secret so dark I couldn’t share it with Jake.

“But when I saw him, it was glorious. Oh, he was a bit bruised and had a deep cut across his forehead. I just couldn’t stop crying. I was jumpy, and I wouldn’t let him out of my sight.” The tremor in her voice reflected the years of sorrow.

“It was dawn when the police arrived. It was that damned Drummond. Antonio was dead. And they wanted Jake for questioning. I’ll never forget the look in Jake’s eyes when they took him. He was handcuffed, those bastards. And he just stopped in front of me as if he knew, but he was still going to take care of me.

“Oh my God, I thought I was going to die. Jake hadn’t killed that black devil. He didn’t kill him. He’d been held and beaten by some of his men, but he’d never seen him.” Her look was frantic as if I was Nate’s grandfather and she was still trying to convince him. “He didn’t do it.”

“How did he die?” It was my patient voice, fearful of learning something I would regret.

"He was shot," she spat the words at me as if a simple bullet was far too good for the recipient.

I felt a sense of relief and didn't fully know why.

"It was the worst time of my life. They kept Jake for days. They searched our house and found some guns but none of them matched. I was sick scared. I couldn't sleep. Finally, they released Jake. There was a big trial and all, but they never did pin it on anyone.

"In a strange way, Jake was kind of a hero. With Antonio dead, the rest of the goons went back home and left us alone. No one saw any of them after that night. Rumors had it that all of them were killed back East, that when they returned the Cosa Nostra gang killed them all out of vengeance for spoiling their chances at our territory. But that was the end of big-time running for us. We hung together, the three of us and Chin, because that's what partners do. But we were different. Stoney never fully trusted me again. He never knew where I'd been, but he was suspicious.

"Jake felt it between us and wasn't sure what to make of it. All that was important to me was Jake never know what had happened. I would do anything to keep that from him, even risk losing Stoney Black.

"I lived in fear. Stoney and I grew further apart. Finally, he took what little money he had left and bought himself a purse seiner and moved up to Alaska, southeast part. Got married too. I was relieved but really missed him."

The rain was slanting, hitting the window. In spots, the drops slid together, making rivulets twisting down the long glass. Even the skies were joining in our sorrow as it hung around us.

"I'll never find it, and I'll never know." Her whisper chilled me.

"Yes, we will." I left the downpour to face her. "Tomorrow will be bright and shiny, and we'll go there and find it."

"No. I can't. I can't make it."

"Yes. It'll be just fine." I could feel her fragile spirit sinking and was determined to be its buoy. "But you'll need to rest up. Come on now." I stood to give her more room on the couch to stretch her long legs.

"Yes, that's right." She turned onto her side, filling the length of the couch.

I put the cover over her, tucking and pampering as my mother had for me. She drew the blanket's warmth closer, almost hiding her face.

"I'll check the tide and be here early. The sun will be all cheery tomorrow."

I reached for the scrapbooks.

"Leave them," she pleaded. "They help me sleep."

I patted the covers, comforting her one more time. Then I left Alex, wrapped in her blanket and memories.

CHAPTER 23

It was just after noon when I arrived at the Wilson Library. I was exhausted. The emotional morning had been more draining than a day's work of digging. I wanted to share these stories, to have another set of ears hear the words to verify their depth and meaning.

With great frustration, I realized I still didn't know what it was we were searching for. I had been too involved in the journey to see the trail's end. What was she hiding that kept her from explaining the search? Bound to my silence, I crossed the rain-drenched lawn to the hall of knowledge.

Lissa's surprise was apparent as she sat behind her desk. Then rising, she pulled me behind the counter. "Look what I've got for you."

I looked toward the direction her hand waved. Waiting in a neat stack were five books of various sizes and shapes.

"That's the complete list he's checked out this summer, except for the ones you've already seen. And he has just one out now."

"Good." I didn't sound convincing as I looked at the work in front of me. "Can you have lunch?"

"Ten minutes," she proclaimed, handed me the pile and turned back to her duties.

I sat in the small room with high windows, the muted colored glass of pale greens and purples soothing. Bent over *Skid Road* by Murray Morgan, I jumped when a finger tapped my shoulder.

"Shhh." It was hard to tell if Lissa's distress was over my racket or the fact I was so nervous.

"Sorry." I was following behind her, juggling my load of books. We stood on the library porch, looking at the big drops or rain.

"Lis, you're sure these are all the books he checked out?"

"On that subject."

"But these all deal with Seattle." She looked puzzled so I hurried to explain myself. "They don't talk about this area."

"Well, there's *The Fairhaven Folktales ...*" Her thought was broken mid sentence. "Why the interest?"

"I don't trust Nate." I wanted to get her off the track.

She stood now, unmoving, rain hitting her unprotected hair, soaking it. "Why?"

"Just a feeling." We'd passed the enormous sequoia tree when I grabbed her arm and coaxed her toward my car, checking for movement, before climbing in.

The large drops pounded against my roof as we pulled into the empty street.

"Lis," I started cautiously, "do you know where I'd find police records from around 1931?"

"No. They probably keep them in the county records." She turned toward me now. "I thought you said the job was over. I thought the books were because you were interested in Nate."

"I am interested in Nate. I want to know what he knows about all of this. Why he's following me."

She looked at me in awe. "He's not following you ... Is he?"

"I think so," I whispered as we pulled up across from the Leopold Hotel, the very hotel where Alex had met up with the goons that night. The ornate, brick building took up most of the block. I hurried Lissa into the Blue Water Bistro, which wasn't crowded, insisting we sit near the window. Placing the stack of books between us, I sat quietly with the morning's memories, giving Lissa time to adjust to her hero's demise.

We were snuggling up to our warm bowls of vegetable beef soup, discussing the stack of reading, when a familiar figure passed through the heavy shower to enter the restaurant.

"Good afternoon." His smile was broad as he peeled his dripping yellow rain slicker off and hung it over the back of a bentwood chair. "Mind if I join you?"

Lissa was aghast when Nate plopped between us. He nonchalantly ran his fingers through his long, thick wet hair, slicking it back, so the drenched strands no longer hid part of his eyes.

"Nice break in the weather." His approach was casual, friendly. "Good for the plants and makes the earth softer," he continued to no one.

I tried to keep the smile from my face, but his magic was powerful, and my spoon hung, waiting for me to regain control.

"Who's doing the research?" He pulled the yellow-bound *Steamers Wake* from the stack. "This is great. Faber did a fantastic job on this book."

I filed his comment and silently pledged to scan that book first.

He leaned back on his chair and flipped through the book. "How's it going? Finished?"

"No," my response was muted as I concentrated on the chunk of beef that bobbed among carrots, green beans, and barley. "The weather was too bad."

"Same here," he brought his chair back down to lean on the table. "Bad for building, but the rum runners would have loved this sloppy stuff."

Nate had his green eyes fixed on me, so I nodded. "So I would imagine."

He was after information. That could only mean he held pieces to the puzzle.

Lissa was caught in our tension and rattled her spoon against the side of her bowl. "Why the interest in rum runners?"

I was surprised by the defensive tone of her interrogation. Holding my breath at her boldness, I waited with her for his answer.

"There was a lot going on during that time. It was pretty lawless, really. Strange happenings back then. Murders. Mafia. I just find it interesting."

"I agree." I wanted to cut him off before he upset Lissa more.

"That's good." He smiled, his words directed solely at me, "I like it when we can agree."

He was teasing me, and I wanted to continue his banter but not now. Not here.

"I'd better get back to work." Lissa was dismissing us. She stood to emphasize her point.

Nate followed us to the counter and ordered his lunch while we paid our bill. We were separate yet very much together.

I watched as the young waitress stumbled though her attempt at flirting with the tall, striking figure beside me, and it made me angry.

"It was nice to see you," I blurted to regain his attention.

"Then you'll have dinner with me tonight?"

The waitress, suspended by his comment, forgot her duties and spilled hot soup on the rim of his plate.

"I can't. I'm busy."

Nate moved closer, insisting, "Then tomorrow?"

The eyes across the counter scrutinized me as she moved to clean up the mess.

"No."

"Please? I just want to talk," his voice was barely audible over the slamming of the ladle onto the counter.

"All right."

"Great." His hand caught my arm. "And, Jean, call me if you need anything." He turned my palm face up and slipped a piece of paper into it. "Keep your doors locked."

He smiled now and walked with us to the door. "I'll talk with you tomorrow then."

Lissa, shifting in her discomfort, strutted past us to stand in the downpour next to the car. Her actions drew me from Nate to her side.

"I thought you said you didn't trust him?" her feelings hurt and confused.

"I don't." I hurried to get us away from Nate. "But maybe he knows something about what went on around here during that time that isn't in these books. He must if his grandfather ever told him stories."

"About what? What's going on?"

"Nothing."

She was angry but smart. Lissa didn't ask any more questions, and I had to wonder what her approach would be. The rain lightened a little as we pulled up to Wilson Library.

"Where are you going?" She didn't reach for the door handle.

"Home to read."

"Call me when you get there."

She gave me a half smile as she left. I sighed in relief, not realizing the tension of our push-pull existence. Keeping secrets was hard and dangerous work.

I waited until her soft pink slicker was swallowed by the old doors before I reached for the slip of paper Nate had pressed into my hand. It was sealed with only my name printed on the outside. Unfolding it I read, "Jean, I might have some information you'd be interested in. If you need anything, call me. Nate. 522-5111."

I touched it over and over again, whispering for my ears only, "Please don't let Nate be my shadow. Let him be my friend."

⸻⸺•⸻

My room was warm and cozy. I slipped into a hot bath, letting the stories drift through at their own pace. The pictures themselves, of smiling faces and happy times, belied the core of the situation. Friendships had been destroyed by the fear of discovery and the inability to re-bridge the gap. The value of trust had never been so latent.

I let my mind recreate the situation, playing each character like an old-time movie. I searched the plot for motives for Antonio's death. There must have been several people who would have liked to have claimed credit for his murder.

And that picture of the three small girls was very curious. Why had she not wanted to share who they were but snatched it up to tuck into the back of her memories?

Eased by the water but not by my thoughts, I dragged myself from the tub to my bed. There had not been any movement on the street, and this comforted a small portion of my anxiety. I snuggled under the covers like the distraught Mrs. McKenzie to set about my task of reading.

Suddenly, I sat up into a new fear. Nate wasn't being my protector. He was following me to be sure I didn't stumble on any new information, something that would implicate his grandfather. Alex had said the police wanted Antonio dead. Maybe Drummond killed him and blamed it on Jake all these years.

The thought of Nate's betrayal sliced deep. I didn't realize how disappointed I was until the full impact hit. Nate's motives were gilded with his own interests.

The uncomfortable discovery stayed with me into the evening. I couldn't shake the effect. The walls of my room seemed to close in on me. The constant splatter of rain added to my confinement. I then realized this was just an inkling of Mrs. McKenzie's restlessness. The depth of her simple act, to leave her home and be among the living, was plastered on every wall I turned to face as I paced the short length of my room.

The course of action was showing itself through my blindness. Get Mrs. McKenzie to the island and be done with it. Help her to alleviate some of her misery by going through the actions of looking. Then, get rid of Nate.

Tomorrow was truly a day of reckoning—a day to clear up the past and open up new futures. Confident in my decision, I tumbled onto my bed to gather sleep.

CHAPTER 24

The clouds and rain had dissipated to a thin layer of fog by morning. Moisture clung to me as I left my dorm and headed for my Volkswagen Bug. All seemed undisturbed in the morning grayness.

The deep sleep, brought on by the rain, was hard to shake. I was apprehensive as to what I would find at the house, and the feeling followed me down the hazy streets to the McKenzie home. Anxiety edged the car down the drive.

The house sat quiet, a beacon of silence. No lights showed through the mist. I sat in my warm car, afraid to knock, afraid Alex was still huddled with her past before the large empty windows. Uncertain of the atmosphere within, I remained in my car, gathering courage.

Suddenly, the back door opened, and Alex stood there, arm waving me forward.

"Come on," she was shouting. "We'd better get started."

With that, her long legs began across the moist grass toward the shed.

I hurried my door open to fall in behind, glad to see her lively step.

"Here," she was pointing toward the tools hanging above the counter, "let's take that shovel and this one here."

She moved to a tall, thick cupboard and opened the door. "I have the flashlights in the house, and we'll grab those too, but we'll take these gloves and a lantern." The lantern clanged in protest as she pulled it from the shelf. "Well," she turned toward me for the first time, "that should do it."

Her eyes, having shed the misery of yesterday, now shone with excitement. "I wasn't sure I'd see you today after all those horrible stories." Her hand took hold of my arm. "I'm tickled pink you're still with me."

I smiled in her shower of appreciation. She handed me the lantern and signaled for us to leave. Loaded with equipment, feeling strong once again, I stepped into the yard.

The sun was filtering through the fog, changing the gray to a brilliant cover of light. We crossed the yard, piling our tools at the top step.

Inside we busied ourselves preparing jugs of water and a hearty lunch. We mixed hard-boiled eggs with pickles, celery seeds, mayonnaise and stuffed it into large pieces of sourdough, then added lettuce. Next, we packed cut carrots, apples, banana bread, and immense slices of dense chocolate fudge sparkled with walnuts. My mouth watered as we filled the basket.

It was eleven when we stood at the break in her hedge, looking down the steps. Below, a thin haze hovered just above the water. Slowly, the sun's heat would dissipate the moisture, and through the thin film, the mouth of the channel would appear. We stood a moment and watched as the fog curled back, opening our path.

We started down casually, hats bobbing, juggling our food and equipment. Piling our load on the sand, we decided to maneuver the empty *Blue* to the water's edge. We set off, steam rising around our ankles as we trudged with the boat. A dense, briny scent hung around us, the perfume of the sea's soul.

Peace surrounded us, the water's surface gentle and smooth as we started out in the mist. With just a few strokes, we were deep in fog, surrounded by gray. The sun's light glistened on the moisture, creating crystal lights that moved with us, spiraling in waves of magic. We were cruising in the mist, swallowed by fog, yet our path was clear.

The exercise felt good after my long sleep, and I leaned into my stroke, bringing with it the deep thoughts provoked by the day before. My eyes wandered to Alex, her head bobbing gently with my pull on the oars. I would miss her. I made a private pact to visit as often as possible. I did not want to lose this jewel with her many facets of light and dark. I had to turn away, for tears were threatening to expose my vulnerability. I had been a shadow dancer, grabbing at the words as footholds along another's path.

The sun drove the rest of the grayness away, and the steep cliffs were far from us now as we left behind the glassy bay to enter the open water. I looked over my shoulder to get my bearing. Across the ripples of deep blue sat the lush, tree studded, emerald mound of Barry Island. In the distance, a large vessel edged into the lingering mist caught between Cypress and Guemes Islands. It promised to be a glorious day. Hitting the port oar, I lined us up for the crossing.

I pulled against the boards, dipping deeper into the cresting waves. Our progress was slower now, and beads of perspiration sparkled across my brow. We nudged along, each lost in her own thoughts and anticipation of what lay ahead. My stroke held the confidence of our pursuit, for truly today would hold long-awaited answers.

"You've been a great help, Jean." Her voice was steady as we rocked through the water. "I don't know how I'll ever repay you." Her eyes, as deep a blue as the surrounding water, didn't flicker as she spoke. "Thank you for listening yesterday."

"I like hearing about your life. It's the best history I know."

"Well, yes, I suppose you could call it history," she chuckled.

I seized the moment and reworded my approach, "But you still haven't told me what we're looking for."

"Haven't I?" It was her rehearsed, high-pitched voice attempting truth.

"No," my stroke matched my frustration, "you haven't."

"Oh." Her finger began to tap against the side of the boat. "A box."

"A box?" I couldn't let her stop now.

"Yes. About this big." Her hands left *Old Blue* to form a foot-and-one-half distance. "Thin." Again the demonstration as the bent fingers moved closer. "Silver. Inscribed with Old English style letters 'J. M. E.' Jonathan Edward McKenzie. I gave it to Jake our first Christmas." She looked away now, concentrating on the green of Guemes.

Accustomed to this approach, I kept rowing in silence, hoping for more.

Finally, she turned back towards me. "He used to keep money in it. 'Funny money' he used to call it. For emergencies or just for fun. He liked to hide it in different places."

At the thought of unearthing a box filled with money, my starboard oar missed the water completely. I leaned forward on the boards, eyes wide. "Money?"

She laughed at my childishness, my imagination longing for a treasure chest.

"No, dear. That's long gone. Oh, it used to be filled, stuffed with big bills. With the trial and us going out of business, well, times got tough. But Jake was a good provider. The best." Her back straightened. "Don't worry. I'll make do."

For the first time, I realized her situation. It had never crossed my feeble mind to wonder how she survived, how the bills were paid, or even where she got enough money to pay me. I was embarrassed by my blindness and wanted to move swiftly past my shortsightedness.

Quickly, my mind picked up the trail of our hunt. A silver box. If it didn't hold money, then what was to be found inside and why had Jake hidden it?

"When was the last time you saw it?"

She blinked at me now, calculating my inquisitiveness. Weighing her words, she began slowly, "Jake was like me. He hated to go to the doctors."

I settled into an even stroke, recognizing the beginning of a chapter.

"My God he was stubborn." Her legs shifted with the agitation of her story. "Damn fool must have known he was going to die. We kept that box on the coffee table for fifty years. We kept pictures in it. I polished that buzzard even when I was mad at Jake. Why," she leaned forward, halting my progress, letting the words slide between us in private, "he even had a secret cubby hole built in our bedroom wall just to hold the box in case of emergency. Fit like a glove."

She leaned back now, concentrating on her tale. "When the money was gone and things were real bad, I wouldn't let him sell it, being silver and all. Then we got back on our feet, and it was about all we had left from our old way of life."

"Towards the end, Jake got kind of restless. He was always digging and sort of jumpy. Sometimes I'd catch him staring at me with a faraway look, as if he'd already left me and I'd never get him back. It was disturbing, and in a way, I felt soiled. I hated myself at those moments." She pushed her chin up, as if tilting back her head would prevent tears from spilling.

"One day, about four years ago, I left Jake digging in his garden and went to town to have my hair done and do some shopping. When I got back, I was walking past the coffee table, and I noticed something was not right. I must have stood there a while but couldn't figure it out. I kept walking over to the table and looking. Jake was watching me from behind his paper but said nothing. After dinner, it hit me, and I went crazy. I looked everywhere while Jake denied knowing anything about it. Everything else was in its place, but the silver box was gone.

"Jake tried to act calm at first, but when I kept coming up with 'Who took it?' or 'Where was it?' he started to get mad at me. It got so bad we couldn't mention it around the house.

"About three months later, September 18, Jake was feeling funny, thought he had the flu, so he went to bed early. When I went up a while later to check on him, he was gone. Poof, just like that. His heart.

"Oh, I was so mad at him for not going to the doctor. But that was the way he would have wanted it. To die in his sleep. We had an agreement, see, no hospitals probin' with their insensitive needles, no machines just to keep us breathing and making the one living go broke." She paused now, looking above at the shore and sky.

I was awed by the concept of their decision. My twenty-two years had taught me nothing.

"But you're never really ready for death when it comes," her voice was as light as the air. "I was in shock for some time. I guess I'd always thought I'd be there to sing him along, sing his damn 'Happy Trails' song or something. Life and death never happen the way you think they will. Those damn dark clouds didn't lift for well over one year. There were days when I didn't think I'd make it alone without my Jake. It was then I started wanting that stupid silver chest more than ever. Something to hold that was just Jake and me. A few months back, I started thinking about how mad Jake got when I suggested he had done something with the box. That maybe he didn't love me anymore. That's when I realized, for some reason, he'd hidden the box."

She looked straight at me now, and her lips curled into a makeshift smile. "So, here we are!" Her hand went up to include the sky, sea, and *Old Blue*.

It sounded so simple. So easy. I watched the mischief in her eyes and wondered at the transformation from her cocoon of yesterday to this lively creature of today.

The shore of the cove was creeping up behind me. The water, flattening near the land, now glittered. Through the seaweed, which now fanned below us, I saw two starfish, one purple, another bright orange, clinging to the same rock, the artist of the sea world at work.

The waters close to shore were warmed by the sun's heat. The cool, deep silt oozed over my tennis shoes as I stepped from the boat and stretched my back. I wasn't exactly tired. I was energized by the excitement of the search. I dipped my hands into the salt water to cool them before pulling the boat up onto the sand.

Mrs. McKenzie worked her way to the bow and stepped onto the sand. She squatted beside me to join in the ritual of splashing water of Neptune onto our faces. It was a glorious, vibrant sensation as the liquid ran down our cheeks, refreshing, then tightening the skin. We sat, huddled, watching the blue waves and sky, salt gathering in rivulets around our ankles like bracelets.

"Shall we go see?" she whispered.

"We'll find it," I turned toward her. A drift of salt had caught in the soft hairs along the side of her face. They glistened in the light.

"I wonder what Jake is saying now, watching us." She raised her face and voice to the heavens, "Enjoying the show? You devil."

Her laughter followed her accusation. Feeling a part of this twisted trail, I joined in. We continued our gaiety as we slowly stood and prepared to hoist *Blue* farther up the shore.

Checking the horizon, she signaled for me to leave the tools. "Let's take a walk."

I watched her in dismay as she started off in the opposite direction, giving her back to the large gray rocks, which covered our destination.

"Bring the lunch," floated back to me from over her shoulder.

I didn't ask but fell in behind her. We covered the distance of the small beach in minutes.

"Go up there," her pointer was directing me up the cliff, "and see if anyone is around."

I set the lunch in the shade of some driftwood and scampered up the dirt-studded face, sensing the draw of the hunt. From my vantage point, the view was reassuring. Nothing moved across the rocky meadow, which led to the stand of trees. The tips of the Two Lovers were barely visible as they dipped in the light breeze, which moved through them to brush against my cheeks.

I did not forget my mission but noted the scenery and water. In the distance, a white sail luffed against the deep green mound of the mainland.

Below, Alex was pointing to the side above the cave. I walked past the peeling, red bark trunk of the madrona to the other side not visible to my boss. A pleasure craft, long, sleek, and white, sporting large work lights suspended aft of the bridge, cruised past in search of the ideal slip from whence to be seen. It was an extreme pleasure craft with the capability of flooding the cherished darkness with its obnoxious city lights. I watched as a woman, precisely dressed for the outing carried her cup down the passageway toward the stern and the blaring TV. I smiled at the vision of the owners of this monstrosity, decked in their whites, venturing into the dankness of our cave. Entertained by my own conjuring, I left their grandness to return to the bluff.

Alex was gone. I didn't dare yell but was suddenly angered by my feeling of desertion. Using the lunch as a marker, I slid down the bank. Where was she? I headed across the beach for the gray sentinels when suddenly I realized the smoothness of the sand, the undisturbed line of seaweed and kelp laced together. I turned back to the brightly striped lunch basket and followed her deep prints until they disappeared behind the rocks on the opposite side.

With each step, my frustration grew. She had purposely sent me up that cliff to ditch me. The cave was just a decoy. The real cache was elsewhere. Convinced by my own conclusions, I squeezed behind the gray mass and hurried in my pursuit of the large brimmed hat, thankful for the easy markings in the sand.

The small inlet ended with more rocks. But instead of her footprints heading inland, they went into the water. I followed only to find myself standing knee-deep in cool water with no shore for quite some time to boast of her path. Water met rock time after time.

The muscles in my legs tightened with the cold now, as I pushed through the chilling liquid. Something splashed behind me. I turned to see the expanding rings from where the object disturbed the surface. Another splash. A rock. I followed the direction of its arch. There above me on a knoll, where grass met rock, stood Alex. She signaled me to return. And in unison, we began back toward our goal, Alex above kicking dirt with her shoes while I pushed through the salt water, watching for barnacled rocks on the sea's carpet.

When we had reached the last mound of rocks before her footprints had disappeared, she waved for me to follow the water to the base of the rocks.

"See the path?"

Before I could answer her, she had started her descent down what appeared to be a ledge, which sloped to the sea.

She was directly above me now, her feet at about my shoulders. "This was another way we'd reach the cave. We'd get up there and walk around to the far side so we wouldn't leave a trail."

I understood what we had been doing now. We were confusing any binoculars trained on us. Making prints in all directions. My head shook in amazement at her crafty ways.

I was just turning to leave when suddenly there was a splash followed by a groan. Alex had slipped on the last part of the ledge. I ran to help her up.

"Stupid," she was mumbling at herself. "I wasn't watching where I was going but checking the boats. Stupid."

I held her arm as she stood, pants drenched to the waist. "Well, that ought to cool me down a bit." Her attempt to make light of the situation worked, and we both giggled.

We headed for the small strip of land with Alex leaning on me for support. She had injured her right ankle, and we wouldn't be able to tell how badly until we emerged from the water. Slowly, the deep cut became visible. Her ankle and the side of her foot had been gouged, and the fine lines left by barnacles tracked up part of her leg.

"Boy, I wish I had some lime juice to squeeze on these barnacle scratches. Keeps the infection out." Her voice was even, not painful, as she looked around. Then her point came up, showing me what she was after. "Hand me that brownish seaweed attached to that rock. I'll crack the bulb open and put it on the cut to slow the bleeding."

I looked at the vegetation and held it up, and she nodded.

"Are you okay?" The deep cut in her leg looked awful, and I hesitated.

"I'm fine." She nodded, signaling for me to bring the slimy greenish-brown bulb to her. "Dumb. But I'll be just fine. I'll keep it in the water for a few minutes, then squeeze some of this in it, helps stop bleeding. But let's get back to the shore."

I steadied her through the slate gateway. A rock protruded out of the water, and we sat her on it. She looked content swirling her leg through the cold.

"That's better." She kept trying to convince both of us.

To keep her mind off, I set about skipping up and down the beach. When I'd reached the boat, I'd take a piece of equipment, shield it from view, deposit it at the mouth of the cave, then emerge again, and run to the other side. Humored, Alex watched my dance of deception, cheering me on.

My task complete, I poured us each a cup of lemonade and walked it out to her.

"Jean, you are a dream. To us," she held her cup high in the ceremony of those who clink their glasses to bind their vision.

"To us," I repeated, never wanting the moment to end.

"Let's have a bit before we're too dirty to want to touch food," she suggested, lowering her injured leg onto the sea's bottom to return to shore. The green salve of the plantain had stopped most of the bleeding.

"Great," I, who am always willing to eat, agreed.

We spread our fare on a flat board tossed ashore in a storm. One side was of rough wood while white paint clung to the other, a reminder of its former self. Someone's dream had found its resting place, and we were preparing to use its scraps as our table. I turned the splintered edge, chewed by the sea, away from us, and brushed the remaining sand from the surface. It was lovely, perched on other logs between us.

The egg salad sandwiches were the perfect temperature and had not gotten mushy, with lettuce that snapped with each bite. I hadn't realized how hungry I was until I saw my first half disappear before Mrs. McKenzie had finished her second mouthful. I forced myself to show some decorum and lingered over the other thick wedge. Carrots crunched and, from seemingly nowhere, chips appeared.

"Let's save the banana bread and brownies for later."

I nodded, hiding my disappointment. I had reached my limit, but that had never come between my mouth and chewy, moist chocolate.

It was harder to stand than I had thought, the food filling both legs, anchoring them. I helped Alex as she favored her bad ankle. The bleeding had stopped, and the cold water had kept the swelling down. Packing up our remaining treats, I hid the striped basket in the shade and followed the undistinguishable set of prints to our destination.

Safe behind the rocks, we set our plan—make the entrance wider and get inside as fast as possible. I took up my old friend, the shovel, and started in, shaking the lazy feeling that follows a large meal. Shortly, the opening was large enough to crawl through, and I began to toss our equipment into the hole.

Alex had been busy collecting branches, which she placed around the entrance, giving us privacy from within. Her ankle, dripping new blood from time to time, didn't seem to bother her as much. Taking off her large brim, she slid into the cave. We stood just inside with our flashlight pointing up, giving an eerie, elongated look to our faces. Our eyes sparkled with excitement as we set about lighting the lantern.

Holding the glowing glass high gave us a perspective on the size of the cavern. It was much bigger than I had expected with what appeared to be a bend in it. At one point, the bumpy ceiling where the roots of the madrona were visible must have been about thirteen feet high. The hard clay earth was spiraled with color and twinkled with moisture. It reminded me of the creatures that live in dark, damp places.

I shifted with this uncomfortable thought and had to force myself to check my legs and pants to see if I had collected any of the unwanted squiggly things on my way in. My flashlight assured me nothing of the kind had found me. Then I noticed the beam hitting something shiny, and I stooped toward it.

"What's that?" the sound of my voice hit the back wall and came at me again. I would have to remember never to raise my voice in the small space.

"Fool's gold. There's a large vein of it in here." She turned from me now, taking the lantern with her. "Here, let's find a place for this."

She searched and settled on a ledge, which jutted out high above us, almost at the center of the cave. "Jean," her voice was low, "can you get this up there?"

We felt for footholds but found none.

"If we had rope, we could loop it through that root and --"

"That's my girl," she was off toward the bag of equipment, leaving me with only my small light.

Her body shielded the lamp and enlarged her shadow, which flickered along the wall in her hip-hoppity way of moving with her injury.

I started laughing and enjoying the magic of our seclusion. I had never known such a thrill, such adventure. My heart raced with excitement, sending a surge of tingling exhilaration throughout my body. Life was good. Mrs. McKenzie was a marvel. And I was lucky.

"Here it is." She stood from her rummaging through the bag. "Now, let's see. Throw it up from this side."

There are certain personalities one learns never to question, and at this juncture in our relationship, I was well aware that Mrs. McKenzie numbered among them. Complying with her request, I went to the other side of the cavern and began one of several attempts to toss the rope through the loop of root dangling from the ceiling. Finally succeeding, we attached the lantern and raised it. Light filled our surroundings.

"This is where Jake used to hide his stash in an emergency. Better than throwing it all over and losing it to those who found it first. It was risky, and we only used it a couple of times, but it came in handy.

"We never kept his money here, though. That's why I'm not sure if that old box is here." She was using her flashlight, running it slowly along the wall to check the shadows. "I can't imagine he would, but with Jake, you could never be sure about anything."

"Would he have buried it?" As if hypnotized, my eyes followed the stream of her light.

"Don't think so. Let's check the walls first." Her hand moved through the air, indicating I was to use my torch to do the same. Flipping it on, I started with the other wall, slowly checking for the silver box. I wandered around the far side of a large outcrop, which formed a bend. There the ground became soft, moist, and my feet sank, covering my already wet and dirty tennis shoes in earth. I stepped back, not liking the sinking feeling and the mud around my ankles.

Our silent search continued for some time before we both ended up back under the lantern. The coolness of the air was making my nose run, and I was growing impatient with this dead-end chase.

"Nothing," I said in disgust.

"We don't know that yet," she soothed, trying to bolster my spirits. "What was back there?"

"Mud." It was a flat reply.

She disappeared around the rocks and was gone for some time before she returned. "Grab the shovel, Jean." Then she was gone again.

I jumped at the shovel and was by her side in seconds. "What?"

"Well, it's a long shot but all we have. This used to go further back. The earth settled here, see." Her bent appendage pointed at a recent slide. "Now this is the place he would hide his special bottles because the walls had holes in them and you could practically just stick the bottles in, cover them with dirt, and pull them out when you wanted. They were easy to find later because the dirt was a different color from the clay. Let's try here. Maybe, just maybe, he stuck that silver box in one of those holes."

I looked at her blankly. Then I saw her crooked pointer go up to indicate my task once again, digging. I followed her direction and stepped back into the mud to begin. Slowly the heavy dirt was moved from the slide. It was hard labor, lifting the damp soil, and my back grew tired.

"Here," she snapped, impatience guiding her command, "I'll try."

She took my place in the mud, sinking past her ankles, past the deep gouge.

"Maybe you shouldn't." I was not comfortable with the exchange.

"I'm fine." Her frustration carried the earth for her.

A short while passed before Alex, spent by emotion and work, leaned on the shovel. We looked at the progress we'd made and could actually tell where the new dirt met the older, hardened clay.

"There's more," she lifted her tired hand only part way. "You can see the difference."

"Here. My turn." I extended my hand to help her. I could feel the weary tremble pass from her to me as she took hold and slowly gained the higher ground.

She sat on a rock, resting, the dankness of the cave filtering through our optimism, soiling it with its darkness. The mood hung around us, defeat reflecting from every wall "It's been so long maybe nothing is the same."

I realized now the adventure was coming to a close as my shovel lifelessly struck the ground. Suddenly, the loosened dirt began to slide, exposing the hard claylike earth. I jumped back, the mud now hidden under soft earth.

"Well," she clapped her hands celebrating the newly exposed walls, "somebody is on our side."

I had to agree, for the wall, now visible, shone with its multi-colored streaks. Empty holes, as she'd promised were dark where the light did not penetrate. The pile at my feet drifted halfway up but would be easy to clear. I began again the draining process of the dig. Nothing. And still nothing as I worked to clear the bottom half of the wall. Each small opening, which surfaced, was empty of treasure.

Alex insisted on taking another turn, sinking past her deep gouge in mud as she stepped up to the task. We played dig tag until only two feet of wall was not exposed. Time worked past us as we continued, determined not to let go of our dream.

I had grown accustomed to the tiny, wiggling creatures whose space we had invaded. Finding them in my hair or crawling up the back of a leg was now part of my occupation, and with a deft hand, I'd fling them from me. I was too tired to hold even fear.

The shovel felt heavy, my back wouldn't straighten, and my feet were iced to the bone from standing in the damp earth when a horrible thought struck me. The row home. I looked at her helplessly, stunned by my realization.

"Yes," she nodded, her voice far away, "I was just thinking the same thing."

As if in agreement, more sand slid from the wall toward my feet.

Alex straightened, blinked twice, while leaning forward on the shovel. "Jean," she drew my attention toward her, "let's pick up and call it a day. We can finish it tomorrow. We have to get home yet."

She was ushering me toward the opening. "Leave the tools here. Jake won't mind. The ornery cuss is the one that got us into this."

Her limp had gotten much worse as she stopped, grabbed her hat, then wiggled out of the opening. "The lantern," she shot back in at me.

After checking the tools, I lowered the rope and blew out the light. The darkness made the cavern move in around me, and I was suddenly scared of being inside the earth. I hurried to the opening.

My eyes burned in the bright sun, and I was disoriented by the brilliance. Mrs. McKenzie also seemed dazed as she leaned up against the sleek gray rock.

We were a pitiful sight. Mud covered legs and trousers, hair streaked with sweat had gathered its own amount of dirt, and our skin had a dingy tinge to it.

"My God, we're a mess," she was squinting in my direction, voice hushed.

I wanted to assure her my view wasn't much better, but her finger to her lips stopped me.

Together, in silence, we worked to camouflage the opening. We followed the stone path, leaving no trace, checking the other side of the rocks for visitors, before we slipped onto the beach. Leaning on each other, like a three-legged racer, we headed for the water, which had now come up the shore to greet us. *Blue* was rocking in the gentle waves, rolling from side to side as the water was not quite deep enough to lift her bow. The current drift had pushed her stern so she was sideways.

"It must be later than I thought," Alex was saying as she took hold of the far side of *Blue* and bent to splash herself.

The salty water was warm where it had covered the heated earth and felt refreshing to my tired limbs. Leaving Mrs. McKenzie, I continued deeper into the chilly liquid and dunked myself, now unafraid of the shocking coldness of the sea.

We moaned and giggled as we spluttered, retaining breath, forcing life back into our depleted bodies.

"My heavens. This is grand." Alex had drenched her slacks, face, and hair. "Jean, do you still believe me that it might be in there?"

I nodded, for surely that cave could hold anything, then dunked one last time. As I reached the hot sand, Alex already had found a seat on a log by our table. I tried to hide my anxiety at the sight of her ankle. It was swollen, and even the salt water did not remove the dirt, which clung to the blood, lingering deep within the cut.

"How about that cake?" She tapped the makeshift tabletop, her fingernails still showing the dirt of our work.

I walked beside my original prints, which led onto the harder sand at the base of the cliff to the shady bushes, which held our tasty morsels. Suddenly, I stopped. The brightly striped basket had been moved, ever so slightly, but moved. There were no animal prints, only mine. But now looking back, I could see what had happened. Someone had come ashore and walked in my tracks to check the basket. The prints that had once held my size-seven shoe were now larger, ridged with a wavy design.

"What is it, Jean?' She was watching me.

"Nothing." I turned and put my feet into the prints, trying to guess at the size of the wearer. When I reached Alex, I realized how stupid it had been to leave the table out, a beacon of our activity.

"I think I left something." I handed her the basket and was off before she could stop me.

I was relieved the same prints did not go near the rocks as I approached the stone gateway. Not wanting to go near the entrance for fear of exposing the path, I turned and headed back along the cliff. The wavy prints were only on the far side of the beach. I turned and ran back to Alex, waving my hat, which I pulled from my back pocket. "Here it is."

I sat across from her, my eyes alert for boats. Where had he come from? We had been lucky. But where was he now?

The chocolate brownie stuck to the wrap, but that did not deter me. I devoured every morsel.

When I was just finishing mine, Mrs. McKenzie handed me the second moist wedge. "I'll stick with the banana bread."

I didn't question her, but accepted the offering. We drank nearly an entire thermos of cool lemonade, leaving just a touch for the row home. I was worried about Alex's ankle and wanted to get home so she could rinse it out properly.

The sun was in my eyes as we started off in *Old Blue*. We were between Barry and the point of Samish when I began to worry. My arms were shaking, and the weekend boats were starting early for the Island Jazz Festival on San Juan Island, making the waters choppier. Vessels, large and small, were emerging from everywhere, filling the horizon with colors.

Mrs. McKenzie slumped against the starboard corner of the transom. The uneven balance of weight made my stroke off center, and I had to compensate by pulling harder on the opposite side. Her eyes were half closed in the afternoon heat, and her ankle, exposed below her dirty and salt-stained tan pants, looked red and festered.

The wound bothered me, but also the distance to shore had my heart racing. I pulled with what little strength I had left, but we didn't appear to be making any headway in the sloppy water. The droning sound of engines blended together in my ears as I attempted to keep my course straight.

I suddenly realized a motor boat had drawn closer and was beginning to slow. I hadn't noticed the Boston Whaler until it was upon us.

"Throw us your bowline."

I didn't question the request but pulled the oars aboard and turned to crawl to the bow to toss the rope.

Alex had pushed herself up and was eyeing the passengers of the Whaler.

"You okay, Mrs. McKenzie?" A mass of blond sun-streaked curls escaped from under the cap of the skipper.

"Hello, Henry." Alex half waved, shifting her bad ankle out of sight. "You remember Nate."

I was fumbling with the bowline when I heard his name, and my head shot up in disbelief.

Henry had cut his engine to an idle. Nate, a blue bandana, rolled and tied around his head, looked more like a warrior than a Scot as he moved aft to catch our line.

"We're building over on Barry, " Henry continued to Mrs. McKenzie above the engine.

"Are you? How nice." Her sing-songy voice held a bit of overacted surprise while Alex's expression was devoid of emotion. "This is Jean."

I nodded at the mention of my name, avoiding the questioning stare of Nate, willing him to silence. I began moving back toward the center seat.

"Stay in the bow," Nate nonchalantly requested as he finished securing the line.

Mrs. McKenzie's arm lifted through the air, signaling for the parade to begin. Henry obligingly shifted around in his seat and gently pushed the throttle forward.

I squirmed from Alex's piercing glare to face the back of the Whaler and the approaching shore.

A thought struck me, and I sat eyeing Nate's feet. I was waiting for a glimpse at the soles of his shoes. Henry had on tan work boots, which covered his ankles, with dusty cotton socks folded over the top of the boot to expose more leg. His heel was up as he rested his weight on his toe. The pattern was straight lines.

But Nate wore tennis shoes. Even though I realized the size of his shoe would have smothered my print, not just covered it, I did not leave my search for the pattern of his shoes' sole.

The Boston Whaler did not throw much of a wake. Nate had fastened our line so we rode the smooth opening of the small rooster tail, my weight holding the bow into the water.

The breeze cooled my burning cheeks, and I was more than thankful for the ride. I kept my face etched in stone as we slid along the water.

Nate leaned forward to talk with Henry, nodded, then turned back to check on us, a smile lighting his face. He toyed with the end of rope, which dangled from the cleat securing us, his hand unwilling to leave its post as guard of our connection.

I turned toward the shore, afraid of the smile bubbling up in reply. But I had carried his vision before me—the broad shoulders, the tan muscles splotched with freckles below the gray tee shirt, and that smile with twinkling eyes.

We passed a deep green sailboat as it tacked its way along the shore. Rounding the tip of Samish, we motored into the bay. Mrs. McKenzie, revived by the light breeze, kept a smile on her face as we scooted along. Ever the stoic performer, there was no trace of the drudgery we had just left except for the streak of dirt that clung to her. But from under the brim of her hat, I could feel her stare.

Realizing her appearance made me conscious of mine. The blush had pinked my cheeks, and I sneaked a glance at Nate. Relieved his back was to me now, I trailed my fingers in the water, then lifted them to splash my face, attempting to erase the sweat from my brow. My fingers caught in my hair, massed together by the salt water and wind, which was now designing my errant strands with its force. My blouse was damp, but luckily, the dip I had taken had removed most of the dirt, only to replace it with the salty stench of the sea.

Whereas Nate had missed my attempt at primping, Alex had taking in my futile process with great interest. I studied her raised brow and tight line of lip. I felt trapped between two strong forces.

Focusing back on the cliffs, I tried to relax. Being the passenger, not the pilot, I enjoyed the ride as we glided along the bay, which was quiet in comparison to the open water. The warm, lazy shore, basked in afternoon light, rose swiftly to greet us. Gulls sailing above the cliff swooped down for a closer inspection, then drifted off again.

Henry cut his engine to an idle as we neared the shore and steep stairs, marking McKenzie terrain. Nate stood and began to untie our line, keeping our boats from hitting by using his foot as a bumper on our bow.

My prayer had been answered. His large shoe was inches from me, its waffle-grid sole a relief.

"See you around six-thirty?" Nate's voice was hushed as he leaned forward to hand me the rope.

"Yes," I gladly accepted, beaming back, comforted by what I now knew. It was not Nate who had followed my prints on the shore.

CHAPTER 25

Henry looped his Whaler back around and waved as we drifted toward shore. Nate and Henry looked like Vikings of the sea, strong, young, fearless, as they set their boat on a swift course for rougher waters.

"Thanks for the ride," Mrs. McKenzie hollered, waving after them.

I watched them for a moment, Nate offering one last salute before he bent into the wind. Alex was watching me again, I knew that, as I moved to regain my position. I dropped the oars into the water to guide us the few feet to the shore. Though the distance was short, the pain was intense, and I opted to slide over the side of the boat splashing thigh-high in chilly water, rocking Alex as I landed. The shock ran through me as I pulled my feet from the muddy sea floor, guiding *Old Blue* to the beach.

Alex's eyes were fixed on me, lips tight, finger tapping the side of the boat. *Blue* was barely on sand when she stood, forcing me to halt my progress. She lifted her bad leg over the side and stood a moment, splashing it. I lifted *Blue*'s bow and hoisted her as far out of the water as possible. Leaning on the boat, Alex limped to the side of *Blue* and waited for me to take my position across from her. The beach remained deserted as we struggled *Blue* to the safety of high ground.

I felt awful, trying not to watch Alex's face, certain I could not endure seeing her pain. I knew her ankle was hurting and she would say nothing. Taking my arm, she made it to the base of the stairs. They had never looked steeper, more angular, more dangerous.

One step at a time, with only an occasional grunt from Mrs. McKenzie, we worked our way to the top.

"Too bad we don't have a trolley," I offered feebly towards the halfway point.

"Humpf," was her only response. Her anger and suspicion of Nate followed us up the stairs.

At the break in the hedge, breath coming in short intakes, she paused. "Oh, God. That was really something." Laughter bubbled in her throat at the journey's end, relief showing in her watery eyes.

"Go on, Jean. I'm fine."

She wasn't, but I didn't want to agitate the situation.

I went on ahead to open the door. My load lightened to a mere empty basket and depleted thermos. Pretty Boy eyed me suspiciously, running up and down his perch silently, cocking his yellow head in his stilted fashion, feathers ruffling.

I dumped the basket on the turquoise counter as he squawked at me, and went to open the sliding glass doors on the side of the house. The afternoon sun blaring through the large glass had heated the room to a stuffy intensity. I heard Alex as she entered, a grunt announcing her approach.

"Jean," she called from the kitchen. "Oh, there you are, dear," greeted me as I rounded the corner. "I can't reach that old cane that's out there above the dryer. Will you get it?"

I went toward the back door. Behind the folding, wood-slatted door, which hid the washer and dryer, I found a deep-hued, wood cane, thick and sturdy with a rubber tip and a beautiful carved dolphin handle.

Alex hadn't moved from her post at the counter. "Here," I offered the walking stick, keeping my fear from my voice. "How are you feeling? Does it hurt?"

Her shaking hand gripped the cane, and she leaned on it with expertise. "There," she tested it, "that's better." She was off down the cool, dark hallway leading to the bathroom.

She winced as she emerged from the half darkness towards me a few minutes later. Seeing the cleaned thermos and the tall glass of waiting cool water, she smiled.

"Before you go, will you help me a little?" She sat at the table, and using her cane as a pointer, she listed her instructions. "Get that pot and fill it with water. Cold water. There's a whole chicken in the fridge and some carrots, celery, and onion. Garlic is on the counter in that jar there."

I drifted through the kitchen in an attempt at following the guiding stick.

Alex gulped down some water before continuing, allowing me time to gather my materials. "Scrub that bird and plop her in the water, throw in a whole carrot and celery stick and just one half of the onion. Add about two cloves of the garlic. Put it on low, and I'll let it sit for a few hours."

I followed the instructions uninterrupted as swiftly as my sluggish body would allow.

"I'm making my German noodle dumpling soup for tomorrow night. Stay if you want." She stood after her second glass of water, inspected my progress, grunted once, and then shuffled toward the living room and the comfort of her large couch.

Watching her, I was beyond concern. "Are you okay? Can I do anything else? Put something on that leg for you?"

"I'll be fine in the morning. Don't worry. Just go over to that cupboard."

The cane led my way to a wood-carved sideboard, which adorned the deep bluish gray slate wall next to the fireplace. I opened the doors to find a few bottles of liquor tucked neatly to one side. Glasses of all sizes and shapes lined the rest of the shelves.

"Pour me some Scotch, dear." It was her innocent voice.

I filled a small glass with Famous Grouse whisky.

"No ice. A touch more. That's fine."

As I brought the brown liquid toward her, she smiled. "Atta girl. Would you like one?"

"I wouldn't be able to drive home." I grinned at the truth.

"Do you go with that Drummond boy?"

Her question caught me off guard, and my hand jerked. A small drop of Scotch ran down the glass.

"No." The statement was too strong and too fast.

"I think he'd like to go with you," she took the glass and sipped, enjoying the flavor before continuing, "and that you'd like to go with him."

My flaming cheeks signaled my response.

"Well," she started up again, interrupting the awkwardness she had created, "I'll see you tomorrow then. After nine. I want to sleep a little."

"Don't you want to soak—?"

"I'm fine," she snapped, eyes unblinking.

I knew it was time to go and left.

———

I barely recognized the reflection in my mirror with my newly tanned body. The lime green cotton blouse with its soft ruffled collar was a dramatic contrast to the sculptured muscles. A new floral print wrap-around skirt hid the defining line where my shorts had protected my white skin. My toenails, now cleaned of the mud they had collected, looked neat and trimmed where they showed through my beige sandals.

I smoothed my curls and hated not having the popular straight hair all the fashion magazines told us we should sport to be attractive. It will have to do, I told my nervous stomach as I hurried to answer the rap at the door.

Nate's smile was mixed with concern.

I immediately stole a peek at my blouse, skirt, and sandals—all were in order.

"You look fantastic," his voice was soft. "But," he held my full attention now, "how did you know it was me behind that door?"

His words worked across my face until his statement hit home, and I nodded at the concept. My excitement had made me vulnerable. I would have to remember that.

"Well," Nate picked up the stilted conversation, "I'm glad it is me."

He brought his hand forward from behind his back. A small collection of flowers sprouted from his large fist.

"Grandmother's garden," he half blushed. "Someone should enjoy them."

"I hope I get a chance to meet her someday." I took the offerings from him. "She must be very interesting."

"Most older people are if you give them a chance. Like Mrs. McKenzie." His eyes were laughing. "Now, I bet she's told you some interesting tales."

"Yes." I turned from him, scooping up a mug and filling it with water as he watched. "There. Thanks, they're beautiful. Shall we go?"

Nate had barely edged into the room before I was ushering him out. "Where are we off to?" I knew I was verging on rudeness, but I just didn't want to talk about our meeting this afternoon until I was sure what he wanted.

"Italian okay?"

"Great."

We were outside now, the sun still high on its arch, filtering through the trees in the mellowness of evening. Instinctively I headed for my VW and stopped short when I realized Nate wasn't beside me. Turning, I saw him standing, watching me.

"Where are you going?" A half laugh escaped. "I thought we'd ride together."

"Oh, yes," I murmured as the pink embarrassment spread across my cheeks.

He waited for me to reach his side before he headed for an old pale green Chevy pickup truck. The water still clung to the edges around the hood from a recent cleaning. He held the door for me as I slid onto the plaid seat cover, impressed by the neatness.

As he rounded the front of his truck, I blatantly followed his form, devouring him with my eyes. My stomach wouldn't stop bubbling at his smile. I wanted to squeal with delight like a child on her first roller coaster ride. His tan pants and pressed shirt eased next to me, and I forced my stare out the large windshield, over the rounded hood to the street.

The truck sputtered, and he coaxed it to life explaining, "She's a little temperamental."

I smiled, avoiding his gaze.

Whistling to Cat Stevens' "Peace Train," filling the emptiness between us, Nate guided us through the back roads of Bellingham to Fairhaven. The old brick buildings made a rich contrast to the newer cement slabs of downtown Bellingham.

"You don't mind a short walk do you?"

The storefronts were lit for night even though the sun was still reflecting off some windows. Not far down the way, nestled between a gift shop and a clothing store, Nate slowed to open the restaurant door.

We stepped inside Vito's, a wonderful, old-style family restaurant with red and white checkered tablecloths and napkins, with the pungent aroma of garlic instantly making me hungry.

The middle-aged hostess, black hair piled in a half-bun, half-French twist, threw her arms around Nate's neck, pulling him down to her. "Nate, so good to see you. How's school?"

"Fine, Joann." Nate released Joann, towering over her and put his arm casually around me, ushering me a few inches forward for the introduction, "This is Jean."

"Welcome, Jean." She looked me over before delivering her verdict. "Such a nice girl." She took my arm to lead us to a private table in the corner by the window.

"So," she was watching Nate, being sure he held my chair for me, "when are you coming back to work for us?"

"I couldn't do that," he was adjusting his own chair to the table as he spoke, grinning, all teeth. "I'd eat all my wages."

Her head went back in a squeal of laughter as she patted Nate once more before leaving. She sang out as she went, "Vito, Nate's here. Get out the cannelloni."

I was memorizing the colors of his short-sleeve shirt, the freckles, and the toned muscles when I heard my name and looked up.

He didn't say anything more, just studied me as if the answers were somewhere scribed across my face. Leaning forward, his work-roughened hands gently took mine and turned them upward, exposing the thickened skin and dents from the blisters.

A carafe of red wine slammed onto the table, followed by a shrill, "Aye! What are you doing to this poor girl? Look at those hands."

I curled my fingers back, but Nate had a steel grip.

"I'm not doing it. I'm trying to get her to stop. Tell me, Joann, what do you see here?"

Nate leaned even closer to me to whisper in a teasing loudness, "Joann has special powers. She can read palms."

"Well," I began shyly, the marks of my work the center of attention. "I doubt she could read anything through these calluses."

Joann picked up the challenge and my right hand, pulling a chair closer with her left. She motioned for Nate to bring the red candle closer before she put her half glasses on and bent her neatly coiffed head over the map of my life.

"Good strong head line, stubborn at times." She winked at Nate over the tops of her eyeglasses. "She won't leave this job until it's done. Don't try to discourage her. Give her support." Her head bent in silence again.

Nate picked up the carafe and poured two full glasses of ruby red Chianti before Joann spoke again.

"Excellent health, very sensitive," she stared in again, her finger poking the flesh around my thumb. She flipped my hand on its side. "Oh," her eyes grew large, "three children. That's good."

Her intensity drew me closer.

"Here," she poked again, "here, there could be trouble, very soon. You have a crack in your lifeline." She grabbed my other hand and sighed with relief. "You'll be fine. You just be careful for a while. I'd like to meet those three children." She put my hand back down on the table, patting it for comfort. "You marry soon. And when you do finish that job, you can always come here. I'd love to have you work for me. Maybe I'd see more of Nate that way."

She stood and put the chair back at the other table. "Are you going to have cannelloni too?"

"It's the house specialty," Nate leaned back, resting his hands on his belly, drawing out the words. "It's the best."

"All right," I gave in, nodding, and reached for my glass of wine to steady my nerves.

We were alone now, and the thumping in my chest was making speech a scary prospect.

"How's your back after all that rowing?" Nate began slowly.

"Fine," I shrugged.

"That's a long row."

"Yeah. Thanks for the ride."

"Do you two row every day?" He was holding his wine now, ready to sip.

"Sometimes," I ventured, not knowing how to answer.

"So how far did you make it today on your excursion?"

"Look," I put my glass down, my stomach knotting, "what is it you want?"

"To help you."

"Right," my sarcasm dripped between us.

A dark look crossed the chiseled face. "Okay. You're right in a way. When I heard you were working for McKenzie, I was curious. I wanted to meet you, and I did. I thought you were nice, and I, well, then I realized you were being followed. I knew you were getting into something you didn't have a clue about."

"Trying to be your grandfather?"

A look of hurt crossed his face. "No."

I stood, "I don't need your help."

"The ladies' room is behind the door to the right." Joann motioned with her head as she approached, putting down two large salads and a basket spilling with fresh, thick bread.

"Thank you." I scurried past her, forgetting my purse.

Behind the safety of the closed door, I looked at the mirror, its rim of ornate, fake gold, a small chip missing from the lower left corner. The room was spotless but small, and it only added to my frustration.

"Nice!" I found myself saying. "He doesn't like me at all. He's just using me because I'm nice. And he wants to know what I know. Nice."

I shook my curls and checked my profile. I wasn't a beauty, but I was tired of being nice. The cold water did not cool my anger, and a big drop found my blouse, darkening it where it landed.

Thwarted by my clumsiness and the path the evening was taking, I flung the door open and stomped into the hallway with its deep red and gold rug. It was a tight passageway where the amber light from overhead threw shadows. Joann emerged behind me from the kitchen, following my stride.

"Jean."

I fought the urge to hurry on and, instead, turned toward her ambling frame.

"Nate's a good boy." Her stare was even as she watched me, and I wondered if he'd encouraged her to speak on his behalf. "You must be special. He's never brought anyone here before." She winked at me knowingly.

"Thank you." I smiled back and turned to enter the main dining room with a lighter step.

He stood to hold my chair as I approached the table, and I noticed his salad remained untouched.

"Truce?" His legs bent as he folded into this seat.

I nodded, a smile replacing my confusion.

"Then I propose a toast." He lifted his glass as his voice rang out, "To Mrs. McKenzie ..."

I listened wide-eyed.

"For having the wisdom to hire you."

A giggle escaped as I reached for my glass to solidify the proposal with a clink.

As our glasses touched, Nate continued in a soft voice, "And, in fate's roundabout way, for bringing us together."

My cheeks resembled the deep red of the wine. I wanted desperately to believe his words.

The crisp salad was chilled to perfection and lightly dressed in a tangy, sweet balsamic vinegar and rich olive oil dressing. I offered my cucumber slices to Nate but coveted the homemade croutons, roasted in garlic, and thick wedges of tomato.

"Vito said enjoy." Joann proudly placed a long, white, oval dish bursting with an array of pickled vegetables, meats, and fresh cheeses.

"Thanks," Nate acknowledged her gift. His face lit up as he hovered over the delicacies. "I used to eat jars of these when I worked here." He pointed to the small yellow corn. "And Vito's cousin makes this sausage. Here," he had grabbed my antipasto plate and was loading it with helpings of every variety.

"Wow, that's enough." I had to take my overflowing plate to make the avalanche of food subside.

We tasted and teased, relaxing now over the age-old comfort of a well-prepared meal. I wasn't certain there would be room for the main course, but when the hot dishes arrived, I unhesitatingly dove into the white cream sauce smothering the dish. I was surprised to find under the blanket of white a spicy red sauce. Lifting the large homemade noodle, I found crab and shrimp meat protruding from inside.

"This is fantastic." I didn't look up but concentrated on my next bite.

"Cannelloni di Mare," his accent was perfect.

I speared a fresh mushroom tempting me as it stuck out of the stuffing, all the while trying to slow my progress.

Where, at first, it was inconceivable I would finish my dinner, as I lifted my last bite, I knew I could devour more.

With some embarrassment, I realized Nate was watching me. His portion had been larger, an extra cannelloni accompanying his serving, and I had been eyeing what remained of the mound of flavorful thick sauces longingly.

"Do you want more?" his hands went toward his food.

"No!" I was horrified by my own intentions.

"It's all that rowing." He used a chunk of bread to push the bite onto his fork.

The comment slid by me in the mellow moments brought on by a delicious meal and the soothing ruby red liquid. The spumoni ice cream had long disappeared, and we sat now enjoying the silence, no longer holding the twitching nerves of awkwardness but the contentment of peace.

"Jean," my mind was pulled back to the table from its wanderings, "I have something I want to show you. Do you want to go and take a look?"

"All right." My smile was trusting, genuine.

Joann followed us to the door while she and Nate exchanged the rituals of parting.

Vito came out of the kitchen for introductions and farewells. He smiled at me while he cleaned his hands on his apron and spoke with his smooth Italian accent, "Tell Nate to bring you more often."

Nate answered for me as he held the door, "Fine by me."

CHAPTER 26

The sun had given into darkness in the warm evening. We drove with the windows down, the balmy air sweeping past my cheeks, lifting my hair. Life was good. I nestled deeper, stretching my legs.

We stopped in front of a large white house. A long porch followed the front to wrap around the side, its ornate railing marching with it. Above hung a single light fixture, illuminating a green door and casting a shadow on the matching shutters, which framed a big window. The rest of the home was in complete darkness.

Nate ushered me from the car to the door, checking the street and his keys.

"Isn't it late to go visiting?" I half whispered, afraid of evoking the wrath of the owners.

Inserting the key, he pushed the door and flipped on a hall light. "No one's here."

I froze just inside the door as I heard Nate lock it behind us.

Passing under an arch, he easily walked through the half darkness to a round table at the end of a large couch. Holding the top of a glass lampshade, he reached under to pull the chain, then moved to a floor lamp behind the overstuffed armchair by the fireplace. As he moved from light to light, neat antique vignettes bloomed into view.

The green couch was spotted with crisp, white, crocheted anti-macassars. The large one, pinned in the center, was flanked by two on the armrests, secured just above the carved wood handles. An overstuffed armchair by the fireplace, somewhat worn, like a loved teddy bear, looked cozy and inviting. Across from it, an old, wooden rocker with fine lines sat motionless with a frail, empty look. A basket overflowing with multicolored yarns brightened the setting.

"Come in," he beckoned. "I'll be right back." He hit the top of the arched wooden clock, and the room was filled with a light melodic ticking.

As Nate disappeared through the far arch, I walked past the one above me, lingering at the photographs, which adorned the walls. On the mantel, a gilded frame held the picture of an elderly couple. The man's imposing figure occupied most of the picture. His arm was draped around the petite figure next to him. Not even reaching his shoulder, stood a small woman with a cap of tightly curled white hair. She held her purse in both hands in front of her bright floral dress.

The face of the man drew me closer, the older image had the same full lips and shape of broad brow as Nate. I turned with fresh eyes to examine the home of the man who had put Jake McKenzie behind bars.

I heard Nate upstairs now as he went down the hall, the sound of his steps spilling down the front stairs. With a few giant strides, he was beside me.

"Want something to drink?"

I checked the snide remark edging toward my lips and replaced it with a terse, "Water."

Nate was off, flipping on lights again. I followed his path this time, past the polished dining table and sideboard displaying plates with green ivy leaves trailing around the edge. The kitchen had a high ceiling with long, tall cupboards. It was, if possible, even cleaner than the rest of the house.

"How long has your grandmother been sick?" I was standing by the shining enamel stove and didn't see a speck marring the smooth surface.

"She's been in the nursing home for about two months." He didn't register surprise at my question but remained concentrated on his task, turning on the cold spigot to let it run.

"So, I've been staying here."

I regarded the broad back with new insight. "You don't cook here, though."

"Usually every day. I'll make you dinner sometime," he extended a glass in my direction.

"You must have cleaned all day."

"Just the truck."

I didn't want to touch anything. I thought of the time he had come into my room when the floor space was hard to find beneath the mess I had left in my exhaustion. My heart sank. Anyone this neat was beyond my comprehension. My private hope of Nate seeing me as anything but "nice" burst, dragging me with it.

"What's wrong?"

"Nothing."

"Well, come on then. I want to show you something."

I led the way as directed through the dining room to the living room. He went to the mantle and held the picture towards me. His voice held the reverence he displayed, "This was the last picture of Grandpa."

"The famous sheriff?"

"Among other things," he shifted, brushing off my rudeness, continuing with his description, "he loved to fish, grow rhododendrons, and work at the Boys' Home."

I took a closer look at the resemblance between the man holding the picture and the one captured there in print. "And your grandmother?"

"She lost her spirit when Grandpa died. She tried hard, but she fell a few months back and really hurt herself. We tried having her at home, but she just got weaker. I hate the nursing home. It's killing her." He turned back now, the muscle on his cheek contracting as he held back his frustration.

"I'm sorry." I wanted to reach out to him, to mend the wound, to hold him tight until every ounce of guilt was replaced with the knowledge and understanding he had tried. There is no stopping time.

"But that's not what I wanted to show you." A grin pushed his long face up, "Come on."

Nate took the lead this time, excitement in his step. He was at the base of the stairs, looking up them.

"You won't believe what I've found," he waited for me to approach, his voice drawing me closer.

I hesitated, looking up the wooden railing.

"I didn't know anything about Mrs. McKenzie or her husband until a few months ago."

I was hooked. If he had information, I needed it more than he did. I cautiously began to climb.

"They were quite famous around here, you know." Nate fell in behind me.

"No, I didn't," I was thankful he couldn't see my face as I lied.

"When Gram got sick, I moved in here to take care of things." He hurried past me, leading me down the hall.

The second door, cracked slightly open, emitted a shaft of light. As Nate went on ahead, I paused at the door to take a peek.

Inside, the walls were covered with dark wallpaper, a farm scene running down them. The deep brown bedspread only half covered the bed. Nate's work belt hung from the back of a chair, and shoes were sprinkled across the floor. A pile of newspapers haphazardly spread out in a corner.

"No fair," his voice made me jump. Then he pushed the door open wide. "Take a look, but it's a mess."

"It's human," I was embarrassed by my own reply. "Sorry, I didn't mean to snoop."

"Snooping isn't always bad." He started down the hall again to open the far door. "If I hadn't been going through Grandpa's papers, I never would have found it."

He paused briefly, checking my expression, which undoubtedly told him what he expected. I couldn't wait to see what he had.

The door opened to a room with walls covered in knotty pine. A bay window extended out over what must have been the side garden. The slightly faded, deep red cushions covered a widow seat. Clearly the sheriff's domain, a massive oak desk and worn red leather chair occupied the side closest to the windows, while bookshelves adorned other walls. A rich oriental rug spread out before us.

Nate went to the bookcase, which had cupboards at its base. He stooped to open the wooden doors.

I walked to the opposite wall and slipped behind the desk to get a closer look at the photos hanging in pride, tributes to a lifetime. Dead center was a picture of two men draped in tailored suits, shaking hands. The one on the left could have been Nate, except the one on the right was President Theodore Roosevelt.

"Wow," my awe escaped.

"Isn't that great?" He carried a wooden box towards me. "Roosevelt was staying at Roche Harbor Resort when Grandpa met him."

"Roosevelt was in the San Juan Islands?"

"Yep. Only someone stole the page from the log book at the Hotel de Haro. You know, the one he'd signed when staying. Too bad."

"Disgusting."

"I think he was more proud of this," He moved closer, his arm reaching toward the wall, pinning me.

It was a plaque which held the crest badge of Drummond on top of a piece of clan tartan and a Scottish phrase below. "Gang warily," Nate read for me, adding his own intonation of the Scottish brogue.

I looked up at him.

"Go carefully," he interpreted the phrase as his eyes met mine.

We were almost touching, and I couldn't breathe. I adjusted my stance.

My action propelled Nate into movement. "Oh, right." He turned and headed for the red cushioned window nook. "Have a seat."

When I stepped from behind the desk, I noticed a long, dark brown leather couch and realized he'd chosen to sit in the middle, giving me little option but to sit near him. I sat avoiding his touch, eyeing the oblong cedar box secured between Nate's large hands. Across the top, two copper hinges ornately spread into an intricate Scottish thistle design.

Nate reverently ran his hand along the smooth, shiny surface as he spoke. "When I asked Gram about this," he tapped the top of the box, "she told me to leave it. Let the past be. Said it haunted Grandpa until the day he died."

My mind would not be still. I sat before a wooden box, which could easily hold the silver one I had spent my day in search of. My fingers twitched to pry it from his grasp and fling it open.

Finally, Nate opened the lid, and to my relief, the glint of silver did not meet my anxious stare. Instead, stacked neatly, layers deep, were clippings from newspapers. Nate slid his hand into the box and with a practiced flip of his wrist, lifted the entire pile of newspaper, exposing an old, green file folder.

I sighed, slightly glad the box held nothing more. My reprieve was momentary. Nate handed me a page he had selected, and I opened the yellowed newsprint. There across the top in bold letters was the bold heading, "McKenzie Being Questioned, No Murder Weapon, Only Motive."

Below an insert held two pictures, one of Jake smiling in a nice suit, the other one I had never seen. "Antonio Vitrona, Mafia bootlegger."

I studied the handsome Italian face with the practiced glare, emitting a feeling of superiority. There was no questioning of Antonio's authority, his disdain for the common. A refined exterior disguised the slime that oozed within. Hatred etched his handsome face with the scar that ran from ear to chin, giving him a curious attraction all his own.

"Here's where McKenzie was released," Nate pointed out, interrupting my thoughts.

There was a small picture of Alex, Jake, and Stoney, arm in arm, leaving the courtroom.

"But he didn't do it." I took the paper from him, hoping my action would cover the fact I had lied early, that I did indeed know how famous the McKenzies were and had knowledge far beyond the printed word of this newspaper clipping.

"Who did then?"

"Maybe it was one of Antonio's men." I was relieved he had let my admission slide.

"No. They would have done it execution style. A bullet in the head."

"Maybe it was a policeman."

He stiffened beside me. "They would have been heroes if they had. But it wasn't."

I didn't push the theory. "Maybe it was someone from back East."

"So, she has talked to you about it a lot."

"No," I spoke too soon, afraid I had exposed too much of the information. I would have to be more careful. "I mean she has mentioned a little about it. Just that the Mafia wanted in this territory."

"You bet." Nate smiled. "And whoever killed this scum," his finger rested beside the photo of Antonio, "is the one who stopped the Mafia from spreading out here, as far as I can figure." He retracted his hand to push a strand of hair behind his ear.

I watched the simple motion and was drawn in by his honesty. I desperately wanted to believe he was on my side. Maybe the contents of this box would help me to trust. "Have you read all of these?"

"Three, four times."

"What's this?" I pointed to the green folder. I needed to know everything he had on the subject.

"That," he heightened my interest by taking it out, "is a copy of what the doctor wrote."

"The coroner's report? You're kidding!" I checked my overeagerness by faking a yawn, "Well, that must be interesting."

It was clear to me now what I had to do.

He was watching my performance, unconvinced, when suddenly the color drained from me. The scream wanted to come, but I made no sound in my fear. My body shook, and I raised a hand toward the window.

It was too late. The face, darkened in the half-light, had disappeared, leaving only the sound of footsteps as the intruder hurried along the roof.

Nate was across the room and out the door, shouting back at me, "Stay here." I heard the pounding beat as he ran down the stairs, the turn of the lock, and the screeching sound of tires as a car farther down the street pulled away.

Regaining my breath, I picked up the folder from where it had landed on the rug and slipped the doctor's report from the cover.

"Damn." The door closed again, and the lock pounded into place. He was racing back up the stairs.

I stuffed the article with the pictures and the autopsy report inside a magazine cover on the desk and was just piling the other news clippings and papers back inside the box when Nate entered.

"You okay?" He grabbed my arm and pulled me towards him, the tightness of his grip a reaction to his anger and frustration of what we suddenly both acknowledged. The shadow had been tailing us, probably all evening.

"Yes."

He released his hold, but his eyes didn't leave me. "Did you see who it was?"

"No. Just a dark face. Do you think he was there long?"

"I don't know."

"Who knew we were going out tonight?"

"Lissa."

"She talks too much."

"What? Don't you ever—"

"I mean in a helpful way, but she doesn't realize how much she tells."

He had used her for information about me. He was blatantly admitting the fact.

"Look, Jean," he pulled me away from the window to the couch. I sat with the box on my lap, watching him pace, his hand in frustration running through his thick hair, the copper color intensified by the overhead light and the gruffness of his mood, the Scot in him evident.

"I don't know what Mrs. McKenzie is doing with you, but she's obviously stirring up dust. Old, dangerous dust. This just proves what Grandpa believed. The murderer is still alive. He said so just a few years ago in some notes I found tacked onto the doctor's report."

"Nate," I startled him, suspending his movement for the box, "I'm tired and scared. Can I go home, please?"

The steam drained from him as he plopped down beside me. "Jean, you have a right to be scared. I think you must be getting close to something."

"Not now. Tomorrow night," rushed from my lips. In a further attempt to draw him from the room, I stood and spoke calmly, "Put the box away, and let's go through it tomorrow night. It's late."

Dutifully he took the closed cedar box from me and started for the cupboard. "All right. We can eat dinner here and work on this."

He carefully secured the doors. Nerves buckled my knees. How was I going to get the magazine out? How would I explain my actions when he discovered the papers missing?

"Are you sure you're okay?"

"Exhausted," I admitted, near tears.

His arms went around me and drew me toward him. "It'll be fine. We'll work together and get this settled. Let me help you."

I tried to speak, but my throat contracted into a tight lump, restricting my breathing to small, shallow bursts of air. My head slumped against him. Something was not adding up, and I needed to find out without giving away any of what Mrs. McKenzie had entrusted to me. I had to do it. I had to get those papers, I told myself. I pressed my eyes closed, squeezing tears onto my cheeks, letting him hold me, knowing when he discovered the missing papers we would never touch again.

My desire to stay was overpowered by the reality of what I had just done. What had possessed me to attempt to steal those papers? How would I get them back into the box? I stepped away from his hold.

"Want to go?"

I nodded, afraid to speak, my eyes fastened on the corner of the desk where the magazine held the secrets. I was overwhelmed with the feeling of failure as I realized there was no way to escape with what I had stolen.

The fresh air made my damp cheeks tingle. I tucked the address and description of the house into the folds of my memory. There must be some way to get those papers.

My mind was drained, blank, as we pulled up in front of my dorm. Nate's opening my side of the car vaguely registered. I hated myself for my behavior and knew, once I was discovered, he would never trust me again.

"Nate," I attempted to explain to both of us why I had hidden the papers, but the whisper of his name was all I could get out.

I unlocked the building door, and we started through the halls. We were an odd couple as we trudged along. Nate was a cat on the prowl, muscles tight in concentration, ready to spring, where I was a limp rag doll, deflated, vulnerable.

We opened my door, and Nate followed me inside. I stood motionless while he moved from window to closet, his actions nailing my feet with solid fear.

"I'm sorry, I …" I began to shake.

"It's not your fault." His arms went around me, offering his strong chest and comfort. I snuggled into the calmness, only to discover the fast beat of his racing heart.

"I'm so sorry," I leaned back, my strength and speech prepared, "I shouldn't have taken—"

His lips stopped mine as small, gentle kisses caught my breath, stalling my courage. Slowly I returned a kiss, and his arms tightened as did the passion of his lips.

The tingling spiraled, swirling, journeying through me at will, reaching hidden and secret coves of yearning. Desire held us as we clung to each other, exploring the tantalizing sensation. Hunger built our fire.

A knock sent new shock waves through us. We stepped apart, our blush forgotten by the urgency to identify the intruder.

Nate slid to the far side of the door so he would be concealed when opened.

"Who is it?" my voice cracked at first use, passion tumbling to fear.

"Me," Lissa whispered. "How was it?"

I hurried to open the door before my friend barraged me with embarrassing questions. "Fine."

"Great. What happened?" Her eyes reflected her surprise as Nate emerged behind me. Now it was Lissa's turn to blush.

"Oh," she gathered her bathrobe, "sorry. I was just checking in."

"Good," Nate moved past me into the hall. "Keep checking." His stare backed Lissa across the hall to her room.

"Sure. Good night." She hurried behind her door for one final peek.

"I'll see you tomorrow," his voice was warm, reassuring, as he grinned in my direction. "But keep these doors locked. Both of you."

Lissa closed her door, and I couldn't help giggling. Nate took my face in his hands and gave me one last kiss.

"Get some sleep," he commanded, closing my door for me and waiting to hear the lock secured into place.

Alone, still reeling from his sweet affections, I jumped onto my bed, wide-awake with the lingering warmth of his touch. Suddenly, my eyes clammed tight. My mind, a neon print of disturbing memories, flashed my actions before me. My heartbeat quickened as I saw my hand snatch the folder, fumbling the evidence into hiding. Over and over, the scene repeated to mock my joy as tears, spilling from tortured depths, slid down my face.

CHAPTER 27

Morning broke slowly as I dragged about my small quarters. I was glad this week was ending. My time with Mrs. McKenzie seemed to have extended a lifetime instead of just two weeks. I felt drained, like a prisoner waiting for the verdict, and I slumped in my chair.

On a whim, needing the tranquil tones of my mother, to know the entire world was not spinning at such a pace, I called home. There was no answer. I pictured where my family might be and longed to be at their side, still pressed to the innocence of family and friends.

I could leave now, I told myself, and be home in four short hours. There I could find peace. There I could find the strength to erase all that had happened and start all over. Be a nice girl and marry a boy from home. I never should have left.

My head was resting on my desk when a pounding on my door snapped me back to reality. Nate had found I had taken the papers.

"Wake up. Let's go have coffee."

"I'm up." I opened the door, relieved it was Lissa. She bounced past me.

"You don't look awake. Come on. Let's go. Then you can drop me off at work."

I studied Lissa's modest shorts and matching blouse, the bouncy trim of her hair. My condition reflected my anxiety, my usual precision reduced to a wrinkled shirt and dirty shorts.

"Change out of your pajamas first," she coaxed and tried for a smile.

I didn't want to tell her I already had, so I rearranged myself as quickly as possible.

"So?" she rocked from heel to toe, "tell me."

"What?"

"What happened last night?"

"We had dinner," I shrugged, brushing my mop of curls.

"And?"

"Nothing. The food was great."

"Is that all?"

"Yes."

She attempted to bury her frustration yet could not stop her question, "But you're seeing him tonight?"

"I doubt it." I was as complete as any kit could get, given the components. "Come on, Lis, let's go."

<hr/>

We sat on the library steps, looking across the green lawn leading to the brick structure of Old Main Hall. Our paper cups of steaming brew rested between us. Lissa, having left her prying back at the dorm, settled into a light conversation about graduation. I listened with little interest.

At nine, I briefly followed her inside to toss my empty cup away. As I stepped back into the morning haze, I saw a car slow next to mine. I jumped back into the shadow. The car sped off, racing as fast as my heart.

I was overreacting, I told myself as I carefully circled through the city, backtracking, watching. Soon I was in front of the white house on Knox Street with green shutters and a long covered porch.

In daylight, the details of wood around the bay window showed the craftsmanship of old. The neatness of the railing, the sconces, and the pillars bore the pride of the owner. Sheriff Drummond had kept his home in impeccable order.

An engine from across the street stopped, silence filling the drone of the mower. I turned to see a neighbor. Leaving his task of cutting precise grooves in the deep green lawn, he watched me. Hand on hips he stood, waiting.

I nodded and pulled away. I couldn't break into a house in broad daylight. I was swiftly losing my senses. My only comfort was by this evening all would be over. Nate would have discovered the papers missing, and for the last time, Mrs. McKenzie and I would have ventured to the cave.

The cave. The thought of ending this chase put me in motion for the first time all day. We would go there. We would solve this mystery. If only I knew what those papers held.

I had grown accustomed to seeing the house dark in early morning. Unconcerned with the stillness, I forged forward with intent. The back door was unlocked, and when Alex didn't appear, I let myself in.

"Mrs. McKenzie?"

There was no answer from the kitchen. I stepped toward the light of the living room windows.

"Mrs. McKenzie. Alex?"

The couch held only a dent from its former occupant. I sought other clues as to where she might be—the crumpled blanket, remnants in an empty glass, but the book of photos gone.

My heart started beating faster, an unusual fear gripping it.

"Here," the voice sounded weak, uncertain. "Here, Jean."

I went toward the downstairs bedroom, the extra room just past her office. There in half-light, curled in a fetal position was Alex.

"Are you all right?"

"Yes," she sounded tired. "My leg's a little sore. Kept me up."

I stood confused. We had to get to the cave to finish what we had begun. There was no time for delays.

"Here," she lifted her arm, "help me to the couch for a spell. Then we'll go."

Relief at her words flooded through me, unfreezing my feet.

Slowly and with caution, for she moaned with movement, I helped her stand. She was heavy today, heavier than she had ever been, and I realized I was not assisting her but carrying her. My heart, the heart that knows more than the mind, beat faster.

"Have you eaten? Would you like some coffee?" I had lowered her onto the couch. In the bright light of the room, I could see she had changed her clothes but they were wrinkled. She must have slept in them.

"Coffee." Her eyes rolled back, and she fixed them on the sea outside.

I hurried to the kitchen. Pretty Boy eyed me as he watched me scurry about the kitchen in a state of harried concern. Even he was subdued with anticipation. This could not be, I kept telling myself. I'd make her eat something so we could go. We had to get to the cave soon.

I noticed the pot of chicken soup I'd started for her was in the refrigerator when I opened it for some butter for her toast. Taking a tray of coffee, toast, and fruit, I placed it before her.

"Here you go." I had to help her sit up, pour the coffee, and insist she eat. My nerves rattled continuously by her lack of strength and spirit.

"Let me see your leg." I moved swiftly before she could stop me.

It was oozing, surrounded with bright red inflammation.

"Shall I call a doctor?"

"No," she half spit at me.

"How about Mr. Chin?"

She waited before she answered, "He knows. He's coming."

"Good," it was my mother's tone. "We'll wait for him."

"Get the book, Jean."

I knew what she meant and went to the small bedroom to find it. Searching, I uncovered it between pillow and sheets. She had taken her memories to bed with her, to cling to their existence, living vividly yet in her mind.

She was sipping her coffee, now a light color returning to her cheeks. "That's better."

I took up my place next to her, gently offering the photo album.

She flipped through the first few pages we had already seen to slow at a page filled with pictures of a building, its curious angles catching my eye.

"This was one of Jake's favorite places to visit when he went to Seattle. It was on what became Lake City Way. But back then, it was considered out of town, just outside the city limits. My god, we had fun there—bowling alleys, underground tunnels that went to houses."

"Houses?"

"Houses," she sounded testy at my ignorant interruption. "You know, houses where the girls were."

She looked at my astonished face.

"Damn it, girl, how am I going to tell you all of this if you don't understand? Whorehouses. Tunnels to whorehouses. They blocked them off after the end of Prohibition. Sold the joint to a foreigner, and the damn fool burnt it down for the insurance money, so they say."

"Here." She pushed the book toward me and slumped back onto the couch. "I can't do it. It's too late. I'm just not strong enough. Take it away. It's over."

I sat motionless, watching her closed eyes.

"Go on. Get it out of my sight." Her hand waved toward me. "I need to rest."

Pretty Boy squawked and paced on his perch, ruffling and unruffling his yellow feathers, the scene disturbing to him as well.

I stood with nowhere to go. Finally, afraid to venture too far in case she wanted to try the journey, I placed myself at the kitchen table and pored over the book.

There were no articles on the incident. No stories of murder and rape. Only the smiling faces of the trio posing, hiding the darkness to shine through on these pages. In each picture, they frolicked at a beach or on a boat without a hint of danger. Stoney's massive, hairy chest exposed as he worked on the boat engine. Alex in her swimsuit, sitting on a beach with tall evergreens behind her. Jake, cap at a slant, holding a large silver salmon and a skinny rod. I remembered the picture of the three young girls with the bows in their hair and flipped to the back of the book. It was gone.

A knock at the back door startled me at first. Remembering Mr. Chin was expected, I hurried to let him in.

There, waiting patiently, stood Nate.

I stepped back, swallowing hard.

"Good morning, bright eyes. Can I talk with you a minute?" He kept a polite distance with a crazy grin covering his face.

"Yes." I did not budge from behind the door.

"Come here."

Only the muscles in my stomach moved, tightening. I hated what was about to happen.

"Come on," he reached for me, and I let him take me. This discussion was best away from the house. His grip was firm but gentle as we headed toward his pickup.

I was surprised when we went beyond the front of the side panel toward the rear of his truck. Relax, I told myself, he's not going to kidnap you in broad daylight. I opened my mouth to speak but then snapped it shut. I had no excuse for what I had done.

"I've got something for you." He released me, and I instantly backed away. Ignoring my movements, he worked the tailgate. It flopped down, exposing a small outboard motor.

I looked from the engine to Nate, not understanding the offer.

"It's for that little boat of yours." He was pulling it toward him. "It's a ten horsepower, so it should get you there and back."

He turned to smile at my still blank face.

"Why aren't you at work?" my suspicion his gratitude.

He stopped to face me full on. "Fridays are slow sometimes. We're waiting on materials and ahead of schedule. If you don't want it, just say so."

"No," I hurried to accept, the realization I hadn't been found out yet slow to work through my jumbled mind.

"Great. Then come on, and I'll show you how to run it."

"Just a minute. I'll check."

"Meet me down on the beach. And bring that red can. Be careful. It's heavy."

I crept back into the house. How was I going to explain this to her? The enemy had come bearing gifts.

Mrs. McKenzie was fast asleep, her wild red hair swirling around her peaceful face. I covered her, tucking the blanket around her legs.

Wasn't it wonderful! By the time she would wake up and be ready to go, we could just jet across the bay with our motor. She would be thrilled. I winked at the silent bird as he watched me swiftly write a note for Alex and Mr. Chin, saying I would be back soon to explain.

Checking for my cap and sunglasses, I hurried to the break in the hedge and had to double back for the red can. Nate was right. The tank was heavy and sloshed as I moved, emitting the stench of gasoline. I struggled with it back to the stairs. Below, Nate was just reaching *Old Blue*, the weight of his gift slowing his pace as he paused for air.

Relieved that my impulsive actions of last night had not been discovered, I paced my steps down to the beach, shifting my load from hand to hand. Nate was sitting on a log, his bandana now secured around his forehead, perspiration marking his tee shirt.

"Those are some steps." He stretched out, catching his breath.

"Where did you get it?"

"Henry's had it in his garage for a long time, and I talked him into letting you use it for a while. That is, of course, if I taught you how to use it."

"Wow," was all that would emit from my bedazzled state.

"Let's get the boat down first."

We hoisted *Old Blue* to the water's edge. Nate enjoyed watching me work, and I couldn't help but return his smile. The sun sparkling on the water and the salt air expanded in my lungs, releasing my tension. This was going to be a day to remember.

He lugged the motor down to the rear of the boat and secured it to the transom. The tanned sculptures of his powerful arms held my attention as they worked to connect the gas tank to the motor. He caught my gaze, and I turned to occupy myself with washing my face with seawater and playing tag with the tide. I felt the child again. Free to explore, to run against the wind and succeed.

"Okay," he drew me back, "let's try her."

I climbed in and sat where he indicated, in my oarsman's seat. He pushed us out, then stepped into the stern, his weight lowering the boat farther into the water than when Mrs. McKenzie was aboard.

"Keep the engine in this upright position until you are out deep enough for the draft of the engine," my instructor began. "Then flip these levers and lower it. Or raise it like this." He lowered the engine a bit to show how it would swivel up and down. "Always check your gas tank. Lift it to see how heavy it is. But if there is water in the boat and the tank is in the water, be sure to lift the tank out of the water. Otherwise, the suction of the fluid around the can will make it seem heavy. You need to get the gas into the engine to get it to start, so give this bulb a little squeeze."

I leaned closer, intoxicated more by his nearness than the fumes. I nodded.

"About three pumps. No more than five. You don't want to flood it." He demonstrated by pumping the black rubber bulb lodged on the hose running between the tank and the engine. "Set your throttle to idle and then cross your fingers." He grabbed the pull rope to kick-start the engine, and it trilled to life, blaring noisily back at us, with blue fumes drifting behind.

My hands clapped together in excitement as Nate pushed the lever to forward and steered us out into the deeper water.

We putted along, "When you want to turn, push the handle in the opposite direction." He demonstrated his ability time and time again.

I enjoyed the excuse to watch him move, to observe the child-man in his element on the sea.

"Here. Your turn." He pulled the lever to neutral and was moving before I could react.

I countered to his shifting game as we brushed arms and legs, sending desire through me.

Blue, left unattended, was setting a course of her own, slowly circling. I grabbed the handle tight to regain control and pulled it too swiftly toward me, almost tipping us.

Nate clung to the far side in mock horror. "No drag racing," he shouted above the rattle. "Easy."

As I felt my way through the turns, comfort settled in, and I was thrilled by my new accomplishment.

Suddenly, Nate leaned forward and threw the throttle to full, the bow lifting in response. Terrified, I overreacted and almost swamped us again. This time Nate was pure concentration as he watched my movements, his green eyes hard as steel, the grin now a straight line.

I wasn't sure which I feared most, his unwavering glare or the speed of the small craft. I looped us back towards shore. He reached forward again, throwing the throttle back, killing the engine. In deadening silence, we slid across the water until we sat rocking on the small waves.

"Why are you heading back in?" Nate's voice held a hint of accusation.

"I don't want to leave the bay."

"You don't want her to see you go outside into the straight with me?"

"Yes." I was being honest. It had never occurred to me she might be watching.

"Okay," he dragged out the word. A muscle flinched on his jaw again, the indicator of building steam. "Listen carefully then. Take waves head on and not fast, especially large ones. You have the right of way, but sometimes, large vessels can't see you. Someone might try to swamp you, and if the engine stalls in his path, it could be dangerous. Never go out without your oars and life jacket. If for some reason, you are being chased, remember you can't go fast, but you can get in closer to shore than most boats. And just run the damn thing aground if you have to."

I trembled, wanting to cry. His anger was not at me but at the unknown element staking my movements.

"I wish you'd let me do more."

I blinked back my tears to speak, "Thanks."

"Okay, you start the damn thing."

I couldn't help but feel the brunt of frustrated moods today, Mrs. McKenzie's pain pushing her temper and Nate's anxiety triggering his. I turned my own pent-up feelings loose on the pull cord, snapping it until the engine roared before me.

Time and time again, Nate would shut the engine, forcing me to start it. In silence, he challenged me until finally he grunted and pointed towards Alex's stairs.

"Cut it," he hollered. "Now pull it up."

"What?" I turned the engine off.

"Pull the engine up."

My hand sought the lever. With no aid from my teacher, angered by his abruptness, I struggled until I found the latch that released the engine and pulled it forward with a thud. It hung in the air, dripping water from its propeller. Nate reached forward and deftly locked it in position.

We had drifted down the shore, and Nate jumped into the water to pull us onto the beach. He extended his hand to help me from the boat, but I plopped into the water on the other side, ignoring him, and stood ready to help *Old Blue* further up the beach.

We slid her, engine waving in the air, up the sand a ways.

Nate secured her to a log before falling in beside me.

"Nice job," he complimented me before adding, "I didn't think you'd be able to do that."

"There's a lot about me you don't know."

"There's a lot you won't let me know."

With no response to his truth, I watched my feet sink in the sand as we walked along.

"I'm sorry," his words were hushed, and when I didn't respond, he touched my arm.

I nodded before taking the first step up the long bank.

Halfway up the flight of stairs, Nate's hand went across my backside. Startled, I turned to face him.

"You have great legs and sand on your bottom." His thick waves of reddish hair now lifted free in the mild breeze as he twisted his damp bandana in his hands, his smile deepening.

There was no deeper crimson than on my cheeks. I started a breathless giggle, paralyzed, embarrassed, to return to the journey.

"Go on," he coaxed, "I'll behave."

Conscious of his view and proximity, I counted the last five stairs before me. As we reached the hedge and started across the lawn, my laugh froze on my face. There at the window, propped on her cane, red tufts of hair surrounding a face held in a sour scowl, was Alex McKenzie. A cold, blue glare followed our movements.

Nate smiled and gave a slight nod at the figure. Sensing the situation, he waited until we were around back before asking, "Are you going to be okay?"

"Sure." My plastic smile was unconvincing.

"I'll pick you up at six-thirty."

"Great. Thanks."

I watched the pale green truck back out into the street before I went to my employer.

CHAPTER 28

The tantalizing smell of rich chicken soup met me as I opened the door. She must have been up for some time. Collecting my breath, I went straight into the living room. There, her figure outlined against the bright window, Alex leaned with both hands on her cane. Her eyes were stern, but her lips did not move.

"Nate asked Henry if we could borrow the motor for the boat, and he was showing me how to use it." My words did not change her expression. "We weren't long, and we stayed inside the bay."

"I know," she lingered over her words, dragging their meaning before me.

"There's plenty of gas. We could take a run over there today." My voice held all things, a plea for forgiveness, a hope to continue our search, exhaustion at the impossible tasks.

"Here," she pounded her stick on the counter. "Get out the flour and eggs." She fell back into a chair, taking up her post as commander. "Beat two eggs with a pinch of salt."

I hurried to comply, glad to be allowed her attention on any level. I couldn't lose her trust now. We still had a task to finish.

"Now, add some flour until it's wet and starchy. Not too much. Let me see."

I showed her the mixture and got the nod of approval to continue.

"Flour your board and work the dough for a while." Her manner hadn't improved. "What kind of engine? A Johnson? They stall all the time, you know."

Encouraged by her interest, I turned toward her to answer, but her cane told me to keep my eyes on my work.

"No. I don't think that's the name."

She grunted behind me. "Okay, that's enough. Now roll it out over there and put a lot of flour down. Roll it into an oblong."

I didn't dare steal a look at Alex but kept my back to her as I followed instructions.

"He only wants to help."

"He wants to stick his nose in where it doesn't belong." Her cane's thud resounded in the small room, echoing her feeling toward Nate. "Cut them into strips about an inch wide and about two inches long. Let me see."

I faced her now with a strip in my hand.

"Well, put them in the pot and get down two bowls. Just make up half the batter now."

"What about Mr. Chin?"

She blinked before answering, "He's been and gone."

"Doesn't he think you should go to a doctor?"

"He's smarter than that. Get us a glass of milk."

I bit back my desire to snap back at the woman who had trans-formed overnight. She looked old, tired, and frail, a sad image of her former self. I forced my eyes away, wanting to remember the lively woman of yesterday.

"That should do it. See if they're done."

I lifted the lid, and thick mounds of bobbing dough accompanied the aroma of homemade chicken soup. My mouth watered.

"Ladle's over there."

I followed the pointer and served up large bowls.

"These are my mother's German strip dumplings."

She didn't wait for me as usual but cut into the fluffy mound immediately. "Not bad." She inspected the inside and then lifted a piece carefully to her mouth. "Good."

It was more than I expected. I watched her devour the food, knowing with a full stomach come strength and calmness. From the look of her appetite, she would mend soon.

Finally, I tested my own fare. The desire to sneak some home to impress Nate with my cuisine crossed my mind.

"Is he coming back?"

"No."

"Good." She finished her last drop of milk.

Her eyes closed to slits, her voice a slithering tone I'd never heard before, "What else has he told you?"

I took a deep breath, weighing what I should tell. "He thinks the murderer is still alive."

"What does he know?" Her voice shot up an octave, and her hand waved through the air, dismissing Nate's assessment.

"He has all the articles on the case."

"He's shown you these?" Her head rocked back a little.

"Well, I didn't really read them all."

"Garbage. There's nothing there. He's a fool like his grandfather."

"And he also has, has …" her head snapped up, halting my speech. A voice deep within warned me not to continue.

"Has what?" When I didn't answer her cane beat along with her shouts, "Has what?"

"The doctor's report," I shouted back.

Pretty Boy was the only one talking now. In hysteria, he raced up and down his wooden perch, squawking madly.

Slowly she released her breath, her eyebrows arched. The sickening voice spoke, "It's nothing. Destroy it. Jake is gone now. He needs to rest. I need to rest." Tears dragged her head forward onto her cane. "Oh, my God, get me back to the couch."

Her weight pressed heavily against me when, as one, we maneuvered into the living room and I helped her onto the couch.

"Bring me the bottle of Scotch, Jean." I went to the cupboard, snagging a glass from a shelf. "Pour me a stiff one."

"Is Mr. Chin coming back?"

"Who?" Her eyes were blank, as was her world.

"Mr. Chin?"

"I don't know."

"I'll call him."

"No. And don't mention a word of this to him. He'll be here soon." Her eyes were wide with fear. "Just go."

"I'll clean first." I was mistrusting her ranting but didn't know what else I could do but stay for a bit.

"All right."

I lingered over my kitchen duties, not wanting to leave her like this. Finally, her moan brought me to her. Where was Mr. Chin?

"What can I get you?"

"Another drink."

I poured another smaller shot.

"Should I try to go today?"

"Where?"

"To the island?"

"No. You can't go alone. Oh, it's too late. I need the box, Jean. I need to know."

"It's there," I tried to sound strong. "And we'll find it. You rest, and then we'll go."

"All right, dear," it was the sing-songy voice. "Cover Pretty Boy as you go."

I brought her a pot of tea and wrapped the blanket around her. Hours ticked away, and still I didn't want to leave my post in the kitchen. I had all but memorized the pictures in the photo album, becoming increasingly curious about the missing snapshot that had fallen to the ground the day before. On a hunch, I snuck down the hall to the guest bedroom where I had found Alex this morning. There on the side table, tucked into the frame of another picture was the photograph of the three girls. I studied them closely—the matching dresses with Peter Pan collars dipping over the tucking across the breast and then the straight line of their shifts with the hem midway down their skinny, youthful legs, exposing their socks folded down over scuffed shoes. They were all so happy, linked by arms and love. Gently, I removed it, exposing the picture of Jake on a boat, with his dashing smile. I flipped the photo over, and in very light script on the back, were three names: Julia, Al, Gin. I had heard her mention Ginny Dillard, the one who could dance, who killed herself after going blind from bad hooch, and who they had named one of their boats for, the *Dancin' Gin*. With reverence, I replaced the sacred picture and headed back to the kitchen to wait. Still, no Mr. Chin. Finally, bored, convinced her deep breathing was a positive sign, I jotted a note, reminding her I'd return, to call me, and then left.

———◇———

My nervousness brought on a bout of cleaning as I whirled through my small space, arranging piles into modest displays. As I worked at straightening my desk, I uncovered the list I had made a few days back of all the elements to this puzzle, which still remained unsolved. My eyes followed my writing past "unidentified item, syringe, guilt re: quitting." My eyes and mind went back up to the word "syringe." I had completely forgotten seeing the needle sticking out from under the magazine that day when Mr. Chin was there. A new fear tore at me. Was he injecting her with some drug? Is that why the mood swings?

I wanted to return immediately, to be there to protect her in her weakened condition, but I knew I couldn't. My plan to return soon was now even more imperative.

I hid the list again. *Get through this evening*, I told myself. *The morning will surely follow.*

The clock read six forty-five when a new dread tightened my muscles. Nate wasn't coming. He would have discovered the papers missing by now, and he wouldn't come. I started to undo the neat blouse I had chosen with care, a white, lightweight cotton with small flowers embroidered along the left breast-pocket. The solid blue A-line skirt slid easily to the floor and I left it there, now the only mar in the tidy room.

I was at the sink, washing off the little bit of mascara I'd applied when there was a knock at the door.

"Lissa?"

"No, it's me," Nate boomed.

"Oh, just a minute." I was still buttoning my blouse when I opened the door.

"Sorry, I'm late. I was talking with my neighbor." He looked at me closely and spoke hesitantly, "You missed something." His finger indicated my eye.

I ran back to the mirror, and the eye I had been washing now dripped black mascara. Great.

"I didn't think you were coming," I shot at him over my shoulder.

"I said I'd be here," he shrugged in confusion.

"How did you get in? Oh, let me guess."

A sheepish smile confirmed my suspicions, "She was just coming in."

"Shall we go?" I'd slopped more mascara on the clean eye and ushered him out.

I wanted to crawl under the seat of the truck as we approached his grandmothers' house. Once inside, I would have to face my actions. A new hope sprung before me. Maybe I could get the papers back inside the box before he noticed them missing. Then I could decide what to do with them once I knew for certain what they held.

Suddenly I sat upright, smiling brightly at the handsome figure beside me.

He gave me a look of surprise. "Going to share the thought?"

"No," I beamed, feeling lighter than I'd felt in days. All was going to be just fine.

In the daylight, the house had a bright, cheery feel about it. Nate took me straight to the kitchen to show me what he'd planned for our meal.

"I caught that," he announced, pointing at the sleek, gray-blue salmon. There was an unmistakable pride in his voice, a basic instinct of the provider. "Do you like these?"

Set in a straight line on an old cookie sheet on the counter sat one dozen oysters. "Like them? I'll shuck them for us."

He grinned in surprise. "Okay, raw is fine with me. We have salad and corn on the cob. A real barbeque." He picked up the salmon, headed for the back door, and paused while I fell in behind. Just outside, built of brick, was an outdoor oven with a grill over the fire pit. A concrete patio surrounded it. It was secluded from the front lawn and surrounded by massive rhododendron bushes. An evenly cut, green lawn fanned out to the side of the house and back toward a two-car garage. It was a larger lot than it appeared.

The cedar chips had been soaked and were already in place. Nate set about spreading them on the hot fire. "What can I get you to drink while I watch you shuck oysters?" There was laughter in his voice. The challenge was on.

The ice clinked in our drinks as I watched Nate prepare his sauce for the fish. The scent of mounds of simmering garlic and sweet basil in butter filled my nostrils, making my mouth long for our meal.

He took out a knife to cut the lemon and handed me the shucking knife for the oysters. "What did she say when I left?"

"Wanted to know if the motor was a Johnson." I looked for something to hold the oysters with.

Nate pulled an old potholder out and held it toward me, amazement in his voice, "She's a sharp one." He shook his head in amazement. "She didn't look too good. She okay?"

"I think she's just really tired is all. It's been hard on her."

"What has?"

I had to cover myself, "She slipped and hurt her ankle a little."

"Seen a doctor?"

"Won't go."

"Gram is the same. Doesn't want any more needles poking her."

I wanted to change the subject as I picked up my first oyster and slid the knife in at three o'clock as Alex had taught me. The shell gave way and I sliced through the muscle.

"Where did you learn that?"

"Come at 'em at three o'clock. I know a few things, Nate Drummond."

His gaze was calculating.

"Where did you catch the fish?"

"I know this nice, deep hole where the salmon like my bait." He squeezed the lemon in the sauce. "I've been thinking, Jean. Who have you seen come and go from her house?"

"Why?"

"Because if the killer is still alive and she's drawing him out, then he knows what she's doing and that you're somehow involved."

"I'm not involved. I did her gardening."

"So what's on the island?"

"We go there for picnics."

"There used to be stashes all over the islands. I'm sure Jake had quite a few."

"Probably," I shrugged, concentrating on the oyster in my hand.

"Maybe she's looking for something herself."

"Like what?"

"Like the murder weapon. When people get older, they like to clean things up. Leave a neat and tidy slate behind them."

"I don't know. She just likes to be on the water," I nodded toward my empty glass, any distraction.

He was pouring my second vodka and tonic as he tried another approach, "They aren't certain what was used to kill Antonio."

"A gun." The shucking knife slipped, almost catching me.

"There weren't any bullet wounds in him."

I didn't reach for the drink he was offering me. My eyes fixed blankly on his gaze, the oyster dripping its salty juices, still not open completely. Hadn't Alex said they'd never found the gun? Who was lying?

"Maybe it was his heart," my voice was flat, devoid of emotion.

"Nope. You'll see when you read the report."

"What?" My face went white.

"Look. Let's not talk about this now. I'm making you the meal of a lifetime." He offered me a smile I couldn't return.

"Can I use the ladies' room?" I had to get upstairs to get to those papers.

"First door on the left down the hall," he pointed in the opposite direction from the stairway.

He watched me as I stoically followed his directions.

My head rested against my hand on the closed door. Where was the truth in this jumbled mess of tale? Alex had definitely said a gun had killed the mobster. I splashed cold water against my cheeks and stepped back into the hall.

Nate turned at the noise. "The coals will be ready soon. How do you like the oysters? With lemon juice or cocktail sauce? I make my own."

I headed back under his watchful eye. "Raw. Just plain raw."

His eyebrows shot up in surprise. "You're tougher than I thought."

We settled across from each other at the table outside, and I slowly put aside my growing confusion, letting the vodka and oysters ease me into contentment. Avoiding conversations about our mutual topic of concern, I watched Nate. He paraded in and out of the house past me, first showing the filleted fish, then giving me another whiff of the buttery garlic, basil sauce. He stood now, talking to his kill, encouraging it onto the grill, tasting the butter mixture and seemingly thrilled at his own abilities.

In no time, salad and corn appeared before me, as did the beautiful pink flesh of the cooked salmon. The chunk he lifted for me was still steaming, and the juices oozed onto my plate. From nowhere new potatoes, small and red skinned, dripping in butter, sprinkled with parsley, landed next to the fish.

"Quite the spread." I was truly impressed with the food and in need of it with the drink.

"I hope I didn't ruin your meal earlier." His earnestness lingered in the air as he stood with the spoon from the potatoes still in his hand.

I shook my head no.

"Then eat, and we'll work after dinner." He sat to join me, humming in his excitement over his well-planned meal.

I did as told, and my job was not a difficult one. The fish was rich, not overcooked, but tender, flaking with the mere tap of the fork. The corn stuck between my teeth as I attacked it, and I remembered the meal I had shared with Alex and her old friends. A horrible thought entered my mind. Could any of them have been the killer? I pushed the question away and reached for more fish. Hunger once more guiding me, I easily gave in to the sumptuous meal.

"How far will that tank of gas take me, and how do I get more?" The thought popped up from nowhere in particular.

"About two crossings to the island. I can bring you another can. Don't try it alone, Jean."

"It's Mrs. McKenzie who likes the water, not me." I cleaned my fingers of the buttery corn.

We lingered over our empty plates, watching the gentle breeze push the thick rhododendron leaves. It was as if we were both reluctant to go back inside, to climb the stairs and begin that which we had come to do. We thought up every excuse, dishes, coffee and ice cream. Finally, we blew out the last remaining candle on the picnic table and let the night push us inside.

The house had grown long shadows in the darkness, which smothered us. And like any old creature, it creaked. Nate's hand felt the wall for the light switch. It clicked in response, but no light followed.

"Damn. Wait here." His form was swallowed by the dark as he passed through the arch.

Again the click and again no light. He was moving faster now, bumping into furniture as he worked his way around the living room. Nothing. Suddenly he was beside me, his voice an urgent whisper.

"Get outside. Go to the truck. Stay there."

He pushed me out the back door. The sky was light enough so I could see the grass, and I started around the side of the house. The pounding of my heart overpowered the sound of my steps. I tried to listen. No lights appeared in the house. As I rounded the front, staying wide of the porch, I noticed the front door was ajar. The sound of a crash came from above, from the room with the bay windows.

I went to the far side of the truck. A tan car was parked farther down the road, and the head of a man appeared from below the seat. I tugged open the driver's side door and climbed inside the truck. The engine of the tan car sputtered, and the driver backed down the street toward me.

My hand grasped the steering wheel, and I applied all of my weight to the horn. The loud blare halted the car momentarily. I flipped on the car lights.

From across the lawn, a second figure, dressed entirely in black, features hooded, sprang at the small car. With his right hand, he opened the passenger side and jumped in. The light barely illuminated what he gripped in his left hand, the cedar box with the engraved emblem of the Scottish thistle.

Chapter 29

The neighbor with the manicured lawn appeared on his porch in his pajamas at the continuous blaring of the truck's horn. He had opened the truck door before I released my frozen arms from the wheel.

"Are you all right?"

"It's Nate." I was frantic. "Do you have a flashlight?"

The pajamas were covered by a robe when he emerged from his house and hurried across his lawn, guided by the amber beam. I snatched it from his grasp running to the Drummond home. I pushed past the front door, up the stairs, and down the long hall. The small light showed little disturbance until it hit on the sole of Nate's shoe. Slowly, guiding the torch up his body, I held my breath until I reached his face, eyes closed, blood dripping from a gash on his forehead.

Kneeling beside him, I could hear him breathing as he let loose a deep moan.

"Nate. Nate, are you all right?"

The neighbor was dialing for help by match light in the dark corner.

Nate stirred, wincing at the light I had anchored on his face.

"I didn't see him." He rolled, reaching for my intruding light and pointing it towards the ceiling, the beam now casting a mellow glow over the room. Next to Nate's large frame was the bent shape of the desk lamp.

"What'd he take?" He tried to sit up but decided against it.

"The box," I whispered.

"Shit." He took my hand and held it.

The police and aid car arrived at the same time, their swift arrival still marking the importance of the owners. The older officer was familiar with the sitting room. The younger one was sent to the basement to check the power.

"What the hell's going on, Nate?"

The lights flickered on.

"That's your job, Gus."

"They get anything?"

"Not as far as I can tell," Nate mumbled. He was sitting on the couch now, holding ice to his head as a medic prepared a butterfly bandage.

"Get a description?"

"Nope."

"How about you?"

My eyes widened as I shook my head no.

"We'll have a look around."

The neighbor followed the police down the stairs and out the front door. He drifted across the street to fill in the other gathered residents with the details.

"Keep him awake for a few hours. Call us if he shows the slightest sign of dizziness or disorientation, slurred speech. See your doctor first thing. It's not deep, but there will be a lump for a while." The medic applied the bandage, closed his case, and left us.

"He was small and wiry, but quick and strong," Nate's voice was low. "Martial arts would be my guess."

With the blood-chilling confirmation of who had sent my shadow, I sat next to Nate.

"They were after the doctor's notes," I hadn't meant to talk out loud.

"Who, Jean?"

"They'll be back."

His hand left his forehead to grab me.

"What are you talking about?"

"They didn't get the report."

"They got the box."

I floated across the room in a subdued state and picked up the magazine. I turned towards Nate as Gus entered.

"You catch the fish you barbequed?"

"Yep."

"Someone pried a basement window. But we have it nailed tight. We'll post someone on the block tonight. They may be back."

"Just kids," it was my voice sounding in the room.

"Maybe. But I've never known kids to go for a fuse box and then make a gash in someone's head like that."

Nate had not stopped watching me. "It's fine, Gus. Have the boys take a sweep by every now and then if you'd like."

"I'll be by in the morning. Better have that checked out good," he used his commanding voice while his thumb went towards Nate's head.

"I'm fine." Nate stood to prove his point. He followed Gus down the stairs.

"What were you using as bait?" their voices trailed down the hall.

When Nate returned, I was standing in the exact same spot. "What are you saying, Jean?"

I handed him the magazine. As he opened it, the papers popped out from between the pages where I had wedged them the night before.

I could see his face as he struggled to comprehend all that their appearance implied. "I don't know why I did it, but I put them there last night. I tried to tell you but couldn't. I'm sorry. I guess I just wanted to get them away from everyone. I don't know why I did it."

He shifted, weighing the papers and his thoughts. "Do you trust me now?"

"I think so," I whispered and looked away.

"Jean. Do you trust me now?"

I remembered what Mrs. McKenzie had said, without trust you had nothing. "Yes," my voice stronger, calmer now as I looked across at him.

"Who knew I had these papers?"

"I told Mrs. McKenzie this afternoon. But she couldn't have done it." I didn't want to believe any of them had been the killer.

"Who did she tell?"

"I don't know. She was so sick when I left. She swore me to secrecy. Told me to destroy them."

He handed me the papers. "Before you do, read them. But let's get out of this room."

He led the way to his own room and ushered me inside. "You'll sleep here tonight."

I deserved his abruptness as he shut the door behind me. I heard his steps go down the stairs. Letting my feet lead, I crossed the room and sat on the edge of his neatly made bed. I snapped on the lamp and began to read through the report.

I'd read the same lines several times, the old type imprinted in my memory, as I left Nate's bedroom and started down the now brightly lit, wooden stairs, my heavy steps softened by the worn oriental runner.

I found him sitting in the living room, drink in hand, his head resting against the back of the couch.

The paper vibrated with the shake of my hand as I read aloud sections of the report. "There was a two-inch cut in the lower right quadrant of the back of his skull, originating three-eights of an inch from the lobe of his ear … where a piece of broken glass was lodged. The glass matched the broken lamp found near the body. There was a scratch originating just below the left eye leading to the left ear … The cause of death: A needle punctured the left eardrum, angling upward, penetrating the brain. One superficial puncture mark was noted on the left chest, just above the heart area, penetrating …" I could read no more and let the paper slide onto the side table.

He lowered his glass of brandy as I approached and stood to pour me one. I sat back into the deep couch and took the offered brown liquid. My hand still shook a little as I accepted it, all the while remembering the long syringe Mr. Chin had brought to Alex's home.

"What will happen to him now if they catch him?"

"We have to prove it first. That's the hard part. What's his name?"

"Mr. Chin," there was no emotion in my voice. "He was one of Jake's best friends. He did it for her."

"Chin? Do you know where he lives?"

"He has an herb shop. I don't know." I turned toward him. He needed to see my sincerity.

"Well, he sure knows where to find you."

"He doesn't want to hurt me. He's had several opportunities. And I don't think he really wants to hurt you."

"Maybe. He could have run me over that night or done worse tonight. But if he knows I have the coroner's report and it's not inside the box, he'll change his mind."

I let Nate take my hand.

We finished the soothing drink, and Nate escorted me up the flight of stairs. Digging into his top dresser drawer, he pulled out a large tee shirt for me.

"Here," he tossed it on the bed and pulled back the covers. "Sleep. I won't be far away."

The shirt smelled of Nate as I pulled it over my bare skin. Funny how the clean scent brought back the desire of his touch from just a few hours before. And now I was tucked into his bed alone.

Sleep came easily but did not stay with me for long. Needles long and dripping a sickening green fluid chased me down hallways where dark eyes watched from the ceiling and the floor. The faster I ran, the more needles appeared. I screamed at them to go away, but they grew larger, surrounding me. I rocked back and forth as the points pressed closer. One pricked me.

"Jean," I heard Mrs. McKenzie's voice call me. "Jean," the voice deepened. My eyes flew open, and I tried to pry away the big hands holding me.

"Jean, wake up."

The tears flooded from my eyes as I felt Nate's chest against my cheek. I gasped for air, which did not come.

"It's all right," his voice was soft and comforting as he stroked my hair.

He folded me back into the bed and lay down beside me, holding me close. "You're okay."

A kiss brushed across my forehead. Another found my cheek as I turned my lips to his. I could taste the brandy on his breath, the smell of his body as his hunger grew, the feel of his touch igniting my lust.

———◦———

The night had been our playground, and the birds now sang to us of its end. I sat watching the twitching form beside me as sleep took hold, draining his power, a strong arm and leg possessively draped over me, the thick waves dampened at the temples and the bandage covering the gouge.

I drifted, waking with the slightest movement, knowing this would end soon and savoring every moment.

We both jumped from the bed, sheets gathering around us, at the pounding on the front door. Nate struggled into his jeans and disappeared to meet the intruder.

"Hey, lazy bones, how about some tennis?" Henry's voice rose an octave. "What the hell happened to you?"

"Nothing. Um, I can't now."

He must have indicated I was there because Henry backed off the porch without any further comment except he'd check in later.

Nate was back as I was finishing putting on my clothes, and I dismissed the look he gave the bed. I had to get home.

As I passed the dresser, I noticed more pictures adorned the tall burl wood structure with crocheted doilies on top. I froze.

"Whose room is this?" I blurted out.

"The guest room and mine for now. Why?" He was picking through the top drawer for a clean shirt.

"That picture," I had not budged and was now pointing at it as I continued, "who are they?"

Nate looked at the photo, which was creating my distress and shrugged. "That's Gram as a little girl, on the left."

I continued my inquisition trying to remember the names on the back of the photo of the three girls with bows in their hair and matching dresses I had first seen at Mrs. McKenzie's home and which was being proudly displayed here at the Drummond house. "What's your grandmother's name?"

"Julia Ann Dwyer Drummond. Why?"

"They were friends?" my voice a squeal as this was beyond expectation.

"Who?"

"Your grandmother and Mrs. McKenzie."

"Could have been. This was a small town, and everyone practically knew everyone else."

"No, I think they were very close. That's Alex in the middle."

With heightened interest, Nate picked up the photo to scrutinize the three girls. "How can you tell that?"

"She has the same picture." I quickly told him about the photo falling to the floor and then finding it in a place of honor, partially covering Jake on her bedside table.

"Jesus, what the hell …" He turned toward me as the impact of their relationship sunk in, repeating something he'd casually mentioned before, "No wonder when I told her I'd found the papers on this case she said to leave it."

The implications of their friendship created a new avenue of suspicion. My mind was racing. Why did Sheriff Drummond focus on Jake if their wives had been friends? What was he hiding? Or had he somehow been protecting them?

Nate put the picture gently back in its spot. "Do you know who the third girl is?"

"I was hoping you could tell me."

He shook his head, his hand running though his hair, a habit when distressed, exposing the bandage on his forehead.

"I think it's Ginny something."

"I've heard of her. Gram was so against drinking because of what happened to her."

"But Ginny drank the bad stuff. Not the good whiskey."

Nate looked at me, and I stopped myself from continuing with more of what I actually had learned from Alex and her friends, how

Alex and Jake had insisted on running only good whisky to supply a growing need and to prevent people from buying liquor that would make them sick or worse, kill them.

"What a mess," he finally shouted into the room. "How the hell were you supposed to know what to do back then?"

Not wanting to dig us deeper into the despair I was seeing in his eyes, I attempted to change the subject. "Let's leave if for now."

"Okay," he agreed and shook off the mood the knowledge of the friendships the picture presented and gave me a winning smile in its place. "Then how about breakfast? Norwegian style."

I returned the smile and felt the urge to return to the twisted sheets of our lovemaking and had to bite my lip before I became bold.

He pulled on a shirt and whistled me down the stairs to the tune of "Good Day Sunshine." In the kitchen, he gave me orange juice to make as he opened the fridge to take out the remains of the fish. When he put the plate before me, I thought he was kidding.

"Fish for breakfast is a real treat, good for you too." He sat across from me with a mischievous twinkle in his eye, watching, waiting.

There are some things in every relationship that must be overcome. Fish for breakfast was not one of the things I could easily work around. Reluctantly, I lifted my fork to my mouth and was surprised at how delicious the cold salmon tasted.

"Toast and cold salmon. This is a first for me."

"It's nice sharing breakfast with you."

"Yes," I was hesitant. This was all so much so fast, and I needed to give him an out, as I was certain he was looking for one, just like my last relationship. "I'd better get back."

"What are we going to do about Mr. Chin?"

The "we" stopped me cold. When had the "we" settled in and to what extent? And what about my promise to Mrs. McKenzie?

My anxiety must have read like a book across my face.

"Jean," Nate started slowly, "last night was—"

"Yes, I know." I needed to cut him off before he said the cutting words I would never forget. "We should never have done that."

"Oh, yes we should have." His eyes held me in a stern glare. "What I was going to say was we need to figure out how to find Mr. Chin. What all do you remember about him?"

I was still back at the "Oh, yes we should have," but my mind resurfaced at the name Chin. "Not much. He brought a syringe to Mrs. McKenzie's home. I don't know what he gave her. But he is known for his use of herbs. He has an herb store in Bellingham somewhere."

"I'll shower. Do you want to join me?"

My scarlet blush answered him.

"I'll be right back. We can go to your dorm, and then we're going to find Mr. Chin." He was gone.

I gathered the dishes, rinsed them, and wandered into the living room to study the pictures again for more clues.

———※◦◈———

The bell sounded our arrival in the cramped shop in Fairhaven. The sign, sporting a gold dragon on red wood, boasted of Chinese herbs, groceries, and specialty imports. It was almost noon, and the air held the scent of incenses and stir-fry food cooking. From behind a large curtain, covering the opening to the back rooms of the shop, a plump woman, dressed in a nondescript brown Chinese frock, sequestered herself behind the counter. She pushed her glasses further up on her nose to watch us more closely. Her hair pulled tightly from her round face, was mostly gray, yet her skin was baby smooth.

Nate and I walked down a few isles, intent on what the shop had to offer. I stopped before a bin that held black shoes, made of a soft material, simply cut like a Mary Jane with a strap across the arch, which snapped to close. The sole was a soft, tan leather. They were simple, functional, and I was tempted to try them on for the price. But I was reminded of our mission and moved further into the store, past the small dolls, coin purses, back scratchers, and other trinkets.

Behind the women, who now smiled a welcome, were row after row of large clear jars, each filled with dried herbs, mushrooms, twigs, or unidentifiable objects.

"Good day," her accent was old country. As her smile broadened, her uneven teeth showed signs of staining from black tea.

"Is Mr. Chin in today?" My smile and voice attempted calm.

Her attitude stiffened as she did not recognize me. There was a slight movement of the curtain behind her.

"He no here." She nodded at us, not knowing if she should be welcoming or not.

"Is he with Mrs. McKenzie?"

"No."

"Has he been to see her yet?"

Her eyes did not leave me, but she made no comment.

"I'm sorry," I started over, taking a step in her direction. I felt no movement from Nate behind me. "I've met Mr. Chin at Mrs. McKenzie's home, and she said she was going to call him because she hurt her ankle."

"No."

The bell on the door sounded as it opened, then suddenly slammed shut again. We both turned toward the sound. Nate was in motion, rushing toward the door and the slim Asian figure running across the street and into an alley.

Turning back to the woman behind the counter, I noticed her eyes were wide and her breathing had all but stopped. Somewhere behind the curtain, another door slammed shut.

"Please, tell Mr. Chin I need to speak with him. He knows where to find me."

Nate was back inside the shop, a dark look on his face. When I reached him, I turned back toward her, imploring, "Please, we are only trying to help."

———◦———

I wasn't sure if Nate was just being polite or if he didn't want me out of his sight. Our morning together had expanded into the afternoon, and now we had plans for the evening as he steered us toward Lummi Island and a barbeque with his friends.

A golden, long-haired dog came bounding across the sand as we headed from the truck toward a few cabins nestled on the beach. Her bark was loud and deep. Nate put down the cooler and bent to greet her, "Grace Marie."

The fur on her thick tail faded from golden tan to blond to creamy white as it furiously wagged, and her lips curled over her teeth in a smile.

"Gracie." Nate hugged her, and she whimpered. Then she drew back examining me. "Don't be jealous, Grace Marie. Say hi."

Gracie's head bent as she sniffed my legs.

I reached to pet her soft fur and admired the long lashes around her dark brown eyes. She blinked and then ran back toward the beach, then circled back toward us, and kept up this routine until we hit the bottom step of the path and landed squarely on the sand before a shake cabin. The deck stretched across the front of the sun-faded, silver-toned, one-story home with turquoise trim and shells pasted to a small window. There was only a small incline to the beach, fire pit, and water beyond.

I recognized the Boston Whaler lulling at anchor just off shore. "Is this Henry's home?"

"Mine." He put the cooler on the kitchen counter and, with pride and familiarity, opened a cupboard, and extracted a dog biscuit for his faithful companion, who had trailed sand on the broad planked floor.

"Did you think I lived with my Gram all the time?" His chest puffed in indignation.

"I guess I didn't really think about it." I turned to take in the hallway, old sofa, stereo on boards balanced on cement blocks, and view. A large chart of the San Juan Islands almost covered the top of the long, wooden table where it had been sealed in place with a quarter inch of varnish, protecting it.

"So you rent?"

"No. Henry rents from me. This was Grandfather's retreat. I'm buying it."

Gracie's wet nose found my bare skin and shook me out of my overwhelmed state.

"And Grace Marie?"

"We both claim her. Shall we?"

The bandage on Nate's head raised a few eyebrows as we joined the small gathering of half-clad bodies on the beach. Henry reached into the blue cooler and handed Nate an icy beer, making some crack to Nate about ducking next time.

Nate smiled and snapped the can open, offering it to me. Then he turned to catch the second can as Henry tossed it high.

I recognized a few of the faces from around campus but still felt the outsider after the brief introductions. Steve and Jan waved from where they were soaking up the rays on their towels. Molly was walking from the cabin with a sack of potato chips, while Mary and Jim headed for the water.

Nate ushered me to a standing of rocks, and we sat looking out across at the emerald islands floating on the horizon. The cold beer slid down welcomingly as we skipped rocks on calm water. It was still warm, and the tide was coming in over the hot sand.

"Want to take a swim?"

"Maybe after another beer." Who knew what would happen then when the beer, mixed with the sun, adjusted my caution level.

I watched as Nate stripped down to swim trunks and started toward the water. A Frisbee zinged past my head. Nate and Grace Marie dove for it. Henry was right behind him. Steve and Jim joined in as the water sport was now in full swing. The testosterone pushed them even further as they raced to Henry's Boston Whaler, anchored with a few other boats drifting in the windless sea.

Suddenly hot, I stood and waded past the warm water close to shore, to the coolness, just a few feet beyond. A blonde, devoid of makeup, hair nonchalantly pulled back into a pony tail, sidled up to me.

"Hi." Molly's sunglasses fit her perky nose perfectly. "I'm with that one there, who is constantly in competition with Nate." Her beer moved toward the pack of young male bodies working their way back to land. Nate and Henry were in the lead, matching stroke for stroke.

"Henry?"

"How'd you guess?"

"He's the only one I know here."

"They do everything together—lifeguard, fish, work, camp, you name it."

"Gracie, here girl," Molly coaxed the paddling dog back to shore. Gracie, thin and muscular in her wet coat, sauntered up to us and then shook with all her might. The cooling drops rained down on us before she headed off to roll in the warm sand.

Revitalized, our focus went back to the water. Nate had edged forward, and Molly was laughing when suddenly her attitude changed. "Oh, no you don't," her tone more a challenge than a command.

I turned to see what she was referring to as she started to back out of the water. Emerging, like gods of the sea with Nate slightly in the lead, the two were heading straight for us. In my ignorance, I stood smiling. Molly, laughing so hard she could not get away, was holding her beer high.

"Don't you dare," she kept her eyes on Henry.

"Give it up, Molly," Steve laughed as he floated in the water.

Before I could react to the look in Nate's eyes, I was in his arms and heading for the water. I squealed and kicked, but the end result was pure torture as I went flying into the frigid salt water.

Molly landed close to me, beer held high in the air, not allowing the influx of salt water in her drink. Sunglasses dripping but still held on the perky nose, she emerged to a round of applause from Jan and Steve, who had not yet joined the dunking festivities.

The battle was on. In our excuse to touch in the ensuing game, Nate and I pressed together as we pushed and pulled each other in the pure pleasure of warm bodies in cold surroundings.

Exhausted, we dried in the warm sun. I took my cue from Molly and followed her as we set about putting out mounds of potato salad, corn, and beans to accompany the barbequing chicken and halibut. I sneaked a peek at the deep rich brownies Molly was constantly guarding from the long reach of the guys.

"Nate likes you," Molly beamed across at me, having driven the last of them away with her long wooden spoon. She re-foiled the pan to a crinkling sound.

"What makes you say that?" I wanted to believe her but was still afraid of letting go of my fears of relationships.

Gracie came to the table where the two of us still sat, put her head on my lap, and gave us the most pitiful look in her hope for scraps.

"We girls just know these things. Don't we, Gracie?"

Abandoning her effort of begging from me, her tail swished across the floor, her paw found Molly's lap, and she batted her big brown eyes.

"I don't know." I was doing a bad job at digging for clues.

"God, just look at him. He's a goner."

I turned in the direction she was facing. Strolling toward us, two beers in hand, smiling from ear to ear, came Nate.

"What have you two been talking about?"

I blushed as Molly grabbed one of the beers, popped it open, and headed for the door. "Thanks. And bring the brownies when you join us."

Nate opened a beer, placed it before me, and then disappeared down the hall. I didn't budge as he returned, carrying an old Cowichan sweater.

"Come on." He handed me the cream-colored sweater with the deep brown pattern of a thunderbird sprawled across the back.

I was admiring the precise, hand-knitting of the Vancouver Island tribe when his words drew my attention.

"This is just getting started." He picked up the beer and motioned for me to bring the prize dessert.

The sounds of Cat Stevens lilted through the air as we settled in around a large fire to continue our evening, devoid of suspicions and shadows.

There was no wind, and the fire was warm and relaxing. Nate, taking up the role of fire king, stoked the blaze constantly through-out the evening. Henry brought out his guitar and we all joined him on various tunes. The brownies long gone, the songs and laughter continued to flow across the water, while the stars drifted above us. It was perfect. An evening dreams are made of.

Suddenly, Grace Marie let out a low growl, head down, and started toward the street.

Nate was instantly on his feet slinking behind her. He caught up to her at the edge of the trail, and the two stood a moment, looking into the semidarkness.

I watched intently, the evening shattered as they came back toward the fire.

On the far side of the flames, resting his back against a log, Steve let out a long snore as Jan nudged him awake. The laughter that followed eased the tension.

Molly rejoined us, carrying a large white bucket. "Oysters anyone?"

Nate took a few and tossed them on the red coals of the fire, just in front of us.

"What are you doing?" My voice was hushed.

"I figured," his profile lit by the blaze as he moved the sizzling oysters into a neat line at the edge of the fire with a stick, "you haven't tasted oysters until you've had them straight from the fire."

"You always this good?" I didn't mean to sound skeptical.

"You want to catch a fish, it's not the hook. It's how you bait it." His face turned towards me now, half in the amber light of the flames, half in cool darkness of the night. Yet both eyes shone equally.

I couldn't help but smile back. Snuggling into the scent of his large sweater as I drew it closer, I knew full well the exquisite craftsmanship of his Cowichan and the thunderbird would be no shield for his powers.

Breaking from his gaze, I easily adjusted to the warmth of the blaze and the company. The fire had a way of bringing us closer. Stories, songs, and jokes filled the night with a communal haze of joy and laughter under a canopy of stars with the water gently lapping in the darkness. The half-moon was just beginning to poke up from the island across from us, it's golden hue adding to the majestic evening.

Henry tossed an empty oyster shell into the water and jumped up. "Hey." He pointed as he threw another. Slowly, some begrudgingly, we all stood and began to follow suit. We saw the magic as we moved closer to the water. Where the shells hit, a trail of light lingered just below the surface. Like fairy dust, sparkling in the sea, the phosphorescence had come out to play with us. I waded in, leaving a trail of shimmering drops of light in dark water behind me, which Nate quickly followed. He wrapped his arms around me, and we watched as others splashed about, creating the amazing transformation as the blue-black water glittered to life where disturbed.

Our toes cold, we journeyed back to the warmth we had abandoned and threw more wood on as sparks drifted towards the heavens. Nate picked up his stick and coaxed a partially opened oyster shell in our direction. The smoky fire flavor combined with the oyster for a succulent treat.

Feeling heady, I laughed a little. "You are good." And I followed the tradition of tossing the shell into the gently rolling water.

"It's not the hook …," he started.

"It's how you bait it," we finished in unison.

We were inches from each other when Nate gently pulled me closer. I could taste the mix of beer and smoky oysters on his lips.

"Hey, lovebirds" broke our spell as Henry motioned from the porch, signaling us inside.

Grace Marie rolled and snorted before she, too, stood to make the journey up the small incline.

I lagged behind, picking up one last empty can and praying Nate's intentions were true to the moonlight making a glistening path across the dark water. I paused just outside the large picture window. An old kerosene lamp cast a light on the table where four male heads bent and fingers pointed to spots on the chart just below the shellacked surface. A pure Norman Rockwell setting as the gleam from the amber glass cast a mellow glow on the young strong faces and their long, sun-lightened trusses glinting of golds and reds.

Molly emerged from the shadow. "They're planning their next fishing trip."

"Must be a good map." I didn't realize my comment was far too nonchalant in the world of fishermen.

"Has all the depths, rocks, coves, you name it," her tone was that of a gentle instructor. "They say Sheriff Drummond put it there so he could study the waters even while he ate. Some say he was a bit possessed, especially about that one case, something about rum runners."

"What has Nate told you?" I could tell I startled her.

In the half-light, I watched her head bend to one side as she tried to get a better look at my face. "He never liked Jill. She was chasing him. And he never brought her here." She reached out and patted my arm, which had unwittingly gathered the large sweater tighter to my body.

My limbs relaxed as I realized the innocence of her comment. "Thanks."

"I hope you're almost done in there because I'm tired," she half scolded as she reentered the cabin.

A chuckle caught in my throat as the heads popped up, and reluctantly, the four fishermen abandoned their map, leaving just the lamp light bouncing off the high polish of the table's finish.

<hr />

Nate bundled us up, and we headed for his green truck. Grace Marie tried to follow us but was told to stay. With a sigh, she turned back toward the warmth of the cabin.

I had no objections to the path the Chevy took us. My thoughts were replaying the evening, the bond that is created over a fire under the stars and moonlight. We parked across the street from the solid white house, and I snapped back to reality. Nate went ahead, almost tripping on an object under the mat on the front door. When he pulled back the mat, his grandfather's cedar box glistened in the porch light.

Nate signaled me to silence, handed me the keys to the truck and went inside first. The Cowichan sweater kept me warm as I stood under the glow of the porch light, listening intently. I could tell his whereabouts by the lights switching on as he worked his way through the house.

Soon he was beckoning me inside, "Sorry. Everything looks good."

We hurried to the couch taking the box with us. Inside were all of the articles and papers. Nothing had been taken. They all lay in the same order.

Exhausted by the sudden rush of adrenalin, we didn't speak as Nate took my hand and we started up the stairs, both minds working on what the appearance of the box meant.

―――――――⊶•⊷―――――――

Morning had again come early as flesh met flesh. The temptation to linger was not as strong as the desire for answers. We sat across from each other now, trying to read the silence surrounding us, the box between us, a glaring reminder we were far from the truth.

"It is just too crazy," Nate's voice rose an octave as he lifted the lid for the one-hundredth time and pawed though the articles and assorted papers. "Nothing is missing. So why did they take it? Unless it was the doctor's report they were after."

I could not share the fact Mrs. McKenzie and I were also seeking a lost box, and the guilt showed on my face. I shrugged.

He pushed the box aside. "I could get used to this."

Afraid to ask what, my confusion spoke for me.

"Spending my mornings with you." The smile which followed held the hint of a blush, exposing the truth behind his statement.

"I really need to get home," I put down my coffee, afraid to linger any longer. It made me uncomfortable when he said the right things. I needed time to think alone. Something was missing.

―――――――⊶•⊷―――――――

My room was undisturbed. The stuffiness indicated no one had opened my door. Nate still searched before he relinquished it entirely to me.

"I'll call you in a while." He kissed my lips, lingering, sending my body into desire. "We can get together later and get this all sorted out."

"Sounds good. I'm going to take a nap."

A Cheshire grin and twinkling eye followed my movement toward the door.

"Alone," I insisted and pushed him towards the hall.

He tipped his cap as the door closed.

CHAPTER 30

Carefully, not moving the blind, I watched Nate's truck pull away from the curb. There was no time to linger in the bliss that follows two nights of love. I had to get to Mrs. McKenzie and tell her of the danger. We would go back to the cave and bury the entrance forever.

I hurried my VW Bug along the road and pulled into her driveway. I was relieved to find no car occupying my usual spot. The back door was locked. I was considering what this might mean as I walked past the sliding glass door off the living room.

I quickly stepped back.

Through the glass, I had seen Mr. Chin's back, bending over Alex who was still on the couch. I crept around again and pressed against the window. I blinked to be sure what I was seeing was correct. In his hand was a syringe. He was removing it from her arm to put it down on the table.

I thought I was going to be sick. What was he doing to her? My fist hit the door, sending a loud rattle through the living room. Mr. Chin turned, startled. Alex didn't move.

He hurried to open the door, his words rushed out, "Good morning, Miss Jean. You're here. That is good. Alex has been asking for you."

I brushed past him to Mrs. McKenzie and picked up the needle, "What is this?"

He eyed me for a moment before answering, "She's diabetic and has not been giving herself her shots."

For the first time I turned to look at her, my breath catching in my throat, my knees crumpling, forcing me toward her. I felt disgusted with myself. While I had been selfishly in the arms of her enemy's grandson, the two nights had taken most of her life.

"Have you called the doctor?"

She struggled to breathe, each effort producing a tiny rattle in her chest. She had bloated a little, giving an unreal puffiness to her cheeks and hands. Sweat poured from her forehead.

"Mrs. McKenzie?" Not knowing if I should whisper or shout, I tried again, "Mrs. McKenzie? Alex."

Eyes opened. Eyes filled with fluid, devoid of life and yellowed with impending death. "Jean?"

I took her hand. It was clammy, no longer smooth. "Yes. I'm here."

She fixed her gaze on Chin. Gathering a deep breath, she let out a low growl, "Go, please."

He bowed and disappeared into the kitchen.

"Don't cry, Jean." She squeezed my hand with little of her old strength. "If you start, then so will I."

I quickly wiped away the tears I didn't know were falling.

She coughed, and I waited, willing her strength.

"Go bring me the box." Her blue eyes had cleared with resolve. "I saw it. I want it. I can't die without it, and I want to die now."

"No," my voice trembled. "No, you're not going to die."

"Bring me the box," she insisted. "I saw it just above, when the dirt—"

Mr. Chin returned with hot tea and placed it on the coffee table. An awkward silence filled the air, and Alex closed her eyes.

We waited as she coughed, deep and dangerous.

Mr. Chin bent beside her and busied himself with the tea. Alex's eyes barely opened as she recognized the back of Mr. Chin's brown robe. Her finger floated toward the island and she struggled with her words. "Jean, yes, of course you can take the boat for a row."

I thought I saw a wink.

Chin turned toward her, teacup in hand. She coughed again, struggling to get out the words, "Just remember, dear, the world is your oyster, and remember how to open a shell with ease." Her look was searching, desperate.

What didn't she want to share with Mr. Chin?

"You hang on."

"Yes, dear," she said in a mere whisper of the sing-songy voice I had grown to love. Her hand drifted toward the bottle of Famous Grouse Scotch.

I poured her a small amount of the bottle, which was almost empty, and held her head as she sipped.

She coughed. "I'll be here waiting."

Her eyes closed, but her chest continued to struggle.

"The doctor was here last night," Mr. Chin informed me as he followed me into the kitchen. "But Alex refuses to go to a hospital. At home, there is nothing even I can do. It is too late. The infection has spread up her leg. Her lungs are heavy with fluid. He told me just to keep her comfortable."

I didn't believe him. I didn't believe any of this. Mrs. McKenzie was not going to die. I was going to get her the box, and she would spring back to her old self because she would be so thrilled to have it again. I had to find the box for her. Nothing else mattered now.

"Call him again," I spit between clenched teeth. I was frantic. "Get him out here." I watched Mr. Chin as he turned toward the phone book and picked up the receiver.

With his back to me, busy at his job, I ran past Pretty Boy for the sliding glass doors. I stopped briefly to look at the bird. He was huddled in the corner, not moving or singing, just trembling. He turned his head toward me. He knew.

"No," I repeated to anyone who would listen. My feet barely touched the stairs as I raced down the landing. The tide was in a ways, and *Blue* was listing to her port in the shallow waters. Untying her, I backed her into the deeper water. Following Nate's instructions, I struggled the engine into the water, counted five pumps on the black bulb, and pulled the starter rope with all of my might. Within minutes, the motor roared, and I pointed her for the open channel. Looking back, I saw the figure of Mr. Chin. He was waving. I paid him no mind and hurried forward.

The blue water skimmed below my bow. It was fairly smooth in the open, and I played with the throttle to get a speed I felt I could handle. My heart was racing, and the wind was washing my tears from my cheeks. Please let it be there. And let the sight of it bring hope and strength back to Mrs. McKenzie.

Looking back at the jagged, rocky mound of land and trees, I scanned the water for boats. Only a few were bumping along in the morning sun. Minutes seemed like hours as I pressed *Blue* forward. I had the narrow strip of beach in sight now, and I checked the lever to lift the engine.

A noise from behind startled me. There, bearing down on me at full speed was the bow of a white boat. I pushed the throttle forward, bracing myself for the landing. As Nate had predicted, the large boat was forced to turn at the last moment, sending its wake spilling over the side of *Old Blue*. I cut the throttle back and struggled with the engine, landing with a thud. Jumping from the boat, I scurried up the bank.

The white hulled boat and its driver circled, like a shark, just off shore. I ran the wrong direction along the edge of the cliff, and the boat followed. When the bank got too jagged, I ducked into the trees to circle back. The sound of the powerful engine still hung just off shore, idling where I'd left it. I crawled back across the patch above the beach and eased down on the far side of the madrona tree, sliding above the opening, taking sand and dirt with me.

With my bare hands, I tore into the small pile of loose earth, removing just a few handfuls, visualizing in my mind where I'd left the flashlight and matches. I crawled through the opening to get the light so I could cover the hole back up. I fumbled in the dark, my hand groping across cold, wet dirt until it struck something warm. My hand curled back instinctively, then slowly reached out again.

A flashlight flipped on. I was holding Nate's knee. I started to scream, but he had his hand over my mouth, muffling the sound.

"Shhh." His eyes were burning fire. "They don't know where this is." He was loosening his grip. "Are you all right? I heard their boat."

I could not say anything, my pounding heart was forcing my chest to heave with uncomfortable pressure. I backed away from him.

"Jean," his voice a warning as he reached for me but I countered. "The murderer doesn't want to be found. This is dangerous business. What were you two doing in here?"

"What are *you* doing in here?"

"I just want to help you."

"No. You want to be the hero your grandfather wasn't."

"Where's Mrs. McKenzie?" He was shifting his footing, placing himself between me and the opening.

"She's dying."

Nate stopped, noticeably shaken. "So, why did you come?"

"She wants something she thinks her husband hid here." I wasn't going to get past him if I didn't tell him part of it, I reasoned.

"Jean, you have to trust me. I want to help. I can't piece it all together, but I do know they are after something and won't stop until they find it. What is it?"

"A box."

His look was incredulous. "So that's why they took Grandpa's box?"

"Possibly, but this is a silver box."

"Where is it?" He looked around at the stack of mud we had excavated, as if inspecting the room for the first time, and lit the lantern we had left hanging.

"I don't know," I answered truthfully and looked him straight in the eye.

He nodded accepting my statement before asking, "Then how do you know if it's even here?"

"She said she saw it. I don't know. I panicked and said I would try."

He grabbed a shovel, "Where?"

"I don't know. Mr. Chin came in and she started telling me life was my oyster."

"Great timing." He thrust his shovel into the mud behind him.

"And that I was to remember ..." My voice trailed off.

He stopped and looked at me.

"How to open the shell with ease."

"How to what?" He shook his head and began digging again.

"Come at 'em at three o'clock." I moved as if in a trance to stand on the dirt we had piled.

Nate slowly stood and backed up to the opening. "Three o'clock, like the oyster." He swung his arm toward the wall where the mud had slid just before Alex and I had left, not quite two days ago. "There somewhere."

He sank into the mud and began to dig while I watched from the rock where Alex had sat. "No, there." I pointed, adjusting his search slightly.

Nate's strength ripped the wall, and a slide began. He stepped back so his legs would not be buried. An object, black, but solid bumped along with the loosened dirt.

I dove for it, gathering it, mud and all, close to me. Nate stepped aside as I carried it under the light. Our fingers worked together to loosen the dirt. A corner emerged, a flat surface of the top, three more sides, the bottom. An oilcloth, caked with earth, coved the object. We reverently unfolded the wrapping from the tarnished box, blackened with moisture. There was no mistaking it as my fingers worked the engraved lettering, "J. M. E."

"Open it."

"No." I snatched it, clutching it to my chest. If Alex wanted her box, no one was going to do anything to it until I got it back to her.

Nate's chest heaved in frustration. "Let's get out of here." He grabbed my arm, thrusting me toward the opening.

"The light," I squealed.

Nate's hand instantly left me. "Damn."

He had his hand on the rope, lowering it when I slithered out the opening and wedged between the rocks. It was too late when I realized my mistake, my movement having aroused the figure bending over the motor on *Blue*. A small gray rubber boat bobbed just beyond him.

"What do you want?" I yelled at the back of the intruder, trying to signal Nate.

"Give it to me," was all he said as he rushed forward. I recognized him now as my shadow, the one from the saloon in Edison, the one from the pizza parlor, the one from Chin's herb shop.

I ran for the water, and he moved to cut me off, but that was all Nate needed to hear, and he was through the rock fence. The muscular Asian didn't even see him coming as they both hit the sand.

He tumbled and rolled, flipping onto his feet, ready to return the attack. Nate stood slowly, weighing the trained abilities of his opponent. They circled like cats, the smaller, wiry man with his sleek, black hair, preparing for battle in the manner of his ancestors.

Nate stood like a bear, ready for the fight, when suddenly the small man leapt at him. He landed a blow to Nate's chest as Nate emptied his fist filled with sand into his opponents face, sending him screeching to the ground. Nate's foot found his stomach while his hand hit the back of his neck, just below the fine hair. The motionless figure slumped further onto the sand.

"Get to the boat, Jean, by the construction site." Nate turned toward me and pointed up the bank. "I'll be right behind you."

I didn't hesitate but began to climb the bank as Nate, mud and sand still clinging to his legs, jumped into the small gray rubber boat and headed for the white hulled craft, anchored off shore. Halfway up, I checked, and Nate was aboard, just going below. I reached the top, breathless, and turned around.

Something was wrong. Nate was leaning over the motor, but something was missing. I looked again. The man on the beach had disappeared. I checked the bank, and he wasn't following me, so I scanned the shore again. Movement drew me back to the white boat. I opened my mouth to shout as the figure from the beach, now poised on the side of the boat, sprang at Nate.

Hideously, they knocked each other from side to side until, with one blow to the gash on Nate's head, he toppled backward. The slim man kicked Nate's legs and they buckled, sending him over the side, a large splash sounding his untimely arrival.

I saw the black head move up the bow, searching. My breath wouldn't budge from where tension held it captive. Then suddenly, the wind in my chest forced his name across the water, "Nate."

The figure looked up at me from the side of his boat, keeping me in view as he stood on the transom, calculating his easy prey. At that second, a hand burst from the water, attaching itself to my foe's ankle, dragging him forward. As he landed, Nate's other fist came up to greet him. A groan accompanied the splash. With his arm wrapped around the neck of the slim body, Nate swam to shore.

They lay side by side, now, at the water's edge, as Nate caught his breath. Slowly he stood and, picking himself up, started for the cliff. He reached the top and sat at my feet, watching the dark head below. The figure moaned and curled into a ball.

"Where's Mr. Chin?" Nate stood.

"At the house." I looked up at his bruised face, feeling weak.

"Let's go."

I ran beside him to keep up with the pace he set, the box not leaving my arms. We were across the sloping field of dry grass and barren rocks, past the old, crumbling log cabin, and into the patch of trees. Nate did not stop but grabbed my arm and pulled me on. The turned-up field was quiet now without the pounding of hammers or the buzzing of saws. A bird, worm in his beak, flew from the exposed soil, startled by our approach.

The broken earth was harder to walk across. Nate didn't slow but steadied me when I faltered. I was merely along for the ride as this steam engine blazed forward. We were headed, I realized, right for the Two Lovers. We brushed past the small clump of bushes, a fluorescent marker dangling from the branch.

I brightened at the news I would be able to tell Mrs. McKenzie. They weren't going to cut the Two Lovers. The marker was for the bush. Suddenly, my mind was drawn to the figure on the couch. My God, I had to hurry.

I snapped my arm free from Nate and began to run. There, nestled in the small inlet just below the famous trees, was the Boston Whaler.

"Hurry," I shouted at the bruised face.

Nate worked his way along the rock-face, stepping gingerly on the ledge until he reached the end where the rock ducked into the deep blue-green water. He pulled the rope, hand over hand, and the Whaler slid easily to him.

I sat midship as he pushed us off, and he took up his position across from me. The engine perked and sputtered before Nate pushed the throttle full forward, and we streaked into the channel.

My mind was anchored on only one thing, Alexandria McKenzie. "Hold on," I prayed into the wind.

With the end of my shirt, I stroked the top of the case, attempting to recreate its luster. Slowly, some of the black tarnish worked free from across the top of the box that had triggered all of this chaos. No. I would not disturb what it held. The box did not belong to me. I brushed temptation over the side of the boat.

Nate briefly watched me before his eyes returned to the inlet before us. No one appeared on the ridge of the steep bank.

Where was Mr. Chin? Concern drew me over the side as we neared shore. I splashed in knee-deep as Nate shut the engine. I hurried for the stairs, leaving him to secure the lines.

Fear propelled me up the steps, and I could feel Nate's weight shake the rickety stairs as he bounded up behind me. Once my feet hit the grass, I broke into a run. The sliding glass doors were locked and a curtain was pulled across them.

I went to the back door. It, too, was fastened tight. I crossed the garden to the front wooden door with the round portal window. It wouldn't budge.

Nate was backing away from the chipped white back door when there was a creak behind us. The shed door moved open to no one. I passed the neat garden where my journey had begun and cautiously moved through the opening, Nate at my back.

I flipped on the light. Mr. Chin stood at the far work counter, just below the empty space where the shovel had hung in Jake's order of his world.

"Bring me the box, Jean." His words were a threat as his hand came from deep within his sleeve and extended toward me, the long fingernail on the pinky finger casting a shadow across the floor.

I didn't budge.

The door behind us slammed shut. Two more young relatives of Mr. Chin, similar in age, stature, and obvious ability, stood ready to pounce, guarding the door.

"I am sorry I have caused you trouble. But you have been too persistent. I must have the box." He snapped his fingers.

Clenching the box, I remained glued to my fear.

"Give it to him," Nate growled behind me.

I stepped forward.

Chin took it from me.

"Come here young Drummond. How is my great-grandnephew, Andrew?"

"He's alive," Nate answered, towering inches from the old man.

"Good. Again, I apologize for having to take such measures." The old man fingered the box, eyeing Nate. "Your grandfather was very clever, but he never suspected this. Open it."

Chin offered the box to Nate.

I saw Nate's jaw tighten. He looked from me to the box. I nodded, and for the first time, he touched the silver.

His fingers struggled where time had made a seal. With a pop, the lid gave way. I watched his face go from confusion to startling knowledge. He fixed his gaze on me and held the opened case in my direction.

I grabbed it to look inside. There were only two items in the box, a tarnished picture of Alex, smiling waving, and the large, ruby-and-pearl incrusted brooch in the shape of a half-moon, which had been her engagement present, the long pin bent and the clasp broken.

With lightning speed, Chin snatched the piece of jewelry, hiding it in the folds of his coat. "Go. Show her the box now."

Numbed by the truth I refused to believe, I stumbled toward the light of the doorway now flung open for me.

"In shock, she lost the brooch at Antonio's house," I heard Mr. Chin explaining to Nate as we trudged in an awkward line past the newly manicured garden. "She came home with her hands and dress stained with blood, but her deepest fear was Jake finding out what she had done. She did not want him to know how foolish she had been. She sent me to get it, but I was too late. The brooch was gone. She lived the rest of her life trying to find this special piece of jewelry, her engagement present."

I led the morbid parade as Nate asked what I couldn't.

"So how did it get into this box?"

"Jake. He had gotten away from Antonio's men but recognized my car and went back inside to help me, or so he thought. He found Antonio's body and the brooch. He had not seen Alex, but realized what had happened. When Jake came out of the house, he just missed Alex as she drove my car home. Your grandfather was quick to blame Jake, to put him out of business. Jake would have taken the blame for Alex."

I stumbled, tears blocking my vision.

"Jake found it stuck in Antonio's body and hid if for many years. But before he died, it worried him Alex would find it. He made me pledge, at all costs, I would keep both of their secrets separate. He was not expecting either of you."

Mr. Chin moved in front of me now to unlock the door, our eyes meeting. "Yes, Jean, for Alex and Jake, I would do anything. Even risk my own family. I have now repaid the life Jake's father gave me."

I nodded and hurried past him. The young men elected to stay in the bright sunshine and not enter the gloom within.

"Mrs. McKenzie?" I tiptoed toward her.

"I've been waiting," she coughed, her chest racking with deep phlegm. Her dry tongue worked over pale lips. "Did you find it?" was a mere whisper.

"Here, I've got it." I held it high, over her so she could see it.

"Open it." She pushed with dwindling strength to raise her head. Yellow eyes fixed on the once shiny box. She squinted.

I opened it, showing the picture of her I knew she could not distinguish from that distance.

"What's that?" She fell back, her crooked finger poking in the direction of the open box.

I brought it closer to explain, "A picture of you, very young, very pretty."

She pointed toward the glass of water, and I lifted her head to help her drink.

The moisture revived her momentarily. "Is that all there is?"

"Yes."

She closed her eyes as tears spilled from them. She was laughing. "Chin."

"Mr. Chin," I called for her.

Her eyes beamed from my face to his, and she struggled, "He didn't know. My God, Jake didn't know." Her voice became a whisper of Jake's song, "Happy trails to …"

She smiled broadly, her excitement bringing on another bout of deep coughing. Struggling for breath, she turned to face the large windows and her beloved sea. Deep from within came a mumbling sound of a familiar tune, feeble and soft. She sighed one last, long breath, and her spirit drifted out across the gentle waves beyond.

"Mrs. McKenzie? Alex?" I grabbed at her lifeless form.

Mr. Chin's head slumped to his chest.

There was a bang as the back door flew open.

"Where is she?"

I turned my head in time to see Mr. Chin reach Josie as she rounded the corner.

"She is gone."

Josie's ring encrusted hand covered her face, partially smothering her words, "We got here as fast as we could." Her body heaved with her sorrow as Charlie and Stew emerged from behind to lend their support.

The three edged forward. Josie sat on the couch by me, taking Alex's hand, wailing long and loud.

I watched the three remaining pillars of old that someday would crumble to lie as Alex did now. I wondered what secrets they had stashed, hoping they would never find light again.

"Was she singing?" Nate was amazed.

"Hell yes, she was," Stew bellowed.

Charlie snapped into action and headed straight for the cupboard by the fireplace. Scooping up two bottles, he brought them to the table. Mr. Chin had taken the cue and brought in a tray with glasses.

Josie busied herself by running her fingers through Alex's red, hair, smoothing it, then down Alex's cheek. As Josie went to straighten the covers, she noticed the tarnished silver box. "My God, she found it."

Eyes traveled to me.

I picked up a glass filled with dark liquor.

The others followed suit. We stood now encircling the fallen queen of rum runners, lifting our glasses containing that which she had risked her life to provide, which she had fought and killed for.

"To Alex," Stew boomed.

"To Alex." All heads snapped back in unison.

"Happy trails, sweetheart," Charlie led the next toast.

We all stood, emotions like the ebbing tide, leaving us barren, raw, exposed.

Josie came toward me, taking my face between her plump hands, kissing both of my cheeks. "You have been such a big help. She really cared about you. But, you go home and rest. We'll take care of things."

Nate stepped up behind me, putting his hand on my shoulder, "Come on, Jean. Let's go."

I kissed each old cheek good-bye, unable to form the words, before I turned to leave. I moved as if in a dream with Nate subtly guiding my path.

We were at my car door when Mr. Chin's voice stopped me. "Jean."

We turned toward him.

"You take this to keep safe." He pressed the bent ruby-and-pearl brooch in my hand. "And come back for the rowboat. Alex would want that."

"Yes, thank you." I hugged the little man, then turned to hide my tears, which were now falling beyond control.

Nate took my keys and helped me into my car before squeezing into the driver's seat.

"Where to?" Nate backed out of the driveway.

I shrugged, not wanting to be alone.

He smiled, shifting the car into forward.

Gingerly, I toyed with the piece of jewelry, the half-moon, given with the promise of love and a future together, as one. I rubbed at the tarnished gold, pondering how many lives these gems had affected. Tears ran freely as I leaned into Nate. I clutched the pin, which had held lives apart, thanking it for drawing ours together.

I would teach my classes what I had learned from Mrs. Alex McKenzie. I would encourage those young spirits to live life filled with strength and conviction, teach them the importance of the tides and the wisdom in riding out the storm when following what you love.

About the Author

Denise Frisino spent her summers playing and working in the numerous islands that define the Pacific Northwest, where her family spans four generations. At age five, she took to the stage and has been involved in theatre and the film industry in Seattle and L.A. as an actress, writer, playwright, and producer, winning awards for her writing and acting. Denise has published several articles and a short story. In the public school system she taught English, drama, writing, and video, receiving the A+ Award for Excellence in Education. She was raised by a journalist and editor for the *Seattle Post-Intelligencer* who taught her a love for and the power of the written word. Denise and her husband proudly call Seattle their home.

For more stories of bootlegging and that era go to
www.whiskeycovebook.com